OUT OF THIS WORLD

A Novel by
Janice Subers

Scripture quotations taken from The Holy Bible, New International Version®, NIV®. Copyright © 1973, 1978, 1984, 2011 by Biblica, Inc® Used by permission. All rights reserved worldwide. Scripture quotations marked (ASV) are taken from The American Standard Version. Copyright © 1901 by Public Domain. Scripture quotations marked (ESV) are taken from The Holy Bible, English Standard Version. Copyright © 2001 by Crossway Bibles, a division of Good News Publishers. Scripture quotations marked (NASB) are taken from The New American Standard Bible. Copyright © 1960, 1962, 1963, 1968, 1971, 1972, 1973, 1975, 1977, 1995 by The Lockman Foundation. Scripture quotations marked (NET Bible) are taken from The New English Translation NET Bible®. Copyright ©1996-2006 by Biblical Studies Press, L.L.C. http://netbible.com. All rights reserved. Scripture quotations marked (NKJV) are taken from The Holy Bible, New King James Version. Copyright © 1982 by Thomas Nelson, Inc. Scripture quotations marked (NLT) are taken from The Holy Bible, New Living Translation. Copyright© 1996, 2004, 2007 by Tyndale House Foundation. Used by permission of Tyndale House Publishers Inc., Carol Stream, Illinois 60188. All rights reserved.

Blessed Be The Name, by Beth Redman and Matt Redman, © 2002 Thankyou Music (Admin. by EMI Christian Music Publishing)

Praise Him, by Gateway Worship, from the album "God be Praised," release date, November 9, 2010

www.xulonpress.com

To Lauren,
with eyes set on
things above!
Col 3:1-4

♡ Janice Aubers

DEDICATIONS

Lovingly dedicated to my grandsons:

William Eaden
Haven Isaac
Waters Everett
and those grandchildren yet to come...God knows your names!

And in loving memory of:

Matthew Batterson
Barrett Burchak
Daniel Bush
LuAnn Henry
Shepherd Oswin Hodgson
Gabriel Houston
"Glory" Meadows
Kenny Moyer
Erica Morales
Baby Boy O'Donoghue
David Arthur O'Donoghue
Ricky O'Donoghue
Charlie Power
Michael Stiles
Baby Subers

...and to all God's precious children who have gone ahead of us to Glory, whose destinies and purposes could not be stolen, who are part of the Great Cloud of Witnesses watching and declaring over us in Jesus' name that we fulfill God's purposes for our lives on Earth and that His will is done on Earth as it is in Heaven, who are living lives of adventure, having more fun than we could ever imagine, who want desperately for us to join them there, who can't wait to show us all the supernatural, awesome and fun things awaiting us, who are beholding the indescribable beauty of our God, and who are living completely awashed in His all-consuming love!

We'll meet you at the Gates!

ACKNOWLEDGEMENTS

To my dearest, Jim, thank you for your unending love, support, and encouragement. You believed in this book from the start and always encouraged me to pursue my dream. You listened to hours of manuscript reading, offered sound and helpful input, ran the house—which has nothing to do with a house!—for days so I could get away, joyfully bought the publishing package, and proudly bragged about me to our friends and family. After ten long years, I have crossed the finish-line. I could not have done it without you. Thank you does not seem adequate. I love you with all of my heart.

To my children, Joy, Jason, Jake, Jon-Zac, son-in-law, Chad, daughter-in-law, Trinity, and honorary granddaughter, Lindsay, thank you ALL for not rolling your eyes at me! You must be so tired of hearing about my book, but you never let on; instead, you cheered me on! Thank you. I have been blessed with the greatest kids in the world. I love you all more deeply than you could ever know.

To my son, Jon-Zac, you are the one who *had* to put up with endless readings, because I wisely made it part of your home-schooling! Thank you for being my eyes and ears. Thank you for telling me when you really liked something, and when you thought it needed tweaking. I so-o appreciate your honesty! I love you to the moon and back.

To my son, Jason, thank you for faithfully using the gifts God placed within you. You have been a creative genius for as long as I can remember. The book cover is truly amazing! I am beyond thrilled to have your work as the signature piece of my dream.

To my parents, Art and Alice, thank you for teaching me about Jesus. I have loved Jesus since I was a toddler. Thank you for making sure I knew that God is a God of love, that He hears us when we pray, that He answers prayers, and that He still heals today. Thank you for living out your faith both in public and behind the walls of our home where only our family saw. You are my heroes and my inspiration.

To my in-laws, Joe and Jean, thank you for loving me like a daughter. And thank you for raising sons who love and honor their wives. Your boys are rare gems among men these days, and I'm so blessed to have one of them as my own! Jim is a man of great integrity and character, and that can be traced back to you. I love you both.

To my dear friend Kris, my sister-in-law Leigh, and my daughter Joy, you three are the truest of the true! Thank you for taking time out of your very busy schedules to read the manuscript and offer constructive feedback. I am more grateful than you will ever know. I owe you girls, BIG TIME.

To Priscilla, you are a gift to me from the Lord! I could not have published this book without your many hours of meticulous editing! You went over every page with a fine-tooth comb. Thank you, thank you, thank you!! I love you to pieces and I'm so glad our kids fell in love and brought our two families together.

To Jason H., thank you for your willingness to jump in last minute with the wonderful illustrations. You are incredibly talented, and your sketches bring the book to life! You are not only gifted, but you are a gift and proof to me that God is in this book. A million thanks.

To Don and Julie, Steve and Rujon, and Wayne and Buena, thank you for allowing me the generous use of your homes so that I could have a place to "get away and write." May God return manifold blessings for your kindness and hospitality.

To Thad and Virginia, Wow! Thank you for your prayers, encouragement, and help to make this book a reality. Virginia, we were supposed to be roommates at the University of Florida, and God in His faithfulness has reconnected us. Wish we lived closer together; glad we have all of eternity to make up for it! You're officially and cordially invited, anytime, to my mansion for tea!

And a big, heartfelt thank you to the many friends and family, too many to mention by name, who prayed for me and encouraged me along the way. I am blessed indeed to have each of you in my life.

NOTE FROM JANICE

Heaven is beyond my ability to fathom. My physical brain cannot begin to grasp what great and wondrous things God the Father has in store for us when we, who love His Son, join Him forever and ever in eternity. We are told in Scripture that He has prepared things above and beyond our imaginations. Isn't it wonderful, though, that God has given us permission to use our imaginations and dream of Heaven? He didn't say not to imagine Heaven, He said it was beyond anything we *could* imagine—beyond anything we could conceive! He did say, however, to set our mind on things above where Jesus is sitting at the right hand of the Father. Well, that certainly sounds like Heaven to me.

So, I set my mind and imagine Heaven. As a matter of fact, I dream of Heaven. I long for Heaven. I wonder about Heaven. And I have decided, if I can dream and imagine Heaven, and if you can dream and imagine Heaven, then how much more amazing is the real thing which God says is above and beyond *anything* we could *ever* imagine? Wow! It has to be absolutely incredible!!

I am convinced that Heaven is a real place: vast; sustained by the One who is Light; clean, pure, holy; filled with music, fragrances, wonders, and astounding beauty; every ounce of it reflects God's glory; multidimensional; with wondrous textures, materials, and architecture; supernatural; exciting; adventurous; fun; overflowing with joy; without sin and having the complete absence of evil; but most of all, ruled by love: pure, unselfish, staggering love.

Heaven is God's abode, His house. It is home to angels and archangels, and all the redeemed who have been purchased by the blood of Christ and have gone on before us. It is the place He has prepared for you and me. And the Father wants ALL of us to join him there.

This spiritual realm is not bound by earthly laws but exists in a multidimensional complexity that the physical being cannot begin to comprehend, understand, or explain. It must be experienced, and even then it will take us all of eternity to discover its depths.

This is a fictional story relating my imaginings of Heaven. I have never seen Heaven. I have never been taken on visits to Heaven. I do not pretend to be an expert on Heaven. I humbly admit that many of my ideas and my inspiration came from studying the dreams, visits, ideas, and revelations of others. I have poured over the Scriptures. I have poured over every book I could get my hands on about Heaven. If you think you recognize something in my story that you've heard or read somewhere else, it is very likely that you are right and I thought it an idea too good not to include. If you disagree with any of my descriptions and imaginings, you are absolutely free to do so.

According to 1 Corinthians 2:8-10, the NKJV, "Eye has not seen, ear has not heard, nor has it entered into the mind of man the things that God has prepared for those who love Him, BUT God has revealed it to us by His Spirit." I love the "but'" on this passage. I believe that we are living in a day when God is revealing Heaven to His children. I am so thankful that right there in that verse, He promises that He does reveal these things by His Spirit.

There are many people who claim to have seen Heaven, either in a near-death experience or revealed by His Spirit. Those who claim to have seen Heaven have this in common: they say it is wholly impossible to find the earthly words to describe what they beheld, and that every attempt falls woefully short.

Here I go, admitting that this book will fall woefully short right off the bat. But thankfully, the real deal will *far* surpass our expectations!

Come along with me, Masumi, Henri, Cristen, Edgas, and Abel as we go on a journey to explore through both the gift of imagination and the revelation of the Spirit of God, the most beautiful place in all of creation. I have fallen in love with my new friends, and I hope you will too. I pray this book will ignite in you an excitement, a passion, an expectancy, and a desire to dream of Heaven yourself. For it truly is *Out Of This World!*

PROLOGUE

Edgas looked up, way up, into the chiseled face of an exceedingly handsome creature, "You're an angel of the Lord!"

"Yes, I am." A smile broke across the angel's glowing face.

"Are you here to take me to Heaven?"

"Well, Edgas, how would you like to go on a little adventure with me?"

"Adventure? Now?"

"Yes, right now," the angel chuckled. "Are you ready?"

"Oh yeah, I'm ready!" Jumping to his feet, he stretched both arms towards the radiant being who filled the small room. The large angel reached down and scooped Edgas into his brawny arms. High in the air and nose to nose with the angel, Edgas' face beamed joyously, "Let's go!"

Wrapping his arm around the angel's neck, Edgas turned to say good-bye to Isabel, the missionary who had tenderly cared for him, and was surprised to see his body lying in her arms. He turned a puzzled face to the angel.

"Your earthly body will remain with Isabel, but your spirit has been set free to come with me."

Edgas turned back, and seeing the tears on her face, cried out, "Please don't cry, Isabel; I'm going with God's angel. I'll be all right. Don't be sad. I'm not sad."

"She can't hear you anymore, Edgas."

"Will she be okay?" Lines of concern creased the boy's forehead.

"Yes, she knows where you are going. She will miss you, that's all."

Edgas looked at the woman cradling his body. Her tear streaked face suddenly wrinkled with bewilderment. She turned her head and looked right at Edgas. He smiled at her and started to say something, but as he opened his mouth, he realized she was looking right through him, as if she didn't see him. She looked back at his body in her arms and then back up through him again.

"She knows I'm here with you, but she can't see me," the angel explained. He then turned to Isabel's guardian who was standing quietly out of the way, "She will look back at this moment as one of the highlights of her life, but right now I'm afraid we've startled her. Glad I'm leaving her in good hands." The two angels nodded to each other.

Edgas, so caught up in watching Isabel, completely missed the fact that the angel was talking to someone other than him.

"I love you, Isabel. Thanks for taking such good care of me."

"Are you ready to go?"

Edgas nodded enthusiastically.

"Hold on tight."

"BLAST OFF!" shouted the boy.

And blast off they did. With one flap of his mighty wings, the two shot up straight towards the heavenlies.

Edgas looked down and saw his orphanage and then his city grow smaller as he and the angel lifted higher into the air. He turned his face upward and felt the rush of a cool wind.

"This is the area we call the First Heaven. It's where the birds of the air fly."

"I feel like a bird!"

The angel smiled, not missing the fact that the boy had a death grip around his neck.

From his perch in the angel's arms, Edgas looked back towards the ground and saw the outline of the continent of Africa take shape, then he noticed Europe and Asia as the circle of the Earth began to appear.

"We're really high," said the boy, with no hint of concern.

"Yes, we are, and going higher!"

"I think we're up higher than the airplanes."

"I think so, too."

"We blasted off just like an astronaut, didn't we? I feel like an astronaut; is this what an astronaut feels like?"

"I bet it is, Edgas. I bet it is."

"The Earth looks like a giant, whirly, swirly marble." The boy watched his world grow smaller and smaller.

"Ah, it certainly does look like a whirly, swirly marble, Edgas. Those white swirls are clouds, the blues are the oceans, and the greens and browns are continents."

After a few moments of silence, Edgas said, "I can't even see the Earth anymore; it's like an itty bitty dot." He pointed down in Earth's direction. "Is that it?"

"Yes, Edgas. Earth is that itty bitty dot almost lost in all of this vastness. Earth seems unimportant from way up here, doesn't it?"

The boy nodded.

"Yet God's attention is riveted to that little speck," the angel looked into the boy's eyes and smiled, "because He loves you so very much."

The boy and the angel continued at great speed and were soon engulfed in a black sea teeming with millions and millions, perhaps billions and billions, of twinkling lights. Edgas shivered slightly, and the angel brought him closer to his chest.

"This is also the area where God hung the sun and the moon, the planets, and all the starry host," the angel whispered softly.

"Wow." The boy whispered back, in awe at the wonder of God's seemingly endless universe encompassing them.

As they rose through the twinkling stars, it reminded Edgas of once when he looked down on his city from a large hill. He had watched the sun set and had loved the way the city had disappeared and been replaced with twinkling lights. He had sat on that hill and watched those lights for hours. Now, wonder of wonders, he was watching the twinkling of heavenly lights. Could this really be happening? Was this a dream? He hugged the angel tighter, bringing his face right up next to the face of this mighty being. He felt the angel's muscles ripple under his grasp; he felt warm breath on his cheek. Edgas shook his head. No, this was no dream. He was really and truly flying with an angel through a sea of stars.

Before leaving the Milky Way, Edgas asked if he could see the planet Mars.

"My pleasure," the angel said, and in a flash he was flying Edgas right over the planet, really close to the surface, just so the boy could see for himself whether or not Martians lived there.

"No Martians," Edgas stuck out his chest, triumphantly. "I knew nothin' lived on Mars! My friend, Philipe, said, "There were so Martians," but I said, "there were so *not*." I was right, wasn't I?"

"Yes, Edgas, you were right." The angel could not stop the grin that crossed his face.

Rising above the Milky Way, the angel pointed out numerous Galaxies, Nebulae, and other wonders of space, calling it, "Space Art." Edgas was overwhelmed by the vastness and beauty of Space Art. It was the most amazing thing he had ever seen.

"Look! God made a butterfly in outer space!"

"Yes, I see it. It does look like a butterfly stretched across the expanse of space, doesn't it?"

"It's huge, and that one," Edgas pointed excitedly, "looks like a great big blue eyeball."

"Some people call that nebula, 'God's eye.'"

"Is it?"

"No, more Space Art."

"Golly, God's a good artist," Edgas admired. "He makes really good Space Art."

"Yes, indeed He does. Everything He makes is really good, especially you." The angel smiled at Edgas, and the boy replied with a planet-sized grin.

High above the galaxies and spectacular Space Art, the angel slowed his pace and looked at Edgas, "We are about to enter the area called the Second Heaven; let's do some damage."

Edgas took his amazed eyes off the Space Art and looked curiously into the beautiful face of the one holding him. "Damage? Why would we want to do damage? This is all so beautiful—is that okay with God? I don't understand."

"This is where Satan has set up his spiritual kingdom which includes his palaces and even his throne room. It's also where he keeps people's stolen destinies."

"Ooh! But I thought Satan lived in hell," the boy's face crinkled with question.

"No, he does not live there. He is ruler over hell, but he can come and go at will. It is a horrible place, filled with evil and torture. Many of his minions are stationed there, but he rules from the second heaven."

"So, how do we damage it?"

"Every time one of God's children passes through Satan's kingdom on their way to Heaven they bust big holes in it. As a matter of fact, every time someone on Earth even claps their hands in praise or lifts their voice or instruments in praise, they bust holes in his kingdom. You should see what happens when a whole congregation claps and lifts their voices in praise to the King of Kings—they send missiles through the Kingdom of Darkness. Satan is always having to patch and repair." The angel snickered, "He honestly thought he could get between the Father and His children, but building his kingdom in the Second Heaven was one of the biggest mistakes he ever made."

"Oh! I hate Satan! Let's bust a big hole in his kingdom!"

"Al-righty, then. What's your favorite praise song?"

"That's easy, 'Praise Him'!"

The angel smiled, "I know that one! Ready?"

Edgas nodded, and the two immediately burst into song, Edgas belting it out with all his might.

"Praise Him! Praise Him! Let all the people praise Him. Praise Him! Praise Him! Let all creation sing!"

The angel shifted Edgas and grasped him firmly with his large left arm. "Stay close to my chest," he commanded.

Without missing a song beat, the boy lay his head on the massive chest. The angel then made a fist with his right hand and held it straight up over their heads. The two ascended through the Second Heaven, soaring upward with tremendous speed. Edgas heard loud, explosive sounds. Curious, but still staying obediently close to the angel's chest, Edgas turned his head and peeked over the massive shoulder. He saw bits and pieces and chunks of stuff flying away from them in every direction. Putting his head back on the angel's chest, he closed his eyes and continued to sing his little heart out. "Worthy to receive the glory, honor belongs to you, forever our King and Lord, all praise belongs to you. Praise Him! Praise Him! Let all the people praise Him. Praise Him! Praise Him! Let all creation sing!"

The angel abruptly spread his wings out wide and slowed his speed, "Good job, Edgas!"

The boy lifted his head, revealing a bright smile. "Did we bust a big hole?"

"You bet we did!" The angel looked directly into Edgas' eyes and returned the smile. Then he threw back his head and laughed heartily. "They hate it when we do that!" He shook his head and chuckled, clearly enjoying himself. "They'll have to start patching that pitiful excuse of a palace all over again!"

Edgas grinned.

They flew on quietly for a few moments.

"Now this," the angel swung his arm in a wide arc, "this is the Third Heaven. Look over there."

Edgas turned his head and looked in the direction the angel was pointing. "I see something glowing, but it's not the stars or the Space Art or the sun or any of that stuff cuz we passed all them back there," the boy pointed down, "in the First Heaven."

"You are seeing the glory of God, Edgas."

Edgas and the Angel ascend through the Second Heaven

Edgas' heart leaped. He kept his eyes trained on that glow, watching it grow brighter as they drew nearer and nearer. Soon it was a dazzling light, brighter than the sun or any star they had just passed, and it radiated and flashed brilliant fiery colors. From this distance, it looked like a beautiful diamond suspended in space.

"Wow! God's glory is really sparkly." Edgas was completely mesmerized by the flashing spectacle of light and color. "It kinda looks like Isabel's ring when the sun hits it, only a gazillion million times more."

"It does look like the flashes of a diamond, doesn't it? God's glory is reflecting throughout the whole world that encompasses Heaven."

The boy turned his head and peered expectantly into the radiant face of the angel. "Is that where you're taking me? To Heaven?"

"But of course, Edgas, that is exactly where I am taking you!"

"HURRA! I knew it, I just knew it!"

The angel laughed heartily, fully enjoying the boy.

The two gazed at their sparkling destination. The angel admired anew, through the fresh eyes of the boy, the many colors bursting from the sapphires, emeralds, amethysts, topazes, and other precious stones inlaid into the foundations and situated all over Heaven. It truly was a sight to behold.

"It's HUGE!" exclaimed Edgas, as they quickly approached. "It's way bigger than Earth!"

"You're right about that."

"Like way, way, WAY bigger than any of the planets, and I don't know why, but I thought it would be flat, but it's not flat, it's round like Earth and the planets and the sun and the moon!"

"It's a whole world, Edgas, and it's unlike anything your earthly eyes have ever seen. It has dimensions and wonders which no one can even imagine."

"Oh, wow! Look at that!" They were close enough now to begin discerning more than just flashes of light and color. "It's so beautiful! It's so beautiful! I knew it would be! I knew it! I knew it!" Edgas could hardly contain himself for the joy that flooded him as he fixed his eyes upon the glory of Heaven.

Very shortly, the space travelers had entered Heaven's atmosphere and were flying over luxurious and varied landscapes.

"There's the wall! There's the wall!" Edgas pointed it out, excitedly. "It's huge! I knew it would be! I just knew it! Did you know it's made of jasper?"

"Yes, I did." The angel's eyes crinkled with delight.

"Did you know that there are twelve gates in the wall, made of pearls?"

"Yes, I knew that, too." The angel laughed out loud, as he continued flying this talkative boy to their heavenly destination. "I can tell you have been a serious student of the Bible."

Edgas beamed. It felt good to be praised. Then he turned a quizzical face toward his angelic spacecraft. "I thought all of Heaven was inside the wall? Most of it's outside. Mostly ALL of it's outside the wall."

"That's very observant of you, Edgas. As you've already said, Heaven is huge. The part within the wall is the Eternal City, the New Jerusalem. It is the dwelling place of the Most High, where the Father and the Son sit upon their throne. It is a beautiful city, the most beautiful city that ever was or will be. But there are many other places to visit and explore throughout the world of Heaven, and they are very beautiful, too."

"Look! There're the streets of gold! And look at all those beautiful buildings sparkling! Are those jewels in them?" Edgas pointed excitedly from one thing to another. "Wow, the city looks so green from up here. And colorful! Is that an ocean? Are those mountains? Wow! There's a river, and it's really sparkly! Look at all the trees! Aren't they beautiful? They're so tall! And LOOK at the flowers! They're huge! Are those waterfalls? Oh, Wow! Oh, Wow!" Edgas continued his excited play-by-play as he caught glimpses of the beautiful land on both sides of the wall.

"Edgas, did you know that God prepared Heaven with you in mind? He knew what would thrill you, and He can't wait for you to see it!"

"He knows about *me*?"

"Of course He does! Who do you think sent me to fetch you?"

Edgas thought he might burst with joy.

"Am I gonna meet Jesus today?" He hoped with all his heart the answer would be a resounding, "Yes!"

"Very soon."

"HURRA!"

They were flying so close to the wall now that Edgas could have reached out and touched it. The angel pointed out one of the twelve Gates of Pearl the little scholar had mentioned, and soon after, Edgas lost sight of everything except a lovely garden and the enormous jasper wall, fairly pulsating with life.

The next thing he knew, he was being set down, ever so gently, right next to the wall on the brightest, greenest grass, *ever*! Edgas wiggled his toes in the soft luxuriousness of the grass, noticing that every blade was absolutely perfect. Bursting with joy, he began to dance about wildly while the angel folded his large wings. "I'm here! I'm here! I'm really here!" The boy's joyous shouts echoed off the jasper wall and reverberated throughout the garden.

"Welcome to Heaven!" Edgas heard the angel's announcement and turned to see three other children, just a tad older than he, standing on the other side of his new angelic friend. Edgas was so tickled by the look of surprise on each of their faces that he began to laugh in amusement, snorting even. He had never felt so good and so much joy in all his life. His little body was free from pain, and he was going to meet Jesus. Indeed, it was the best day of his whole, entire, ten-year-old, life.

INTRODUCTION

MAPUTO, MOZAMBIQUE
11:50 a.m.

"Let me hold him." Missionary Isabel Power spoke softly to the nurse at the bedside of Edgas Seca. "Why don't you grab yourself some lunch while I'm here?"

Grateful for the reprieve, the nurse stood and slipped quietly out of the room.

The 10-year-old was losing his battle with complications from an AIDS-causing infection. Edgas had drifted in and out of consciousness throughout the morning, and Isabel knew it wouldn't be long before this brave little soldier would meet his savior, Jesus Christ. The hospital staff had done all they could. Thanks to donations, their crude, little hospital at least had the means to keep young Edgas comfortable.

Isabel slid her strong, slender arms under his frail body, easily lifting him off his cot. *Skin and bones,* she thought. Holding him in her arms, Isabel sat down and drew him close. She would have been thankful the rocker was near the open window, but on this hot and sticky day there was no breeze to bring any relief to the relentless heat. Isabel liked to say she was "glistening" with perspiration, but today, there was no way around it, she was sweating, plain and simple.

"Your Heavenly Father is waiting to welcome you home."

Hearing the whispered words, Edgas' eyes fluttered and slowly opened. He looked intently into Isabel's eyes and she looked lovingly back into his. They held that gaze for a long precious moment. He was saying goodbye, and it moved Isabel to her core. Oh, how she had grown to love this boy. As she looked at his thin little face and hollow cheeks, she saw the edges of his lips begin to curve upward, if ever so slightly. He was smiling at her! What a gift he bestowed. Isabel could not help but give the gift back to Edgas.

Her emotions were a mixture of pain and gratitude: a topsy-turvy conglomeration of joy and sorrow. She had seen too many little ones die. It just wasn't right. Yet, as horrid as that was, another child was leaving his pain and suffering far behind, and for that she was grateful.

Edgas, struggling for his next breath, closed his eyes.

After a minute or two, he opened them again and moved his mouth as though he was trying to say something. Isabel leaned in close, straining to hear him.

"I'm—not—a—fraid."

His words were choppy and slurred between raspy breaths.

"I'm — gon — na — meet — Je — sus — to — day."

"Yes, Edgas! You're going to meet Jesus today!"

Isabel laughed out loud and hugged him close, tears streaming freely down her cheeks. She knew this precious boy was *very* excited to meet his Maker. He had asked her endless questions about Heaven over the past few months. In fact, Heaven was almost all he had wanted to talk about. It was a great comfort to him in the midst of his pain.

Now, his heart, mind, and soul were settled, and he was at peace within. He wasn't asking any more questions. He was unafraid, truly, as he had said.

But his inward peace stood in stark contrast to his outward battle. Edgas was a fighter, and right now he was fighting for every breath.

"Sing — to — me." His words were barely audible.

Isabel began to rock, back and forth, quietly singing Edgas his favorite hymn while her anguished heart cried out to the God of Heaven: *Please Lord, end his suffering. Don't let him hurt for another minute. He's ready to go home and live in Heaven with you. Oh Jesus, send your angels to come and gather this precious son of yours so that he will never again be an orphan.*

Before the unspoken prayer left her heart, the curtain in the window rustled and an indescribable peace filled the room.

Isabel looked at the rustling curtain. *That's strange. I wonder what made the curtain move on this breezeless day.*

"Is someone there?" She thought perhaps one of the orphans had sneaked over to see Edgas, so when no one answered, she called out again, her voice barely above a whisper, "Who's there?"

Edgas jolted and his eyes popped wide-open, startling the breath out of Isabel. Stunned, she noticed his face begin to glow with a radiant glory as a wide smile covered his face. Edgas was suddenly filled with a strength and vigor he had not had in months. His raspy breathing stopped.

"You're an angel of the Lord!" he said, looking up towards the ceiling.

"Do you see an angel, Edgas?" asked Isabel, excitedly.

"Are you here to take me to Heaven?" Edgas continued his one-sided conversation.

"Edgas, is an angel here to take you to Heaven?" Isabel looked up at the stained ceiling and then back at Edgas, and then back at the ceiling.

"Adventure? Oh yeah, I'm ready!" Edgas sat straight up in her lap and stretched his arms out, then shouted excitedly, "Let's go!"

Then just as suddenly, Edgas went completely limp and fell back against Isabel's chest. Again, the curtain in the window rustled, and all was still.

MAPUTO, MOZAMBIQUE
UNSEEN REALM

Her guardian could tell she was weary. He had been watching over Isabel for years and knew her well. She had a strong belief in the Triune and he knew that her faith could not be shaken. She had taught these little ones about her sweet Lord, leading perhaps hundreds to faith in Christ over her many years of service. She could take their little hands and say, "Follow me," because she truly lived out what she believed.

Isabel sang softly as she rocked the child, and Michale lifted his own arms in worship. It was a holy moment, and he was very aware of the sweet presence of the Holy Spirit living within the woman.

He felt something akin to pride the past few weeks as he watched Isabel help Edgas through the most difficult battle of his young life. The boy had faced death with more strength and dignity than most adults he had seen over his many, many years, and many assignments. In this case, he could easily shout, "O death, where is your sting? O grave, where is your victory?"

He glanced over at Sancto, Edgas' guardian, who was gazing tenderly at the boy as he struggled for his last few earthly breaths. Michale and Sancto had served side by side for several years. It was not an angel's job to question. Michale fully trusted in the Lord's wisdom, but, still, that didn't mean he wouldn't miss his friend.

Just as expected, Abel flew in to fetch Edgas. He greeted the guardians who returned the greeting and then retreated out of his way. Michale knew that Sancto would miss guarding the boy. Neither felt sad about it knowing they would see him, and each other, often in Heaven, but there was a bitter-sweetness in this season coming to a close. Sancto had enjoyed this assignment, yet he was looking forward to a short rest before being given his next charge. He knew he had served the Lord, and the boy, well.

The two guardians watched with delight as Edgas recognized their friend, Abel, as an angel of the Lord. They hung back, out of the way, so as not to interfere with Abel's assignment. They were tickled at Isabel's confused face as Edgas hung for a moment between the two realities. Isabel had been given a precious gift, and Michale felt his heart soar with gratitude at the kindness of his Creator.

When Abel and the boy left the room, Sancto saluted Michale. "Good bye, my friend. Take care of sweet Isabel. I shall see you soon."

Michale grinned and returned the salute. "Enjoy your break, you lucky fellow!"

"Whatever." The angel made a "W" with his thumbs and forefingers like the kids in the orphanage often did. He laughed and shook his head, "It's not luck, and you know it! You're picking up bad habits from those kids!"

The two friends shared a laugh and then a hug and slap on the back.

"Keep an eye on Edgas for me."

"You know I will. Goodbye, my friend." Sancto spread his wings and leaped into the air. He followed Abel and Edgas all the way to Heaven. Edgas did not see him following, but Sancto would not have missed Edgas' discoveries for anything.

Michale waved goodbye then turned his attention back to Isabel. He saw the scrawny demon out of the corner of his eye, had smelled his presence for a long time, but gave him no indication, no acknowledgement. He'd deal with him soon enough, but for now his focus was on strengthening Isabel and on that alone.

TOKYO, JAPAN
6:50 p.m.

"Oh no! Masumi, we gotta go!" Michitaka Hara jumped up from the table, crammed his books in his backpack, and began running towards the door.

Startled by the unaccustomed ruckus, other students in the quiet library stared as his embarrassed sister hurriedly followed his example.

Michitaka, *Michi* as his family and friends called him, had been helping Masumi study for her high school entrance exam. The two had lost track of time, and, as they both knew well, trains in Tokyo waited for no one. The sun was setting behind towering skyscrapers, and Masumi knew her parents would soon begin to worry. The library was about a ten-minute walk from Higashi-Shinjuku Station where the siblings took the Tokyo Metro Fukutoshin Line. They would have to run if they had a chance at catching the Express, and with only one train transfer, and a short walk, they'd be home in about forty-five minutes, but if they missed it, and had to take the "local," it would stop at every station between here and the moon, and they wouldn't be home until—well, until forever.

"Can't you just call Okasan and tell her we got caught up in our studies?" Masumi hoped her voice would carry to the bobbing dark head running in front of her.

"No! Phone died this afternoon."

"Ugh. This is why I need my own phone." Masumi muttered her frustration as she scurried to keep up with her brother. "I told Okasan I needed my own phone; maybe now she'll believe me." Raising her voice, she called out, "You know we're gonna be grounded for *life*!"

"YES! I KNOW! And I'm not taking all the rap for this, Masumi; you have a watch, too, you know."

"I know, I know. I'm sorry. I wasn't paying any attention," then she whispered to herself, "because—I figured *you* were."

Michi chastised himself for forgetting to charge his phone and for not noticing the time. *Way to go, Michi-san! You blew it again, you big dope!* He glanced down at his watch, the digital numbers glowed 6:54. *You're gonna miss the 7 o'clock, too, you idiot.* He hollered over his shoulder, a little too harshly, "COME ON! HURRY UP, MASUMI! We canNOT miss this train!"

Masumi ran hard to catch up with her brother. "Michi! Let's just ask someone if we can borrow their phone!"

"What, and miss the Express? No way! Just come on, we can make it."

His longer legs pulled him ahead again. But, realizing his sister's idea was probably a good, practical one, he turned his head and called back to her, "We'll ask somebody once we get on the train!"

Presently finding himself trapped in a sea of dark-headed commuters, Michi knew they would never make it in time if he stayed within their slow-moving current, so he plunged ahead, rudely knocking into people as he worked at slipping past them.

Masumi tried her best to keep up, but then she too got trapped in that sea of humanity although she was not about to bump into them as her brother had done. She completely lost sight of his black crop of hair in the ocean of dark crops in front of her. A tad of panic threatened to choke her, and she determined not to lose him. Hopping off the sidewalk, she ran in the street next to the curb until she passed the congestion. Her mother would have had a fit if she had seen her do that. It was not only dangerous, and probably illegal, but even more importantly, it was extremely rude.

Masumi ran as fast as she could under the weight of her loaded backpack. Her heavy books pounded painfully into her back, bouncing with every step. She finally managed to catch up with her brother, and, just when she did, they reached and rounded the all-familiar corner. Immediately, she saw the entrance to the train station just across the street. *Almost there.* Michi took another quick glance at his watch: 6:58.

"I think we can make it, Masumi!" He yelled, glancing back at her as he darted into the crosswalk. "Come on!"

He was jolted by a long blast of a horn and tires screeching.

"MICHI!" Masumi's scream came loud and shrill.

Michi looked up and saw the headlights of a car barreling down on him. He froze. For an instant, he couldn't think what to do, then he quickly spun around and dove back in the direction he had come from. He exploded into Masumi, sending her tumbling backwards and then landed with a thud on top of her. The car skidded to a halt just inches from where the two lay in a heap on the pavement.

He lay still for a second or two, his heart pounding wildly, relief flooding his body. He pushed himself up and brushed the dirt off his uniform. "I am so sorry, Masumi. You okay?"

She didn't answer. She didn't move.

He looked down at her and repeated, "Masumi, are you okay?" Again, there was no response. He grabbed her, shaking her gently, "Masumi! Answer me!"

He felt a thick, warm liquid on his hand—blood. It was coming from the back of her head.

"Oh God, Help! Somebody, help me!" Michi looked around desperately. "HELP! PLEASE! I NEED HELP!"

He felt for a pulse. His heart was beating so loudly he couldn't tell if hers was beating or not. Already a crowd was gathering around him, and someone holding a cell phone said they had called for an ambulance.

Michi held his lifeless sister in his arms. *Oh my God...What have I done? What have I done?*

TOKYO, JAPAN
UNSEEN REALM

"No you don't!" A large, glowing, and very handsome creature appeared out of nowhere, picked up a small, grotesque demon and easily tossed him aside, and then, just as suddenly, pushed Michi out of the way of the vehicle which was barreling down on him. The car screeched to a halt, rolling straight through the angel as he stood, protectively, over the brother and sister.

"NOOOO!" The insidious demon scampered to his feet and ran full steam toward the children.

"Oh, YEEESS!" The angel stood his ground, tall and erect, carrying all the authority of Heaven. With hands on hips, he spread his massive wings and faced the beast head-on, shielding the children from the demon's fury. There was no way this little weasel was getting to the children, not on his watch.

The demon spit out vulgarities, raging mad, knowing full well he could not get past this envoy of Heaven and that he had been unsuccessful in his mission, earning him a severe beating which would most assuredly follow.

Zimbu and Thigma, the children's guardians, joined the newcomer in spreading their wings protectively around the young pair, and the three angels became an impenetrable hedge.

Hiding in the shadows, too cowardly to come out and face his sworn enemies, was another demon, bigger and more deformed than the first. Furious that his plan had failed, he cursed a long spew of vile but kept himself hidden from the angels' view.

Presently, another of Heaven's envoys, magnificent in both appearance and strength, flew to the scene. "Ready, Raphia?" His booming voice was as powerful as his mighty presence.

"She's all yours, Tooma."

Immediately, Tooma reached out and scooped Masumi up in his massive arms. He wrapped her tightly in light, saluted his comrades, and then with a grin, shot like a bullet into the heavenlies.

Raphia spoke quietly to the guardians, "All set?"

"Yes," they responded. "We understand the plan."

Zimbu added, "I will watch from the perimeter like we discussed, and then at the precise moment, I'll distract the horde while you transform."

"Good," Raphia smiled, then looked to the other guardian.

"I will discreetly back away until Masumi is taken to the ambulance. At that point, I will not leave her side until she returns," responded Thigma.

"Heaven has sent me in answer to the girl's prayers," said Raphia.

Thigma nodded, remembering Masumi's prayer uttered only this morning. This was going to be a great day; he could feel it in his bones.

"Heaven is with us," said Zimbu, loving that he was from the kingdom that could say that with full assurance of its truth.

"Okay, then," Raphia smiled at the guardians, "here we go."

In the minutes that followed, as witnesses and curious onlookers pushed in toward the children, the two guardians retreated clandestinely into the crowd, blending seamlessly with the other guardians present. If all went as planned, the demons would not be able to tell which guardians were assigned to whom in this sea of humanity milling excitedly about. And although Thigma had backed out of the picture, he never once took his eyes off of Masumi.

Raphia turned and looked for the little pest. *Probably hiding in the shadows.* He leaned over the boy pretending to study him for a moment. "Well, well, well, what'd ya know...I do believe I see a mark on this one." He straightened to his full nine feet and announced, "Michitaka belongs to Jesus!"

At the mention of that holy name, all demons within earshot grabbed their ears and cowered. A smile tugged at the edges of Raphia's mouth. He couldn't see the traitors, but he knew what they were doing; he'd seen it many times before. He was almost tempted to say it again—just for pure pleasure—but he had an assignment to carry out, and he mustn't miss his opportunity.

Knowing Thigma's keen eyes were attentive on the boy and girl, Raphia, unhurried, left them and walked amid the crowd, dimming his light as he went.

At that exact moment, Zimbu shot like lightening into the sky, leaving a trail of glory in his wake.

Every demon within miles looked up; and while their curious eyes followed the blazing streak across the sky, they did not see the angel change form.

Raphia quickly returned to the boy, looking to all the world like one of the men in the crowd. As he watched the unsuspecting demons, the angel could not stop—nor did he try to stop—the smile, which lifted the corners of his mouth. His eyes twinkled as he thought, *Oh, how I love my job!*

KANSAS CITY, KANSAS, USA
4:59 a.m.

Cristen Maples' parents waited helplessly in Room 421 mocked by colorful flower arrangements and a bright balloon bouquet. Taped to the walls were dozens of cards—some store bought, some handmade—filled with prayers and good wishes for a quick recovery. A muted television set hung forgotten above their heads; a blue and yellow privacy curtain was pulled to one side along its ceiling track; a hospital tray loaded with several magazines, a book, an iPhone, an iPad, a small Styrofoam cup with a bendable straw, and a plastic water pitcher filled with melting ice chips was pushed over by the wall; and an assortment of machinery, oxygen tubing, and red emergency signs hung on the wall behind where the bed had just stood. Now, both bed and occupant were eerily missing, leaving a void in the room and an aching void in their hearts.

William Maples had arrived just moments earlier. Awoken out of a deep sleep, he had thrown on a pair of track pants, thrust his feet into sneakers, and sped to the hospital after receiving the frantic call from his wife. Thankfully, there was plenty of parking at this hour, and he had found a close spot right away. Why this Emergency Room didn't have valet parking was beyond him, even if it was the middle of the night. He threw the car in park, opened the door, and raced towards the entrance, his only thought to get to the side of his wife and daughter. How he managed to turn off the motor, grab his keys, and start running without getting his leg slammed in the car door, he'd never know.

"Come on. Come on. Come on."

The elevator came no faster at his urging. He rushed in before the doors fully opened and simultaneously pushed the number four and the close-door buttons in rapid succession. Oblivious to his distress, the doors paused, then calmly slid closed, and then with great relief he felt the elevator rising.

Almost there. He wiped his forehead on his shirtsleeve and paced back and forth waiting for the doors to now reopen. The moment they did, he burst through the gap and sprinted down the hall towards Cristen's private room.

Just as Will reached for the handle, the door swung inward. He had to jump out of the way to avoid being run over. Two aides and several nurses were pushing the hospital bed out of the room. Frantically looking between the bodies of running staff, Will caught only a glimpse of his daughter as the bed whizzed past him and rushed down the hall.

Feet frozen to the floor, he stared in shock at the disappearing group. Turning, he faced his wife who had moved to the doorway. The two held each other's gaze, eyes and hearts communicating without words. Will looked down the hall and then back at his wife. Elaine nodded followed by a deep breath. Will reached out and squeezed her hand, then tore off down the hall after his daughter.

Catching up to the hustling group, he could not wedge in close enough to touch Cristen, so he ran along beside them. Her attendants noticed him for the first time when he hopped on the elevator behind them. Ignoring the hospital staff, Will reached over the side bed railing and placed his hand on his daughter's arm as the aide pushed the button for the second floor.

"Cristen. Cristen, can you hear me?" There was no response from the girl. "Cristen, it's Daddy. I'm here, baby. Daddy's here."

The staff quietly exchanged glances, sorrow for the father filling their eyes.

"You're gonna be okay. You're gonna be okay, sweetheart."

The elevator quickly descended, and within seconds the doors opened on the second floor. Will jumped off the elevator and out of the way but continued to run beside his beloved child. Though she was now a teenager, she would always and forever be his little princess.

As they approached the operating room, one of the aides turned to him. "This is as far as you go." He spoke with authority, but his eyes were kind.

"I love you, Cristen. Oh Father, be with my baby girl. Jesus, help her, help her, Lord. It's gonna be okay, baby. It's gonna be okay."

Wasn't it? He hoped so. With all his heart, he hoped it was so.

Will kissed his fingers and stretched them towards Cristen one last time, managing to touch her foot just before the staff ran her through doors into a restricted area.

Oh God! Have mercy. Help the doctor know what to do. Heal her, Lord. Oh God! I trust you. Help me trust you. Be with my baby. Be with her Lord. Oh God! Oh God!

The doors before him closed, and she was gone.

Will stood, alone, at a red line he couldn't cross before doors he couldn't enter. His shoulders sank along with his spirit. He had never been so scared in all his life. He was out of breath, and it wasn't from the constant sprinting of the past few minutes; no, it was from the panic trying to overtake him. He felt as though his heart might beat right out of his chest.

After staring blankly at the closed doors and the No Admittance sign for a full minute, he sighed heavily and dropped his head. Every ounce of him wanted to slump to the floor. He tried to calm himself by taking deep breaths and letting the air out slowly. The last thing he wanted to do was leave his baby girl, but he was no good to her standing here in the hall. Reluctantly, he turned and began the trek back to his wife.

The moment Elaine saw him, she bolted out of her chair and ran into his arms. They held each other in a long embrace before Elaine pulled back and looked desperately into Will's eyes.

"I went with her as far as they would let me. I tried to talk to her, but she didn't respond." His voice was choked with emotion. "What in the world happened?"

Elaine quickly brought her husband up to speed. Cristen had suddenly spiked a fever after complaining of great pain. She seemed to be falling in and out of sleep, but when awake she was talking nonsensically and was confused and disoriented.

The alarm on a monitor had sounded, and Elaine thought it sounded different from the alarm that alerted nurses when the IV bag needed to be changed or had a kink in the line, and a nurse had immediately rushed in. After a quick check of her vitals and a glance at the monitor, the attending intern was called in—that's when Elaine had phoned Will to get to the hospital as quickly as possible. By this time, Cristen was coming in and out of consciousness, an alarm had been sounded and a decision was made to rush her back into surgery. And that's when Will got there.

Beside himself, Will paced back and forth around the empty room while the completely drained mother sank wearily into the green vinyl recliner where she had slept, or rather tried to sleep, for the past two nights. The adrenaline and shock of the last few minutes now settled into a tangible fear.

The blasted alarm echoed over and over in Elaine's mind. *Oh dear Jesus! Please don't let her die!* She searched her husband's face for any sign of hope.

Will collapsed onto the small metal chair next to Elaine and ran his hands through his thinning hair. *How could this be happening?* They never expected this. He stared blankly at his feet, never even noticing the untied laces.

Elaine had been fighting back her tears, but now that her husband was here she gave in to them. "Oh Will, I'm so scared!"

"Me too, baby." Instinctively, he reached out to hold his wife's hand, his own eyes brimming. He tried to think of something to say, something which might encourage his wife, but his sluggish brain came up with nothing. Breathing heavily, he rubbed his crying wife's back for a few seconds, but then feeling completely helpless, he popped up and began to pace again, round and around the tiny room.

The incessant circling made Elaine feel sick to her stomach, so she closed her eyes. One more pass around the room, and she might throw up.

Suddenly, Will dropped to his knees in front of his wife and clasped her hands in his. He looked deep into her eyes, "We need to pray!"

Tears splashed on him as she nodded her head in agreement.

Slipping silently out of the recliner, Elaine turned and kneeled beside her husband, placing both elbows on the seat in front of her. Will leaned forward and rested his elbows next to hers. Still holding hands, they bowed their heads, and together, began to pour out their anguished hearts to their Heavenly Father.

KANSAS CITY, KANSAS, USA
UNSEEN REALM

"You cannot touch them!" An angelic being turned to face a spirit of fear lurking in the doorway of the hospital room.

"I can do whatever I want," spouted the demon.

"That is a lie! And these are not yours to torment."

"They are if they listen to me." The demon knew the couple would be vulnerable to his attack right now. He was titillated by the taste of easy prey, and his lizard-like tongue licked his cracked lips in anticipation.

"Even if they listen to your accursed lies, they do not belong to you." Obed swept to the doorway and boldly leaned down, nose to nose, and glared into the bloodshot eyes of the odious creature. "You are not welcome here." He opened his wings and blocked the demon's view of the couple as they collapsed in their chairs.

In no way deterred by his former ally, the spirit bared his fangs and snarled at the angel, determined to find a way past the guardian's defense. He would not be bullied by these towering lights. He had as much right to be here as they did. He spread his scaly wings, and with a hefty thrust, leaped over Obed, hovering only a moment before landing on a beam above the ceiling. His hideous form cast a dark shadow over Will and Elaine and brought a heavy foreboding into the air.

Instinctively, Innesto, the guardian who had watched over Elaine since the day God had breathed her spirit into her dot of flesh, spread his strong, feathery wings over her. His assignment was to shield her from the fiery darts of the enemy, and shield her he would. This insect was defeated at Calvary, and he would have no victory over Elaine. She belonged to the Most High, a cherished daughter of the King, and Innesto would do everything in his power to protect her.

Presently, like sharks drawn to blood, two more demons joined the spirit of fear on his perch.

Obed moved to the center of the room, "Leave them alone, I tell you."

But the demons had no intention of leaving them alone. Like rabid animals, they began their frenzied attack.

"Cristen's going to die! My baby's going to die! She's gonna die!" The spirit of fear squawked from his perch.

"God is going to take her!" The spirit of accusation was quick to join in, "God is going to take my girl! He doesn't care about me. God is going to take her."

"Stop it!" commanded Innesto. "You and your kind are the ones that kill, not God!"

"It's no use." Hopelessness joined his depressed voice with the tirade of lies. He slinked across the ceiling until he was directly above the couple. He lay on his belly and spoke with slow, almost slurred words, "It's no use. God has never answered my prayers. Cristen is as good as dead, and God doesn't care."

But just then, the couple slipped to their knees in prayer, and as Will called on the name of Jesus, the demons covered their ears and shrieked.

Light flooded the room as Heaven opened above them. Heaven was receiving their prayers.

KANSAS CITY, KANSAS, USA
4:54 a.m.

Bursting through double doors, hospital aides hurried Cristen Maples into the operating room. The scrubbed surgeon slapped on a mask, rammed his hands into gloves, and rushed through the doors behind the wheeled, gurney-like bed, being careful not to touch anything. The icy room was a flurry of activity as doctors, nurses, and assistants scrambled to prepare for the emergency surgery. Bright lights hovered in the center of the room like UFOs. Packages of sterilized utensils were flung opened, thudding on a cold metal tray draped in green. Everything, it seemed, was draped in green. Everything except for the scurrying staff who were draped, head to foot, in blue.

The aides scooped up Cristen and easily transferred her limp body to the operating table. After making sure she was secure, they seized the bed and rushed back through the doors and out of the way. With one fluid motion, a seasoned nurse swept back the teenager's long blond hair, twisted it, stuffed it up under a cloth cap, and then immediately covered Cristen's mouth and nose with an oxygen mask. When the mask was secure, she then snatched up numerous wires and expertly connected Cristen to a series of computer monitors. Glowing numbers, words, and green graph lines flickered to life, beeping and bleeping as they ran across the screens filling the room. Meanwhile, the anesthesiologist checked the IV line and began making his preparations.

They were a well-oiled machine—gifted, talented, rehearsed, each knowing their part and flawlessly executing it; and yet, in spite of the untold hours of experience constituted in this small room, there was a palpable tension in the air as concern for the young girl was mounting. The teenager before them lay unconscious, looking much more dead than alive. Contrary to the way she appeared, however, the heart monitor displayed a racing heart. Her life was in their hands, and they were fully aware that one mistake, or one momentary lapse in concentration, could mean the difference between life and death. Their faces reflected a mixture of compassion and professionalism as they readied Cristen for surgery.

Dr. James had a gift for staying calm and steady under pressure, but even he could feel his own heart rate increasing. "Lord, help us." His whispered prayer flowed from his heart and his lips as he adjusted the lights and began to examine his young patient, who looked utterly helpless and vulnerable lying on the table before him.

What in the world went wrong? James' mind raced, searching for answers. Mental images of the late night surgery he had performed just two nights previous flew through his mind. He was an excellent surgeon; there was no doubt about that, and by all indications, this girl had initially appeared to have had a successful appendectomy. In fact, he had just read in a report that her pediatrician was planning to have her released later this morning, assuming no complications.

What could have caused such a sudden turnabout? An infection? Dr. James knew there was no time to spare and that he must ascertain the problem—quickly—if he were to save her life. Every eye was steady on him, as this group of highly trained professionals awaited his instructions.

Give me wisdom, Lord.

"Let's open her up." He lifted his eyes and nodded to his attending staff. "We're going back through the original incision." With that, everyone immediately flew into action. Like a well-rehearsed orchestra, with the surgeon as conductor, the symphony to save the life of Cristen Maples began.

KANSAS CITY, KANSAS, USA
UNSEEN REALM

The operating room was filled to overflowing with spiritual beings of all shapes and sizes. The stark contrast in the room between good and evil and light and darkness was unmistakable as both beautiful, glowing guardians and hideous, deformed demons crouched, stood, and hovered in close proximity, watching over their human assignments.

Guardians live in a battle zone; it is the nature of their gifting and assignment. So, as always, the angels in the room kept a sharp eye on the demons around them, knowing that every intention of these evil beasts was continuously cruel and vicious. The guardians knew that most of these bloodthirsty savages had legal right to be there, having been invited, albeit unknowingly, by the actions of their hosts. They also knew that the demons' sole quest was to steal, kill, and bring destruction in any form, by any means, whenever and wherever possible. The demons preyed especially upon the vulnerable, always taking advantage of any weakness, no matter how young, how defenseless, or how frail. The vermin were never nice, never thoughtful, never considerate, never compassionate—not ever. To them, mercy was a sign of weakness, and they loathed it. They were hateful and malicious to their core, and they fed on inflicting as much pain and torment as possible, especially when they had an audience. And to top it all off, every demon in that room knew that any failure would be met with swift reprisal of a dreaded and painful punishment.

As always, Ziv stood right behind Dr. Arthur James, the man he had lovingly attended for forty-six years. He had spent hours upon hours in this very operating room blocking arrows of accusations against his charge and driving out tormenting spirits of death and fear. Ziv loved the intensity of emergency surgery and, on many occasions, had skillfully guided the surgeon's hands, helping his man successfully execute some very difficult, and sometimes impossible, operations. It was a wonderful privilege that Ziv would never take for granted, nor would he ever get over the wonder of God's human creation.

This quiet guardian had been gifted with exceeding intelligence and was always one step ahead of his enemy. He never acted impulsively, out of anger or frustration but handled every situation swiftly, with calm confidence. It was natural for him to take a leadership role in this room, as did his human charge. The other angelic beings deferred to him, but they were unified in heart and purpose and worked well together as a team. It was this advantage that gave them the upper hand on most occasions. The demons were too occupied in tearing each other apart, both figuratively and literally, to ever work in unity. And, as every angel not only knew but had also witnessed, a house divided against itself simply cannot stand.

Ziv watched the team make ready and knew routinely what actions Dr. Art would take. The guardian's vantage point, being nearly three feet above the surgeon's head, afforded the angel an easy view of the young patient stretched out on the operating table. Gazing at Cristen, he was filled with compassion. He acknowledged and welcomed her guardian with a nod of his head. They were of the same class and rank, and understood this nonverbal message of respect and support. No words were needed.

Ziv remained vigilant. He knew that one of the most successful techniques of the Kingdom of Darkness was to spew lies into the thoughts of humans. It was not without cause that Satan is called the Father of Lies. Ziv had witnessed the enemies of God setting about their evil plans of pain and torment, and then watched them as they successfully flipped it around and blamed their handiwork on the human's own ineptness, and even on God Himself. Century after century, Ziv had seen humanity listen to all manner of sickening lies and, tragically, believe them. The demons were experts at twisting distortion around the hearts and minds of people, binding them in chains of unbelief. And every spirit in that room, both from Heaven and hell, knew well that when a person believes a lie about who they are, and about who God is, they will eventually self-destruct.

The surgeon's guardian glanced at the unwelcome evil in the room. How far they had fallen. It was almost impossible to believe that these hideous, evil creatures had once been beautiful spiritual beings, in love with their Creator. What a horrific testimony of what happens to a being void of light and love and truth. How they had turned their backs on the Majestic One From Whom Eternity Came, Ziv would never understand. But they had. The God of Heaven made no robots. Ziv was grateful that he himself had been given freewill. But the demons had used their freewill and chose to believe that the Father of Lies would exalt them and give them kingdoms and power if they followed him; they willingly, knowingly, chose to follow this created being. Oh, Lucifer was crafty and beautiful, make no mistake. He was the most beautiful of all God's created beings. But he was not God! And after tempting every angel, he had found himself on the wrong side of a lightening bolt, removed forever from the glory of Heaven. Ziv reflected that Lucifer, now called Satan, is still quite handsome to look at, much like a stately prince. That is, until you see his eyes. They are hard and filled only with hate.

Ziv looked up through the hospital roof into the expanse of the heavenlies. The demons were spewing lies, but he knew the truth. A feeling of thankfulness flooded him. He not only knew the truth of the situation—it did not take much discernment on his part—but he also knew *the* Truth! This Truth had a name, and it is Jesus! Ziv nodded his head towards Heaven in great appreciation. How he loved the Triune God.

And how he hated these despicable demons. Having watched them hurt God's beloved creation for so long, he longed for the day when the Kingdom of Darkness will be cast into the Lake of Fire, forever! Never again to pollute the atmosphere with their evil venom. But until that day, Ziv wished that people understood they could have victory, now. He knew without question, that God wants His people free from the chains of deception, and will joyfully shatter the lies that bind them. If people only knew what it meant to take up their spiritual weapons and put on the full armor of God. If they'd learn to resist the devil, he would flee! And, Oh! If people ever understood that angels were given authority to fight on behalf of the believer when they prayed and spoke words of faith, they would never stop praying! Ziv knew that faith is the shield by which angels can deflect the lies shot at the human. And if any arrow gets by the shield, then the truth of the Word implanted in their hearts will keep the lies from penetrating. How Ziv wished God's people understood these principles.

While Ziv was thinking about these things, another angel flew unexpectedly into the room. Ziv recognized Uriel at once. He had been sent from Heaven to escort a newly departed spirit home. Ziv looked compassionately back at the child and knew that she would not make it through this surgery. He knew, without question, that she belonged to the Lord and great wonders and adventures and glories awaited her. He was not in the least sad for her, but his heart went out to her family who would surely grieve her loss.

The newcomer greeted his breed with a broad smile, then landing at the side of the table, stood watch over the body of Cristen.

As soon as they saw him, the demons began bouncing up and down in ravenous anticipation like vicious little hyenas about to get the spoil. The smell of death in their nostrils was a rush to their senses. Experience had proven that their victims were very vulnerable right now, and so with confidence they began an all-out assault on the minds of the medical staff, planting putrid lies of fear and hopelessness. It was disgusting.

Despite the swirl all about him, Uriel never took his eyes off of the girl's spirit, and at the very moment Cristen began to rise out of her body, Uriel wrapped her in his light.

"Guard her well, comrades, she'll be back in a bit." Uriel shot out of the room, traveling through space faster than the speed of light—he flew at God-speed. Holding the teenager tightly in his arms, he turned his face towards Heaven. He closed his eyes with a grin, thoroughly enjoying one of the most fun parts of his duties.

There was a moment of confusion among the demons. Only a few had heard the angel's declaration, and they were furious with the news. Robbed completely of any pleasure, they shot menacing looks at the ones who were still carrying on as if nothing had happened. They knew that this was not the feeding frenzy they'd envisioned, and the tables would soon turn.

If this child really came back from the dead, it would not go well for any of them. In fact, it would be a hand's down defeat.

Demons began jumping on demons to shut them up, and several quietly slithered, unnoticed, out of the room.

While in complete contrast, the guardians whooped and laughed and even danced, completely overjoyed with the wonderful news. They knew that The One Who Sits On The Throne was working a marvelous plan, and this battle would most assuredly be theirs.

PARIS, FRANCE
11:56 a.m.

Celeste Leonard lifted the lid off the pot of homemade soup and gently stirred. She loved the way her little kitchen smelled of freshly baked bread, roasted garlic, and sautéed onions. She found cooking therapeutic and spent many of her well-earned days off right here in this kitchen. She hummed unconsciously as her thoughts traveled back to happier days. Just as she was placing the lid back on the pot, she heard a bloodcurdling scream followed by a loud thud which shook the house as if a bomb had exploded.

"What in heaven's name?" Celeste dropped her spoon and ran towards the sound of the crash. She rounded the corner to find her teenaged son, Henri, lying motionless at the bottom of the stairs. Blood was coming out of his mouth and a broken arm was twisted in an unnatural position.

"HENRI!" Celeste threw her hand over her mouth and rushed to his side. "Oh my God! Oh my God! Alison, Call SAMU!"

Henri's twin sister stood wide-eyed, frozen at the top of the stairs.

"NOW!"

Alison shook off her stupor, tore herself away from the railing, and flew down the hall to get her cell phone. Her fingers trembled as she dialed 112.

Crouching over her son, Celeste laid her cheek close to his mouth and prepared to administer CPR. She felt a faint breath and saw his chest lift.

"Oh thank God." Relief flooded her body. "Henri? Henri, can you hear me?"

No response.

"Stay with me, son," she begged.

Leaving Henri for only a moment, Celeste raced to the kitchen, switched off the burner and grabbed a dishcloth. Back at his side, she wiped his mouth so he wouldn't choke on his blood.

Fear and panic were closing in. Her eyes brimmed with tears and her hands began to visibly shake. She had no clue what to do. Seeing his twisted body made her feel queasy, but after a failed attempt to adjust his bent arm, she decided it was best to leave it and wait for help.

Henri's twin slid next to her mother on the floor. "He tripped on the stairs and fell all the way down!" Tears welled in Alison's eyes. "Maman, is he gonna be all right?"

"I don't know, honey." Celeste tried to control the panic in her voice. "Did you call SAMU?"

"Yes. They're sending an ambulance."

"What did they ask you?"

"The doctor asked if he was conscious."

"Is that all?"

"No, he asked how much he weighed and if he took any meds."

"So they're sending an ambulance?"

"Yes, Maman."

"Is a doctor coming, too?"

"I don't know; he didn't say."

"Oh, please hurry!" Celeste whispered. "Please, please hurry!" She leaned over her son looking for signs of life...*still breathing but barely*.

Feeling completely helpless, she shrieked, "Don't die on me, Henri!" startling Alison, who burst into tears and began to sob uncontrollably.

Celeste glanced at her sheepishly; she hadn't meant to upset her tender daughter. The twins had celebrated their fourteenth birthday just last week. They looked so much alike with their light brown hair and big brown eyes. Henri was several inches taller than Alison, but Ali, as he called her, was older, *by a whole half an hour*, and she loved to rub that in.

Now the older twin was collapsed at his side, willing him to live.

"Come on RiRi, please be okay." Staring at the motionless body, she choked the words out through hot tears. "Hang on, little brother, people are coming to help you." She leaned into her mother, who pulled the young girl into an embrace, holding her tightly. Alison buried her face into her mother's shoulder.

Celeste, one hand on Henri and the other around Alison, could not stop her own tears. Taking a deep breath, she lifted her head and shook it slightly, determining to be strong and forcing herself to believe everything was going to be all right—although she was beginning to get frustrated. *Where is that ambulance? What's taking them so long?* With a wave of panic, she looked at Alison. "Today's not a holiday is it?"

"No," whimpered Alison, "it's not." She lifted her head, revealing tears still streaming down her cheeks.

"Did they say they were coming?"

"Yes. They said they would send an ambulance right away."

"Did you give them the right address?"

"Yes," Alison's lip quivered as she wiped her sweaty hands on her jeans. "Oh, Maman, I'm so scared!"

"Me, too, Alison. I am, too." Celeste felt like the earth had given way, and she was free falling. Her resolve, made only moments ago, had already melted away. Her hands were no longer the only things shaking; her entire body was trembling as fear began to overtake her. She reached her shaky hand out and placed it back on Henri's chest. She couldn't feel any movement, but perhaps that was due to the trembling. Scared out of her mind, she cried out, "Oh God, if you are real, PLEASE HELP US!"

PARIS, FRANCE
UNSEEN REALM

Three massive angels huddled together over their human assignments. Starlin looked awkwardly at the other two and shrugged. "He tripped."

"He wasn't pushed? By one of *them*?" Heston nodded his head in the direction of the shadows.

"No, pure accident. He tripped."

"What were *you* doing, reading a book?" Capri teased.

"Very funny, Capri. Come on, you know Henri. He never walked anywhere. Perhaps if he had listened to his mother about running on the stairs—"

"Did you know?" Heston interrupted, looking directly at Henri's guardian.

"No. I didn't." Starlin slowly released a breath he hadn't even realized he'd been holding.

"So then, he must not die, otherwise you would have been advised." Capri's puzzled expression matched the other two guardians.

"Yes, that is true." Starlin agreed.

"Well, this is good then," added Capri.

"Of course it is good," stated the more solemn Heston. "Everything from The Master is good."

Starlin lowered his voice, "If it was held in secret, even from us, then He is planning a surprise attack."

"Ah, I love a good bushwhacking," Capri whispered, his eyes bright with mirth.

Starlin turned his gaze on the boy he had grown to love and said compassionately, "But in the meantime, poor Henri's not looking so good."

His comrade winced at the wrangled arm. "I'm glad he is unconscious."

"Yeah, that's gotta hurt," Capri agreed.

"The brat's as good as dead." A low, beastly voice growled from the shadows.

The muscles in Starlin's face tightened, and he instinctively squeezed his hand into a fist.

"Looks like you losers were left out of the loop."

Oh, how that sandpaper voice grated on one's nerves, especially when it was followed by an even more unpleasant laugh.

"He's forgotten all about you losers. He doesn't care about you. Look at you, you think you're so high and mighty. Suckers, all of you! He's just using you, working you. He doesn't even know you exist. You're his puppets. That's what you are—puppets! Stuck down here in this little apartment with these losers, these insignificant mortals. You've been overlooked, you know, You should—"

"Oh, SHUT UP!" Three heads snapped towards the irritating voice. "That's enough!" Their humans listened to these confounded lies, but they certainly didn't have to. And if anybody in the room was an unnoticed, uncared for sucker and puppet, it was him. The very lies he spouted were actually quite true—of him!

"Make me." The emboldened demon snarled, as he began crouching towards his human victims.

"I'll make him," Starlin clinched his fist and turned towards the demon. Heston gently grabbed his arm. "Wait," he kept his voice low. "Don't even give him the satisfaction of acknowledging him."

Everything in Starlin wanted to attack the annoying pest, drive him out of the house with his tail between his legs, licking his wounds, but Heston was right; it wasn't time. He quietly turned back, took a deep breath, and trained his eyes on Henri, trusting that the orders to fight would come soon enough.

Capri leaned close, "How many do you think there are?"

"I don't know, four or five maybe. They're waiting for more, or they'd already be out here."

Heston was absolutely right, for the moment Henri had fallen, one of the foul minions had flown off for reinforcements.

Typically, the demons had more access to spew their lies into the thoughts of their human assignments, but seeing the guardians huddled together, on high alert, gave them pause and a reason to be a little more guarded. A face-to-face with the guardians right now would be too risky. They would wait for backup or be shredded. So for now, they stayed hidden, obliged to sling their fast-pitched, hardballs of fear from the shadows. But make no mistake, those hardballs were well-aimed directly at their victims.

Capri looked at his sweet charge. He hated seeing her so upset. *Someday she'll be able to see this from HIS perspective, I pray that day will be soon.*

Something moving caught Heston's eye. "Here they come."

The guardians could see directly into the other room—doors and walls were no obstacles in the spiritual realm in which they lived.

"Must be about ten of 'em," Capri instinctively spread his wings over Alison, shielding her from the onslaught about to be unleashed.

The small horde of evil sprang into the living area immediately launching an all-out verbal assault. Like rabid animals, putrid saliva foamed in their mouths, oozing down their chins, and the taste of it aroused them into a near frenzy. Hatred burned in their eyes towards both the angelic beings and, most especially, the humans in the tiny room. How God could love these pathetic creatures was beyond them, and the very thought of it made them hate the humans even more.

All manner of accusations against God, against His love and His faithfulness, together with all manner of accursed lies—laced with fear—were shot directly at the two leaning over Henri. The demons saw the fire of the Holy Spirit inside the girl and knew their actions against her were limited, so long as the girl refused their lies, but there was no fire in the mother; she was fair game.

"You do not have permission to touch this one." Capri glared at the grotesque spirits and stood his ground over the girl.

"We don't need to touch her to destroy her," a demon hissed and snorted, sickeningly, while the group of evil crept closer and closer.

"Ah, but the mother is all ours." The leader of the pack licked his cracked lips, green ooze dripped off his chin.

Heston spread his wings over Celeste. "Not for long!"

"Oh, the angel makes a profession of faith," mocked a lying demon of false religion.

"Back off!" Heston pulled his sword out of its scabbard, daring a demon to try something. Light reflected off the silver blade, temporarily blinding the demons who flinched and shielded their eyes. How they hated the infuriating light and anything that made them look weak. These creatures inhabited darkness. They craved darkness. Darkness was their only protection and only in the domain of darkness did they have power over humans. Darkness is where they solely operated, was their sole desire, and keeping people prisoners of it was their sole objective.

Like mad wolves, the angry pack turned on the offending guardian preparing to pounce on him en masse. One-on-one they were no match for the angel and his sword, but perhaps jumping him together they could disarm him.

But without warning, a blinding light exploded into the atmosphere—an open portal! A heavenly being descended; he was much larger than the attending guardians, and in his extended hand he held a saber completely consumed by light as if on fire. This sword could easily disintegrate a demonic being or anything else that got in its way. With shrieks of terror, the unsuspecting demons cowered from the light and raced to find a shadow. Starlin, Capri, and Heston turned and greeted the newcomer with a salute of respect.

"Welcome, Aloys." Capri smiled. "It's good to see you again. Impeccable timing."

Aloys returned the smile and nodded. "Heaven is at hand."

Landing softly, he tucked his massive wings and then glanced around cautiously before extinguishing and sheathing his weapon. No demon in sight. The three guardians parted, letting Aloys stand closest to the strewn body of Henri.

"The Everlasting One is working a masterful plan. I've been sent to borrow Henri." Aloys examined the boy, narrowing his eyes as he looked him over carefully. "Don't leave your posts. The boy will sleep for a short while, enjoying a sampling of his heavenly destination. He'll be back when his tour is over."

The guardians exchanged excited glances. They now knew that this would be a life-altering, view-changing event in the boy's life. The Kingdom of Darkness was about to be pushed back in this Paris neighborhood. It was all they could do not to dance in abandoned joy.

"Welcome, Aloys."

The fourth angel waited and watched alongside the others. When Aloys observed the first sign of the boy's spirit lifting away from his body, he swept him up, engulfing Henri in his massive arms, and swaddled him like a pupa in a cocoon of light.

"Have fun fellas!"

With one thrust of mighty wings, Aloys catapulted through the ceiling, reentered the portal, and vanished from sight. Immediately, the portal sealed shut, and the heavenly light vanished with him.

The guardians knew exactly what Aloys meant by his last remark and grinned at each other. Adrenaline pumped through their angelic veins, for a battle was about to wage for the soul of the mother and the faith of the daughter—and, oh, how they loved a battle!

ONE

Jesus said, "Let the little children come to me, and do not hinder them, for the Kingdom of Heaven belongs to such as these." — Matthew 19:14 (NIV)

I t was as if the children were snatched from Earth. Gently, lovingly, protectively, but snatched just the same. For in one moment Masumi, Henri, and Cristen were struggling for life, and in less than a heartbeat they were enveloped in a brilliant light and whisked like reverse lightning through the atmosphere. Securely wrapped in a cloak of peace, they felt absolutely no fear.

When they opened their eyes, they found themselves standing together on the lushest grass imaginable, in a place so clean, bright, and undefiled it drew their breaths away. The sky above them was an electric blue, and the air around them was crisp and easy to breathe. It was a perfect day, if ever there was one.

Time stood still, it seemed, as the wide-eyed children stood spellbound by the scene of indescribable beauty. They had been deposited in an exuberant garden, generous with lush, lavish vegetation, and bursting with bright, colorful flowers. This glorious garden was hedged in on one side by a mammoth wall—the children could not see the top of it, nor the ends in either direction—which, quite remarkably, seemed to be filled with light and imbued with life.

The children's minds swirled, wild with wonder, as realization of where they might be began to register. Their absolute delight was evidenced by wide, unbidden smiles as they eagerly drank in the extraordinary beauty surrounding them.

Abruptly, a large, luminous angel landed beside them with a delicacy that belied his massive size. If the children had seen this being on Earth, they might have been terrified at his powerful presence, but as it was, they felt no fear, just complete and utter astonishment. Mouths agape, they watched him set a young, jubilant boy down on the grass and then furl his mighty wings.

This heavenly being was dazzling; every ounce of him radiated light. These children had never seen such a glow and could not take their eyes off of him. He must have been nine feet tall, at least, with broad shoulders and strong, rugged features, and he towered like an oak tree over the children. His blond hair was thick and curly, and his glowing skin was deeply bronzed. He had a handsome face with sparkling, blue eyes that twinkled with kindness and pleasure, and a magnificent smile of perfectly straight, white teeth. His long, white garment, which seemed to be a part of him rather than a separate piece of clothing, was made entirely of light and elegantly embellished with rich, gold trim. Soft, opaque rainbow colors, reminiscent of an opal or oyster shell, coursed through his large, snowy white wings with every flutter of the feathers. Those wings, now folded behind him, rose up high above his head and added an extra foot or two to his already Goliath-like height.

The angel chuckled at the children's stunned faces; his eyes danced with mirth as joy literally, and liberally, spilled from him.

"I'm here! I'm here!" The children tore their eyes away from the glowing presence and discovered a slender boy dancing joyfully about.

"Welcome to Heaven!" said the angel, with a booming voice that was both kind and powerful.

"I thought this *had* to be Heaven." Cristen's eyes darted about the garden.

"Am I dead?" Henri, quite incredulous, could not fathom the notion; he didn't feel dead.

"Ah, Henri." The angel's eyes twinkled wildly. "*You* are very much alive!"

"You know my name?" The boy's eyes widened in surprise.

"I know all of your names." He looked at the girls and smiled; his kind eyes brimmed with tenderness, "You are Cristen, and you are Masumi." His warm smile could have melted ice and butter; it certainly warmed the hearts of these girls.

"And this excited one," he turned and patted the dancing boy on the head, "is Edgas."

The children, bright with wonder, shared smiles with each other, for this seemed to be their own introductions, as well.

"We're here! We're here!" Edgas was about to burst from elation.

"We're here all right, but how did we get here?" Cristen ventured tentatively, still surveying the gorgeous garden in which she found herself.

"Yes, how?" Masumi looked questioningly into the most beautiful blue eyes she had ever seen.

"You have left your physical bodies behind on Earth, and your spirits have been transported here to Heaven."

"That's weird." Henri's mind raced for answers. "I mean, I was just walking in my house, and now I'm here."

"Don't you mean *running*?" the angel teased with a wink.

Henri's eyes popped. "Uh, yeah, I guess I *was* running."

"Me, too!" Masumi nodded and looked at Henri. "I was running to catch a train, and then I was here."

"I wasn't running or anything," Cristen chimed in. "I think I was telling my mom I didn't feel so good, but same as you guys, I was in a bed one instant and the next thing I knew, I was here."

"How do you feel now?" her glowing host asked.

"Um," she thought about it for half a second, "perfect!" Laughing, she shook her head in amazement and added, "Absolutely perfect."

"Me, too!" squealed Edgas, "I feel absolutely perfect, too!"

Smiling, Masumi and Henri nodded in agreement, conveying that, *Yep. Absolutely perfect* was exactly how they felt, too.

"Good," their host said with a definitive nod, looking very pleased.

"Can you feel better than absolutely perfect?" Edgas turned his innocent face up towards the angel. "Cuz that's what I feel like!"

The angel grinned back at the boy. "Yes, Edgas, I believe you do!" He tousled the boy's hair and chuckled.

The angel took a moment to smile at each child, and then he spread his arms open wide, saying, "Come and see great things your Father has prepared for those who love His Son."

Instantly, a path of light appeared out of nowhere and began to stretch out ahead of the angel, rushing rapidly through the garden.

The children gasped, frozen with surprise, gawking at the ever-extending, supernatural path of light.

"Follow me." The angel laughed heartily, turned, and stepped onto the path. He began to coast away from the children as if riding on a conveyor belt or moving sidewalk. "Now, don't dawdle!" he called over his shoulder, "Wonders untold await us!"

The astonished children looked back and forth from one to the other, giggled hysterically and then ran after the angel. The moment they stepped onto the path of light, they too were carried effortlessly along. Their whirling minds didn't know which was more amazing: the towering angel glowing in front of them with rainbow infused wings, the colossal wall pulsating with life beside them, the impossible, intricate detail of everything growing in the garden, or the path of light that suddenly appeared and now was magically transporting them along.

They followed their leader in stunned silence, trying desperately to take it all in.

MAPUTO, MOZAMBIQUE
11:55 a.m.

Floored, Isabel sat unable to breathe. Edgas was gone. She stared at his lifeless body, dead in her lap, hardly believing what she had just observed with her own two eyes.

Did this boy, on death's doorstep, really just sit up, glowing with life and vitality, filled with more joy than she had ever witnessed in her lifetime, and speak with a clear, strong voice? She saw it. She heard it. The trouble was comprehending it. *Oh my heavens!* He could barely whisper only moments before. Yet, he just chatted with an angel—an *angel!*

Isabel blinked her eyes and looked back at the stained ceiling. *An angel was just in this room! A real-life angel just took Edgas home to glory.* Hadn't she just prayed and asked God to do that very thing? *Oh my stars! Oh my heavens! This is the most glorious thing I have ever seen!*

She felt a giggle rise up in her throat. She looked down at the precious boy in her arms, dead to this world but very much alive in Christ. "Your Father just took you home, didn't He Edgas?"

Isabel felt a thrill course through her. She had been given a glimpse, through Edgas' eyes, into the spiritual realm. By faith she had believed that Heaven was real, but now she had been given this blessed gift to "see" it. And like a seed, that sweet, unmerited gift was implanted down into the depths of her soul, and along with it, came a deep longing to go there herself one day.

It was like he was alive in both realms for a moment. Isabel replayed the scene in her mind, trying to understand what she had just witnessed, as she rocked Edgas' empty shell. *He was here with me in both body and spirit, then his spirit awoke to the other realm, momentarily bringing his body along with it, and then his spirit went on with the angel, leaving his body behind.*

"I will never forget this moment as long as I live, dear Edgas," she barely whispered, "and I will never forget you." She kissed the top of his head with all the tenderness of a mother. "Thank you for the way you lived for Jesus, thank you for the way you loved Him, and thank you for the way you faced death. You were a brave little soldier. I learned more from you than you ever did from me."

Isabel simultaneously felt a lump rising in her throat and a song rising in her heart. Swallowing the lump, she sang the song, quietly, as a prayer to her Lord...

Blessed be Your name
When the sun's shining down on me
When the world's 'all as it should be
Blessed be Your name

Blessed be Your name
On the road marked with suffering
Though there's pain in the offering
Blessed be Your name

Every blessing You pour out
I'll turn back to praise
When the darkness closes in, Lord
Still I will say

Blessed be the name of the Lord
Blessed be Your name
Blessed be the name of the Lord
Blessed be Your glorious name

Blessed be the name of the Lord
Blessed be Your name
Blessed be the name of the Lord
Blessed be Your glorious name

You give and take away
You give and take away
My heart will choose to say
Lord, blessed be Your name

TWO

The twelve gates were twelve pearls, each gate made of a single pearl. The great street of the city was of gold, as pure as transparent glass. — Revelation 21:21 (NIV)

"This is so-o weird!" Henri's voice shattered the silence of the dumbfounded troop coasting behind the angel on the remarkable path made of light. He hadn't meant to be so loud. He lowered his voice slightly. "I don't get it, though. I mean, if we're dead, shouldn't we be floating around on clouds or something?"

"I already told you, you're not dead; you're very much alive." The angel's tone was kind. The children could sense he was smiling although at the moment, not his face but his feathery wings filled their vision.

"I thought we'd look more like ghosts or vapors." Masumi scrunched a puzzled face.

"No," the angel turned towards her. "You still look like you."

"I saw my body, and I wasn't in it." Edgas faced the others to see if they were listening. They were. His eyes lit up, and he nodded his head enthusiastically, "I really did!"

The group was all ears.

"I just stepped right out of my body cuz when I turned around to say goodbye to Isabel, she was still holding me, and I was lying there, looking dead." Edgas stuck his tongue out to the side and rolled his eyes back for emphasis. "And boy was I surprised to see me like that, and that's when *he* told me," Edgas pointed to the angel, "that Isabel couldn't hear me anymore. Then we flew all the way to Heaven, and we saw all kinds of cool stuff on our way. Right?" Edgas looked at the angel expectantly, hoping he'd corroborate his story. The angel nodded and winked at him.

"You saw yourself?" Cristen eyes widened.

"Yep."

"But how? I mean, I see your body right now." Henri was trying hard to understand what had happened to them.

"I guess I have two bodies cuz one is back there with Isabel, and this one," the boy patted himself, "is walking on a magical path in Heaven wearing—" he paused, astonishment covering his face. "NEW CLOTHES! Hey! When did I get these new clothes? I've never had new clothes before!" Edgas' astonishment quickly turned into a great big lump that lodged in his throat and silenced him for a moment.

The others looked down at their own clothes and for the first time noticed that they, too, had on new clothes. They had each arrived in Heaven wearing a pair of trendy jeans and a graphic T-shirt.

Henri pulled his shirt out and turned his head. "'Heaven Rocks'" he read the upside-down words aloud, "Hmm, that's cool," he said, nodding his approval, "and true. What is this a picture of?" He twisted his shirt, trying to gain a better perspective of the design.

"I have no idea, but I like it." Edgas said and then asked Henri, "What's my shirt say?"

"King's Kid," read Henri.

"It has a really neat crown and sword design on the back," added Cristen.

"Yours has wings on the back; they look kinda like his wings," Edgas volunteered, nodding in the direction of the angel in their midst.

Masumi pointed to the small font on the front of Cristen's shirt, "It says here, 'I walk with Angels.'"

"I love the flower on your shirt, Masumi," said Cristen.

Masumi looked down and touched the small, colorful petals. "Is there anything on my back?" She turned her head, trying to peer over her shoulder.

"Yeah, the back has the same exact flower that's on the front, only bigger. The design takes up the whole back," Cristen said.

Delighted over the fun surprise, the group could not wipe the wide grins off their faces. Each of them really liked their own T-shirt and would have picked it out themselves had they been given the option.

Reaching down, the angel placed his large hand on the top of Edgas' head, sending a gentle wave of energy through him. Repeating the action with each of the others, he picked up where the conversation left off before the clothing discovery, saying, "This body is your spiritual body. When you live on Earth, this spirit-body lives inside your physical body, knitted together as one entity and invisible to the physical world. Your earthly body acts as a house, or a shell, for your spirit. When your physical body ceases to live, your spirit being—the real, eternal you that will never die—is immediately separated from it."

The angel continued his lesson gliding backwards along the moving pathway.

"Now you know why John the Apostle said, when he had been caught up to Heaven, that he didn't know if he was in the body or out of the body. Your spirit being is a spiritual body as real, solid, and tangible in this spiritual realm as your physical body is in the physical realm. You have already discovered that you still have your five senses: you can see, hear, taste, smell and feel just like you could on Earth. But now, because your spiritual bodies are not confined by Earth's laws, you are about to discover some wonderful things you can do and experience which would be impossible for your earthly bodies to do and experience."

The happy children bounded behind him fully absorbed in his words.

"Another thing you've probably noticed is that you still look like you and act like you—only you're the best, most perfect version of you, and you are completely without sin. You see, your spirit is eternal. God created your spirit to live with Him, forever. Here in Heaven, a spirit never ages, never gets hurt, and never feels pain."

"So, we *are* spirits?" Masumi scrunched her puzzled face again.

"Yes."

Henri, pondering Masumi's earlier comment, said, "We're spirits but not ghosts."

"Or vapors," Edgas threw in.

"Correct." The angel laughed. "You are not a vapor or a ghost! Granted, some people use the two words interchangeably. For instance, they may call the Holy Spirit, the Holy Ghost. That's perfectly fine, and that's not what I'm talking about. Technically speaking, however, there is no such thing as a ghost."

"Really?" Henri looked surprised.

"Really. The spirits of those currently living on Earth are still knitted to their earthly bodies, and the spirits of the departed have been freed from their earthly bodies and now either live in Heaven or the other place. You see, when you depart your earthly body, whoever owns you, takes you. Period. There are no human spirits wandering around Earth as ghosts."

"I heard that some houses, hotels, and stuff are haunted by the ghosts of dead people," said Henri.

"You may have heard that, but if you believed it, you were deceived. Some houses, hotels, and stuff are occupied by demons, pretending to be the ghosts or spirits of dead people. Believe me, there are no human ghosts."

"Oh, I do believe you! I'm just processing. Wow, demons pretend to be dead people." It was another statement, but the angel answered as if it were a question.

"Yes."

"That's weird!" Henri looked up and grinned at the glowing giant in front of him. "Man, we have a lot to learn, don't we?"

Edgas, the giggler, couldn't help himself, "He's not a man, he's an angel!"

Cristen interrupted the banter with a loud shriek. It was unclear who was the most surprised, Cristen or her new acquaintances. They stopped and quickly questioned if she was okay.

"My staples are gone!"

The group curiously watched her as she patted and mashed her tummy. "They're gone!" She looked up at the others, a grin of realization spreading across her face. "I just had surgery, and my staples are gone! They're not there!"

"Of course they're not there," agreed the angel. "The staples were never in your spiritual body."

Masumi quickly scanned herself. "Oh. My. Goodness!" She pointed to her arm. "Look at this! I had a big scar right here, and it's gone, too!"

The angel chuckled, relishing their discovery. "See? What did I tell you? These bodies are not physical, they're spiritual, and they're perfect—no diseases, no defects, no imperfections, no scars, and no staples."

"This is so weird," muttered Henri as he turned his arms this way and that. He hiked up his pants and examined his legs. He raised his head and looked at the others, stunned. "Mine are gone, too. All my scars and bruises are gone." He gave a sheepish look and added, "I tripped a lot."

"Look at me! Look at me!" Unable to contain his joy, Edgas jumped off the moving pathway which immediately came to a halt, and turned one cartwheel after another. He jumped straight up and pumped his fist in the air, "HURRA! HURRA! Look at me! I got meat on my bones and no more pain!"

The others watched, laughing and giggling, as Edgas whooped and hollered, spun circles, shimmied to the left and shimmied to the right, and turned more cartwheels. They held up their hands when he ran back to high-five all of them, including the big angel.

On the move again, they quickly became a chatty group of friends, excitedly pointing out beautiful and unusual things to one another as they glided along the magical path of light.

They asked each other scores of questions and quickly learned about each of their families, their homes, where they lived, their ages, and how they came to Heaven. They were quite surprised to discover that Edgas had had AIDS; it seemed impossible because he was so healthy and vibrant.

"I'm so happy." A contented smile lifted the corners of Masumi's mouth.

"Everyone is happy here," the angel enjoyed piping in lessons between the children's excited chatter. "Nothing will ever make you sad in Heaven."

"Isn't that called joy?"

"That's right, Cristen. Very good." She felt her face flush from the angel's praise. "Joy saturates all of Heaven: 'For in the presence of the Lord there is fullness of joy, and at His right hand there are pleasures forever.'"

"Oh, that's in the Bible!" Edgas beamed, glad to recognize the angel had quoted a verse of Scripture.

"You're quick," the angel acknowledged with a grin. "It's Psalms 16:11." Continuing his lesson, he added, "One of the ways joy is expressed in Heaven is happiness. It's okay to be happy, and everyone here is."

"Well, I'm sure happy." Edgas turned another cartwheel to prove it. The girls laughed and joined him in cartwheeling down the moving path. Cristen couldn't get over how effortlessly she could turn them. *Now that's different! I could go on forever without getting dizzy or tired.*

Henri eyed the others turning down the wide path of light; he had never done a cartwheel before, but it sure looked like they were having fun. *Oh, why not?* He decided to join in the fun; but instead of a cartwheel, he jumped straight up in the air, tucked, and managed a decent looking front flip, greatly surprising himself.

"Wow! These bodies really are better than the other ones! I can't believe I just did that!" He did it again with the same success.

The happy group twirled and flipped and giggled and spun and laughed as they moved along on the moving path of supernatural light.

Presently, they came upon an arbor of tall, resplendent trees. Thick, leafy branches interlaced high overhead forming a seemingly endless canopied corridor. The ever-extending path of light coursed ahead like a long aisle leading them into the tunnel of trees. A hush fell over the children, and they proceeded silently. The tree trunks were a masterpiece in and of themselves, while the mingling of high, stalwart branches created delicate lacy patterns of unimaginable beauty. When not gazing up at the intricate lacework, the children were gaping at the running path peppered generously with a vast array of colorful, fragrant flowers. These lovely flowers popped up out of nowhere as the path sped on. It was mind-boggling, and the aroma was divine, quite literally.

When at length they emerged from the foliage canopy, the children stopped, frozen in sheer amazement at yet another incredible sight.

"What on Earth?" Henri's mouth dropped open.

"We're not on Earth anymore, remember?" Edgas, for once, wasn't giggling. He, too, stood with mouth agape.

"No duh," whispered Henri.

The moving path of light ceased, and instantly the children were back on solid ground. Then a new and different kind of path appeared. It looked to be made out of something similar to cobblestones, and it formed ahead of them as if by magic. The openmouthed children watched as the path traversed briefly through another lovely garden before, to their amazement—as if watching a computer graphic—it became a stone bridge across a small stream, where it then continued to a quaintly nestled door at the bottom of the massive jasper wall and stopped.

The children's eyes followed the path every step of the way as it unfolded before them, but now they were completely captivated by the beautiful door at the base of the wall. They had never seen anything like it. It looked more like a gate, and was beautiful even from a distance.

"I think that's what's on your shirt, Henri," breathed Masumi.

Henri tugged his shirt out again, and although the design was upside down to him, he could still tell that a graphic design of this door-in-the-wall was exactly what was on it. "Cool."

"Is that a pearl?" asked an amazed Masumi.

"Indeed, " answered the angel.

Cristen abruptly turned to the angel. "Are those the Pearly Gates?"

The angel chuckled, "Well, it's one of them."

The children stared in awe. Could this day get any crazier? Gazing at the beautiful door, or gate, whichever it was, they could see that it was remarkably made of one, enormous pearl.

"Cool!" Henri repeated before laughing. "How big ya think the oyster was?"

Cristen and Masumi snickered.

"I think it musta been ginormous!" Edgas laughed and turned to make sure Henri had heard him.

"It's amazing," Masumi whispered.

"Yeah, totally." Cristen was mesmerized by it.

Indeed it was totally amazing. The pearl itself was considerably larger than the angel and was set into a gate of luminous golden filigree, making it look much more like a giant ring or brooch than a gate. Bright white and shining with opalescent rainbow colors much like the angel's wings, it was the most spectacularly amazing thing the children had ever seen.

"Well, go on," urged the angel.

The group tore off down the newly constructed path and ran, laughing, across the miraculously built bridge. As they neared the giant pearl, they noticed it had words in a beautifully etched script running across it. But after closer examination, they discovered that the words were not etched on the pearl at all! The words just appeared, as if being written by an invisible hand, and then after rippling across the surface, disappeared.

Their minds reeled! The beautiful, scripted words seemed to be alive.

"What does it say?" Edgas' tone was reverent.

The angel smiled broadly, for he loved showing off the glories of Heaven. "It says 'Judah' first in Hebrew, then in Aramaic, then Greek, Latin, and—"

"How *does* it do that?" Henri interrupted, pointing at the pearl excitedly, for he had suddenly noticed that the pearl was suspended in thin air! It was just floating within its setting.

"Oh my goodness!" breathed Masumi, "How *does* it do that? There's nothing holding it in place!"

The others moved in to check it out, and as they did, the pearl began to slowly rotate, revealing 360 degrees of moving, living, script.

"—and all the languages of men," finished the angel with a satisfied nod.

"It's fantastic." Henri's voice was thick with admiration. Feeling irresistibly drawn, he reached out to touch the pearl with its living script. The others followed suit.

"Is it alive?" Edgas was sure it was, but how could an object be alive? And even if the pearl was alive, how could the writing be alive? It was completely out of his frame of reference, as well as the others'. But they had to admit it sure looked alive.

"All of Heaven is alive!" The angel spread his arms wide.

"Why does it say Judah?" Cristen could not take her eyes off of the script. She didn't believe in magic, but this was magical and beautiful and amazing.

"It's not magic, Cristen. It's supernatural."

Cristen's eyes shot to the angel. Had he read her thoughts?

"Each of the twelve gates has one of the names of the tribes of Israel inscribed on it; this is the gate called, 'Judah.'"

The angel walked in front of the gate and turned to face the children, "Wait here. I'll go tell the sentry we have arrived."

"What century?" Edgas asked, confused.

The angel could not stop the grin. "You'll see."

Facing the gate, he spread his arms and commanded, "Swing wide, ye heavenly gate," and instantly, it obeyed, and the angel disappeared through it.

MAPUTO, MOZAMBIQUE
UNSEEN REALM

Alone in the room with Isabel, Michale turned and immediately began encouraging her spirit. He was determined to do his part. He knew God was at work, for the flame of the Holy Spirit was strong within her.

He stood protectively over her and the body of the boy. He raised his arms and with a deep voice sang an angelic song of Heaven. He put both hands on Isabel's shoulders and calmed her spirit. He spoke words of faith, filling the room with the glory of the Lord.

He had almost forgotten the little weasel in the room until a nauseating stench wafted past his nose. He scanned the shadows.

There's the scuzzball. His attentive eyes saw the Accuser's pawn hiding in the shadows; these hideous creatures always showed up at times like this to spew their blasphemies against God.

He was not the least bit concerned about this little nuisance, for Michale knew two things very well. One: the demon would not step foot in the glory cloud that filled the room, and two: Isabel was a rock. She'd sail through this attack. Indeed, she would sail with flying colors, of that he was sure. He looked at Isabel; she was laughing and praising the Lord. Yes, indeed, she was a rock.

"Ah, come to have your fun, I see," he decided to let the rat know he saw him. "She doesn't belong to you, so why don't you just crawl back into your hole?"

The demon did not respond. He kept his beady eyes trained on Isabel, waiting for a break in the glory or for a moment of weakness when he could launch his attack.

Michale turned his eyes back to Isabel, and for the first time noticed the weariness in her eyes. He suddenly realized that she was more vulnerable than he had thought.

"Keep worshipping, sweet Isabel," he encouraged lovingly. "Keep worshipping."

Hiding in the shadows

THREE

But the righteous shall be glad; they shall exult before God; they shall be jubilant with joy! Sing to God, sing praises to His name; lift up a song to Him who rides through the deserts; His name is the Lord; exult before him! — Psalm 68:3-4 (ESV)

The gate swung opened at his command! And as it did, brilliant light, thrilling music, and a marvelous aroma burst upon the children from the other side of the wall. They were stunned silent by the suddenness of it.

Watching the angel disappear into the light was like staring into the brightest sun, yet they did not have to squint or shield their eyes from its intensity, for their spiritual eyes adjusted to it immediately.

The air swelled with a multitude of melodic voices and instruments lifted in song. This harmonious music, rich and vibrant, swirled around them like garments of praise while an exhilarating fragrance permeated the air with aromatic pleasure. It wasn't too flowery or too sweet or too spicy or too anything. It was perfect. Absolutely perfect. The happy children inhaled it deeply.

Awash in the unexpected thrill of sensory bombardment, the children stood transfixed, experiencing firsthand how their spiritual bodies were capable of so much more than their physical bodies.

As their senses seemed to have no limits, so also their capacity for joy seemed limitless. Never before had they felt, nor even imagined they could feel, so utterly, so unreservedly, so euphorically, happy.

Henri could not stop smiling. He looked at his new friends and saw that they, too, had ear-to-ear grins plastered across their faces. He swallowed a chuckle. "Being dead is AWESOME!" His proclamation brought with it a string of giggles.

"I thought you said it was weird?" Cristen asked with a laugh, recalling how many times her new friend had said the word.

"It *is* weird." Henri shook his head, incredulously. "Very weird."

"But it *is* awesome, right Henri?"

"It sure is, Edgas."

"I know!" Edgas threw his hands in the air. "It's *awesomely* weird!"

"Hey, that's it!" Henri agreed, patting the boy on the shoulder. "Or," he paused and tapped his chin, teasingly thoughtful, "could be that it's *weirdly* awesome." He shrugged, "Either way works for me."

"I like you, Henri." Edgas smiled up into the older boy's eyes, "And I think *you* are awesome."

"Thanks, but would that be *awesomely* weird or *weirdly* awesome?" Henri crossed his eyes and wiggled his thick, brown eyebrows.

Edgas, laughing at the comical face, answered, "Hmm. I think *awesomely* weird!" He turned his bright face to the girls and added, "And I think you girls are both awesome, too."

"*Awesomely* weird or *weirdly* awesome?" A grinning Masumi mimicked Henri's eyebrow wiggle.

Edgas belly laughed. He couldn't have held back that laughter anymore than he could have kept a wave from crashing on the shore. "*Weirdly* awesome!" he eked out between breaths.

Cristen suppressed a laugh threatening to escape, "Ya know what Edgas? We think you're awesssss—" She doubled over in giggles, unable to finish the word. She had no idea if she was laughing at the silly joke or something else, for at this moment everything was hilarious.

Contagious laughter spread to Henri and Masumi. Within moments, they too, were doubled over. The four friends were laughing so hard they began to plop, one by one, to the soft grass where they rolled around like small children, laughing hysterically without a care in the world.

Fountains of joy burst from somewhere deep inside them, flooding thirsty spirits and souls with irrepressible bliss.

Just as the laughter was subsiding, Edgas caught his breath and asked, "*Awesomely* weird or *weirdly* awesome?" which set them all off in hysterics again.

"Yes!" they chorused between breaths.

When at last the waves of laughter did subside, the sprawled out children laid back contentedly in the soft grass, awashed in light, listening to heavenly music and breathing deeply of the glorious fragrance.

The song, which danced in and around and through them, was so complex it was mind blowing. It wasn't really a song; it was more like a symphony. But, it wasn't really like a symphony; it was more like a myriad of symphonies playing all at once. It wasn't even like different symphonies playing at the same time, in the same key, with complimentary chords. No, it was more like each individual and unique song—no matter how intricate the composition or how complicated the arrangement—was only a single thread that was woven together with a myriad of other threads, creating a musical tapestry so inconceivable it made the children's heads swim.

How their ears could hear and distinguish the different threads, one from another, they had no clue, but they could, and they did. Never had they even imagined of such a possibility. Every song was only one thread, one single, thin thread, in a symphonic score beyond imagination.

Totally enraptured, they closed their eyes and let the heavenly music infuse them with immeasurable pleasure. They wanted to sing out, to join their voices with the heavenly chorus, to become part of the tapestry, and for it to become part of them. They instinctively knew that if they did sing out, they would be perfectly in tune with the other threads.

Henri rolled over and propped himself up on his elbows. "I have a confession to make," looking a little sheepish, he added, "though I'm kinda embarrassed to admit it."

Immediately, the others rolled over and, propping up on their own elbows, looked questioningly at Henri.

Overflowing with joy, Cristen was surprised by this sudden turn, "What's wrong, Henri?"

"Oh, nothing's wrong, it's not like that." He studied a blade of grass, plucking it from the ground and running it through his fingers, amazed by the intricate detail and soft feel of it.

"Oh good, I'm glad." Masumi rolled back over and gazed at the beautiful Pearl Gate.

"So...what's your confession?" Edgas prodded.

"Well, it's just that I thought music in Heaven would be kinda boring, you know, like church music is sometimes. I thought Heaven would be more like that, and if you had told me that I'd really love the music in Heaven, I'd'a probably thought, 'Yeah, right. I doubt it!' But I'd'a been so wrong. I never in a million years could have imagined how amazing this is. It's so much better than anything I've ever heard before. It's like, really, really, really, cool."

"Well, not me," said Edgas, looking at Henri. "I thought it would be really cool, but I didn't know it would be really, really, really cool."

"Oh, I agree, I don't think I could ever get tired of this!" Masumi sat up and smiled at Edgas.

Cristen put her hands behind her head, "I could listen to this forever."

"That's good," Edgas chuckled, "cuz you probably will!"

Cristen giggled.

"Now don't start us all laughing again, Edgas, or we'll never find out what's through that gate!" Masumi teased.

"Speaking of gate," Henri said, turning his full attention towards the giant pearl, "wonder what's keeping our angel." He stood to his feet, and as he did, he absentmindedly dropped the blade of grass he'd been fingering and gasped.

Cristen looked curiously at Henri who was staring wide-eyed at the ground. "You look like you've seen a ghost. What's the matter?"

"There's no such thing as ghosts, remember?" snickered Edgas, getting up to see what Henri was staring at. Henri didn't return the laugh but kept staring openmouthed at the ground.

Edgas bent way over and looked at the grass, then turned his head and looked up at Henri. "What are we lookin' at?"

Speechless, Henri could only point.

"What in the world happened, Henri?" Masumi regarded him with genuine concern.

"We're not in the world anymore, remember Masumi?"

"Yes, thank you, Edgas, but don't worry, I *totally* remember!" She laughed at the boy's continued reminders.

Cristen reached out and touched Henri's arm. "You okay?"

Henri shook his head as if to wake from a dream. He stared at his friends. "Now, *that* was weird."

"Awesomely weird or just plain weird?" Edgas, serious now, looked intently at Henri's face.

Henri broke into a wide grin. "*Awesomely* weird. Totally."

"Well, what happened?" Edgas couldn't take the mystery another moment.

Henri had the groups' full attention. "I was playing with a piece of grass, and when I dropped it just now, it totally grew back into the ground," he pointed, "right here."

"What?" Masumi and the others turned to look at the grass.

"It was this one," Henri pointed to the blade which had magically grown back in place, "and it totally reattached like I never even touched it, much less plucked it."

Cristen's hands flew up over her opened mouth.

The new friends all bent over and plucked a piece a grass just to drop it and see if it would reroot. It did. They dropped to their knees and plucked again, and again, and again. Furiously, they plucked! And every blade instantly rerooted as if it had never been touched.

"Oh my goodness! This place is like a fairy tale!" squealed Cristen.

Edgas reached over and picked a flower, all eyes on him. He dropped it, and it rerooted. The astounded group shook their heads, looked at each other, and then burst out in giggles of delight.

"This place is going to take some getting used to," said Masumi. "I keep thinking, *I don't believe it* because that's what I always said whenever something really cool happened, but that just doesn't feel right anymore, not here anyway, because I really *do* believe it. I just can't get over it!"

"HURRA!" Edgas hopped up and turned another cartwheel. "Isn't Heaven really, really, really cool? Isn't it amazing? It's wonderful just like I knew it would be, and we haven't even gone through the gate yet! Hey, I wonder if the angel has found the century? You'd think he'd be back by now." Turning abruptly, the boy ran towards the gate.

"I think he said, *sentry*." Henri said, standing to his feet. He turned and followed Edgas with Masumi and Cristen right behind.

"That's what I said, he went to find the century."

Henri and the girls chuckled. They were already smitten with the enthusiastic boy and his irresistible joy.

The group moved closer for a peek through the gate. They were surprised at the thickness of the wall and a bit disappointed to see nothing but bright light. It felt as if they were peering at the sun through a tunnel.

Then, all at once, the children heard a thunderous whooshing sound coming towards them, and the brightness dimmed slightly, blocked by a large shape. Whoosh, whoosh, whoosh. They froze with excitement. Surely the angel was returning for them. Would they now go through the gate? They held their breaths in anticipation.

PARIS, FRANCE
NOON

"He will help us, Maman; I know He will." Alison took a deep breath and let it out slowly. She took her mother's hand and closed her eyes. Mustering up her courage, she whispered, "We need to pray for him." Celeste nodded her head.

Alison opened her mouth to pray but was surprised to hear her mother's voice first. "Oh, God! I know you're really busy and have really important things on your mind, but right now, I hope you hear me because Alison and I need you, and most importantly, Henri needs you."

Celeste rose up on her knees, and with one hand on Henri's chest she wrapped the other around her daughter and squeezed her eyes tightly. Lifting her face toward Heaven, she pleaded for the life of her only son. "Please, oh please, God, hear our prayer, and have mercy on us. I'll do anything for you if you'll only let Henri live. Not for me, dear God; I know I'm not worthy but for Henri's sake. He's so young and he's such a good boy and he believes in you and he loves you. Please don't let him die, dear God, please, please don't take him! I need him more than you do, and Alison needs him too. What would we do without him?" Tears coursed down the cheeks of the desperate mother.

"Oh God, we need him here with us," she begged. "Please God, please!" Celeste fell across the boy's chest, her fears erupting into a rush of hot tears.

Alison reached her hand out and placed it softly on her mother's back, rubbing gently. Her heart was breaking for her mother, but she suddenly felt an unexplainable peace wash over her. She inhaled deeply, willing the peace to fill her, body, soul, and spirit.

Her thick, brown hair, wet from tears, stuck to her face. She smoothed it and tied it back in a ponytail using a rubber band she handily wore most days on her wrist. She blew her nose and wiped her tear-streaked face on her shirttail without so much as a conscious thought.

She looked at her brother and then closed her eyes to block out his twisted body. Taking another deep breath, she clasped her hands under her chin and then quietly began, "Jesus, I know you hear us. We need you, Lord. Yes, we are unworthy, but it's not because of our worthiness or our goodness that we can come to you but because of your blood. Have mercy on us, Lord. Have mercy on Henri. Forgive us our sins and wash us clean that we may boldly come before your throne and ask for grace in time of need."

Celeste straightened and looked over at her daughter. Who in the world was this girl praying with such bold confidence? *When had she become a young woman?*

"You are the Lord of the whole Earth," Alison continued earnestly, "and you hold healing in your powerful hands. It's an easy thing for you to heal Henri and let him live if it's your will to do so. Oh, Jesus, I love you so much. I don't know what your will is for Ri, but Maman and I want to have him here with us. So, please give us faith, and the ability to trust you, and to believe in your goodness. Amen."

Alison opened her eyes and caught her mother staring at her as if seeing her for the first time.

"Alison, that was amazing! When did you learn to pray like that?"

"I'm just talking to my friend."

"Do you really believe that?"

"Oh yes! I know Jesus is my friend."

"No, not that."

"Do I really believe what?"

"That it's an easy thing for God to heal Henri?"

"Yes, I really believe that."

Celeste looked down at the strewn body of the son she loved so much and whispered, "I want to believe that, too."

"I don't know if He *will*, but I know that He *can*."

"But God is...well, you know, He's *God*. Isn't he too busy watching over nations and wars and natural disasters to have time for us?"

"No Maman. He cares about us, very much, and He is never too busy for us. He's here with us now. Pastor Jacques has taught us this, and I believe it with all my heart. It's true. God loves us, and He loves Ri, too. I don't know why this is happening, but I know that God is good and that He will help us through it. Please believe, Maman. Please believe in Jesus."

FOUR

Nothing impure will ever enter it, nor will anyone who does what is shameful or deceitful, but only those whose names are written in the Lamb's book of life. — Revelation 21:27 (NIV)

The angel filled their view as he came through the short, tunnel-like pass through the wall. "It is time. Come, children!"

Their excitement was palpable as they moved to follow their angelic leader. The pass in the wall was so high that there was plenty of room to spare above the angel's comfortably folded wings, and...was it their imaginations, or did the opening just expand to make room for them to walk comfortably abreast? The eager girls, giddy with wonderment, grasped each other's hands tightly.

The magnificent wall was easily twenty feet thick. The children hardly noticed its smooth, gleaming quality though, for their full attentions were immediately riveted to a mind-boggling sight straight ahead—a foot. One, gigantic, bright, shining, sandaled foot.

As they emerged from the gate, they looked up, and up, and up, discovering that the foot belonged to the biggest creature they had ever laid eyes on. He was ninety feet tall, at least. Beside him was another, of the same height and stature; and the two of them shone like polished metal, reflecting light as if made of bronze. Although very similar in appearance, they had their own distinct features, like brothers in a family. The two were muscular and fierce looking, yet there was kindness in their eyes. Their hair, which flowed freely to their shoulders, looked like pure gold spun into soft, wavy, glowing strands. They stood at attention, each with a flaming sword securely grasped in an enormous hand. Surely no one would pass through this gate without their permission.

The hushed children gaped, unabashedly, yet safely tucked behind their leader.

"Holy cow—the sentry." Henri's breathy whisper brought instant understanding to each of the children.

The angel chuckled, "They are holy, Henri, but I don't think they appreciate being called cows."

It was funny, but no one laughed, that is until much later. Standing in the presence of these sentries, who guarded this entrance called Judah, was just too intimidating.

Looking around, the group noticed a fourth, luminous angel walking towards them carrying a set of books. He was strikingly beautiful and about the same height as the children's leader. His radiant skin was dark, his hair was black as night, and his eyes were the color of the ocean depths. His smile flashed a set of pearly white teeth, and his eyes welcomed the children without words. The children loved him instantly.

The four, very large books he was holding seemed weightless in his muscular arms. Light danced wildly off the volumes which were covered entirely in gold. A tall golden table suddenly arose in front of him, and he gently set the books down on it. Taking the topmost book, he opened the cover and held it up before him like a hymnal.

Cristen drew in a sharp breath. There on the cover, etched in beautiful lettering, was her name in full: Cristen Louise Maples. To think that there was a book in Heaven devoted entirely to her. She felt her eyes brim with tears, and she heard these words run through her mind, *"This book is your life story, Cristen."*

The guardians with flaming swords got on one knee, then leaned way down to see Cristen's book. The angel holding the book took hold of a lovely satin ribbon and turned to the marked page.

"Wait here, children." Their leader joined the others of his kind in examining the book.

The four children dared not move. They huddled together and breathlessly watched the unbelievable scene unfold before them. The angels read the open page carefully.

Satisfied, the group of angels looked at each other with knowing smiles and then turned and smiled at Cristen. She thought she would melt from the warmth of those smiles.

The angel holding the book announced, "Cristen Louise Maples, you may enter the Gate of Heaven!"

Goose bumps ran up and down Cristen's body and she felt her heart pounding with excitement. After a quick squeeze, she released Masumi's hand and began to walk toward the group of angels. She will never, throughout all eternity, forget the rush of thrill she felt at this moment. She had just passed through one of the twelve Pearl Gates right into the very Kingdom of Heaven.

She was greeted by a cool, no, it was warm, no, it was a cool and gentle breeze. Cristen closed her eyes and let it kiss her face. She noticed for the first time that the temperature was perfect. It was a perfectly glorious day. She thought it was the kind of day that makes you glad you're alive, or rather, dead. She smiled. Who would have ever thought that being dead was this wonderful? Certainly she never had.

Opening her eyes, she quickly surveyed the scenery before her. There was a meadow of emerald green grass stretching straight out in front of her for miles and miles, thickly blanketed with clusters upon clusters of vibrant flowers; some of them were as big around as dinner plates. The meadow was bordered by a rich, green forest of beautiful tall trees to her right and rolling green hills to her left.

Cristen spotted a grand river which looked like a winding ribbon of light sparkling wildly in the distance as it wound through hills and out across the meadow. She was enthralled by the demonstration of light it created. And high above, the sky was dotted with fluffy white clouds and was a hue of blue she had never seen before; and in the far distance, out over the horizon, the sky was ablaze with living color. It reminded Cristen of a sunset with its pinks, peaches, purples and oranges but with many more colors and much more magnified. Something blazing like the sun must be just beyond the horizon to cause such an impressive display.

Oh! Heaven is glorious! it's simply glorious!

At this moment, Cristen from Kansas was not unlike the fictional Dorothy from Kansas, who stepped out of a black and white world into an unfamiliar land bursting with color. Had she, like Dorothy, lived in a black and white world all her life? Perhaps. All Cristen had ever known, every lovely thing, paled to the brilliant vibrancy of the panorama spread before her. As a black and white photograph of an autumn day cannot even begin to capture the actual vibrancy of a tree fully adorned in fall's finest clothes, so it was with life on Earth compared to life in Heaven. The Earth is but a shadow: a black and white photograph.

While Cristen enjoyed the beauty spread before her, the others waited for their turn. Each of them saw their very own name beautifully etched on the cover of one of the golden books. The angels repeated the process of opening the other books, one at a time, and studying the pages carefully.

I wonder what they're studying so intently? The moment that thought crossed Masumi's mind it was followed by an answer.

It is not by good works or righteous acts, Masumi, but only by believing in, and the receiving of, the shed blood of Jesus Christ, my Son, that you can enter through this Gate.

So, that's it! They're checking our life records to see if we've accepted Jesus as our Lord and Savior!

Soon each of the four children had been gloriously smiled upon and invited by full name, to enter.

"Masumi Hara...you may enter the Gate of Heaven!"

"Edgas Isaac Seca...you may enter the Gate of Heaven!"

"Henri Eaden Leonard...you may enter the Gate of Heaven!"

With that marvelous invitation, Masumi, Edgas and Henri, one at a time, passed by the ninety-foot sentries with flaming swords, the angel holding the golden volumes, and the magical table and joined Cristen. Together, they stood amazed and surveyed the indescribable beauty.

PARIS, FRANCE
UNSEEN REALM

The portal closed as quickly as it had opened to the relief of the demonic spirits; they hated the blinding light that burst forth from the realm of God's glory. It hurt their eyes and exposed their distorted, hideous forms, but even more than that, they hated the reminder that they would never again experience peace, beauty, or joy—not ever—for they had chosen Lucifer as leader and were cast out to an eternity void of the Lord of Glory and His living Light.

Aloys had taken Henri's spirit to the assigned meeting place in Heaven, but as the boy's body lay lifeless on the floor, the emboldened demons came rushing out of the shadows immediately on the attack. They wasted no time in screaming out their hate-filled accusations against God and His character and in trying to get past the guardians.

Starlin, Heston, and Capri stood backs together with wings opened protectively as they hemmed in the mother and daughter. Raging spirits of fear, despair, doubt, unbelief, idolatry, false religion, hopelessness, helplessness, and deception encircled the angels trying relentlessly to reach their victims. Poisonous venom spewed vehemently as the demons sphered dizzily over, around, and under the angels and the women they stewarded.

A brazen beast stretched out his scaly, taloned hand trying to snatch hold of Celeste and received severe blows from her guardian, driving him back on his rear. Others tried to break through the angelic barrier with no success. Blow after blow was delivered to the head or twisted body of a wretched demon. The three guardians kept more than a dozen monsters at bay.

Capri ferociously protected Alison. He felt strengthened by an unseen power and knew that the God of Heaven was with him. He battled tirelessly to prevent these demons from touching his charge, but he could not stop the barrage of lies aimed at her. And those lies hit their target more often than not. These vile demons were well aware that accusations against God were their greatest weapon against the girl and her mother, and they were unrelenting in their attack.

Starlin's ward was in no danger at the moment. He was safe in the arms of Aloys, but the guardian was responsible to watch over Henri's body, and protect it he would. He fought valiantly beside his comrades.

Heston put a demon to chase and then turned in time to see several more charging Celeste. With extraordinary effort, he lunged back in front of her, extending his wings to shield her from the sudden attack. He grabbed one demon with his hand and pushed him aside, he used his wing to slam another back on its haunches, he tripped another, and with the force of his knee, winded another in the gut.

His comrades, while beating demons themselves, hailed his valiant effort with shouts of praise and encouragement. Undaunted, the trio continued their defensive stance, fearlessly protecting the women.

A small, fiendish demon slithered undetected under the angels' defense and lunged onto Celeste. Heston yanked him off and slung him like a beanbag across the room. Fear seized the opportunity to jump on her back, and then Hopelessness piled on.

The one who'd been slung stood to his feet—more embarrassed than hurt—and seething with anger, charged back towards Celeste. This time Starlin snatched him up and flung him with all his might. The pest sailed through the atmosphere and landed in a heap several blocks away. He slunk bitterly into the shadows, hoping against hope to dodge a beating. The guardians did not see him again.

Fear, however, clasped his hands tightly around Celeste's head and neck, digging his spiny talons into her spiritual body. Heston tugged, but the spirit held fast, spewing lies into the mind of Celeste. The woman, seized with fear, immediately collapsed over her son, sobbing.

Then, the most amazing thing happened—Celeste began to pray. As she did, the demon's grip loosened slightly, enabling Heston to pluck him off of Celeste like a piece of ripe fruit.

"That's my girl!" the angel encouraged. "Run to The Source." Heston turned a lopsided grin towards his comrades, "I know, I know, her theology's a little messed up, but, hey, she's moving in the right direction."

"TRUTH!" Capri shouted excitedly as Alison began to pray. The instant truth came out of Alison's mouth, every lying demon was pushed back by an invisible force.

"Ya hear that, fellas?" Capri said to both the good and the evil in the room. "You go, baby girl!"

His companions grinned openly. Thanks to Alison, the trio got a moment to catch their breaths, but they maintained their protective stance.

"That a girl," Capri felt he could burst with pride. "Use your sword, sweetheart. You got the power! God's word will never return to Him void. It will accomplish His intention, so use it, baby!"

Starlin chuckled. "Ha! She's been asking for an opportunity to share with her mother—looks like one has been delivered!"

"On a silver platter," agreed Heston.

"Though not the platter she had in mind." Capri said, gazing compassionately at his sweet charge.

"No, but according to God's infinite wisdom and goodness," reminded Heston.

"Yes, of course!" replied Capri. "That is an absolute."

At every mention of the name of Jesus in the young girl's prayer, the cringing demons were repelled. Covering their ears, they screamed out in pain-filled, high pitch tones. The echo of Truth in the room began to replace the lies; demons were loosing power as Truth took over the atmosphere. Before long, they were cowering in the shadows again, and their reinforcements had abandoned them completely.

"Hey lookie there, fellas!" Starlin pointed to Alison's mouth, "The sword is forming."

"If she keeps this up," added Capri, "we'll be on the offensive in no time. Keep on praying sweetheart, keep on praying. You're creating a spiritual no-fly zone for your enemies!"

Capri ferociously defended Alison

FIVE

Night will be no more, and they will not need the light of a lamp or the light of the sun, because the Lord God will shine on them, and they will reign forever and ever. — Revelation 22:5 (NET Bible)

Flabbergasted, the children stood speechless trying to take in the wonder of the panorama that stretched out before them. The continued rush to their senses was beyond astounding; it was simply impossible to grasp. Again, they instinctively, without thought, inhaled great big gulping breaths of sparkling, invigorating air.

The light that had burst through the gate seemed even brighter now that it was unobstructed by the wall. Yet again, the children's eyes had no difficulty adjusting to its intensity; no one even blinked. There was a purity in the light they couldn't explain, but it gave everything the appearance of being fresh and clean and new. They could not see the source of the light although everything within eyesight reflected it. There was not a shadow to be found. Every tree, every flower, every blade of grass, every angel, even the children glowed with reflected radiance.

Music, music, music! Where was it all coming from? Even the flowers looked like they were singing! The heavenly orchestra saturated the air, drenching the children in its richness as it flowed around, in, and through them as before. Songs of praise drifted by on invisible air currents and hung over everything like a vapor canopy.

The children beheld many things that, though familiar, looked nothing at all like anything they had ever seen before. They knew they were looking at flowers, they knew they were looking at trees, but they had never even imagined these common things could look like this.

The seemingly endless variety of both flowers and trees was mind-boggling. Some flowers were as big as a tree, some changed colors while the children gazed upon them, and some looked like a faceted, colorful gemstone. Were they gemstones, or were they flowers? They honestly couldn't tell. There were all manner of shrubs and bushes, some of them positively overflowing with colorful blossoms. The leaves of the trees were of all shapes, colors, and sizes. Trees grew in abundance and were also of all shapes, colors and sizes. Some of the trees were of a flowering variety, some were laden with large, succulent fruit, and some towered seemingly miles into the sky. There were trees in every shade of green, trees covered in rich autumn colors, and trees adorned with millions of shimmering golden leaves. The children would not have been a bit surprised if those leaves were really made of gold.

They also discovered that they had exceptionally good eyesight. Every single thing they beheld, no matter if it were close by or far away, was clear and distinct; things at a great distance were so visibly clear that it was almost as if they were looking through a telescope. And the same was true for things up close. The children could discern the tiniest of details, almost as if they were looking through a microscope. Every blade of grass, every leaf, every petal on every flower, stood out, defined with great detail. Even the ground itself seemed more solid, more real somehow.

Compared to Heaven, Earth was like a flat screen television. No matter how real looking or how high the definition, it was still flat. Nothing the children had ever seen or even heard about on Earth came close to what lay before them.

One of the most fascinating things they discovered was colors they didn't even know existed. The color spectrum was limited on Earth—but not so here. There appeared to be no limits to the possibilities.

"I've never seen so many colors," whispered Cristen when at last she found her voice.

"I had no idea there *were* so many colors." Masumi leaned into Cristen and sighed contentedly.

"There aren't!" Henri shook his head and chuckled, "How is this even possible? My brain is on overload!"

Slowly, Edgas turned in a circle, trying to comprehend the magnitude of the scenery. "I thought the garden was beautiful, but I was wrong."

"No, it *was* beautiful, Edgas." Cristen's eyes continued to sweep the scene. "It's just that this is beyond beautiful; I can't even think of a word to describe this."

"Maybe that's 'cause there are no words," Henri offered.

The children were silent as they surveyed the incredible landscape, completely unaware of the lovely image they themselves cast as they stood together by the wall just outside the Pearl Gate. If their parents could have seen them, it would have taken their breaths away and most certainly eased their pain, for every precious face was aglow with joy and wonder as they admired their surroundings. A gentle breeze played with their hair as the light shone through and highlighted each strand. They were "a picture worth a thousand words" as they studied a scene for which there were no words.

Oh, what a place! How it thrilled them from the tops of their heads to the tips of their toes! Wave after wave of pleasure, and love, and peace, and joy continued to inundate them. If this was all there was of Heaven, it would have satisfied them forever. But it wasn't all there was. No indeed, this was just the beginning.

TOKYO, JAPAN
7:10 p.m.

Michi's anguish grew as he waited what seemed an eternity for help to arrive. His worst fear was taking root and strangling him heart and soul. Now, blaring sirens and flashing red and blue lights announced the ambulance's arrival with typical fanfare. The traffic-clogged road parted somehow, just enough for the ambulance to narrowly, though slowly, slip through the congestion. That feat in itself was almost miraculous.

Swallowed up in hopelessness, Michi didn't even look up. *You're too late.* He was sure he had felt life leave his sister and knew in his heart she was dead.

An EMT jumped from the approaching, slow moving van and rushed over to where Michi sat cradling Masumi; her head draped back limply over his arm.

"You're too late; she's dead." The mumbled words were barely audible.

Two medics pushing a gurney glanced at him compassionately as they joined their comrade who was already bent over examining the lifeless teenager. Michi didn't notice. Pushed aside, he scooted back out of the way. Hating to give Masumi over to them, he watched helplessly as the three medics quickly began accessing the situation.

"She's lost a lot of blood. Trauma to the head."

"There's no pulse."

"I TOLD YOU, SHE'S DEAD!" Michi's anguished shout startled the gathered crowd and gripped the heart of everyone within hearing distance. "And it's my fault," he added with a whimper. He covered his face in shame.

Several people drew near, not really knowing what to do, but feeling the boy's need for support. A woman in her mid-forties offered him her handkerchief. He accepted it without looking at her and absently wiped his face and blew his nose. He was a pitiful sight. His school uniform was covered with his sister's blood. His hair was disheveled, and his eyes were bloodshot and puffy. He felt sick to his stomach. In fact, there was no way to stop it; he was going to be sick. He turned and wretched into the street.

The EMTs feverishly tried to revive Masumi. Nothing. Michi's heart sank. He had hoped he was wrong, but he knew it—she was dead. The medics lifted her limp body on to the gurney, quickly secured her, and rushed her over to the waiting ambulance. Michi stared absently at the flashing lights for a second, then jolted to reality, jumped up, and ran after them.

When he reached the back of the ambulance, he grabbed the handle, put his foot on the step, and was just about to pull himself up when one of the medics put his arm out, blocking him. "Sorry, you can't ride in here."

Before Michi could object, another medic slammed the doors shut and ran around to the driver's seat, leaving Michi standing alone staring at the doors. Through the rear windows he could see the men hovering over Masumi as they continued their efforts to resuscitate her. The siren suddenly began, piercing the night, as the ambulance carrying his sister picked its way through the crowd and then sped away.

This time its fanfare blared his guilt to all of Tokyo: *Masumi is dead, and you killed her! You killed her! You killed her!* The words of accusation echoed over and over in Michi's mind with the rhythm of the calling siren.

Strength drained from him like air rushing out of an inflatable toy. Dispirited, he collapsed to the sidewalk weeping uncontrollably, his body heaving. He had killed his beloved little sister, and there was nothing anyone could do about it.

SIX

For to me, to live is Christ and to die is gain. If I am to go on living in the body, this will mean fruitful labor for me. Yet what shall I choose? I do not know! I am torn between the two: I desire to depart and be with Christ, which is better by far; but it is more necessary for you that I remain in the body. — Philippians 1:21-24 (NIV)

How long the large and handsome angel had been standing among them, the children didn't know; but now here he was with his arms open wide, and he bid them come.

Masumi reached out and grabbed Cristen's hand again. Cristen squeezed it gently and hand in hand they moved toward the angel, boys following. Just as the angel opened his mouth to speak, he was interrupted by a large crowd of people scurrying up and over a nearby hill. The angel's open mouth slid into a wide smile as he watched the exuberant crowd come bustling towards the new arrivals.

Attired like royalty in gorgeous apparels of rich, vivid colors, exquisitely designed of opulent fabrics and textured materials, many of which were embellished with dazzling jewels, a throng of noticeably excited people came rushing towards the children, approaching with great eagerness. Broad grins and bright eyes abounded.

Oh, how beautiful! I wonder if they're people or angels?

Just as the thought crossed Cristen's mind, she heard a cheery voice call out, "Welcome! Oh, welcome, my Henri! My beloved boy! Oh! I'm so glad you're here!"

Cristen spun in the direction of the voice and saw a beautiful young woman, she guessed to be in her early twenties, running towards Henri. She had shoulder length, chestnut hair and big, brown eyes, and looked just like a royal princess in her lovely, long, blue gown.

Henri looked a bit confused, as though he was searching to find her in his memories. A moment later he gasped, followed by a half-question, half exclamation, "Grandmama?"

Old people aren't old in Heaven? The thought rushed through Henri's mind, and then he heard the angel laugh. When Henri turned towards the sound, the angel nodded and winked at him.

So totally weird, does he knows my thoughts?

Turning his attention back to his grandmother, Henri smiled shyly as this lovely young woman made her way through the gathering crowd. Once she reached her precious grandson, she grabbed him and kissed him on both cheeks. The second she grabbed him, he recognized her. He enthusiastically returned her embrace, both of them grinning from ear-to-ear.

"I thought you were dead," Henri finally managed.

"Oh no, Henri! Look and see, I'm very much alive!"

It suddenly dawned on Cristen that her own grandmother might be here, too. She quit watching Henri's reunion and began to search the crowd. Suddenly, she spotted someone with a bright smile making a beeline right towards her. *Is that my Meme?* Right then their eyes met and held fast, and, in that instant, Cristen's question was answered.

"MEEMS!" Cristen ran full speed into her grandmother's open arms and wept for joy. Her grandmother was simply beautiful, and her eyes shone with delight as she beheld her much beloved granddaughter. Love, joy, and goodness exuded from her. She, too, was young and vivacious, and she wore a dazzling gown in her favorite emerald green color which accentuated her bright green eyes. She looked a lot like the pictures Cristen had seen of her from back in her college days, only better. Meme, or Meems as Cristen liked to call her, was her mother's mother, and she and Cristen had been very close.

Now they held each other fast in a tight embrace. Her grandmother planted kiss after kiss on Cristen; she kissed her cheeks, her forehead, and the top of her head. She was delighted to be reunited with her granddaughter, and unabashed in showing it. Cristen was completely drenched in her grandmother's love.

"I love you, Cristen, honey," she repeated over and over. "I'm so glad you've come to join me." Cristen knew she meant it with every fiber of her heavenly being.

"I love you, too, Meems. Oh, I've missed you so much."

Cristen's thoughts veered home. It was strange how distant and far away it felt. Although she loved her family, she had no desire to go back to them. This place was too incredible, too joyful, too exciting to ever want to leave it.

"Oh, Meems! I can't get over this place!"

"I know honey, isn't it something? And you've only just stepped through the gates, just you wait; it's magnificent, truly magnificent! It's a place of wonder and delight. Oh! Let me tell you, I am constantly discovering something new and thrilling or something so surprising that I just burst out in praise. Living in Heaven is living a life of adventure!"

"I can believe that! It's been one surprise after another since I got here!"

"Oh, you just wait, honey, you ain't seen nothing yet! And just wait 'til you meet *Him*. He's love. That's all I can say about Him. He's awesome, and He's love. You just can't even imagine...you just...well, never in your life!"

"Oh, Meme, I'm so excited to be here with you! You're right, I can't wait! It's already so incredible! How can it possibly get any better?"

'Oh, it does, baby girl. Let me tell you, it sure does."

"I want to, like, scream or shout or dance or something!"

"Well, then go right on ahead! No one will mind at all. Just let your praise out, baby girl!"

Cristen laughed. She did feel like doing all those things. She glanced about, suddenly aware of all the people around her.

"What are you waiting for?" Meme laughed out loud. "Come on, I'll join you!"

Meme began to dance and shout and sing. I don't think Cristen would have been any more shocked if her grandmother had said, "Let's go get tattoos together!" Cristen could not help but laugh. Meme reached out and grabbed Cristen's hands, encouraging the young girl to join in the fun. Cristen did. She let loose the joy that was already bottling up, and the two shouted and danced their hearts out. It felt wonderful. And just as Meme had said, no one seemed to mind at all! In fact, everyone seemed to enjoy it immensely. Most laughed with joy, and many joined the celebration, laughing and dancing and spinning Cristen around and around.

"Joy is everywhere!" Meme stopped dancing and turned to face Cristen; surprisingly, but perhaps not surprisingly, the older woman wasn't even winded. Taking the girl by the hands she added, "You'll soon discover that even the best, most wonderful things on Earth can't even begin to hold a candle to anything here in Heaven. And best of all, sweetheart," the woman leaned in like she was revealing a great secret, "there's no evil here, none whatsoever. There is nothing to ever be afraid of! No one or no thing can ever hurt us here. Not ever. And let me tell you, we don't even lock our doors. Ha! Some people don't even *have* doors!"

Cristen, listening to her grandmother rave about Heaven, felt her heart soaring. She was absolutely thrilled that this wonderful place was now her home, too. She knew, way down deep, that this was where she belonged and the only place her heart ever wanted to be.

Meme raved on, "And you'll never get sick or be tired; well for that matter, you'll never even get sick and tired, not of being here," she chuckled at her own joke, "because there is always something to do or new to discover. And you'll never feel lonely, or be frustrated, or get disappointed, or be stressed out, or freaked out, as you kids used to say. You left all those things behind, sweetheart. Oh, hallelujah!"

When Meme shouted hallelujah, there was an eruption of spontaneous hallelujahs among the throng. No matter what anyone was doing or saying, they stopped and shouted, hallelujah! It was wonderful and hilarious all at the same time.

A man and woman, bubbling with contagious joy, stepped up behind Meme and teasingly poked their heads over her shoulders, grinning at Cristen. When Meme felt their presence, she turned and burst out laughing. She grabbed the couple by the hands and turning toward Cristen, announced, "Cristen, baby, it's time you met my momma and daddy!"

Cristen's eyes popped open wide, then puddled with happy tears.

"You're my *great*-grandparents?"

"Yes, sweetheart. We are indeed." The lovely woman hugged Cristen as if she were her own child. "We are so happy you've joined us here."

"You look the same age as my Meme," Cristen pulled back and gazed at the lovely young woman, her voice carrying the surprise she felt.

"Isn't that wonderful?" The woman grabbed Cristen's grandmother around the waist and squeezed, "We're more like sisters now."

"Yes," replied Meme. She turned to the woman, adding, "But you will *always* be my Momma!"

Then the handsome young man picked Cristen up and twirled her around and around. "Our baby has come home!" he shouted with joy, hugging her tightly before placing her back on the ground. Cristen could not stop the giggles or the tears of joy which simultaneously erupted.

She turned, and immediately discovered another set of young adults smiling brightly. They appeared ready to scoop her up, as well.

Cristen ventured a guess. "More great-grandparents?"

The beautiful woman replied, "We're your great-great-grandparents! And you, sweet girl, are precious to all of us. Hope you're ready for some serious hugging." Cristen's great-great-grandmother, brimming with joy, tittered and hugged her tightly. Then her great-great-grandfather called out, "My turn!" and then he, too, picked her up and spun her around.

"Goodness, I have a lot of family," said Cristen, peeking around behind the lovely woman when she noticed a line forming.

In the meantime, Edgas looked around for a familiar face. He lit up when he recognized dozens of children he knew from his village. Boys and girls of all ages, big and small, gathered around him with joy and dancing.

"Edgas! Edgas! Welcome, welcome!" was repeated over, and over, and over, again. Then they put Edgas on their shoulders and paraded him around like a sports hero who had just won the game of the century. He thought his heart would explode from all the love being showered on him. Hugs, pats on the back, and enthusiastic welcomes were followed by excited chatter about the joys and wonders of life in Heaven. Edgas had never had so much attention in his whole life; he felt happy and special. This was certainly not the reception he'd expected for a poor, outcast of society, orphan boy with AIDS.

There is no class division in Heaven; all who come enter these Gates as a son or daughter of the King! You are not an outcast in My Kingdom but a son of the King. The thought came unexpectedly into his mind. If he had been alone, the words might have brought joyful tears.

Wow! I'm a son of the King!

There were others around him that he did not recognize but who embraced him warmly and said, "We have prayed and prayed for our Mozambique people to know

Christ. We welcome you with great joy and celebration!" Edgas was completely blown away by his reception, and his face reflected the joy he felt.

Masumi's greeting committee was smaller than those of the others but no less joyful. There was a dear friend from her church, Inagaki-san, a middle-aged woman who had taken an interest in her a few years ago. Masumi had been devastated when she'd died in a car accident. Now here she was, very much alive, ready to pick up where they'd left off. She, too, looked to be in her mid-twenties, but it took Masumi only a second to recognize her.

"Oh, Inagaki-san, you look wonderful! It's so, so good to see you again!"

"Call me Hiroko, sweet Masumi-chan. We all go by first names here. We are sisters in the Lord!"

"Oh. Okay, Hiroko," Masumi giggled. It seemed strange and a bit disrespectful to call her elders by their first names, but somehow she knew it was right, here in Heaven at least. And it didn't take long before it seemed completely natural.

Gathered around her were also a number of missionaries who had labored in Japan, their joy immeasurable! But the most fascinating to Masumi was the large crowd of Japanese men and women who had come to greet her. Hugging her, these precious ones told her they had been adding to their numbers for centuries and have prayed fervently for their nation to turn to Jesus. They were overjoyed at her arrival and hugged her like she was one of their very own daughters. Masumi tried to bow to them, to show respect in the traditional Japanese custom, but before she could bend over, someone else was grabbing her around the neck and hugging her close, very unJapanese-like! It was so foreign to her, hugging a complete stranger, but she found that she eagerly received the love and affection.

The angel stood back and watched his charges with joy. He would never tire of witnessing these reunions. After a time, he called their attentions and motioned for everyone to gather around.

Lifting his arms to quiet the crowd, he began with a surprising announcement, "These children have only come for a visit. It is not their appointed time to join us here. I have been commanded to show them some of the glories of Heaven. They will have a taste of their eternal home and see many wondrous things. Then they will go back to their earthly homes and tell all who will listen about the realities and splendor of Heaven."

Immediately, disappointment washed over the children's countenances. *What? Not staying? Why? Why not?* They were not expecting this bit of bad news and it certainly wasn't what they wanted to hear.

New tears pooled in Cristen's eyes. Meme immediately slipped to her side and hugged her tightly. "It'll be okay, honey," she comforted. "The Lord's will is always, and absolutely, perfect and is without question, the best for everyone. You can trust Him. He knows what's best, sweetheart. I will wait for you to return and continue to love you and pray for you until that day!"

As Cristen hugged her grandmother and listened to her wise words, she felt a peace envelop her. *Everything will be okay*; she knew it was true. "I do trust Him, Meems." As the words left her mouth, her spirits lifted.

At that same moment, Cristen felt a hand gently touch her shoulder. Turning, she looked into the beaming face of one of her dearest friends.

"I've been hanging out with your grandmother."

"LuAnn!" Cristen squealed and leaped with delight. Her best friend, LuAnn, had died from cancer just one year prior.

"Oh, Cristen, I'm so happy to see you!" The two girls embraced with such joy, it seemed they would never let go. Stopping only for a moment to smile at each other, they excitedly hugged again.

"Let me look at you!" Cristen managed to pull back and really look at her friend. "Your hair grew back! It's beautiful!" LuAnn had lost her hair due to chemotherapy, and now her light brown hair was long and curly and glowed with a heavenly radiance. LuAnn was healthy and strong and glowed with happiness. She didn't look like she had been ill a day in her life.

"You're alive!" Cristen squealed for joy and hugged her friend again.

"Oh, she's alive all right," the angel winked, "only her address has changed." Coming up from behind the girls, the angel smiled warmly and placed his large hands on their shoulders, sending an electric-like wave of warmth and energy soaring through their bodies.

LuAnn smiled at the angel and then back at Cristen, "I use to live in Kansas City, now I live in Eternal City!" she chuckled, "I never stopped living, Cristen, not even for an instant; I just relocated up here, leaving my sick body behind."

"Oh, LuAnn! I understand that now." Cristen gave LuAnn's hand a squeeze as she peered into her friend's eyes. "I didn't before; I hurt so badly when you died. It's hard to explain, but I had an ache, way down deep, that never went away. Oh, I've missed you so much!" She reached out and pulled her into another tight embrace. "Your family misses you, too."

"I know. I think of them always," LuAnn's smile changed to a look of understanding. "I'm so happy here, I sometimes forget that they suffer. But I know they'll join me here one day, and when that day comes, nothing will ever separate us again—not ever!"

Reunions such as these were repeated over and over and over again. The children saw family members, friends, missionaries, Sunday School teachers, and countrymen: everyone who had had anything to do with their journey to loving Jesus, and who had entered their eternal reward before them, had come out to greet them. Each one of them greeted the young visitors enthusiastically, with great joy, while waiting patiently for his or her turn. No one was in a hurry or pushy; no one tried to take time away from anyone else. It was as if time didn't matter. The only important thing was that these children felt welcomed. And boy, did they! The children felt more love than they had ever known, and they hugged and kissed and squeezed all these very special ones and never grew tired of it.

Cristen looked at each face she loved so much with a new appreciation. She recognized their willingness, while still living on Earth, to give of themselves to her in some way or another. She knew for certain that when her grandmother was alive on Earth, she had spent many hours on her knees praying for each of her children and grandchildren. Now, here her grandmother stood, enjoying the fruit of her prayers.

The children had absolutely no idea how long this celebratory reception went on, but when they had visited with everyone who had come to greet them, the angel announced, "Come children, you must say goodbye for now." So, after several more loving embraces, the children obediently took off over the meadow, waving feverishly to their loved ones, blowing invisible kisses, as they began their adventure to experience some of Heaven's amazing glories.

TOKYO, JAPAN
UNSEEN REALM

Shame got right up in Failure's face, his red eyes narrowed as he seethed, "The boy was supposed to die, you idiot, not the girl!" His rancid breath hung in the air as a green vapor.

Failure bowed up under the reproach and retorted, "It wasn't my fault."

"Liar!" Shame screamed. "He flung you aside like a rag-doll and pushed the boy to safety!"

Failure lifted his head and glowered back, "So, who cares? One of 'em died. And besides, now there's one less Christian."

"Who cares?" Shame growled. "WHO CARES?" He screamed it this time. "Minion cares! I care! And by Lucifer, *you* should care!" The scales on the demon rippled with anger; his face turned beet red as veins popped out on his neck. He stretched a taloned hand out, wrapped it around the scrawny neck of Failure, and squeezing hard, pierced the smaller demon's leathery skin.

Failure's eyes widened as pain shot through his body, but he determined not to give Shame the pleasure of seeing him cower. He held his breath and stood his ground, face-to-face and eye-to-eye with Shame.

Shame clamped his reptilian hand as tight as he could; he would teach this idiot a lesson, and, by Lucifer, he was not going to suffer because this fool failed his assignment.

Failure, realizing he would not win this match, lowered his eyes, ashamed, and cursed.

Shame screamed in his face, "LOOK AT ME!"

Failure's hate-filled eyes looked back at Shame, loathing the monster.

"Kill the boy! Understood?"

Failure nodded his head, and Shame released him with a shove. Failure lost his balance and fell to the ground. He got up quickly, coughing and sputtering from the strangle hold around his neck.

Shame stared at the imbecile, despising him for his weakness. *Why did Minion force me to work with such an idiot?* He seethed. *I'd be better off without him, without both of them for that matter. I am so much better and smarter than either of them.*

Shame turned and saw a dark silhouette slink by, and he heard a quick guttural laugh. "OH SHUT UP!" he bellowed, his anger to a boiling point. He hated other demons laughing at him or at his situation. His hands were tied; he had to work with Failure. But, by Lucifer, he would not be made a fool by him, and he was not about to be punished for Failure's stupidity.

He turned quickly, full of vile, "Make it right!"

Failure wouldn't look him in the eye, but knew he better respond if he didn't want back in his vise.

"I got it," he snarled.

Shame got up in Failure's face and in a low breathy voice, growled, "I mean it, kill the boy!" He turned and disappeared into the shadows.

With all beady eyes on the altercation between Failure and Shame, no demon noticed Thigma hop in the ambulance with Masumi nor did they remember Raphia or give him another thought. To them, he was just another guardian foiling their plans, and they were glad he was gone.

Failure breathed out heavily, then muttered, "Nobody calls me a fool." He sprung from the ground and hovered near Michi.

"You killed her, you killed her, you killed her," he began whispering in the boy's ear. Then he changed his accusations to the first person, "It's all my fault; I killed Masumi. I'm the one who killed her; it's all my fault."

"It's all my fault."

75

SEVEN

But the fruit of the Spirit is love, joy, peace, patience, kindness, goodness, faithfulness, gentleness, and self-control. Against such things there is no law. — *Galatians 5:22-23 (NET Bible)*

The merry group traveled rapidly over the lush and color-splashed meadow towards the river that Cristen had seen sparkling in the distance. The disappointment in learning they must go back to Earth was quickly forgotten, replaced with happy chatter about their encounters with loved ones, interrupted by shouts of, "Wow!" and, "Would you look at that!" and, "Weird!" and, "Yes, Edgas, *awesomely* weird!"

Passing under flowers as large as a tree only added to the anticipation of the journey they were embarking on. For they weren't just observing these never-before-seen things from a distance but were now walking among them. Every flower turned to face them as they passed, just like a flower on Earth will follow the sun. As impossible as it was, the flowers were clearly greeting and welcoming the children, honoring them as they passed by.

Truly, it was like walking into a fairy tale, only it was a fairy tale of a magnitude and beauty beyond their wildest imaginations. Big eyes tried hard to take everything in, but found it utterly impossible. It was too much. It was too fantastic. It was too spectacular. It was too unusual. It was too astounding. Their brains were on circuit overload, but their spirits were exhilaratingly aflutter.

The angel led the children into a large orchard filled with fragrant fruit trees, that is, *very* fragrant fruit trees. The trees were quite large, and, not surprisingly, they were unlike any they had ever seen or even heard of before. In fact, they were quite peculiar. Each tree was simultaneously ladened with both blossoms and fruit, but not only that, each tree bore several different kinds of blossoms and fruit—at once!

"How can one tree grow different kinds of fruit? My brain's freaking out! It's so weird!" Henri stared slack jawed at the fascinating trees.

"Awesomely weird!" the others echoed in unison, unable to keep straight faces. But smiles aside, they too, thought it was truly weird.

"Can any of you recite the fruit of the Spirit?"

"Oh, I can!" cried Edgas. "The fruits of the Spirit are love, joy, peace, patience, kindness, goodness, um...gentleness, long suffering—that's the one I've been learning about—and the last one is the one we talk about at the orphanage all the time, self control." Edgas ended with a definitive nod.

"Very good, young Edgas!" complimented the angel, patting the boy approvingly on the head.

"Did any of you know, however, that it is not the *fruits* of the Spirit, but the *fruit* of the Spirit?"

"What's the difference?" Cristen was eager to learn.

"There is but one Holy Spirit, and the evidence of His work in your life produces fruit. The fruit of His work in your life is measured by how much you embrace these godly characteristics and how much you let them operate in and through you. When you are surrendered to the Father, the Holy Spirit will empower you to live a life of godliness, and just like this one tree is full of different fruit, so also will you produce different fruit. One you, one Holy Spirit, one fruit with many different characteristics."

The angel spread his arms and looked around the orchard. "These particular trees are here in Heaven as an everlasting reminder of the work of the Holy Spirit in the lives of men and women."

The enthralled children nodded their heads in understanding. Looking around, they noticed the trees were spaced out in perfectly straight and even rows, with enough room for the angel to walk between them. They also discovered that even under the awning of the bountiful branches, there were strangely no shadows. Every leaf, every flower, every branch, every piece of fruit, every woody trunk, every thing, gloriously reflected light, making shadows a physical impossibility. Nevertheless, it was not the brilliant light from the meadow but a more subdued light, which emanated softly through the many vibrant colors of the orchard.

The children admired the copious trees as they walked slowly through the lovely orchard. The fragrance was intoxicating. The peace of this place was soothing. They couldn't help but stroke the trunks as they passed, and were more than a little bewildered that the texture, though not smooth, was not rough.

As Edgas passed under a high branch, he was surprised to feel something brush him on the head. He looked up and saw a large branch swaying. The breeze was light and certainly not strong enough to have caused that branch to blow against him. There was nothing but a gentle ripple of leaves. So, with a wary glance back up at the branch, he walked on. Passing under another high branch, just a few trees away, he felt something brush against his back. He spun around. Nothing, and no one, was there. He jolted his head up in time to see a branch springing back into place. He stared, confused.

"Hey! That tree just touched me!" Edgas turned toward the sound of Henri's voice. Henri was staring up at a branch.

"You probably just brushed into it, Henri," Masumi suggested, looking over at her friend to see what had happened.

"No, it definitely brushed up against me."

"Yeah, I think the trees touched me, too!" The look of shock on Edgas' face was humorous.

"They're just welcoming you to their orchard." The angel smiled broadly, then chuckled at the children's faces.

"They're what?" Cristen, wide-eyed, looked at the angel to see if she had understood him correctly.

"You heard me; they're welcoming you to their home."

"OK, am I dreaming?" Masumi looked at the chuckling angel and had to smile. "You mean they're alive? Are you saying the trees are alive?"

"Of course! All trees are alive." The angel gave them a look that said, "Duh."

"I don't think she means that kind of alive," Henri volunteered. "I think she means like people and animals kind of alive, alive. Right Masumi?"

The girl nodded her head.

"Hi there, trees!" Edgas laughed and waved with exaggerated gestures.

The trees waved back.

There was a collective gasp heard above the rustling sound of waving leaves.

Then a new round of giggles.

"Why, I never woulda believed it." Cristen shook her head in amazement.

"Have you not read in Isaiah that the trees of the fields will clap their hands? If the ones on Earth will clap, why wouldn't the trees in Heaven clap?"

Cristen looked at the angel and scratched her head. "I thought it was a metaphor."

As if on cue, the trees began to clap their branches together. They started with a slow rhythm, then picked up the pace and before long were in a full ovation.

When the slack-jawed children could peel their eyes off the trees, they turned to the angel for an explanation.

"They are worshipping their Creator. They do it all the time, and they love to surprise any newcomer that wanders into their orchard." The angel belted out with a hearty laugh. "These are very playful trees."

The grinning children soon found that they themselves could not refrain from clapping. They joined this very strange ovation, giving praise to their Creator, clapping and laughing with all their might, along with the trees.

"The trees want you to notice something." The angel spoke after the clapping had quieted.

"They do?" Masumi furled her brow but did not take her eyes off the branches overhead.

"They want you to look down on the ground, and tell them what you see."

"That's weird," Henri smirked, "I didn't hear them say anything, but okay, if you say so."

The children studied the ground.

The angel studied the children. "Well, what do you see?"

"Beautiful green grass." Masumi was the first to answer.

"Beautiful flowers that turn to face me everywhere I go," added Edgas.

"That's true. Maybe I should ask what you *don't* see?"

"Oh, I get it!" Cristen excitedly began to look around. "I *don't* see any fallen leaves or dead branches!"

"Oh, that!" Henri said as he and the others were catching on. He looked around, "I *don't* see anything dead or rotten. Nowhere."

"Yeah, I don't see any rotten fruit, or any dirt either." Edgas felt smart, and that made him feel good about himself and proud, in a good kind of way. He smiled broadly at the angel, who again patted him on the head.

The trees seemed to sway as if they were proud, too.

"That's amazing." Masumi admired. "With all these trees, there is not one single thing that is dead or decaying. There's nothing to rake or leave on the ground to rot. It's really clean in here."

"Now look at their fruit. What do you see?"

"Do you mean what do we *not* see?" Henri elbowed the angel, then quickly straightened, shocked at how comfortable he had already become with this mighty creature.

The angel grabbed the teen in friendly hug, "Yes, Sir Henri. What do you NOT see?"

Henri relaxed under the congeniality of the angel. It felt good and comfortable to be in his presence.

"Um, well, let's see," he squinted his eyes to better scrutinize the fruit. "Every piece of fruit is perfectly formed. Looks like there are some different sizes, but each piece is perfect in it's shape." Henri laughed, "I guess I went with what I *do* see, after all!"

"There's no bad fruit," Masumi said, reaching out to touch a ripe, peach-looking fruit, enjoying its softness.

"There are no holes or bad spots on any of the fruit," Cristen noticed, and then following Masumi's example, she reached out and stroked a plump, plum-looking fruit.

"All the fruit is ripe and ready to eat!" Edgas' mouth began to water.

"And I bet there are no worms eating any of them!" The angel grinned and patted Henri on the back.

"What about the leaves?" the angel asked.

"Same ol', same ol'!" Cristen and her friends laughed at her joke; there was certainly nothing even remotely same ol', same ol'!

"The leaves are perfect, too, all of 'em," Edgas offered, smiling proudly at the angel.

"Yeah, there are no dead, or torn, or worm eaten leaves either" Henri added, checking out the many trees.

"And all the fruit is ripe and ready to eat!" Edgas repeated, his mouth really watering now.

"You already said that," the angel replied.

"I know, I just wanted to make sure you heard me."

"Sounds to me like you might be getting hungry."

"Whoa," Henri stopped looking at the trees and stared at the angel. "I haven't even thought about food since we got here, not even once." He turned to face the others, "If you knew me, guys, you would have just said, *weird!*"

"I'm not *really* hungry," Edgas answered the angel. "It's just that it all looks so delicious! My mouth is hungry, I guess."

Immediately, the angel turned toward the children, and in a gesture they were quickly getting accustomed to, opened his arms and said, "Oh taste and see that the Lord is good!"

"Really?" they chorused.

Edgas looked questioningly at the angel. "Like, are you saying we can eat the fruit, or are you just quoting Scripture again?"

Another grin crossed the angel's radiant face and nodding his affirmation toward Edgas, he said, "Really!"

"The trees don't mind?" Cristen faced the angel after glancing at the 'living' trees. She thought if they were indeed living, they might not want someone to pick the beautiful fruit off of them.

"They can't wait for you to taste their fruit."

"Sweet!" Henri exclaimed.

"HURRA!" hollered Edgas as he, Henri, and Cristen took off in search of the perfect fruity snack. Every piece looked so delicious; the trouble would be choosing.

Masumi looked at the angel just to be sure it really was okay. He laughed out loud and shooed her off with his hand. "Go on!" She took off after the others.

The children had difficulty deciding which kind of fruit they wanted. Did they want an apple, a pear, a peach, or perhaps they might want to try something they'd never seen before? Decisions, decisions.

"Can we have more than one?"

"Yes, Henri, eat to your heart's content. We eat for pleasure here, not for nourishment."

"YES!" Henri wiggled his eyebrows, excitedly.

Cristen put her nose to the blossoms and drew in deep breaths as she searched the tree. The fragrances were intoxicating. Then, the glistening gleam of a golden, apricot-like fruit, high on a branch, caught her eye. She stood on tiptoes and stretched for it, but it was too high. She tried jumping—no go, still out of reach. A tad disappointed, she was about to start searching for another piece of fruit when the branch it was on swung down low. Flabbergasted, she stared at the branch, then shaking her head, she reached for the gleaming fruit. "Um, thank you, tree," she said and then easily plucked the proffered treat. As she examined it, she thought, *I am quite sure I will never get used to this place!*

The apricot-like fruit in her hand was bright orangey-yellow, extremely glossy, and perfectly shaped with no spots or bruises. Cristen sought out her friends. They had all picked something different. She smiled as she saw similar looks of shock on the other faces. The branches must have helped her friends, too.

Both Henri and Edgas held a piece of fruit in each hand.

Masumi held up her piece, closed her eyes, and then bit deeply into its flesh. It was crisp, juicy, and bursting with flavor! Her taste buds tingled from the robust flavor of both sweet and tart which lingered delightfully on her tongue.

"Is that an apricot?" She asked Cristen, between bites.

"Mm-hmm, at least I think so," Cristen nodded her head, mouth full of the golden fruit.

"How is it?"

Cristen swallowed. "Oh my goodness, it's delicious! What are you eating?"

"It's a peach, I think." Masumi examined the fruit in her hand. "I thought it was gonna be a plum cuz it's not fuzzy, but it tastes more like a peach, only more incredible. Well, in truth, it's the best thing I have ever put in my mouth!" She smiled and licked her lips.

"What did you pick, Henri?" Masumi wiped her mouth with the back of her hand.

Henri looked down at the half eaten fruit in his hand, "Beats me, never seen it before; it's kinda sweet though," he held it out for the girls to see. "It's kinda sour."

"Well, which is it?" Cristen chuckled.

"Both I guess, I don't know, it's kinda tangy."

Now Masumi was chuckling.

"One thing's for sure, it's really good." He took another bite and added with a mouthful of fruit, "Yep, *really* good."

They turned to see what Edgas had chosen and burst out laughing. Eyes closed, head tilted back, he was attempting to chew a chunk of fruit so large that it filled both of his cheeks. He looked like a chipmunk. The hilarious image was completed by rivulets of juice running down his chin. Lost in his own world, the only sound he made was a contented humming noise.

"Well, it obviously taste good, Edgas, but what is it?" A still laughing Henri said as he walked towards the younger boy.

Edgas looked up, and a smile spread over his puffed out face. "Wad ya zay?"

"I asked what you were eating."

His answer was indiscernible; it sounded something like, "Whaa whaa whaa whaa whaa."

The angel threw his head back and roared. His laugh sounded like thunder, deep and hearty, and it resounded through the orchard.

At the sound of the angel's explosive laughter, Henri, Masumi, and Cristen, erupted into more joyous giggles. Bright eyed Edgas just stood there grinning and chewing, chewing and grinning, quite pleased that he was the cause of the laugh.

"Do people always feel this good in Heaven?" Masumi asked the angel.

"Yes, absolutely."

Cristen joined her friend. "What do we do with the pits?" She held up her finished fruit.

"Oh, good question. Is there a trash can nearby?" Masumi revealed the pit in her own hand, "I don't feel right about tossing it on the ground."

Henri, arm raised in a pitching position, froze just as he was about to launch some fruit seeds into the orchard. "Well, leave it to me to be the first person to mess up Heaven." He brought his hand down and gave the girls a sheepish look.

"Go ahead, throw it." The angel mimicked the look on Henri's face.

"No way, I'm not gonna mess up Heaven."

A still chewing Edgas walked up to join the others. "Where do we throw the trash?"

"Yes, is there a trash can nearby?" Masumi looked around, repeating her question.

"No trash cans in Heaven."

"None?" Cristen was intrigued. "Why?"

"No trash, therefore, no trash cans."

A skeptical looked flashed across Masumi's face. "It's so clean here, surely something is done with the garbage. Does someone come pick up the trash later?"

"Nope. Go ahead, toss your seeds, and see what happens."

"Aaall riiiiight," Edgas said in a singsongy voice, "if yooou saaaay so." He figured the angel was about to show them something cool. He grinned and tossed his pit high in the air. Every eye followed the pit as it sailed above their heads, and then, before gravity got ahold of it, it vanished—evaporating right before their eyes!

"Huh?" The stunned group stared into the empty space, and then laughing, quickly tossed their own fruit pits high into the air. Theirs, too, vanished. Delighted, the children clapped their hands, and the friendly trees joined the ovation. The angel belly laughed, thoroughly enjoying surprising the children.

"How'd it do that?" Henri turned wide-eyed to the angel.

"I told you, there is no trash in Heaven."

"Is that how this orchard stays so immaculately clean?" Masumi was catching on to this new revelation.

"Yes, Masumi. The old leaves and falling fruit evaporate completely before they ever reach the ground."

"That's so cool." Edgas nodded his head happily. "I knew Heaven would be cool."

"Hey, where did the juice stain go that was all over Edgas' face?" Cristen looked from Edgas to the angel. Edgas reached up and touched his chin.

"Evaporated just like it did from your sticky hands."

"Oh! I hadn't even noticed! You're right, my hands are perfectly clean."

"Mine are, too!" Masumi scratched her head in new amazement.

"So, what's next?" Edgas' eyes shone bright with expectation. He knew this orchard was just the beginning, and he eagerly awaited the angel's answer.

"Listen. Can you hear it?"

The children closed their eyes and listened for what they did not know.

"I only hear music and singing," said Edgas.

"Listen closely; it's part of the music."

No one moved a muscle as they concentrated on the sounds around them.

"I think I hear the sound of rushing water."

"Very good, Masumi!" She beamed under the angel's praise.

"Come along, children! Let's go find it." Turning, he continued through the orchard.

The children exchanged glances and then scurried to catch up. They looked like a string of toddlers as they trailed behind this large, angelic being with his swift and fluid gate. His wings were folded neatly against his back, and his huge frame filled their view, filling the space between the trees. The angel was the perfect blend of strength and beauty; he was strong and powerful, yet surprisingly gentle and graceful. His pervading glow gave him the unusual appearance of near transparency, however, he was as solid as the trees they were passing.

"Hey, what a minute! Wasn't Edgas' shirt white?" Cristen pointed to Edgas, her questioning eyes looking to the others for confirmation.

"It was!" shouted Edgas, excitedly. "Look! It's GREEN! How'd that happen? When did it happen?" The group stopped walking.

Henri turned to have a look, and Masumi gasped. Covering her mouth, she pointed at Henri's shirt. "Look at your shirt, Henri! It's a graphic of one of these fruit trees!"

Henri tugged his shirt out again, "What...? How...? Where'd the gate go? Okay, now this is weird."

Edgas couldn't help himself, "Awesomely weird!"

The shocked group laughed and quickly examined the girls' shirts.

"Look at Cristen! Look at Cristen!" Edgas clasped his hands with glee. "The angel wings are blowing!"

Indeed, the feathers on the back of her shirt rippled slightly, as if caught in a gentle breeze.

Amazed, Henri said, "How in the world does it do that?" He quickly turned to Edgas, "I know, I know...we're not in the world!"

Edgas grinned at Henri.

"What's mine doing?" Masumi turned her back to the others, and just as she did, a single petal fell off of her shirt and gently floated to the ground evaporating just before it landed.

When the others squealed, Masumi turned around in time to watch it fall.

"This is CRAZY cool!" shouted Cristen, who had never felt so much joy in her life.

"HURRA!" Edgas' joy exploded in the now familiar shout.

The children turned and looked at the angel.

"Oh, the glories of Heaven!" was all he offered in way of an explanation. He laughed out loud and started walking again followed by the happiest, most wonderstruck group of kids you have ever seen.

Leaving the orchard, they entered the loveliest glen, simply purpled over with violets. How it took their breaths away. A hush fell over them, and they instinctively tiptoed, not wanting to crush any of the flowers. But no matter the care, there were just too many violets blanketing the ground for the children to successfully avoid stepping on them. They quickly discovered that the dainty, velvet-like petals and purply blossoms were not the least crushed or bruised by their footsteps. Each bloom sprang right back into place, leaving no evidence that a small troupe had trampled through their midst.

Walking quietly, they listened with all their might for the sound of rushing water while all eyes feasted on the thick purple quilt.

At the far side of the glen, there was a slight incline which hid the source of the sound from the children's eyes.

"I can hear it real clear now; it's been there all the time." Edgas turned and jogged backwards. Looking at his friends, he added, "But I didn't know that it was water." He turned again and ran excitedly towards the sound, pulling away from the others.

"I hear it, too. Come on!" Henri and the girls chased after Edgas, leaving the angel behind.

The closer they got to the sound, the more it seemed to beckon them. They ran steadily and easily up the incline. Upon cresting the short summit, a mighty river burst into view. The children immediately screeched to a stop, bunching up on top of each other like an accordion.

A united gasp was followed by silence as, in heavenly fashion, every jaw fell open. Astounded, each of them could only manage to point at the wonder before them.

The angel belted out another hearty laugh.

"What do you think?" he called over his shoulder, passing by the stunned group.

"Is it on fire?" whispered Edgas when he had at last found his voice.

PARIS, FRANCE
12:11 p.m.

Sirens.

"Thank God they're finally here!" Celeste jumped up to open the door.

The ambulance double-parked in front of Celeste's townhouse, and three men in white lab coats rushed out of the van.

Celeste stood in the door, frantically waving them in, "Hurry, hurry! Please hurry!"

A young doctor bounded up the steps two at a time while the hospital medical staff grabbed the gurney out of the back of the van. Celeste led the doctor to where Henri lay sprawled on the floor, and then she and Alison moved out of the way, clutching each other as the man went to work.

Half a minute later, the others joined him on the floor, blocking Celeste's view of her son. As she leaned to the side, watching intently, she caught the quick glance of one med tech to the other. The look on his face told her what she had feared. Henri was gone. She hoped she was wrong and held her breath as the men examined her boy.

One of the men hopped up and sprinted out to the parked van. He rushed back carrying a load of medical equipment.

The group, ignoring the women, went to work immediately to resuscitate the boy. Several excruciatingly long minutes passed. The scene, which would be sure to haunt the mother and daughter forever, slowly played out in front of them as the team valiantly tried to revive Henri. But it was to no avail.

By and by, the men slowly rose to their feet, averting Celeste's pleading eyes. The doctor turned towards Celeste, building the nerve to face the grieving mother.

"I'm sorry." He paused, grasping for words, then wagged his head sadly, "There is nothing more we can do." Celeste's knees gave way, and she buckled to the floor, still clinging to Alison.

"No, no!" she wailed, "There must be something you can do! He was just breathing! It's not too late, it's not too late! Don't just stand there, do something! Help him! For God's sake, help him!"

"We have done all we can do." The man reached out to pat her, comfortingly, but Celeste recoiled against his touch.

"WHAT TOOK YOU SO LONG TO GET HERE?" she screamed. "He'd still be alive if you had come sooner!" Celeste began to weep inconsolably.

"I am sorry for your loss, Madame."

Alison held her mother as fresh tears poured down her own cheeks. The two rocked in each other's arms while the men transferred Henri's limp body to the gurney and strapped him down. They raised the gurney and began to wheel his body out to the waiting ambulance.

Celeste looked up, "Stop! Where are you taking him?" The men pushing the gurney continued out the door while the doctor turned back.

"We'll transport him to the hospital for you, Madame. The medical examiner will meet you there." He spoke matter-of-factly, hiding his emotion, then turned and hurried out to the vehicle.

Celeste was in shock. Her precious son was just whisked off. She and Alison remained huddled on the floor and watched the door close behind the man. Celeste's heart slammed shut with the door.

The ambulance driver turned off his flashing lights and silently pulled away. No lights, no sirens, no fanfare.

EIGHT

Then the angel showed me the river of the water of life, as clear as crystal, flowing from the throne of God and of the Lamb down the middle of the great street of the city. — Revelation 22:1-2a (NIV)

"Weirdah!" said Henri, his voice full of wonder.

"Yeah," Edgas whispered back, "*awesomely* weird!"

"No, *that* there is *weirdly* awesome!" Cristen gave a slight chortle at their ongoing joke but never took her eyes off the river.

"You're right, Edgas, it looks like it's on fire...but it's not!" Masumi stood spellbound beside the others, gazing in awe at the spectacle before them.

"This is the River of Life," explained the angel, as if that would answer any further questions the kids might come up with.

The River of Life was very wide. As it rushed by, bursts of color-filled light shot out of it in every direction looking much like flames of fire. Simultaneously, the brilliant, heavenly light reflected off of it, flashing like the bulbs of a million paparazzi with every movement of the rushing river. The resulting display was astoundingly spectacular. It put even the best fireworks show to shame.

"Is it alive?" Edgas knew the answer before he even asked.

Before the angel answered, the others chorused what was becoming a familiar tune, "Everything's alive in Heaven!"

"You're learning." The angel looked very pleased with his young students. "It *is* called the *River of Life* for a reason."

"I've never seen anything like this before." After the words left her mouth, Masumi let out a laugh. "Well, that would make sense. I've never been to Heaven before!"

"It kinda looks like liquefied diamonds," said Cristen, continuing to gaze at the light show. "Hmmm," reflected the angel, "that's a very accurate description, Cristen, well said. It does indeed look like liquid diamonds."

"Who in a million years would think a group of teenagers would be mesmerized by a river?" Henri shook his head. "It's like, like, sooo cool!"

"No wonder I could see it from way back across the meadow," added Cristen, remembering how the bright ribbon of light had grabbed her attention even then.

"Are you kiddos just going to stand there and stare?" The angel's eyes danced with pleasure at the transfixed children. When there was no response, he swiftly moved behind them, spread his wings, and gently herded his group towards the riverbank. As if coming out of a trance, they giggled at the feel of angel wings on their shoulders and began the hike to the river.

Here the grass looked like a velvety carpet, thick, green, and lush. It was blanketed with an artist's pallet of colorful, tiny, soft flowers. These, like the violets, were in no way crushed by their footsteps.

They walked along the riverbank for only a moment before coming to a lovely, picturesque bridge which spanned the width of the river. They had not noticed the bridge because it was engulfed by flames of flickering, flashing light. The angel led the children onto the bridge, and when he reached the halfway point, he leaned over the edge and looked down into the fiery water. The children, following his cue, also leaned over the railing and looked into the rushing water beneath them. From this angle, they could easily see that the water was as clear as crystal.

"Look!" Masumi pointed excitedly to the riverbed where golden, ribbon-like veins ran in abundance. "Is that real gold?"

"Yes, Masumi."

"And look there!" Squealing, Cristen jumped up and down with delight as she pointed into the river, "Those look like real jewels!"

The angel's face beamed with pride, "They certainly are!"

The riverbed was covered with all shapes and sizes of colorful gemstones as an ocean might be covered with seashells. Some of them were bigger than a man's fist. These gems were flashing brilliantly as they reflected the intense light shining down through the crystal water upon them.

"I think those stones are making your fire, Edgas," added Henri, still shaking his head.

"The River of Life flows from the Throne of God," said the angel. Curiously, they looked upstream thinking they might see that throne, but they only saw an endless river. They turned back and gawked, mesmerized by the wonder of it.

"I don't see any dirt anywhere," remarked Edgas. "I'm guessin' stuff evaporates in the water, too?"

"You're a good guesser," replied the angel.

The children marveled that there was not one single speck of dirt or debris anywhere—no sticks, twigs, leaves, or anything at all to muddy or pollute the water.

They ran with great joy back and forth across the bridge, peering over the railings, pointing things out to each other, determined not to miss a single thing.

"It looks happy to me!" said Masumi.

"What does?" said Henri.

"I'm happy!" Edgas laughed to prove it.

"It does to me too, Masumi," Cristen nodded her head.

"What does?" Henri asked again.

"The river!" shouted the girls with more giggles.

"A song from *The Sound of Music* just popped into my head." Cristen faced the others.

"I love that movie!" said Henri.

"Do you remember these lyrics, 'to laugh like a brook when it trips and falls over stones on its way?'" Cristen sang the words, her heavenly voice clear and sweet. "Doesn't this river just look like it's laughing?"

"Yeah, it does!" agreed Henri.

"And singing, too!" Edgas had never seen the movie, but that didn't stop him from joining the conversation.

"Yes, but it's not tripping and falling along its way," Masumi said, with a wide grin, "more like dancing and leaping along its way!"

The group nodded their agreement.

"Well, one thing's for sure," Cristen added, her steadfast gaze on the river, "Maria's hills may have *seemed* alive with the sound of music, but Heaven really *is* alive with the sound of music!"

The group laughed, heartily agreeing. It was truly amazing how music was a part of everything they had experienced so far. The sound of the river as it rushed along, dancing and leaping, laughing and singing, blended in perfect accompaniment with the symphony of music still filling the air.

The angel hummed *The Sound of Music* theme song as he crossed over the bridge.

"You know that song?" Cristen looked up at him, surprised.

"Of course! It's one of my favorite movies, too!"

The surprised children looked back and forth at each other and then followed him across the bridge.

"You watch movies?" Masumi was astonished.

"I've had to sit through my share of them. Some I liked, some I didn't. *Sound of Music* is one I liked."

All eyes were now on the angel as they walked off the bridge.

"And we have theaters here, too, you know."

Henri came to a sudden halt. "No, I did *not* know!" He was surprised but delighted to learn this, for he loved to act and had been in several plays at his school.

"But of course! People still use their gifts in Heaven. Just because you move to Heaven doesn't mean you stop doing the things you love! You actually become much better at it. Heaven produces awesome movies!"

Would there be no end to the surprises? The more the children learned about Heaven, the more excited they became.

Their minds began to ponder the endless possibilities of a life in Heaven as they absently followed their tour guide, who was now leading them upstream along the banks of the mighty River of Life. They progressed quite slowly, for it was completely impossible for one, or several, or all of them, not to stop and stare at the amazing, fiery river.

"Living Water!" shouted Cristen, with sudden revelation.

"Yeah, we already said it was alive," Edgas reported.

"I know, but," she turned to face the angel, "you said this is called the River of Life, right?"

"Yes, indeed it is."

"And like Edgas said, it *is* alive, right?"

"Yes, indeed it is."

"Okay, I was just thinking about that, and then I remembered what Jesus told that Samaritan woman, you know, the woman he met at the well, that he would give her *living water*. Is this what he was talking about? Is this the living water he meant? Oh, I don't get it, but somehow, this water is alive with God's power."

"Well, Cristen, Jesus was saying that *He* is the living water. Remember I told you that this river flows right from the Throne of God? Well, the throne is not the source— God is the source. This river is alive because it flows right out of the heart of the One Who Sits On The Throne. This river is not only *from* God, but it is part of Him."

"Oh!" Cristen was excited now as the revelation was becoming clearer."

Masumi joined in the discussion as the others listened intently, "I remember in that story that Jesus told the woman that if she knew Whom she was talking to, she would have asked *Him* to give *her* a drink, and He would have given her living water and she never would have been thirsty again. What did Jesus mean by that because everybody *does* gets thirsty again. I mean, don't we all need water to live?"

"It was an invitation to her spirit being, not her physical being. You are right that her physical body would always need hydration from physical water, but her spiritual body could be satisfied eternally with Jesus' living water. The living water from God Himself. Did you know that the Lord still offers His children to come and drink from the River of Life?"

"I'm confused," Henri scratched his head. "It sounded like He was telling the Samaritan woman she could drink from the River of Life, like right then, you know, with Him, on Earth, before she died? But this river is here in Heaven."

"Yes, it is in Heaven, but it also flows on Earth, through Jesus. The spiritual part of you can drink from this river anytime. You don't have to wait until you move here to drink it."

"Or *visit* here," added Edgas, with an overacted fake pout.

"That's right, Edgas. No one has to wait for a visit to Heaven to drink from this river. It's available right now; they only need ask. Jesus will liberally pour this water, straight from the Father's heart, into the very spirit of the thirsty one so that they never have to be spiritually thirsty again."

Henri couldn't stop his smile from widening. "So just as Earth's water quenches our physical thirst, this heavenly, living water will quench our spiritual thirst?"

"By George, he's got it!" The angel winked at him, proud of the kids for catching on so quickly.

"Who's George?" asked Edgas. The others laughed.

"Nobody," said Henri. "It's just an expression."

Walking along the water's edge, the little group continued to discuss the things of the spirit. The angel smiled quietly and nodded his head as the group got the revelation of living water. He loved being with these sharp kids and appreciated the eager way they wanted to learn.

Coming around another bend in the river, they discovered a place where the river forked. One of the channels was more shallow than the other, and its current was less swift. It looked as if this section could be forded with no effort, and the sparkling stones were within easy reach.

"Can I, I mean, *may* I..." Edgas could hear Isabel's voice correcting him in his mind, and he smiled, "Well, anyway, what I want to know is, would it be okay if I touched one of those pretty stones?" He looked pleadingly at the angel. "I only want to touch it, I promise I won't take it, I'll put it right back."

"Certainly!" There was no hesitation in the angel's jolly reply. "You may each pick a stone! Choose whichever you like."

Again, the children gave him a second glance to see if he was being serious or just teasing them.

"You mean pick *up* a stone, right?" questioned Cristen.

"Nope. Pick one."

"For keeps?" Edgas' eyes were wide.

"Yes, for keeps!"

The children stared at him, speechless.

"Go ahead," he coaxed, "there are plenty, and many more where they came from. Heaven will never run out of gemstones."

In one instant, four merry children became explorers on the great gemstone quest. Trouble was, like with the fruit, there were so many gemstones, and they were all so beautiful, all so perfect, all so unusual. How would they ever be able to choose?

In obvious merriment, the angel called after the scampering prospectors, "And while your down there, feel free to quench your thirsty spirits."

They stopped in their tracks and turned back towards the angel. He had just invited them to drink from the River of Life! Their hearts soared! He smiled and gestured for them to go on with the back of his hand.

With great joy, they began running along the river's edge, peering into its sparkling freshness, thrilled with their prospecting task.

Realizing that any spot was as good as any other spot, Henri stopped running, lay down on the plush grass, and stuck his face near the water to examine the gemstones more closely. The others followed suit.

"Wow!" Henri yelled. "It's like someone dumped out an enormous treasure chest. These gems gotta be worth a fortune!" Then he whispered quite seriously to Edgas, who had lain down right beside him, "We better be on the lookout for pirates!"

Edgas looked surprised, but when he saw Henri wiggle his eyebrows, he burst out in a happy laugh at the joke.

"Maybe that's why it's called a river bank. Get it? A river *bank*?" Edgas was very proud of himself for coming up with that joke.

"I get it." Cristen smiled at him. "That's a really good one, Edgas."

"Hey, maybe we can take out a loan from the river bank," chortled Masumi.

The angel roared with laughter, his deep tones rumbled right through the children colliding with the joyous sounds of the living symphony. The combination produced a sound so delightful that it filled the children with unimaginable pleasure. They stopped searching and turned to watch him. Never had they witnessed anything like it. Oh, how good it felt just to be in his presence.

"Well, Masumi, today is your lucky day: interest free River Bank loans for all!"

The children loved that the angel was enjoying their jokes and having fun with them. Even though it was hard to believe that someone as important and smart and holy as the angel would enjoy their company, but it made them feel very special and very important, too.

"But there's no such thing as luck," corrected Edgas.

"Right you are, Sir Edgas, that was just an expression. Let's see...how about, 'Today, you are blessed indeed.' Would you approve of that?"

"Oh, yes! That's much better."

"Thanks for keeping me straight, young man." The angel winked at Edgas, then continued to chuckle as the children went back to the difficult task of choosing a stone.

"And Henri?"

Henri looked up again, "Yes?"

"No need to watch out for pirates, at least not any bad ones. Any pirate that made it to Heaven can have his fill of heavenly booty; they won't be stealing yours!"

Henri smiled, then stopped. "*Are* there any pirates in Heaven?"

"Of course! Anyone who repents and accepts the sacrifice of Jesus is welcome here, even if he had been a pirate...and yes, there were pirates who repented!"

The children exchanged smiles, yet again.

"And guess what they do in Heaven?"

Dumbfounded, Cristen shook her head. "I have absolutely no idea."

"They take people on real treasure hunts."

The children could not have been any more surprised, and their quizzical looks were quite humorous.

"How does that sound?"

"Really?" Cristen lifted an eyebrow.

"Really."

"I think it sounds awesome!" Edgas squealed.

"I think it sounds weird." The second the words left Henri's mouth, he turned to Edgas and added, "Yes, Edgas, awesomely weird!"

The group laughed at their running joke and then returned to his or her adventure of finding the perfect gemstone.

Henri spoke quietly to himself as he continued his search, "I never, *ever*, would have imagined that born-again pirates took people on treasure hunts in Heaven." He shook his head and chuckled, "Never, ever, *ever*."

Finally, after much deliberation, the sprawled out children narrowed down their choices. One by one, they picked out a stone.

Henri decided on a turquoise-blue one. He plunged his arm into the water. It felt cool and refreshing just as he thought it would. He was tempted to dive right in and swim in the fiery river, but after taking another look at the current, he reasoned that although it was less swift than before, it was still swift enough to carry him quickly downstream, so he willed himself to refrain. He did remember, however, that the angel said he was free to drink from the river. The instant that thought crossed his mind, he felt very thirsty. He cupped his hand, filling it with the crystal water. He sipped at first, then scooped another fist full and gulped eagerly. The water flowed through his body, reviving him completely. The sensation was similar to quenching an earthly thirst but at the same time, all together different. He felt like his whole body came to life.

The cool water ran down his chin, his arm, and onto his chest. Wherever the water touched, it tingled with a rush that felt electric. *Weird!* He was momentarily distracted by the powerful sensation, but a brilliant sparkle caught his eye, and he remembered the blue stone he was after. He plucked it out of the river and held it up in the light. He watched, amazed, as it flashed turquoise-blue rays all around him. He rubbed it admiringly with his thumb enjoying the feel of the stone. It fit nicely in his hand, and he loved the cool, silky smooth feel.

"How can this stone reflect so much light?" Henri offered the question without ever removing his eyes from the stone.

"Heavenly gems have more facets than earthly gems."

"Why is my arm still tingling?"

"Why do you think?"

"Because the river is alive?"

"You are one smart boy, Henri."

Just then, out of the corner of his eye, Henri saw Edgas stick his whole head underwater. When his soaked head popped up, he was laughing hysterically from the sensation. Sparkling droplets filled his dark curls and dribbled all over him. He shook his head like a puppy, sending water flying. Everywhere the water touched him, tingled. It was exhilarating.

Edgas, following Henri's example, then cupped his hand and swallowed several big gulps of the refreshing water. It was the most delicious, refreshing drink he had ever had. It was so delightful that he forgot about his stone until he heard his name called.

"Edgas! Have you found a stone yet?"

Oops. He better choose one. He still couldn't decide; they were all so beautiful. *Here goes! I can't go wrong with any of them.* Edgas shut his eyes tightly and plunged his hand down into the water, plucking up the first stone he touched. He wanted to be surprised, so he kept it hidden in his closed hand as he ran over to the others who had already gathered for show and tell.

Shimmers of bright color shot from their hands as they held their energized stones out for each other to see. The stones vibrated with energy as they twinkled and flashed.

"It tickles!" Masumi giggled from the thrill of it.

The angel was right in the midst of them, enjoying the beauty of the gemstones as much as the children.

Cristen laughed at the tingling sensation as she showed her new friends the canary yellow stone she had chosen; it was the brightest yellow any of them had ever seen.

After much admiration, Edgas eagerly opened his hand and discovered that he had grabbed a bright white stone. It looked very much like an opal; only Edgas had no idea about that. He was thrilled, for he thought it looked like the angel's wings, white, yet filled with the rainbow.

Masumi held up her deep, crimsony-pink colored stone, and everyone oohed and aahed as they looked it over enthusiastically.

"I've never seen a color like that before," Cristen said, marveling at Masumi's beautiful stone.

"I know!" smiled Masumi. "It's the prettiest thing I've ever seen."

Then lastly, Henri showed them his turquoise-blue stone.

"Oh, I love that color, Henri!" Cristen reached out and caressed the stone.

They continued to take turns examining and touching each other's cool, silky, and incredibly sparkly stones. They decided that these gemstones were probably the most beautiful things in the whole Universe.

"Look, Henri!" Cristen pointed excitedly at Henri, "Your shirt has a treasure chest on it!" Henri tugged his shirt out again, trying to get a good view. The rest shook their heads in amazement, then quickly checked to see if their own shirts had changed.

"Mine's blue!" Edgas jumped up and down, "Mine's blue!"

"Oh, Masumi, another petal just fell off your shirt." Cristen pointed and the whole group turned in time to watch the petal float down and evaporate.

"I can't imagine that I'll ever get used to this!" Masumi laughed.

"You're flapping again, Cristen." Edgas was eager to let her know. This time, Cristen reached back and pulled her shirt out so she could witness it herself. "Oh my goodness. That's CRAZY!"

The angel moved in front of the group. "Oh, the glories!" he said again, then added, "Okay, it's time to put your stones away."

"Are they really for keeps?" Edgas looked up into the smiling face of the angel.

"Of course. Now put them in your pockets, for it's time for us to continue our journey; there are many more glories to discover." At that, he turned and continued his progression alongside the river.

Gingerly, the group of friends placed their stones deep into their pockets. With wide smiles, protective hands over their stones, and full hearts, they took off after their angelic host.

"Oh, you guys, this is like the best field trip EVER!" Masumi cooed, running along beside the others.

"Yeah, it is," laughed Henri, thinking that no trip—field or otherwise—would *ever* be able to compare to this Heaven adventure. He wondered if all of this beauty was really a dream, and he would wake up and be disappointed. But then he reasoned that there was no way his mind could have come up with the glorious things he was seeing and experiencing.

Without a doubt, this was the best day of his life—of all of their lives, or more accurately, their entire existence! And little did they know that they were still only at the start of their journey.

PARIS, FRANCE
UNSEEN REALM

Angels and demons spilled into the little townhouse with the arrival of the medical team. The guardians greeted each other with a quick salute; the demons greeted each other with growls and snarls.

"This is our turf," warned Fear, baring his fangs. He said it as much to the arriving angels as to the arriving demons.

Starlin kept a close eye on the men as they examined his Henri. He moved in close.

The light-bearing newcomers joined Heston and Capri in a protective circle around their humans.

The examination confirmed Celeste's worst fear: her beloved boy was gone. When the doctor relayed his sympathy, her knees gave way, and she collapsed to the floor. Immediately, Heston was on his knees besides her, speaking encouragement to her spirit.

Accusation came close as well, whispering, "They let my Henri die. They should have come sooner. If they had come sooner, my Henri would still be alive."

There was no doubt Celeste had heard and believed the lies when she screamed the very words to the doctor.

"Ha! She's listening, which makes her mine!" Accusation gloated. Heston glared at the demon but continued to speak words of peace. Accusation smirked menacingly back at the guardian, revealing a snaggy row of yellowed teeth, but he wisely stayed out of Heston's reach.

Starlin never left Henri's side. The men in white coats lifted Henri's body onto the gurney and began transporting him to the ambulance. As they neared the door, Starlin turned and with a grin, bowed to his comrades, and then hopped onto the gurney. "See ya later, fellas," he said, saluting.

Capri shot back, "That's quite a load for those poor men!"

The guardians shared a smile, then Heston and Capri returned their attention to protecting their charges, and the group of spiritual visitors left with the ambulance.

The barrage of lies never abated.

Celeste felt the full force of the demonic attack, and she thought she might throw up. Covering her mouth with both hands, she sank forward, eyes shut tightly.

Alison found herself down on her knees beside her mother. Her head was swimming with confusion; the paralyzing fear that had gripped her only moments before, however, was gone.

Capri leaned in close and whispered, "Pray baby—" and then his voice was interrupted by another, only this voice came from within Cristen. "Call out to Jesus, Alison. He wants to help you."

The guardians bowed their heads. The Great Counselor was speaking in His still, small voice. Cristen was learning to recognize that voice. It sounded so much like one of her own thoughts, yet she knew that on her own she could never have come up with the wisdom it often brought. The angels remained hushed, not wanting to interfere with the Holy Spirit's work. He began to do what He does best, comfort. He spoke words of comfort to Alison, encouraging her spirit.

Alison was at a loss for words but had a pressing need to pray. She wrapped her arms around her mother and called out from the depths of her heart, "Help us, Jesus! Help us, Jesus! Help us, Jesus!"

Immediately, the demons screamed and covered their ears. Oh, how they hated that name.

And at the same time, Capri and Heston saw a rainbow of swirling energy surge from within Alison. It wrapped itself around the guardians like a cloak, momentarily engulfing them, and then as quickly as it had come, retreated back into Alison. The guardians instantly felt energized by its power. They replied with grateful hearts, "We worship you, Holy Spirit of God, and we thank you!"

NINE

Then I heard every creature in Heaven and on Earth and under the Earth and on the sea, and all that is in them, saying: "To Him who sits on the throne and to the Lamb be praise and honor and glory and power, for ever and ever!" — Revelation 5:13 (NIV)

The luminary in angelic form, with four wide-eyed children in tow, traveled easily along the banks of the River of Life for a few more miles. The children thought it remarkable to reach into their pockets and feel the cool smoothness of their special stones.

Cristen had hoped they were going to follow the great river upstream—all the way to the Throne of God! But as they came upon a new bend, the angel turned and led the children away from the rushing waters. The fiery, "liquid diamonds" carried on its course without them, and the little group quickly lost sight of it—although they could hear its rhythmic melody for quite some time.

Their angelic leader discovered his charges to be a slow moving pack to herd along. He stopped and waited patiently for them more times than he could count as one or another became enthusiastically distracted by a colorful flower whose blossoms were the size of a dinner plate, a tree with heart shaped leaves, or a shining shimmer from something new and unknown. They just couldn't help but stop and gawk at the overwhelming beauty and stunning perfection.

The leisurely pace was of no consequence, time wise, because Heaven exists in a multidimensional spiritual realm where time just *is*. The only awareness of time is the experience of the current moment; and the only measurement of time is the gaining of knowledge from one's experiences and discoveries, and the expectation of new experiences and discoveries to come.

Before them now, appeared another one of those new discoveries. Standing alone, over the path they seemed to be following, were two, intricately carved, alabaster columns supporting two, scroll-like doors swung wide open. There seemed to be no particular reason for this unusual gate, for even if the doors had been bolted shut, the children could have easily gone around on either side of them.

"Why's this big ol' door here? Edgas turned a quizzical face to the angel.

"Yeah," agreed Henri, "it does seem kinda weird to have a door that's not connected to anything. What's the point if it can't keep people out?"

"Or keep them in?" added Masumi.

"It's a gate, and it's used a marker. It lets us know we are entering a new area; you'll find marker gateways all over Heaven."

"Oh! Kinda how the Gateway Arch in St. Louis marks the gateway to the West?" said Cristen.

"I suppose it's somewhat like that," agreed the angel.

"Look up there," Masumi pointed to an inscription suspended between the columns, over the doors. It reminded Cristen of some decorative metal scrollwork she'd seen, only this was a beautiful, glowy white material, not metal.

"Expedition Park?" Henri read the words, then turned to the angel for an explanation.

"Is that the name of this new area? Expedition Park?" asked Cristen.

"Yes, it is."

"It's so green. What kind of park is it?"

"Well, Masumi, it's somewhat like a nature park."

"It looks huge." Cristen moved to the gate and peered through the opening. She chuckled because the view was exactly the same. "Is it?"

"It is."

Edgas turned hopeful eyes to the angel, "Would we by any chance be going on an expedition in Expedition Park?"

"We are but not by chance!" The angel's eyes twinkled. "There's something in the park you are to see. Come along."

The angel passed through the open gate with his little troop following, except for Edgas. He decided it would be kind of funny to go around the outside of the gate. Giggling, he ran around one of the huge columns and then joined the others behind the angel.

"Do these trees and flowers look different to you?" Cristen asked Masumi as the group walked deeper into Expedition Park.

"Different from what? They're certainly very different from anything in Japan."

"Yeah, I can believe that! No, I mean different from the ones we've seen so far."

The angel interjected. "Have you done much traveling, Cristen?"

"I haven't been out of the country," she snickered, "until now, that is! But I've been to quite a few states. Why?"

"Do the states all look alike?"

"No, not at all," Cristen pondered the question, and then added. "Oh I get it! Some states have mountains and lakes and rivers, some have forests and waterfalls, some have deserts with cactus, and some have beaches with palm trees."

"Exactly. Just as Earth has a wide variety of topography and plant life and animal life, so does Heaven. There are mountains, lakes and rivers, forests and waterfalls, deserts and cacti, and beaches and palm trees. Earth was made in the image of Heaven, not the other way around, so all those things, plus some, were here first."

"I think Earth is pretty in places," Masumi added, "but Heaven takes my breath away!"

"Everything is bright and shiny here" Edgas added.

"That's because everything is filled with the light of God," the angel explained, "and everything has been created to reflect His glory, even you."

"Is that why there are no shadows?" questioned Masumi.

"That's exactly why."

"Hey, look!" Henri stopped walking and pointed excitedly toward the wooded area bordering the path. "Did you guys see that?"

"No, see what?" Masumi stopped with the others and scanned the area where Henri was pointing.

"I saw something dart into those woods."

"You mean like an animal?" Edgas' voice went up an octave.

"Yeah, like maybe a deer or something."

Edgas whipped around to face the angel, his eyes bright, "Are there animals in Heaven?"

The angel, having turned back when his little chicks had stopped following, looked at the eager faces. "Of course!"

Their jaws dropped opened, and the angel laughed uproariously.

"Didn't you think there'd be animals here?"

"I hoped there would be," said Cristen.

"Oh, what kind?" Edgas jumped up and down and clapped his hands with glee. "We have an elephant park in Maputo, but I've never been to it. Most kinds of animals I've only heard about; I haven't seen 'em with my own eyes."

"There are all kinds of wonderful creatures here, Edgas!"

"Are there elephants and giraffes?"

"Why yes! Tall, grand giraffes."

As if on cue, several tall, grand giraffes appeared and walked across the path right in front of the children.

Squeals of delight could have been heard for miles!

Right behind the giraffes came three large, wrinkly, gray elephants; but instead of crossing the path, they turned and lumbered right up to the children. The angel greeted the giant pachyderms, and then one of them wrapped its trunk around the angel in a friendly hug.

The squeals were quickly replaced by shocked silence and broad smiles.

"Kneel," the angel commanded kindly. The large creatures lowered themselves down on all fours. The angel turned his attention to the children, "All aboard!" he said, with his best conductor imitation.

The first elephant curled its trunk to form a step, and the angel reached his hand out towards Edgas.

"I bet they don't do this in my elephant park!" said a smiling Edgas as he took the angel's proffered hand and climbed on the elephant step. The elephant raised his trunk, and Edgas easily scrambled up to his large, round back. Next went Henri, right behind Edgas. Cristen and Masumi repeated the procedure and were soon seated high on the back of the second elephant. Lastly, the angel climbed aboard the third.

The children laughed and patted the elephants, surprised to find that the wrinkly skin felt soft and supple, not at all dry and course as they had thought it would feel.

"What about *tigers*?" Edgas picked up where the conversation had ended.

"You *sure* you want to ask about tigers, Edgas?" laughed Masumi. "You *do* remember how quickly the giraffes and elephants showed up?"

"No need to fear tigers, Masumi," said the angel. "Nothing will ever hurt you in Heaven."

Immediately, a set of tigers dashed across the path and disappeared into the woods.

Here was a collective squeal, followed by a string of giggles, followed by a menagerie of animal names lobbed at the angel.

"Are there monkeys?"

"Do you have lions?"

"What about zebras?"

"Kangaroos?"

"Chipmunks?"

"Bunnies?"

"Horses?"

"Kittens?"

"Yes, yes, and yes!" The laughing angel held up his hands to stop the stampede. "We have every kind of animal you can imagine, and even kinds you have never imagined! And why not? Animals display God's creative majesty; they glorify His handiwork; they show off His wonder! Of course Heaven would be filled with them."

The elephants entered a large, flat, grassland where herds of wild animals were wandering freely, such animals that would not normally mix: zebras and lions, antelopes and leopards, gazelles, rhinos and cheetahs, were grazing and playing together. A wide brook meandered through the length of the grassland, offering refreshing water to every creature.

From their high perch, the children watched in amazement. They were on their own private safari, and they were loving it!

"They don't eat each other?" Henri's words were more of an observation than a question.

"This is the greatest day of my life," cooed Edgas. "Everyone in Africa talks about going on a Big Five Safari!"

"Big Five? What's that?" asked Henri.

"It's a Safari to find the lion, the elephant, the rhino, the cape buffalo, and, I can't remember the other one," said Edgas. "It's a big deal if you spot all five!"

"The leopard," said the angel, just as a leopard bounded in front of the children's caravan.

The group gasped.

"Well, Edgas, I think we've been on the Big Fifty Safari!" laughed Cristen.

"And, we've only just begun," returned the angel. "Are you ready for more?" He paused playfully and then added, "How would you like to meet more of Heaven's animals, up close and personal?"

"HURRA!" cried Edgas, bouncing up and down on the elephant's back.

"Many more live here in Expedition Park; it's quite big you know."

The elephants carried the children across the broad grassland and then deposited them on a path that led into another wooded area. The children had been prepared for the elephants to kneel down so they could disembark in the same way they had embarked, but instead, the elephants reached around with their long trunks, wrapped a child around the waist, plucked them up, and then set them gently on the ground.

The elephants were rewarded with squeals of laughter, loving pats, and thank you trunk hugs.

As they angel led the way, the children joyously skipped along behind him. They turned and waved goodbye to the elephants, and to their delight, the elephants lifted their trunks and returned the wave.

Passing under broad trees, Edgas continued to peek up at the branches expecting them to brush his head or grab him at any moment while Henri and the girls kept a sharp eye out for forest animals.

They scaled a hill and came upon a clearing, discovering a picturesque lake nestled charmingly beneath them. A light breeze played with the girls' long hair and ruffled the angel's feathers as the five stood at the top of the hill gazing at the inconceivable beauty before them.

Soft grass blanketed the hill all the way to the water's edge while trees and bushes of varying heights and sizes were peppered about and fringed the lake in many places. The grass itself seemed to be waving to the children as every blade flickered and shimmered in the breeze. A vast array of bright and bold colors were splashed across the entire area by a multitude of cheery flowers.

A sparkling brook emptied into the far side of the lake with a gurgle and a splash while ripples, full of light, danced like a million mirrors across the water, wildly reflecting the glory of God.

The peace of the scene filled the children's souls.

"This would be a lovely spot to live," sighed Cristen.

"Indeed," said the angel.

Masumi sighed contentedly. *Does perfection like this simply grow wild in Heaven, or did someone plant all of this? And I wonder who tends the grounds and gardens of Heaven.*

"People and angels work together caring for the land here in Heaven."

Masumi turned and caught the angel smiling at her. *He knows what I'm thinking? How is that possible?*

The angel led them down the hill, and when they had descended about half way, he had the children sit down under a fruited tree overlooking the lake. Unbelievably, the ground itself molded around them, almost like it was made of memory foam, causing them to be incredibly comfortable. It seemed as if comfort itself was alive in Heaven, for comfort enfolded the children everywhere they went.

"Some people really enjoy tending land and gardens; it's their gift." The angel said, as he situated himself on the ground next to Henri. "If you did something like that on Earth, and really enjoyed it, or if you never had a chance to do it but would have loved to, you get to do it here. You're still you. If you liked it before, you will love it here. One of the greatest joys and blessings of Heaven is the absence of resistance; things do what they're supposed to do.

Relaxing under the tree, they noticed the sky was filled with birds of many colors and a variety of plumage. They flitted about overhead, chirping out their praises; their melodic singing was delightful. Why hadn't they noticed them before? Perhaps it was because there had been so much else to see. Whatever the reason, they were there now, and the children watched them soar in the blue, blue sky high above them. Down and around, up and over, back and forth they flew with grace and ease. Their joyful songs blended into the grand tapestry of the heavenly music. It was a splendid performance, and the children enjoyed it immensely.

Would they ever get used to this magnificence? Probably not.

A flock of perhaps two hundred or so geese-like birds flew past the children, low and close to the water. They were grouped between two and six abreast in various patterns stretching out in a long fluid line. As quickly as they came into view, they were gone. Then suddenly, they reappeared from the other direction. When they were near the center of the lake, the foremost birds lifted off the surface in an upward direction; the ones behind followed in perfect formation and synchronization, creating a long arc of fluid motion into the wide blue sky. They quickly leveled off and flew away with a graceful flapping of wings.

Now a lone, snowy white egret, with long legs, a long neck, and a long beak walked in the shallows, wings outstretched. Folding its wings behind, it stood still, very stately, looking out at the water. After a short while, it began to wade through the water, close to the shore, slowly and methodically.

There were other birds that from time to time came into view over the lake, some in groups of two or three, and some alone as they circled lazily in the air, singing their melodious songs of praise.

A momma duck waddled out from under a flowering bush near the shore. Five young ducklings followed her in a single line as she glided into the water. The children laughed when the last duckling had to hop to get into the lake. The happy family swam around, paddling their little webbed feet and quacking joyously. Every now and again, their heads would completely disappear replaced by little ducktails pointing straight up out of the water. When heads and beaks popped back up, one little shake or twitch and any excess water rolled right off their backs.

"Have you ever heard the expression, *Like water off a duck's back*?" The angel's voice interrupted their reverie.

"I have," answered Cristen while Henri and Masumi nodded their heads, and Edgas shook his indicating a no.

"What do you think it means?" Abel turned his head toward the children.

"I've heard it, but I never really thought about what it means," said Henri. "Maybe it's like, things don't stick to you or something."

"Yeah, that's kinda what I was thinking," Cristen nodded her head. "Like, we shouldn't let things bother us too much."

"Oh, I get it!" Edgas spoke up. "The water doesn't soak in on those ducks but runs right back into the water."

"That's right, Edgas," the angel smiled at the boy. "Do you have anything to add Masumi?"

"Well, I guess if the duck's feathers did soak up water, they would get so heavy that the duck couldn't float, so God made their feathers kinda oily so that the water wouldn't soak in."

"Very good, Masumi." Now the angel was nodding his head. "If the duck's feathers didn't repel the water but absorbed it instead, the duck would be too weighted down and heavy to do what the duck was created to do."

"Like bob around and stick its rear-end up in the air?"

"Yes, Henri, like that." Abel chuckled with the others. "Here in Heaven, no one is weighted down by the cares of the world; no one is weighted down by what other people say or think about them; no one is weighted down by expectations, false or real; no one is weighted down by past mistakes or failures; and no one is weighted down by evil or sin. All those things are repelled by the blood of Jesus; nothing bad or harmful can ever be absorbed here in Heaven. Here you are free to be yourselves; you are free to become all that you can be; you are free to become all that God created you to be; and you are free to become who God created you to be."

"We are free to become ducks!" said Edgas, bending over and wiggling his bottom. The others stared at him for half a second before bursting out in peals of laughter.

The angel grabbed Edgas, pulled him into his lap and tickled him playfully. Edgas squealed with delight.

"No, dear Edgas, you are free to become YOU!" The angel hugged him tightly before releasing him.

The joy the children felt was invigorating. It was lovely to rest here on the lush grass, watching the activity on the lake, laughing with their friends, and listening to the angel's message. The children did indeed feel free. They were free to enjoy each other and God's wonderful creation. For the first time in their lives, they felt a little bit like the carefree birds circling above them. If they could have, they would have leapt into the air to join the birds in flight. How wonderful it must be to have wings. Oh, to be an angel and fly with the eagles. They slightly envied the beautiful creature sitting beside them with the gorgeous rainbow infused wings. Maybe, just maybe, before their visit was over, he would take each of them for a quick flight over the beautiful city. Well, a person can dream, can't they?

TOKYO, JAPAN
7:15 p.m.

Subconsciously, Michi heard the sirens fade away in the distance, then he noticed them began to get loud again. Were they bringing his sister back? He glanced up, hopeful, but was immediately disappointed to see the flashing lights of two police cars approach as they expertly maneuvered through the clogged street. Michi dropped his head.

At their arrival, most of the curious onlookers peeled away.

A massive gridlock had resulted from the accident, so one of the officers went straightaway into the intersection to unjam the traffic and get it moving again. He spoke briefly to the poor driver who'd almost hit Michi. The man was visibly shaken by the impending death of the young girl and had hung around to speak to the police, but after the officer listened to his story and took down his information, he sent him on his way to help clear out the intersection.

Meanwhile, the other officer was surprised to find no evidence of an accident. Puzzled, he scanned the crowd and saw a young teenager, crumbled in a heap on the sidewalk, blubbering. As the officer started towards the boy, a kindly looking older gentleman intercepted him and told him what had happened from his point of view.

The officer, with a pang of sorrow, pulled out his notepad and went over to the young boy. He knelt down beside him. "I'm Officer Tsukahira," he said tenderly. "I'm going to help you, but first I need to ask you a few questions."

Michi never looked up.

"I need to know your name and address and your phone number."

Michi did not acknowledge the officer's presence. He continued to mutter nonsensically.

Officer Tsukahira looked over at the gentleman, who only shrugged his shoulders, as if to say, "I wish I could help you."

The officer rose back to his feet and looked at those gathered around, "Does anyone know this young man?"

He was answered with wagging heads and a few no's.

"No, but I was only a few feet behind them and saw what happened," said a woman, stepping up to the officer. "The kids came busting around me—almost knocked me over—in a hurry to catch the train, I suppose, anyway, I heard him call out to the young girl, he called her...Masumi, I think, then he dashed out into the street. He ran right out in front of that car, almost got himself run over, but he lurched out of the way; unfortunately he threw himself into the girl, knocking her to the ground." The woman shook her head sadly, before adding, "Oh, here, I have both of their backpacks."

She handed the backpacks over to the officer, who for the first time had some hope that he might be able to find out who these kids were. "I think she must have hit her head on the curb and died. Such a freak accident."

Michi, upon hearing the whole tragic event retold, began to wail inconsolably. The kindly gentleman walked over and put his hand on the young man's shoulder. If anyone had been paying attention, they would have seen his lips moving, perhaps in a silent prayer.

The remaining bystanders watched helplessly, eyes moist with tears.

TEN

The wolf will live with the lamb, the leopard will lie down with the goat, the calf and the lion and the yearling together; and a little child will lead them. — Isaiah 11:6 (NIV)

"Okay, now about the business of our Expedition," the angel announced as he hopped up and glided over to a nearby bush. Plucking several things off the bush, he came back to the children and reaching up into the branches above their heads, he grabbed several pieces of ripe fruit. After handing each child a small nut, a piece of fruit, and a leafy twig, he turned and to their surprise and great delight, called out:

"Rabbit, come!"

"Lamb, come!"

"Deer, come!"

"Lion, come!"

"Did you say, l-lion?" asked a shocked Edgas.

"Yes, it's all right, Edgas, I promise."

"Is it Aslan?" Cristen asked with a chuckle, referring to the lion from The Chronicles of Narnia. Henri and Masumi chuckled while the angel broke into a smile.

"No, Cristen, it is not Aslan."

"Who's Aslan?" Edgas had that quizzical look again.

More chuckles.

"Aslan is the name of a lion in a children's allegorical story."

Edgas scrunched his face, "What's an al-le-gorital story?"

"An allegorical story is one with a hidden meaning or moral. In this case, Aslan was like Jesus. He defeated evil by willingly laying down his life as atonement for the others in this wonderful gospel illustration. But don't worry that you do not know Aslan, dear Edgas, for you will meet the Lion of Judah, the true lion who really did lay down his life. You have already met Him by faith, but soon you will meet Him face to face."

Edgas sprang to his feet and started turning cartwheels again! "HURRA! I knew it! I just knew it!" His gleeful shouts sailed across the lake. He ran back to the group, his face lit up with exhilaration, "I told Isabel I was gonna meet Jesus today!"

His unbridled joy was contagious. The new friends felt their own excitement rising with renewed anticipation of meeting their Lord face to face. Wow! How could this day get any better? And yet, amazingly, they knew for sure it would.

Suddenly, something caught Masumi's eye. "Look!" she pointed to a tiny patch of gray in the grass.

"Where?" Henri looked in the direction of Masumi's finger.

"Oh, it disappeared! There it is again!" They all spied it now. Up, down, up, down, up, down, closer and closer it made its way through the gently swaying grass.

"It's a bunny!" cried Cristen. "Look how cute he is!"

It eagerly approached them, not the least bit afraid or timid. It was darling with its long floppy ears and fluffy white, cotton-ball tail. The little rabbit wiggled its nose and hopped right up to Masumi. She held out all of her treats, not knowing which one it would prefer, and it began to nibble on the leafy twig.

Giggling, she reached down and gently rubbed its silky fur; it felt incredibly soft. She scooped the little bunny up in her arms and rubbed her nose and face in its downy fur.

While the children oohed over the bunny, a baby deer poked its small head out from behind a bush. The movement immediately caught Edgas' attention.

"Oh, here comes another one!" he shouted gleefully. The fawn studied the children, then kicked up its tiny hoofs and came scampering directly to Edgas. Edgas carefully held out his hand with all of his treats just like he had seen Masumi do, and the tawny fawn chose to nibble the leaves, as well. It even ate the tender branch.

"That tickles!" Edgas giggled as the deer pushed down on his hand with its little nose. He reached up and stroked its velvety soft, spotted fur. It readily let Edgas pet away while it enjoyed the treats.

Cristen looked up to see a little lamb bounding her way. She stayed perfectly still as it approached. It was precious—and its fleece was whiter than snow! It walked right up to Cristen, and she carefully held out her piece of fruit. It grabbed the fruit then playfully pushed into Cristen. She laughed as it munched the fruit and then plopped down in front of her. She tried to scoop it up, but it was a little too heavy. All she managed to get into her lap was its back half. Its curly wool was fleecy soft and reminded her of a favorite blanket. The little lamb was perfectly content to sit half-in half-out of Cristen's lap, and it seemed to thoroughly enjoy the petting.

Henri surprised himself because he did not feel impatient or jealous that he had not yet been chosen. While watching Cristen try to get that little lamb into her lap, he felt a puff of warm air on the back of his neck. Very slowly, he turned his head and found himself eye to eye with a lion, a huge l-i-o-n, lion. His instincts wanted to scream at the surprise and size of the creature, but he uttered no sound. He immediately realized he wasn't afraid.

The lion, with his broad nose and big, gorgeous brown eyes, crooked his head and looked intently at Henri. The two stared at each other. Henri dared not breathe. After a moment, the lion gently pushed against his back. Henri smiled and let out his breath. Opening his hand, he revealed the treats to the beast behind him. The lion lumbered around, opened his enormous mouth, and gently took the piece of fruit that was offered. It then plopped down on the soft grass right in front of Henri and ate the fruit.

Henri had never before been this close to such a large, powerful, and muscular animal. He felt a thrill of excitement rush through him. He very slowly, and very bravely he later reflected, reached his hand out and stroked its mane. He expected it to be coarse, but it felt like silk. He quickly pulled his hand back, and with eyes wide with amazement, he glanced over at the angel who had taken a seat next to him. The angel broke out in his easy laugh. He was enjoying this moment as much as the children. He patted Henri good-naturedly on the back while rising up on his knees. He gently grabbed the lion's mane and leaned over its large furry head and whispered something to the lion while briskly rubbing its face, like they were old friends. The lion stretched its neck, and with its soft nose, nuzzled the angel's face with much affection. Henri felt, as much as heard, a deep rumbling vibrate through him. The lion was purring like a kitten!

Henri reached out again and patted the lion's golden back, and to his surprise, the big creature rolled over on its side inviting Henri to pet and perhaps scratch him. It was just like something his puppy at home would have done. Henri obediently scratched away, all the while shaking his head and grinning in disbelief. The others stopped petting their animals to watch Henri's interaction with the enormous lion. They, too, shook their heads in amazement.

The children had no fear; the animals before them were sweet and gentle. Nor did the animals feel any fear. Oh! The glories of Heaven!

"Are all the animals this tame?" Cristen kept her eyes on the little lamb as she tenderly pet it.

"Yes, Cristen. All of Heaven's animals live as God originally intended. They are all friendly. They are friendly with each other and friendly with you. You will never, ever, have to fear them, and they will never, ever, have to fear you. They are here for your pleasure and enjoyment."

While the angel was talking, the wooly lamb stood up from Cristen's lap and stretched. Then suddenly, it sprang straight up in the air and ran all about the children. It bounded down the hill, and then back up again, beyond where the children were seated. It ran in and out of the children, bounded back down the hill, and then raced back up again. Its playfulness brought smiles to every face. Beyond the children again it went, and then turning, it ran full speed towards the seated group and leaped right over the top of Edgas' curly head. The air was split with giggles. The daring act excited the little fawn who now wanted to join in on the fun. Without warning, it jumped out of Edgas' arms and began to scamper up and down the hill, with the lamb.

The children laughed as the two romped, and played, and frolicked. Several times, their romping landed one or the other right on top of the lion which only looked at them with those large brown eyes. When they tired of playing, the little lamb came and plopped down right beside the lion, nuzzling right up to its great, big, face.

The lion lifted its ginormous paw, and the children flinched, fearing the lion was also tired of playing and might swat the lamb away, but to their astonishment, it gently placed its paw over the lamb's back.

"I don't believe what I'm seeing!" Henri's mouth fell open. "I'm seeing it, but I don't believe it!"

The lion looked lazily over at the little lamb and then over at Henri, and Henri is positive that he saw it smile.

"Well, I believe it!" Edgas smiled at Henri. "I mean, look at our shirts, who woulda believed that? Hey! LOOK at our shirts! They've changed again!"

Edgas was now sporting a fawn colored shirt, Henry's shirt had the image of a lion's head on it, Cristen's wings started fluttering, and Masumi's was still dropping petals from the flower on the back while the one on the front remained the same. The amazed children shook their heads and checked out each other's shirts...again.

"Come, children. Say goodbye to the animals; it's time for us to go to the Eternal City! There are many more 'unbelievable' things for you to see!" Rising to his feet, the angel winked at Henri and then began walking away from the lake and away from the animals.

"The Eternal City!" A thrill ran straight through Edgas. He jumped up and clasped his hands with joy. He quickly patted the fawn on the head and ran to catch up with the angel, all the while calling out goodbyes over his shoulder to the other animals.

"Let's go!" Henri jumped to his feet and ran after Edgas and the angel. He had taken about ten steps when he stopped in his tracks. "What am I thinking?" He turned and ran back to the lion, then leaning over, faced the beast nose to nose. Feeling suddenly emboldened, he reached both hands out, placing them on the sides of the lion's face, right up into its silky mane, and rubbed briskly, just like he had seen the angel do. As he was rubbing, the lion got up and nuzzled into Henri's face which disappeared completely behind a cascade of flowing mane.

"Goodbye, Aslan," Henri whispered, touching his forehead to the soft broad face. He looked deep into the lion's brown eyes. "Goodbye! Don't forget me." Before Henri could sprint off, the lion stood on his hind legs and wrapped his large front paws around Henri's neck, dwarfing the boy. Stunned, Henri slowly wrapped his arms, at least as far as they would go, around the midsection of the lion. The boy and lion hugged goodbye.

The girls stood, watching in stunned silence.

When the hug ended, the lion dropped to all fours, took his paw and gently pushed Henri in the direction of the angel. Henri walked backwards for a few feet, waving to the lion, then turned and ran on.

The girls took a minute to pet each animal goodbye, even the friendly lion. Then they, too, ran to catch up with the boys and the angel. Just as they reached them, a sound like thunder shook the ground beneath them.

Henri whipped around. "Was that what I think it was?"

The lion's jaw opened wide, and he bellowed another ground shaking roar, causing Henri's heart to beat a little faster knowing he had just been so close to all that power.

"I think he's saying goodbye to you, Henri!" said Edgas, quite amazed.

"Goodbye! Goodbye, Aslan!"

The group waved enthusiastically to their animal friends and then happily skipped along behind their guide in the direction of the Eternal City.

Wait. What? "Goodbye children! Come see us again!" The children spun around. Did they only imagine it?

KANSAS CITY, KANSAS, USA
5:17 a.m.

While Dr. James and his team desperately worked to save the life of their young patient, Will and Elaine begged the God of Heaven for His mercy. They prayed with passion as if their daughter's very life depended on it, and, indeed, they believed it did. Soon their spirits felt quieted, and when they could think of nothing else to say, they knelt in silence, still hand in hand.

"I wish I knew what was happening." Will turned to face his wife.

Elaine pushed up from her kneeling position and sat back wearily in the recliner, her forehead resting heavily in the palm of her hand. "They said they'd come and tell us as soon as there was something to tell."

Will stood to his feet and stretched. He felt stiff all over. As he walked to stretch his legs, he felt his peace fading and his anxiety rising. His mind was racing with questions. Back and forth, back and forth, back and forth he paced the tiny room like a caged animal.

"What's happening? I can't play this waiting game. I need an update."

"I know, honey, but they said they'd come to us, and I'd rather them concentrate on her right now, not on us."

Will stopped his pacing and breathed out heavily. "You're right." He looked at the anxious face of his wife and thought she was beautiful even with her tear streaked face, red nose, and puffy eyes. She was a woman of quiet strength, and even now her peace amazed him. In direct contrast, he was a wad of nervous energy. And that energy was threatening to implode—or explode—if he didn't keep moving.

After a few more turns around the room, he knew his pacing wasn't cutting it. He couldn't escape the torrent of fears and negative thoughts that were swarming around in his head. He had to do something, *anything*.

His forehead creased with worry, "I can't stay here doing nothing, Elaine. I'm gonna look for a nurse, see what I can find out. Any news is better than no news."

He started out the door, "Will, honey?" A lump lodged in Elaine's throat.

"Yeah, babe?" He turned to face her.

"Before you go, could you hand me my cell? It's charging on that night stand." Elaine pointed. "I'm gonna call your mom."

"Texts! I can't believe I didn't think of that." Will grabbed his wife's phone and pulled his out of his pocket. "Call Mom, and then let's get the word out and ask for prayer!" He plopped down in the metal chair beside her and busied himself by sending texts as fast as his fingers would fly.

Within ten minutes, Elaine had brought Will's mother up to speed, had spoken to her son, Scott, had decided not to wake her other two boys, and had reached her father in Florida—a praying man; and Will had called the pastor and had activated the church prayer chain. At least now the word about Cristen was out, and their prayers would be multiplied. And, too, Elaine and Will's best friends were on their way to the hospital. These sweet friends weren't sure what they could do, but they would not let their chums suffer without being there to support them.

Before long, there was a soft knock on the door, and the moment Jon and Ginger poked their heads into the room, Elaine burst into fresh tears. Ginger held her and let her cry. Anguished tears poured from Elaine while tears of compassion rolled down Ginger's cheeks. Jon grabbed his friend and gave him a big, strong hug that said without words, "I'm here for ya, man."

"You guys didn't have to come down here," Elaine whispered, although she was so grateful they had. She wiped her eyes and blew her nose.

"Where else would we be at 5:30 in the morning?" Jon smiled, lightening the heaviness in the room. "We got nothing else going."

Ginger smiled wryly and shook her head at Jon's lame attempt at a joke, adding kindly, "We wouldn't want to be anywhere else." Her friend meant it, and Elaine knew it was true—there was no obligation in this friendship, only love. She would have done the very same thing if this had been one of Ginger's kids.

Jon grabbed his wife's hand then reached out and took Will's. "Let's pray." Ginger took Elaine's hand, and Will took a hold of her other. The four friends stood in a tight circle, and before the prayer was over, they had dropped hands and had their arms around each other's waists and shoulders.

It felt good—comforting—to have these friends standing with them. Jon prayed a simple but powerful prayer, and Elaine felt hope rising up in her spirit.

ELEVEN

Now the whole world had one language and a common speech. The Lord said, "If as one people speaking the same language they have begun to do this, then nothing they plan to do will be impossible for them. Come, let us go down and confuse their language so they will not understand each other." — Genesis 11:1, 6-7 (NIV)

Tirelessly, the young visitors traversed picturesque landscapes of unimaginable beauty; lovely vista following lovely vista. Every, single, solitary thing reflected God's glory. It wasn't a blinding reflection as light reflects off snow on a wintry day but a soft reflection that never once offended their eyes.

"Sunglasses not required," became Henri's mantra.

Sighs of contentment and little gasps of wonder were their constant companions as they witnessed one marvel after another. On and on they traveled, completely captivated by the overwhelming magnificence as far as they could see in all directions. There simply was no way to take it all in.

Masumi happily slipped her arm under Cristen's, and together they walked arm in arm.

"By the way, Cristen, how long have you known Japanese?" ventured Masumi. "You speak the language very well. All of you do."

"Huh?" Cristen's face showed her surprise.

"Did you take Japanese at your school? It's amazing how you and the others speak it so fluently. You must have studied my language for many years."

Cristen stopped walking. "What are you talking about? I don't speak Japanese."

"Sure you do!"

"No, I sure don't! The only Japanese words I know, Masumi, are like, uh…" Cristen thought hard to think of some Japanese words, "uh, sayonara, sushi, and uh, teriyaki."

Masumi's expression changed to bewilderment.

"Oh, and Nintendo, Toyota, and Nissan."

A very confused Masumi stared at her friend.

"Oh, and arigato!"

"Really, stop teasing, Cristen. You're speaking Japanese right now."

"I'm speaking English right now, and so are you!"

"I know a little English but not enough to have a conversation with an American. I'm not speaking English: I am speaking Japanese!"

"How is that possible?" Cristen's expression changed from one of surprise to the same bewildered look Masumi was wearing. "Are you sure?"

"Quite sure."

"But, I'm hearing you in English."

"And I am hearing *you* in Japanese."

The girls stared at each other, stunned.

Henri, noticing the girls had fallen behind, shouted, "Hurry it up, slow pokes!" Then taking a closer look, his voice turned more serious, "Is everything okay?"

When the girls didn't answer, he began jogging back towards them.

"What language did Henri just speak in?" Cristen leaned forward and whispered.

"Japanese."

"I heard him in English!"

"No way! Are you sure?"

"Yeah, I'm sure! He just spoke English!

"Well, that's strange because he just spoke Japanese!"

"Henri?" Cristen said, as the boy reached the girls, "What language are you speaking?"

"Duuuh, same as you." He looked at the girls' quizzical expressions.

"Which is...?" Cristen turned to face him.

"French, of course." Henri looked back and forth from one girl to the other, not knowing where they were going with this.

Huge grins slowly spread across the girls' faces.

"What's up with you two?"

Now Masumi turned to face him, "I don't know French, Henri. I am speaking Japanese."

"What? Don't be silly, you're speaking perfect French!" He looked at Cristen and then back at Masumi. "You're serious."

The girls nodded.

"Don't you know French?"

"Not a lick, or Japanese either, which is what Masumi says she's speaking; and I am speaking English!"

Henri's jaw dropped, "No way!"

"Way!" both girls laughed.

"Okay, this is totally weird!"

Edgas and the angel retraced their steps and joined the others. "What's the matter, you guys? Is something wrong?"

"No, Edgas, nothing is wrong, but something *is* awesomely weird!" Henri shook his head in amazement while Masumi and Cristen tried very hard not to burst out in hysterics.

"Or weirdly awesome," laughed Masumi.

Cristen turned her smile to Edgas, "We've just discovered that we've been experiencing more supernatural stuff, and we didn't even know it!"

"Really? What?"

"What language are you speaking, Edgas?"

"Portuguese, just like you guys," he looked back and forth at their expressions and added rather timidly, "and why is that so funny?"

"Because we're not!" laughed Cristen. "It seems we are all hearing each other in our own languages."

"What?" Edgas exclaimed. "Don't any of you know Portuguese?"

"Nope!" they chorused.

"Not one word!" Cristen added with a chuckle.

Masumi grinned and shook her head. "It's mind-blowing!"

"It's totally, awesomely WEIRD!" Henri's eyes bugged out in wide exaggeration.

They stood silently for a moment, shaking their heads as this newest discovery sank in.

Enjoying their stunned faces, the angel roared with laughter. His blue eyes sparkled wildly, and his whole body shook from the core. "I wondered how long before you'd figure it out!" He delighted in watching them discover the glories of Heaven.

"How is it possible that we understand each other?" Masumi asked.

Henri had a new quizzical look on his face, "Yes, but not just that, our mouths are in sync with the words, so it's even more than just understanding each other because we *appear* to be talking the same language."

"There are no language barriers in Heaven! There is only perfect unity here. There is no English, French, Japanese, or Portuguese. No, it's a new heavenly language, and you all speak it and understand it perfectly from the moment you arrive."

All eyes were glued to the angel as he explained this new, glorious discovery.

"You see in Heaven everyone can understand each other. Different languages were originally given at the Tower of Babel to force separation. It was intended to keep people from uniting in rebellion against God. But that is not necessary here, for in Heaven there is no rebellion—only love, harmony, and perfect unity.

"And at the End of the Age when God has finished gathering men and women from every tongue, tribe, and nation, there will be glorious diversity, blended as one family, in perfect unity. Imagine what it will be like when all the redeemed, from every corner of the Earth, experience the joy of communication just like you kids, from four very different cultures with four very different languages, are getting to do."

Why of course! It made perfect sense.

"Heaven is SOOO wonderful!" Cristen shouted.

"Amen!" shouted Masumi.

"And so is the Lord!"

"Amen, Edgas!" The group heartily agreed.

"No wonder we keep hearing those songs of praises to God!" Edgas tilted his head up and concentrated on the heavenly chorus.

"Yeah, the longer we're here, the more amazing I realize God is!" Henri was not used to speaking from his heart about God, but he didn't feel strange or embarrassed. It felt right and perfectly natural, so he continued. "Before I came to Heaven, I didn't understand that the Lord was great, but now...now that I'm here, I don't just think He's great, I know He is!"

"Indeed, the Lord Most High is great and greatly to be praised; He is marvelous in all His ways." The angel was radiant as he spoke. "Well, now, are you heavenly communicators ready to discover more of Heaven's glories?"

"Oh, YES!" They clapped their hands in joyful anticipation, more than ready to discover all they could about this amazing place called Heaven.

"Well, that's a good thing," the angel's eyes twinkled, "because there are many more glories to be discovered, for the glory of the Lord is everywhere!"

The enlivened troop, filled with mind-blowing wonder, continued their quest toward the Eternal City.

KANSAS CITY, KANSAS, USA
UNSEEN REALM

As the couple prayed, the hospital room filled with Light. The shrieking demons scrambled backwards, scattering like cockroaches out of its path. They hated The Light as much as the name of Jesus because they knew the two were one and the same, and when Light poured in like that, there was only one source—Heaven. Heaven was receiving the prayers of these two, and if Heaven was receiving, then more than likely, Heaven would be answering. If the evil spirits didn't act fast, the towering lights in the room would be too powerful for the demons to breach their defenses.

Obed and Innesto stayed close beside their human assignments, on high alert. They were a great team, understanding and anticipating each other's moves; often communicating without words.

When Will said the name of Jesus, a smile slipped across Obed's face. *Finally!* He could feel his shoulders relax. He knew that he and Innesto would be strengthened in this fight, and chances were very good reinforcements were on the way. The two tipped their faces towards The Light, drinking in its presence. Oh how they missed living continually in and with this Light.

As Light held the darkness at bay, the angels turned and placed their hands on the shoulders and backs of their human assignments, encouraging the spirit-man within them.

There was a sweet presence in the room, and the couple sensed it as they finished praying. They stayed quietly on their knees for a few minutes soaking in the peace. But as the Light abated, the demons crept back towards their victims with renewed vigor, unleashing a new assault.

Elaine felt drained. She closed her eyes and silently repeated the name of Jesus.

Will tried hard to have faith, to be the strength his wife needed, but his mind was bombarded with all manner of fears and thoughts of accusation. He knew to take them captive to the obedience of Christ. He tried. But the moment he'd grab one, a dozen more came barreling in. He had never felt so confused and conflicted in his life—tormented actually. His head was swimming. Not knowing whether his daughter would live or die was making him crazy. He began to pace like a caged animal.

There was a blip of light in the woman's mind, and Innesto knew immediately that Holy Spirit had just given Elaine the thought to call her mother-in-law. When she asked for her phone, Innesto slyly nodded at Obed, and the two guardians smiled but only with their eyes; they were careful not to let the traitors see.

Oblivious to anything but their own tirade, the demons completely missed what was truly happening.

The SOS for Cristen was in full swing as cell phones were lighting up all over town. Men and women were shaking off their slumber and getting down on their knees on behalf of the young girl and her family. In answer to those prayers, angels were being assigned new and temporary missions.

Soon, the couple was joined by their best friends, who were accompanied by their own guardians. This tight group of humans and angels had spent countless hours together.

As the four friends prayed for Cristen, their four guardians encircled them, standing back-to-back and wing-to-wing. The fire of the Holy Spirit burned strong within the humans, and the demons knew, all too well, that their attack had been severely hindered.

A string of profanity spewed from a spirit of Despair as he crouched in the shadows. "You said this would be a cinch," he turned and glowered at Accusation, hate piercing from his red eyes.

"It is!" Accusation straightened, puffed with pride, and returned the hate-filled look, "Don't be a fool."

More profanities.

"Shut up, you idiot! I have a plan." Infuriated by the disrespect of Despair, Accusation—red with anger and loathing, veins popping in his neck—turned his wrath towards the humans and snarled, "Stop praying! God doesn't hear you, anyway. And even if he did, he never answers your prayers. It's a waste of time." Then, perceiving that Will was struggling the most, Accusation moved in as close as he dared and aimed his assault directly at the father, changing his words to the first person, "He doesn't even heal my headaches! Why do I think He'll heal my Cristen?"

Obed and Innesto encourage Will and Elaine

The guardians held their tongues. How they wanted to shut the darkness up, but they were unwilling to enter a verbal fight with these abominable, vile creatures. Their wings blocked much of the verbal rubbish, but some of the lies hit their mark.

Obed knew that a bull's-eye had been drawn on Will. "Stand strong, William! Keep praying," he encouraged. "You're taking atmosphere away from the enemy. Don't give up. You will be victorious."

"The prayers of a righteous man or woman availeth much," added Innesto, quoting James 5:16. "Don't stop, you are helping to make us strong by giving us weapons to use against your enemy."

Tangoori, Jon's guardian, quoted from 2 Corinthians, "For the weapons of your warfare are mighty for the pulling down of strongholds." He looked at the couple, "Come on, keep those weapons coming—give me some Word!"

And adding his agreement to those of his fellows, Chacomel, Ginger's guardian, quoted from Hebrews the fourth chapter, "For the word of God is living and active and sharper than any two-edged sword."

The guardians were proud of their people. They were pushing back darkness through prayer. How the angels wished the humans could see what the angels could see. How they wished the humans knew how much power they had in the spiritual realm through prayer. If they truly believed what God said in His Word, they would never stop praying.

By now, the friends were hugging, and the guardians were eye witness to two very exciting things: Love, fueled by the fire of Holy Spirit, was palpable and was pushing away every fear, and Hope had taken root in the soil of the human's souls.

Yes indeed, it was to be a great day for the Kingdom of Light.

TWELVE

And he carried me away in the Spirit to a mountain great and high, and showed me the Holy City, Jerusalem, coming down out of heaven from God. It shone with the glory of God, and its brilliance was like that of a very precious jewel, like a jasper, clear as crystal. — Revelation 21:10-11 (NIV)

"Yellow! Edgas, your shirt is yellow!" Everyone turned to Edgas as the words flew from Cristen's mouth.

A laughing Edgas danced with joyful abandon. "How does it keep doing that?"

"And there goes another one of your petals, Masumi!" Henri exclaimed. The group turned in time to witness a dainty pink petal drift down and then evaporate.

Edgas peered around Cristen, "Yep, just as I suspected! Your wings are blowing just like his." He pointed to the angel before scooting over to check out Henri's shirt, "What'd yours change to?"

"That's weird," breathed Henri, tugging on his shirt. "It kinda looks like a spaceship." His friends agreed it looked like something out of a Star Wars movie.

"That's cool, Henri. I wonder what that's about?" Cristen leaned closer and studied the graphic design.

"Are we getting ready to go into space, like I did on my way to Heaven?" asked Edgas, hopefully. "Cuz everything on Henri's shirt so far has been about something we've done or about to do, so I'm guessing we're about to go into space or do something in space."

"Very observant, young friend. Yes, it has been, and no, we're not."

"Then what *does* it mean?" The inquisitive Edgas didn't listen for the Abel's answer. Something caught his eye, and he pointed excitedly, "Look over there!"

Everyone turned.

"People!"

A small group of beautifully clad people were chatting together in the not-so-far-off distance. The children waved enthusiastically when they passed by. Gradually, they began to see a growing number of people.

"It *is* a city," said the angel, "and cities are populated with people, are they not? The closer we get, the more people you shall see."

Very soon, they began passing men, women, and children—of varying sizes, skin tones, and nationalities—coming and going in all directions: some along other magical-like paths, some disappearing or appearing over luxuriant green hills, and some traversing brooks as they wound through charming verdant hollows. The group could not get over how joyful, how strong and vibrant, how beautiful and handsome, and how young everyone was. No one appeared to be any older than perhaps, mid-twenties. While some were considerably younger than their twenties—none appeared older. Broad smiles beamed like sunshine from faces full of the joy of the Lord!

"Hello there!"

"Welcome, young ones!"

Everyone they passed smiled and waved, and many called out warm greetings. Some folks looked as though they were simply out for a leisurely stroll while some were excitedly visiting with friends and family. Others looked to be bent on carrying out an important task; yet no matter what the people were doing, there were no hurried, harried, stressed, or angry faces anywhere to be found, only smiles and radiant joy.

The angel explained that there were no deadlines to meet, no schedules to keep, no time clocks to punch, no paychecks to earn, no stress or pressures of any kind. The people looked peaceful because they were indeed, full of peace.

Among the people they passed, there were those who were shouting praises to God; those who were dancing exuberantly; and many were those who were singing, joining their thread with the majestic, overriding tapestry of music that floated by on veiled air currents. In truth, the passersby voiced such lovely tones the children thought the singers must have been professional vocalists. Some of them carried small instruments like zithers, lutes, lyres, flutes, fifes, drums, and trumpets and were skillfully playing them as they went along, as if joining an invisible marching band.

The heavenly symphony swelled as the population increased, but somehow it never interfered with thought or conversation nor did it ever become irritating. Quite the contrary, the blended mixture of sights, sounds, and even smells was perfectly divine; its very presence was an integral part of the fabric of Heaven, and it infused everyone with pleasure.

"Praise the Lord!"

"Hallelujah!"

"Glory to God!"

"Praise to the King!" and other exaltations resounded through the countryside. So grateful were the hearts of the people for what the Lord had done for them and for what the Lord had given them in Heaven, that praise was a very natural byproduct. When someone shouted out a praise, immediately, like a ricochet, someone else would respond with a praise. One exclamation of praise could cause a chain reaction of praises that traversed the world that encompasses Heaven.

The group of friends found themselves joining in with the people in expressing their love and gratitude to the Lord in shouts of praise. When they reflected on the experience later, they were surprised to realize how uninhibitedly they shouted out their praises, never worrying about, nor even considering, what others might think of them. They just shouted out praises because their hearts were full. It made no difference to them who was near or who heard. They were totally free to do what their hearts dictated. How strange and uncharacteristic to feel so very, and completely, secure. They had never felt like this before.

The angel slowed his pace, allowing the children to participate in the praises as they made their journey. He would never tire of the look of wonder and awe on a child's face. And oh! How he enjoyed watching these young ones he was growing to love so dearly, praise his King.

All at once, a thunderous sound rapidly approached them from behind. The children looked up just as a half-dozen light beams arced overhead, leaving streamers of trailing light in their wake as they sped past. It reminded Cristen of an air show she had once seen when jet planes, emitting colorful vapors, whizzed in and out of sight right over her head.

"Wow!" they chorused.

"What was that?" Henri turned an inquisitive face toward the angel.

"My comrades," said the angel, following the trail of light with his eyes.

Edgas gasped. He was the first to see where those light beams were headed. His friends followed his pointed finger and froze in wonderment.

So absorbed in their praises, and in watching all the people, they had not noticed the radiant city before them. Although, gazing upon it now, they had to wonder how in the world they did not notice it, for that seemed a complete impossibility.

The angel winked, "God has perfect timing."

The Eternal City shone like a jeweled diadem rising up from the horizon. *Never* had they seen *anything* like this. It was glorious! It had the gleaming appearance of pure gold, shining brighter than any sun. Flashes of light, in a kaleidoscope of brilliant colors, continuously burst forth from the city into a sapphire sky. It was incredible, truly beyond incredible, and wholly and utterly beyond any possible earthly description.

As they gawked in stunned silence, the angel raised his arms and sang out in a clear, strong voice, "Great is the Lord, and greatly to be praised, in the city of our God, in the mountain of His holiness. Beautiful for situation, the joy of the whole Earth, is Mount Zion on the sides of the North, the city of the Great King!"

Cristen's spine tingled as the angel recited the King James Version of Psalm 48 verses one and two. The Bible seemed to come alive to her and make sense in a way she never understood before. *The King is great*, she thought, *and His City situated on His holy mountain is joyful and way more than beautiful.*

How long the children stood staring, they had no idea. For again, time seemed to stand still. When at last they were on the move, they were so excited that they hurried along, passing their angel guide. He laughed ardently and let them run on ahead. Most of the run was uphill, for the great city was indeed set on high and could be seen from great distances all over Heaven.

Passing homes and gardens outside the city, the children began to notice that many of the buildings were fashioned with precious stones and transparent gems such as, diamonds, rubies, sapphires, emeralds, jasper, pearl, onyx, and more. Many of the gemstones were as large as, or even larger than, the Pearl Gate. It only took a moment for the children to realize that gemstones are the foundation, or concrete blocks, of Heaven! It was flabbergasting! These gems were cut to refract light in such a way as to sparkle and shine beyond anything imaginable. The children, unconsciously, reached in their pockets and rubbed their stones.

Never would the visitors have believed that the Pearl Gate with its iridescent glow, the River of Life with its dazzling and fiery liquid diamonds, or their gemstone treasures tingling in their pockets, could pale in comparison to anything! But...OH! The glory of this city humbled the other things; those were only a minute reflection of the light that exploded from here. Surely the Eternal City itself is what Cristen had first seen shining like a million sunsets over the horizon.

They ran as fast as they could, for all they wanted was to get to this glorious city.

"Look!" Masumi squealed, coming to a screeching halt. "The streets of gold!"

The whole group squealed and clasped their hands, bouncing up and down with sheer joy.

"Oh my! The streets of Heaven are really made out of gold, just like it says in the Bible!" Cristen exclaimed, gawking at the golden road stretching out before her.

Not surprisingly, it was unlike any gold they had ever seen; it was definitely gold but of such purity that it was transparent, almost like glass, and it was polished to a high sheen, like a newly waxed floor.

"I can see myself!" Edgas said, watching himself dance his now-familiar jig. "Look everybody! It's kinda like a mirror! Can you see yourself? I can see myself!"

"Yes, Edgas, I sure can!" Masumi and the others peered at their own reflections and then at each other's.

Bursting with joy, the children skipped and danced and ran and leaped down the golden street; it felt simply luxurious under their feet. It was almost cushiony. They knew immediately that their feet would never tire on these wonderful streets.

"How 'bout that?" Henri murmured, mostly to himself.

"How 'bout what?" asked Edgas.

"God uses gold as asphalt. It's so common, He paves the streets with it!"

"Common? Hmm..." said the angel, who had kept up with the exuberant children with ease, "*abundant* might be a better word choice. Common seems to suggest little value, but, in truth, it has great value. Your Heavenly Father uses only the best materials for His kids, even for the roads; that's how very much He loves you."

"Oh, I agree. Abundant is a much bett—" Cristen's voice trailed, for she was quite suddenly distracted by unusual activity on the road in front of her.

"What in the world?" cried Henri, amazed that something else astonished him. "I know, I know—we are *so* not in the world."

MAPUTO, MOZAMBIQUE
12:18 p.m.

Isabel began to cry softly, her tears washing Edgas' sweet face. She knew she ought to put him down and go get the nurse, but she couldn't force herself to do it. She wasn't ready to let go of this moment or of the precious one she loved so much. How she would miss him. She would miss his enthusiastic questions about Heaven. She would miss his run-on sentences. And, oh, how she would miss his beautiful smile. Heaven was getting more precious everyday, populated with the spirits of those she dearly loved.

"Lord," she prayed, as silent tears slipped down her cheeks, "thank you for letting me witness the answer to my prayer. Thank you for taking Edgas home to live with you. Be a Daddy to him, Lord. He deserves a family. I know he's in a much, much better place and that you'll take good care of him. I know you love him more than I do. We're going to miss him here, Lord."

Tears were streaming freely now; she paused to take a deep breath, trying desperately to keep her emotions in check. "I'm going to miss him, Jesus. I know he's with you, but how many more deaths will there be? I can't take many more, Lord. I can't keep hurting like this. I miss my Daddy, too, Lord. Oh, God! Have mercy! Have mercy on my kids. Bring your healing to this place. Come to Mozambique, Lord. I need you, Jesus. I need you so much."

It was of no use now to try to stop the tears; her shoulders heaved up and down as she wept before her Father in Heaven.

THIRTEEN

The Word became flesh and made His dwelling among us. We have seen His glory, the glory of the one and only Son, who came from the Father, full of grace and truth. — John 1:14 (NIV)

"A hovercraft? In Heaven?"

"And why not, Henri? There are all kinds of transports here," responded the angel, eyes twinkling.

"Then why in the world have we been walking?" laughed a still shocked Henri.

"Cuz like you just said, we're not in the world." Edgas could not let the word go unnoticed and grinned at his own joke. He wasn't quite sure what a hovercraft was, but it sure looked cool as it floated in the air just above the ground. "Hey! That's what's on your shirt, Henri!" Turning to the angel, he added, "Is it a space ship?"

"I don't know why I find this so surprising," mused Cristen. "I guess I just figured everyone walked in Heaven, like we've been doing."

"They do walk," the angel grinned, "and some of us fly."

Right then, two people came out of a gorgeous, faceted building and walked up to the hovering hovercraft. "Open," they commanded, and immediately, as if by magic, a hatch-like door lifted open, and a set of steps descended and hung in the air. The two climbed in, closed the hatch, smiled and waved to the children, and then sailed off, hovering over the golden street.

Henri, with bright eyes and face aglow, turned to the angel, "What other kinds of transports are there?"

"We have many different ways to get around—paths made of light beams," he gave them his best duh-look, then with a bright smile, continued, "hovercraft, hover-boards, cars, motorcycles, planes, trolleys, bicycles, chariots, buses, trains, boats, ships, skate-boards—things you are familiar with and things you've never dreamed of. You name it! If it's something that interests you, then we have it!"

"I'm still so surprised," said Cristen. "It makes sense that all these things would be here, but I just wasn't expecting it."

"I haven't seen very much I *was* expecting!" laughed Henri.

"That's for sure," Masumi nodded.

Walking farther into the glorious city, they began to see increasing numbers of both the familiar, and unfamiliar, kinds of transports traveling down and around the broad golden streets; but even with the increased activity, it never felt overcrowded or congested. There was ample room for all—no traffic jams in Heaven!

"I feel like I just entered the movie *Back to the Future*," said Henri, watching another hovercraft pass by, "only way, way, way forward into the future! This is so cool!"

"Oh LOOK!" cried Cristen, "That, that whatever-it-is, looks like it's from *The Jetsons!*"

"You're right, Cristen. Some people love all things futuristic and spacey. The people that do probably have homes and flying cars that look a lot like they came right out of the Jetsons."

"Who are the Jetsons?" asked Edgas, waving at the people in the flying space-ship-like car.

"A cartoon family that lived in a futuristic space town," Cristen answered. "They had flying cars and robots that cleaned and cooked for them."

"Are there robots in Heaven?" Edgas wondered.

"There are things here even better than robots!" The angel wiggled his eyebrows at Edgas in Henri-like fashion.

"Where are the gas stations?" Masumi glanced around.

"No need for gas," replied the Angel. "Heaven is powered by light; just about everything runs on light energy."

"Well, there doesn't seem to be any light shortage," laughed Henri. "Is it expensive?"

"It's free! Everything is free here."

"I just realized I don't hear a single motor running," said a perplexed Masumi.

"You're right, Masumi, none of the transports are making a sound!" Cristen agreed.

"Is it because of the light energy?" asked Masumi.

"Yes, exactly right, girls," said the angel. "Isn't it marvelous? Light energy generates zero noise and zero air pollution!"

Although the myriad of transports was an unexpected surprise, an expected, yet unprepared for surprise, was the overwhelming abundance of angels. The sight of thousands of angels walking, hovering, and zipping here and there around the city was almost overwhelming.

The visiting children saw angels of varying size and rank, but all were dressed in seamless garments of light that were either trimmed in gold or gemstones or tied with colorful sashes. The children still could not discern if the fabric was, or was not, a part of the angels themselves. But, oh, how brightly they shone!

The busy angels were coming and going at great speeds, employed with very important tasks and responsibilities. Every angel the children saw at present resembled a man, with every shade of skin tone and hair color imaginable among them. The angel guiding the children told them, however, that there were many different tribes of angels.

"Each tribe has its own distinct look, created perfectly for their different purposes and assignments. Some angels are feminine in form and many of these tend the heavenly nurseries. Some are very small and look a lot like delicate fairies. These are filled with sparkling green light, and they tend the streams, rivers, and waterfalls. Some angels are wingless and actually look just like children! These are the happy playmates for many of the young children here in Heaven, especially those who have made it to Heaven before their parents."

The angel continued, explaining that some angels were couriers, some were messengers, some recorded everything they witnessed on Earth, while some collected prayers and worship and brought them back to Heaven. And some, as expected, are guardians sent to Earth with the human spirit at the moment of conception, and these will stay with their assigned human until the day of the human's physical death. He said that all the afore mentioned tribes were under the Archangel Gabriel's leadership.

"And some," the angel's eyes widened as he spoke, "look like nothing you have ever seen or imagined! These are called the Host of Heaven, and they war on behalf of the saints. They report to the Archangel Michael. Many of these tribes are fierce and very strange looking. Some of them have multiple eyes all over their bodies and wings, and some have a band of eyes around their head," the angel laughed. " No enemy will ever take these guys by surprise! Some angels have flowing hair of blue fire coming right out of their heads; these were created to carry the glory of God. And some angels look like fire, some look like smoke, some look like clouds, some are made of metal, and some have bodies and faces that are faceted like a gemstone. Some were created to, not just carry, but *be* a weapon! These shred the enemies of God. And some angels are so big they can hold the sphere of Earth in their hand!"

The attentive children listened with wide opened mouths.

"So, no fat baby angels?" Henri laughed, he had always pictured fat cherubs in Heaven, probably from the Renaissance paintings he'd seen.

"Nope. Raphael's cherubs are not here," the angel shook his head and chuckled. "But you guys don't look too disappointed."

Edgas, with a sudden revelation, looked up into the face of their beloved angel, "We've been with you all day—or whatever time it is—I really have no idea, it almost seems like forever, but it also seems like only a few minutes. Anyway, we've been with you all this time, whatever it is, and we don't even know if you have a name! Do you have a name?"

"Why yes, Edgas, I have a name." The angel smiled appreciatively.

"I figured you probably did, but you never told us your name so I wasn't sure. But I thought you must cuz archangels Gabriel and Michael have a name, and the bad one, Lucifer does, too, so I guessed you had a name. But, I dunno! Maybe only archangels have names. Are you an archangel?"

The angel's smile spread across his face, and his eyes laughed with merriment.

"Oh, may we know your name?" Masumi asked.

"Yes, of course." He looked at the precious faces with their expectant eyes on him. "I am the Angel Abel," he said, sweeping his hand and bowing deeply. "It is a pleasure to make your acquaintances! And no, Edgas, I am not an archangel; I am a guardian."

"May we call you by your name?" asked Cristen.

"Or is that rude?" Masumi quickly added.

"I would be very pleased for you to call me Abel."

"Are you Adam and Eve's son, Abel, who was killed by his brother Cain?" asked Henri.

"No Henri!" Abel said, withholding the laughter threatening to break free. "Contrary to popular belief, and Hollywood, people do not become angels when they die. As you can see by looking around you even now, angels and humans are very different creations, created for different purposes. I have always been, and will always be, an angel. You were made a human in the image and likeness of God, and you will always be a human. At the end of time, you will live again on a resurrected Earth, in a resurrected body, as a human. You will be able to do incredible feats with your perfected body, but you will always be fully human."

"Abel?" ventured Cristen, "Have you always lived in Heaven?"

"Yes, Cristen, though I have traveled to the Earth for many extensive visits, I have lived here in the presence of God for eons."

"Eons! You're kinda old then aren't you?" commented Edgas.

"Yes, Edgas," Abel said, struggling to keep a straight face, "I'm kinda old!"

"I bet, if you're that old, you've seen some pretty cool stuff, huh?" said Henri.

Abel could restrain his laugh no more. He threw his head back, and his wonderful laugh barreled out! He loved being in the company of these delightful children.

"Well, Henri," he said, his expression changing to one of seriousness, "As a matter of fact, I, along with all the angels in Heaven, watched the Creator as He opened a scroll and stretched it across the expanse of the spiritual realm, creating the physical realm with its limitations of time and space. I saw Him name the stars as He flung each one into this new dimension He called space, along with every planet and moon that He placed in every galaxy. I watched him make the sun and divide the night from the day. I saw Him form the Earth and set it on its course around the sun. I was there when the very first animals appeared on the Earth. And I held my breath and watched with great anticipation as God formed man out of the dust of the earth and breathed life, which was man's eternal spirit, into him. At that moment, man became a living soul, and I watched him open his eyes and take his first breath."

"I have witnessed the Master's faithfulness to mankind since that very first day. I've watched His covenant plan unfold. I've seen men and women of great faith believe God and trust Him when they could not see Him. I've seen generations of faithful ones await His coming."

"I was one of the angels singing 'Glory to God in the Highest' to shepherds in a field on that fateful night in Bethlehem. I waited my turn to hover over the manger, hoping to catch a glimpse of the face of the One I had always called The Word—The

Glorious Word. The Word became a tiny helpless, human babe. I marveled and wondered at the unfathomable humility of my Creator, that He would leave all this majesty and splendor," Abel held his arms out and looked around. The children, following his example, also looked around at the splendor. Then Abel continued, "and go to Earth, taking on human flesh, as one of His creations."

"I watched this babe grow and become a man. I was among the few who brought my Lord bread and water and ministered to his needs after he was tempted in the wilderness. I watched him make fishers of men, heal the sick, raise the dead, and set captives free."

"I, along with my fellow servants, did not understand when His own people rejected him. We watched in shock and disbelief as the Holy One was beaten and nailed to a cross. Again, we did not understand why the arm of the Almighty held us back from coming to our Lord's rescue. We waited breathlessly for the order to stop this horror, but it never came.

"I beheld the anguish and compassion on the face of the Almighty as He watched His only son suffer for the sins of ungrateful people. He was fully resolved to carry out His perfect plan.

"I saw the midday sky turn to midnight blackness. I watched the Earth quake and tremble, and I heard its rumble at the death of my God!

"And I will never, *ever*, forget the deafening silence in Heaven.

"I dared not breathe. I dared not move a muscle. Filled with suspense, knowing that the God who created the Universe with the power of His word, could have stopped the slaughter of His own son with a single word or a nod of His holy head but chose, instead, to turn His head away. "Why?" I screamed silently? "Why would He care for fallen and prideful men?" I didn't understand His wonderful plan to redeem mankind and make a way back to Himself.

"Whispered words blew through the celestial city, 'Wait three days,' awakening hope and expectation.

"I anxiously awaited those three earthly days—waiting and watching, watching and waiting—and then I witnessed the resurrection power of God! I shouted praises to the Alpha and Omega with everything in me as The Word conquered death and the grave!

"I watched the Lord of Heaven and Earth make an open spectacle of Satan and his cohorts. This fallen, once fellow servant, who wanted to be worshipped as god, he who had led a rebellion against the Almighty, taking a third of the heavenly angels with him, was rendered powerless—stripped of the keys to death and Hades, stripped of his kingly robes, and stripped of all the gemstones which adorned him and was his pride. Oh, children, how we, the remaining hosts of Heaven, rejoiced and celebrated his defeat! Our victory cheer shook the Heavens with its thunderous ovation!

"I sang out praises, loud and long, and I worshipped as the King of Kings and Lord of Lords ascended, fully man, yet fully God, back to my abode in Heaven, where He reigns forever and ever in glory and majesty.

"And I watch and continue to wait with all of Heaven's citizens for that day when He will set up His everlasting Kingdom on Earth as it is in Heaven.

"Oh yes, indeed, children—I have seen a *lot* of cool stuff!"

The children hung on every word as the angel recounted what they already believed by faith. To watch the Angel Abel's face as he told of his experiences was positively captivating! Imagine, being an eyewitness to the greatest events in all of human history! Hearing Abel tell it will certainly be one of the highlights of their journey to Heaven and is sure to remain etched in their minds forever.

"Wow" they whispered, quietly reflecting Abel's words.

"Did you see David fight Goliath?" Henri asked, curiously.

His question started a barrage of new questions, one right on top of the other.

"Did you see Noah's ark?"

"What about Moses? Did you see him deliver the children of Israel from Egypt?"

"Did they really walk through the Red Sea?"

"How about Elijah and the prophets of Baal?"

"Was Samson's strength really in his hair?"

"Did you see Joseph's coat of many colors?"

"Whoa! Hold up!" Abel said chuckling, holding his arms out in front of him like a traffic cop. "Yes, yes, and yes! I told you I was old! I was not only privileged to witness these events you call Bible stories, but I had an active role in some of them. You see, angels are obedient servants of the Most High. We often have assignments to protect God's children and help them. Some angels minister God's love, some are recording events as they happen, some are messengers, and others are warriors who fight demonic spirits in warfare.

"We, Heaven's servants, joyously celebrate when people give their hearts to the Lord, for we know how worthy He is to receive those hearts. We love it when men and women step out in faith and believe God against all odds."

"You see, children, angels have always had access to the Throne Room, and we behold the One Who Sits Upon the Throne. We behold His glory, and we are witnesses of His creativity and of His might. We *know* His awesome power and His faithfulness. We *know* His character. We *know* His love and His goodness. We *know* that He is worthy of all praise and honor! Which, by the way, is why Lucifer and his followers can never be forgiven. But, oh! How wonderful it is when humans, like you, believe that God is worthy, *without* seeing Him. We esteem that highly! Heaven is full of men and women who dared to believe!"

Then, with piercing eyes, Abel said, "I am so very glad that *you* chose to believe!" That marvelous smile flashed across his face, and the children knew he meant it with all of his heart.

He suddenly shot up into the air like a bullet, taking the children by surprise, and leaving them to stare up after him. He spun in a tight corkscrew, rising higher and higher into the blue sky. Then they heard him shout at the top of his voice, "You are worthy, Oh Lord! You are worthy! Worthy to receive all honor and glory and praise!"

Then, just as suddenly, he flew in an arch and changed directions. He headed straight towards the shocked group still staring up at him. With wings tucked behind, arms by his side, he nosedived straight at them until all at once he spread open his wings, straightened, and landed right back where he had started.

The children instinctively hit the ground and covered their heads.

He burst out with another hearty laugh when he saw them scattered about on the ground.

"I thought you were gonna bowl us over!" said Henri, scrambling back to his feet.

'I did too!" said Cristen, reaching out to help Masumi up.

"I wish I could fly!" said Edgas. "That was the coolest thing I *ever* saw!"

Abel grinned at Edgas. "All things are possible, Edgas! All things are possible to those that believe!"

Edgas, Cristen, Masumi and Henri exchanged shocked looks.

"Really?" they chorused.

"Really!" He nodded his head, and his eyes twinkled wildly.

MAPUTO, MOZAMBIQUE
UNSEEN REALM

Isabel, deep in prayer, slowly, unconsciously, rhythmically rocked the dead child back and forth, back and forth, as unhindered tears streamed down her face.

There was a rift in the heavenlies, as if someone had suddenly unzipped a large black canvas. Bright light flooded the little hospital room.

The demon scrambled backwards out of the light; cowering, he used his leathery wing to both shield his eyes and hide from the light.

A tremendous angel flew directly into the room carrying a bowl and a scroll. He had bright, glowing, copper colored hair and radiant green eyes.

"I'm glad to see you, Jakartur."

"How is she?"

"She is worn thin," Michale said, "but she leans heavily on the Lord and on His word, so she will, without doubt, pull through this trial."

Jakartur nodded with full understanding. He looked tenderly at the woman holding the body of the boy. He got on one knee in front of her and held her sweet face in his hands.

The woman wept.

The angel immediately held the bowl beneath her face, catching the tears as they spilled into the receptacle.

When the bowl was filled, Jakartur stood to his feet.

"Amen," agreed the two angels.

Jakartur touched the boy's head tenderly, "Your suffering is over, young one." He then turned to Michale, "It never ceases to amaze me how forlorn the shell without the spirit."

"Hurry her heart prayer to the Father, Jakartur. Make haste!"

Jakartur nodded. "On my way, my friend."

And with that he leaped into the air, flew directly into the light, and disappeared. Then zip! As quickly as it appeared, the bright light was gone.

Michale breathed a sigh of relief.

So did the demon but for very different reasons.

"So, she's worn out, is she?" The ugly demon hissed, crawling out of his hiding place for the first time.

Michale turned to face the scuzzball as he began launching his verbal attack against Isabel and the God she loved and served. Lies and accusations spewed from his fanged and twisted mouth.

Michale spread his wings, shielding Isabel from the assault. "Buzz off, insect," he said. "She's not going to listen to you!"

"Sure she will," he scoffed. "They always do."

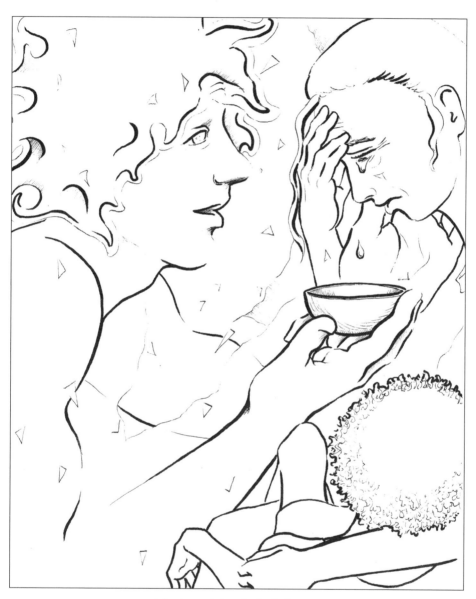

Jakartur catches Isabel's tears

FOURTEEN

You keep track of all my sorrows. You have collected all my tears in your bottle. You have recorded each one in your book. — Psalm 56:8 (NLT)

The up-close-and-personal view of the Eternal City was even more spectacular than the view of it from a distance. The giddy group glided through town on broad, spacious, golden streets regarding so much in every direction that there was literally no way to take it all in.

Like most earthly cities, the Eternal City has lovely tree-lined streets and avenues; beautiful grassy parks with dancing fountains; all manner of buildings—including, but not limited to—homes, shops, galleries, universities, theaters, amphitheaters, museums, libraries, restaurants, and studios; a vast network of transportation systems; a bevy of activity; and inhabitants. Yet, unlike any earthly city, its meticulously clean streets were made of pure, translucent gold; landscapes were fashioned of rich, lush vegetation generously flowered with colors never seen on Earth; the buildings were abundantly studded with gemstones—if not made entirely out of a gemstone; the atmosphere swelled with music and delicious aromas—both of which could be seen as well as heard and smelled; there was no noise or air pollution; myriads of angels filled the air; transports were going and coming and hovering and floating and flying about; and all the people—every single one of them—were radiant and completely happy.

This was culture shock at its best. It took a while for the visitors to get beyond the sheer awe of it. It was both familiar and unfamiliar and entirely unusual. Gemstones they had seen, but an entire building fashioned of a single, faceted gemstone was mind-boggling, especially when a facet opened like a door, and a young man stepped out through it.

But once the group adjusted to the wonder, they began to notice beautiful, intricate designs of impeccable craftsmanship. No detail was overlooked, skimped, or omitted. No two buildings were alike—although many shared the similarity of open and arched doorways and open windows—yet, the integration of the different architectural styles united in peaceful harmony. It was clear that no dissonance or discord existed in this heavenly realm.

When asked about all the opened windows, and even the complete lack of window panes in some cases, Abel answered, "Ah! No need! We have perfect temperature and weather: no dust, no pollen, no air pollution, and no humidity," he chuckled. "No neighbors to hide from, and best of all—absolutely no crime! So most people enjoy wide, opened windows."

"I'll never be able to explain this place" said wide-eyed Edgas, shaking his head.

"I know, Edgas," agreed Cristen, "I was just thinking that I don't even *know* words to describe what we're seeing."

"I guess we could tell people to take their imagination and multiply it by a million," Masumi said.

"Or a billion," added Henri, chuckling.

"You could eat right off the street it's so clean," Masumi said, remembering the streets of busy Tokyo.

"It's crazy clean," said Cristen, "not a smidgen of dirt anywhere."

"Not even a mud puddle," added Edgas, "I guess all that stuff evaporates here, too, just like everywhere else." He looked at Abel.

"Yes, it does, Edgas. The Great Light purifies everything. Even if a germ or virus could get into Heaven—which it can't—the Light would eradicate it immediately."

Edgas smiled back at the angel, "Sounds like Heaven is a healthy place to live!"

Abel rubbed the boy's head and laughed.

"Who built this city anyway?"

"The Lord himself is the Chief Architect, Cristen. He designed every inch of this place with you in mind." Cristen felt a warmth rush through her. "And, He loves to work alongside His kids. People have architectural and design gifts which they get to use to their fullest here. Your gifts don't die with your body but are eternal. You will spend eternity using your gifts. Remember we talked at the lake about getting to do the things you enjoy when you come to Heaven?"

The children nodded.

"Well, these people enjoy designing."

"They're really good at it!" Henri added, admiring one of the many buildings.

"Come." Abel commanded, "I've something to show you."

Immediately, a path of light appeared, and this time the children jumped aboard without hesitation. It carried them deep into the city through effusive neighborhoods of gorgeous mansions set spaciously apart. Each and every mansion had it's own, distinct architectural flavor, but all sat on luscious, sprawling lawns generously peppered with bright, cheery flowers and stately trees. The landscape of each mansion fit its particular home design perfectly, and Abel explained that every mansion perfectly suited the heart desires and specific tastes of the individual who lived in them.

At one point, Edgas twisted around to gawk at a particularly huge mansion, and in doing so, he spied an angel peeking his head out from behind a tree. Their eyes met.

The angel froze, and his eyes popped like he had been caught with his hand in a cookie jar. Edgas smiled and wiggled his fingers in a little wave gesture. The angel wiggled his fingers in return, and then nonchalantly, pretended to study the tree with keen interest. Edgas wasn't sure what to make of it, though he thought it was kind of funny. He turned and dismissed it from his mind.

He did not see Sancto sigh a deep breath of relief.

The path of light came to a stop in front of an enormous and magnificent looking building made entirely of cut crystal. It had for a door an extremely large, arched opening. Abel walked up to it and turned to face the kids.

Seeing the angel stand in front of the arch, Henri suddenly realized that the arches he had noticed everywhere were probably designed with an angel in mind. When angel wings are folded behind them, they extend high up above their heads. With an arched doorway, an angel never needs to duck. This particular doorway was as wide as it was tall; an angel could pass through it even with wings open.

The children peered curiously around Abel's waist, trying to catch a glimpse beyond his wings into the open building. He grinned at them, and then teasingly, spread his wings to block their view. They saw sparkles of light dancing wildly behind him. They looked up at his playful face; the light in his eyes dancing wildly, too.

"The Lord wants you to know what is kept in here."

"Then let us see!" snickered Henri.

A laughing Abel kept his wings spread wide while his little brood tried to peer around him.

"Group hug!" he yelled, wrapping the children in his mammoth wings. The kids burst out in squeals of glee.

Then, just as quickly, Abel folded his wings behind him, turned and marched through the archway. Henri was delighted when he saw that his assumption was correct—angel's wings indeed fit perfectly through arches.

The chortling group quieted as they followed their leader into the crystal building. Crossing the threshold, they gasped and then held their breaths as they looked around. Astounded eyes raced about the room, absorbing the wonder.

Rows of crystal shelving filled the cavernous room. Carefully arranged on the spacious shelves, grouped in clusters, were little crystal bottles of a glistening liquid. The liquid sparkled like the great river as bursts of colors shot from the bottles.

Affixed under each cluster was a small golden plaque.

Right inside the entranceway, an elegant table, beautifully carved of rich wood, stood impressively. Upon this lovely table lay several ornate volumes covered in luxurious silk—or perhaps made of silk entirely—and gorgeously decorated with diamonds, pearls, colorful stones, and gems.

A man emerged from way in the back of this incredible and very large room and began walking towards them. He was a handsome young man with a thick crop of dark hair, a beguiling smile, dark skin, and a lovely, deep purple, velvety garment. In truth, he was a very old man, but his appearance, his gait, and his vitality belied his age.

"Why Abel, who have you brought to see me?" the man asked, his kind eyes smiling at the children.

"Allow me to introduce our special guests, Joseph." Abel slipped behind the children placing his broad hand on the top of each head as he said their names. "This is Henri, Masumi, Edgas, and this is Cristen. They're visiting the Eternal City, and I have been given the honor of showing them some of the glories of Heaven. The Lord would like for them to see what you do in this room."

"Why, yes, of course! Welcome, children. I'm so happy to meet you and show you this wondrous room." A look akin to pride covered his bright face. "Come and see the Room of Tears."

"Tears?" exclaimed Henri.

"Those are tears in the bottles?" asked an amazed Cristen.

"Yes," replied the keeper of the tears.

"I thought perhaps it was holy water from the River of Life."

"Why, yes, Cristen, these tears do shimmer a bit like the Great River, don't they?"

"They're lovely," whispered Masumi.

"Whose tears are these?" Edgas' eyes went from the bottles to Joseph and back again to the bottles.

"Why these are the tears of God's beloved from all over Earth."

The surprised children turned all eyes to Joseph as he continued, "Did you know that your tears are precious to the Lord?"

The children shook their heads, no.

"Tears are unspoken prayers. Do you see the plaques under the bottles?"

All heads nodded.

"Those tell us the name of the Lord's beloved whose tears are in the bottles."

"Wow! Are my tears in here?" asked Edgas.

"Perhaps. This is only one of many rooms just like this. What's your last name Edgas, and what country are you from?"

"Seca. I'm Edgas Isaac Seca from Maputo, Mozambique."

"Why, yes, Edgas Seca! Indeed I do have your tears in here. I am the keeper of all the Mozambique tears." Joseph grinned and looked at the angel, "It would appear that Abel knew just the right room to bring you to."

"Come with me, and I'll show you your tears." He motioned for all the children to follow him to the back of the glistening room. After passing rows and rows and rows and rows of shelving, Joseph finally chose one of the rows and began reading name plaques as he walked along. The children, reading some of the plaques, quickly noticed that the bottles were arranged in alphabetical order. After locating the 'S's,' it wasn't long before Joseph pointed to some bottles and announced, "Here they are!"

Edgas stood spellbound. His name, beautifully etched on the little golden plaque, glowed with life. He could hardly breathe. His very own name was on a book in Heaven *and* on a plaque in Heaven. Unbelievable.

"Those are *my* tears?"

"Yes, they're beautiful aren't they?" Joseph's words sounded more like a statement than a question.

"How'd ya get 'em?" Edgas whispered in awe as he stared at his sparkling tears.

Before Joseph could answer, he was interrupted by a sudden whoosh, whoosh, whooshing of giant wings. The children recognized the sound and swung around in time to see a large, twelve-foot tall angel fly right into the room. As they peered down the long aisle of glistening bottles, they watched him land, ever so softly, just inside the arched entrance.

This angel was stunning—even from this distance the children could tell. His white garment of light was trimmed down the front with a large band of gold. His hair was like glowing copper, and his large eyes were the color of a bright spring meadow. In one hand he carried a golden bowl, intricately and beautifully designed. The golden bowl was filled with a clear liquid. And in the other hand he held a white scroll.

Joseph smiled and winked at the children. "Ah, now how's that for perfect timing?" He led the group back to the front. "We will demonstrate your answer, dear Edgas."

"Hello Jakartur. You have impeccable timing. My young visitor here just asked me how we get the tears. Let's show these children what we do."

Jakartur looked down and smiled at the children while handing Joseph the small scroll.

Joseph opened the scroll and silently read what was written there which the children were not able to see.

"Let's see, Isabel Power, I think you're right over here," Joseph said while scanning a nearby shelf.

"Isabel Power?" Edgas screeched, clasping his hands in surprise! "I know her! She's my friend! She's my orphanage mom!"

"Oh, I see," was all Joseph said as he took one of the bottles off the shelf and handed it to the copper-headed Jakartur. Jakartur, ever so carefully, poured the tears from his golden bowl into the tiny bottle without spilling a single drop. The children were amazed that this giant angel could handle a very small bottle with such delicacy.

Jakartur handed the bottle back to Joseph. The Tear Keeper held the bottle up in the light for the children to see. It shimmered and sparkled fiercely.

"Oh," breathed Cristen, "it's beautiful!"

"Those tears are her heart's cry for the orphan children of Mozambique," Jakartur spoke in a deep resonating voice, "and for you, Edgas." He turned his gaze upon the boy. "She loves you very much." He gave the boy a warm smile and Edgas thought he would melt from the love flowing from this heavenly being.

Edgas looked at Jakartur incredulously, "How did you know my name?" he whispered.

"I know you well, Edgas." Jakartur reached down and tenderly touched the boy's cheek but made no further explanation. Edgas was speechless, pondering the implications. Had Jakartur been the one who had gathered all of his tears?

"Now come over to the table, children, and see what happens next." Joseph led the group to the lovely carved table.

Picking up one of the jewel-studded volumes, he opened it to a blank page and then gently laid it back down on the table. Next, he took the bottle of Isabel's tears and carefully tipped it over the blank page so that only one teardrop spilled out. When the tear splashed on the page, words appeared! The wide-eyed children sucked in a sharp breath of surprise before their mouths fell open. Holding their breaths, they remained as quiet and still as mice.

Joseph repeated the process, one drop at a time, until several pages of words had been revealed. He then closed the book and handed it to the large angel. Jakartur turned to go, but first, with one of those broad grins that only an angel can give, he reached down and tousled Edgas' hair.

"Goodbye, children. May the Peace of the King be with you always."

He then dipped his copper head, acknowledging Abel, whose own blond curls bobbed in return, and then, spreading his enormous wings, he flew out the same way he had entered, leaving the children to stare at an empty doorway.

Answering their unasked question, Joseph explained, "Jakartur is taking the book of Isabel's heart prayers to present as an offering before the Father in the Throne Room."

The children watched Joseph return the bottle of Isabel's tears to its proper place on the shelf.

No one spoke a word as they processed the profoundness of what Joseph had just spoken.

They couldn't have explained it to you, but they felt holiness and reverent awe in this lovely Room of Tears, and it quieted their souls. They had laughed and giggled their way across Heaven, but now this new feeling was arising within them. Understand that joy was in no way abated; it just felt coated in—well, what was it they were feeling? Love. Their joy was coated in love. Not only did they feel loved, but they also felt their own hearts welling up with love for others.

Abel, sensing the emotion said, "How great is the Father's love for you. He not only sees your tears, but He has His angels catch them and keep them in a bottle. Tears shed on behalf of another are as prayers before Him."

"I had no idea."

"Me either, Masumi," whispered Cristen. "I guess there were times I was praying and didn't even know it!"

Abel smiled at her.

"Wow," breathed Henri.

Edgas was so overwhelmed that for the first time in his life he was truly speechless.

"Oh, the Father loves you so much children! Never forget how much He loves you," Joseph said as he walked them back to the entrance.

"Well, are you ready to see some more of the glories?" asked Abel.

"Oh, YES!"

"Then come along, children. Goodbye, Joseph; thank you."

"Yes! Thank you! Thank you!" they echoed.

"You are very welcome! Goodbye, children!"

They turned and walked out of the beautiful room. Edgas slowed, taking one last lingering look, still astounded that he saw not only his own tears but Isabel's too.

They were not twenty feet from the doorway to the Room of Tears when they heard the now familiar sound of angel's wings on approach. The children spun around in time to see a large, raven-haired angel flying directly towards the Room of Tears. Like Jakartur, he carried a golden bowl in one hand and a little scroll in the other. He flashed a brilliant smile and nodded his head to the children as he flew up to the Room of Tears. He, too, landed quite gently for his enormous frame, and then furling his enormous wings, disappeared through the arched doorway.

"More tears?" asked Henri.

"Yes, Henri. This goes on twenty-four hours a day, seven days a week, earth-time. Angels continually go back and forth between Heaven and Earth collecting and bringing the tears of the saints. That should tell you just how precious each tear shed is to the Lord."

"Wow, Edgas!" said Cristen. "That was really something to see your tears in there."

"And Isabel's, too!" added Masumi.

"I'll bet our families have added some tears to their bottles today, huh Abel?" asked Henri.

"Yes, I'm quite sure many prayerful tears have been shed on your account."

"It's hard to remember that our families are sad and worried while we are having so much fun," commented Cristen.

"Thank you for showing us the Room of Tears, Abel," whispered Masumi. "I will always remember this special room."

"You are very welcome," he said, but not with words; he said it with the warmest and truest smile as he looked at each one of them with eyes that spoke of his love for them. The children had never known anyone who exuded such love and kindness; it filled them with warmth and gladness of heart.

A quiet settled over the group. Fingering their stones, they followed Abel down another golden road and pondered the many things they had seen and experienced so far on this fantastic journey to Heaven which by all indications was still far from over.

TOKYO, JAPAN
7:30 p.m.

Guilt-ridden and grief-stricken, Michi walked numbly over to the police car. He had ceased weeping and now felt almost nothing. Mechanically, he followed the officer's instructions to get into the back of the squad car, only half hearing him. The kindly gentleman climbed in through the opposite door and sat beside him. The man had volunteered to stay with the boy at the hospital until his parents arrived, and the relieved officer thought it was a good idea.

"Mr. Ninomiya will ride with you to the hospital," said Officer Tsukahira.

Who is Mr. Ninomiya? Michi didn't know, and he didn't care.

Officer Tsukahira made a quick call on his radio and then slowly pulled out into traffic. Michi stared mindlessly out the window, without seeing. His mind replayed his irresponsibility over, and over, and over. The "if onlys" were already making him crazy.

Tokyo, as usual, was lit up in all her neon glory, but tonight Michi hated it. The blinking fluorescent lights were harsh and annoying, adding to his pounding headache. Neither could those bright lights penetrate the darkest night of his life. The tall buildings of Shinjuku were nothing more than a blur as he rode past them. Tomorrow morning they'd be filled with businesspeople going about life as usual, completely unaware that his life had shattered into a gazillion pieces. Tonight, some of those same businesspeople would be heading home drunk, puking up noodles and sake on the city streets, sidewalks, and train station stairways. It would all be cleaned up by morning, leaving not a trace of evidence. His life, on the other hand, would never be cleaned up.

On and on they drove past buildings so close together that only a small cat could squeeze between them. They passed skyscrapers, markets, noodle shops, sushi bars, department stores, shrines, and railroad tracks—everywhere railroad tracks, a forever reminder of his folly. Tucked here and there, small dirt playgrounds with a few swings and a slide were small evidences that children had not been completely forgotten in this never-ending city. Michi knew—though he gave it no thought at the moment—that there were lovely grassy parks scattered throughout the city; however, most of them had signs that read, "Keep Off The Grass."

Michi was beginning to feel like a caged tiger, sick of his concrete jungle. He couldn't breathe; it was all closing in on him, and he was suffocating. The world as he knew it had spun completely out of control. He thought he might throw up again, so he sat back and closed his eyes tightly. He told himself to breathe. Breathe. Just breathe.

It was no use. Tormenting thoughts ran through his head. He knew he would have these thoughts the rest of his life. *I killed Masumi. I don't deserve to live. I should have been the one to die, not her. I'll make it right. I'll make it right, somehow. I'm the one that should have died. I'm the one. I can't go on knowing that I killed my sister. I can't live like this. My life is over. I might as well end it. My life is over.*

"Huh?" Michi felt someone gently touch his shoulder, and shook himself out of his trancelike state. "Did you say something?"

"I said we're here, son. We've arrived at the hospital."

Officer Tsukahira pulled up to the emergency room entrance and parked his squad car beside several ambulances. Michi took a deep breath, forced himself out of the car, and followed the officer. They trudged through automatic glass doors into a packed waiting room. Every eye in the room looked up at the officer, then at Michi. He kept his head down, but he could feel their stares. If he looked as dreadful as he felt, he was sure he was quite a sight. The sick and suffering, anxiously waiting to see a doctor, suddenly didn't feel as sick as they had only moments before.

This is a nightmare, my worst nightmare. Michi started to pass out, but the kind gentleman grabbed his arm and held him fast. He spoke something into Michi's ear which Michi didn't understand, nor, at that time, give any thought to, but as he spoke, strength flowed into Michi. Later, when Michi did think about it, he also pondered how strong the old man was, but at this moment, he wasn't thinking of that, either—only that he was glad he hadn't fainted and crashed to the floor, adding more humiliation to his shame.

FIFTEEN

I will rejoice greatly in the Lord, my soul will exult in my God; for He has clothed me with garments of salvation, He has wrapped me with a robe of righteousness, as a bridegroom decks himself with a garland, and as a bride adorns herself with her jewels. — Isaiah 61:10 (NASB)

Music billowed and swelled around the little band of visitors as they followed Abel through the Celestial City. Woven within this tapestry was the buzz of excited chatter, joyous laughter, exaltations and shouts of praise, cheery trills of song-birds, and the glorious whoosh, whoosh, whooshing of angels' wings. The sounds flowed in and out of each other, blending seamlessly into a grand symphony of delightful sound.

Four heads in constant motion surveyed the many wonderful sights, sounds, and smells; but, absorbing it all was about as possible as a rock absorbing water. Their brains were on overload, but their joy was boundless. Emerging from the time of reflection, the children found themselves giggling anew and squealing with delight as they pointed out fascinating discoveries to each another.

At first glance, the sapphire sky appeared to be dotted peacefully with fluffy white clouds. A closer look revealed that those were not clouds at all but angels. Angels were everywhere. The sound of a profusion of angel wings beating was completely foreign to the children, yet utterly thrilling!

Multitudes of people either lived in, or came to visit, the Eternal City; it was a busy, bustling, and active place. Again, the children noticed that no one looked to be any older than their mid twenties. And, as with their own grandparents and friends, all had an ageless quality—glowing with life, energy, and vitality! Each and every inhabitant had perfectly radiant skin and healthy, shiny hair, and there were no overweight, infirmed, weak, sickly, crippled, or deformed among them.

The visiting children saw thousands of people wearing spotless, radiant, white, shining gowns. According to Abel, after arriving in Heaven everyone is given a white gown made of a special material that reflects God's glory. Some of the gowns were plain—no, there was nothing plain about them; indeed the very fabric made them anything but plain—simple might be a better description. And of these simple gowns, many were tied around the waist with a sash of any color that delighted the person wearing it, for the children saw every color imaginable.

"These are the ones who probably made deathbed confessions or died very young," explained Abel.

Some of the gowns, however, were elaborately stunning; for although they were made of the same white, shining material, they were exquisitely adorned with the most beautiful gemstones. These decorated gowns varied from fairly simple to extraordinary.

"These are the ones who have lived a selfless life of service to the King. The more they acted in love and obedience, the more gems adorn their gown. Your Heavenly Father loves to honor those who openly followed Him while walking on Earth."

"Don't the people with no pretty stones on their clothes feel bad?" asked Edgas sympathetically.

"Do they look like they feel bad, Edgas?"

"Oh no, not at all, I think they look real happy, but I wondered if they feel bad on the inside."

"They are so thankful to be here, I don't think they care too much; but, if they could go back and do things differently, I'm sure they would."

"Will they ever be able to earn gemstones for their gowns?" Cristen reached in her pocket and rubbed her bright yellow gemstone.

"Not after they come to live in Heaven, Cristen. Earth-life is one's only chance to earn these particular stones. Whatever is on your gown when you arrive is what you will have throughout all of eternity. You may want to remember that, and live the rest of your lives with it in mind."

"Wow, so that guy who just passed us," Henri turned his head towards the handsome young man, "must have done a lot of great things for the Lord—his gown is covered in gemstones."

"Yes, he obviously lived a life for the Lord, and the Father wants everyone to know it. Father's love to brag on their kids, and your Heavenly Father is no different. He doesn't have favorites so anyone can earn these beautiful rewards, and He is so happy when you do."

"You said that everyone has a white gown, Abel?" Masumi looked up at the angel. "I'm guessing they don't have to always wear them, for we've seen plenty of other kinds of clothing."

"You're right, Masumi. You can choose to wear your white gown whenever you want; most people choose to wear them when they go to the Throne Room or for some other special occasion. It's only one option of clothing—you have a whole wardrobe of beautiful clothes to wear."

Clearly, as the children were witness, heavenly garments came in an endless variety of styles, colors, and fabrics exquisitely crafted and utterly luxurious. Each garment appeared soft and comfortable, entirely wrinkle-free, and was remarkably created to reflect light.

"I love fashion," sighed Cristen.

"Then perhaps you'll be a fashion designer when you come to stay," replied Abel.

"Really? There are fashion designers in Heaven?" Cristen's eyes brightened.

"Look around; just like the architecture, someone had to design all these clothes."

"I figured God designed them," offered Edgas.

"He certainly gives the ability and the materials, but as I mentioned before, people still use their gifts and talents in Heaven. So, boys and girls, whatever it is that you love to do—that thing you're really good at, or the one thing you'd very much *like* to be good at, or have a desire to do—that's probably what you will end up doing when you come back to live in Heaven. Earth is the preparation for your forever! Your time on Earth is but a breath; *you,* however, will live forever and ever without end. If The Creator was generous enough to give to man creativity, gifts, and talents on Earth, how much more are those things available here in Heaven? Remember, Earth is a shadow of Heaven, not the other way around."

"What's that called that some people have draping behind them kinda like a long fancy super-hero cape?" asked Edgas.

"Those are royal robes."

"Robes? That's weird." Edgas glanced at Henri to see if he'd noticed the use of his word. "Are they part of the outfit, or did those people do something special to earn them?"

"Oh, they have a beautiful meaning, Edgas," Abel's eyes danced, "and everyone gets one. Wearing a robe is a symbol of royalty. Have you ever seen a picture of a King or Queen wearing a regal robe?"

The children nodded.

"I saw a picture of Queen Elizabeth's long coronation robe. It was trimmed in white fur with black spots," added Cristen.

"That's called ermine," said Henri.

Cristen nodded her head in remembrance.

"Well, that's what these are like. Remember that your Father is The *Great* King. If you are His son," Abel bowed to the boys, "then that would make you a prince, Sir Edgas and Sir Henri, and if you are His daughter, then that would make you a princess," Abel bowed to the girls, " Lady Masumi and Lady Cristen. And princes and princesses get to flaunt their royal robes."

Cristen had a thought that made her laugh.

"Something funny you'd like to share with us?" asked Henri, wiggling his eyebrows humorously.

"Well, I was just thinking that if we tell people everyone wears gowns and robes in Heaven, they'll probably picture nightgowns and bathrobes like my mom wears in the morning when she has her coffee!"

Edgas burst out laughing at the image in his mind, then added, "Or maybe they'd picture choir robes." Still laughing, he added, "That would be funny, too."

"The Japanese are familiar with yukatas and kimonos which can be very beautiful robes," said Masumi, thoughtfully. "Yet I don't think even my people could imagine these robes! I certainly didn't. They're exquisite and really comfortable looking— kimonos are tight and restrictive. I can't wait to wear one of these!"

"Me, too! Not that my mom doesn't look all comfy-cozy in the morning, but who'd want to spend eternity in a bathrobe?" Cristen laughed at the image in her mind. "Like you said, Masumi, these are exquisite. I'm sure I'd feel like a real princess if I got to wear one."

"And me a prince!" agreed Edgas, with a firm nod.

"You know, Heaven is nothing like what I expected," Henri shared as they walked along.

"What did you expect, Henri?" Abel continually amazed the children with his genuine interest in them and what they thought.

"I don't know. Maybe people sitting around on clouds playing harps next to Raphael's fat little angel babies who were dropping grapes in their mouths, I guess." He chuckled at the thought. "I really never gave it much thought, but I figured it would be kinda boring."

"Well, Henri, what do you think now? Do you think this is boring?"

"NO! Not even close! I could never be bored here!"

"I hate to confess this," Cristen dropped her eyes slightly, "I thought Heaven was going to be like one long—*never ever* ending kind of long—church service. I do like my church, a lot, but still, I don't think I'd like it if the service never ended."

"I think God would be bored with a never-ending church service, too. Don't you, Cristen?" The angel grinned and then rolled his eyes before adding, "Especially if it were like some of the ones I've seen!"

"It's strange," added Masumi "my heart is overflowing with feelings of worship. I mean, I've never felt more appreciative and worshipful in my whole life, yet we haven't even stepped foot in a church or temple or wherever it is that people go to worship God here."

"Sometimes it is hard for God's people to know the difference between acts of religion and an attitude of worship," said Abel.

"Do you have church services in Heaven?" asked Edgas.

"There are times in Heaven, many times actually, when both saints and angels gather together and joyously worship The King. If that's what you mean by church service, then I suppose we do; but we don't call it that. We might call it an Assembly or Gathering. Other times we are so overwhelmed with His greatness and His goodness and His glory that we stop right where are and give Him thanks and praise. And when one person starts a-praisin', it's hard for the rest of us not to join in! You'll hear praises ricochet all over Heaven.

"Heaven's citizens are always welcome in The Throne Room, and they can come and go as they please. Make no mistake, most of us run to get there and hate to leave. It's hard to leave the One who loves you so completely. Some people have to be almost dragged out of there, they love being in His presence so much. Oh, children, He is so worthy!"

"What *does* everyone do here, Abel?" Henri asked, then added with a laugh. "It's quite obvious they're not sitting around on clouds playing harps and eating grapes with fat cherubs!"

"God created you for purpose children. Did you think His purpose for you ends when you die?"

"Yeah, I guess I did," Henri answered honestly. "I mean, I never really thought much about my life before, I mean after the Earth part."

"You are not alone in that, Henri. Now think about this: you were created an eternal being which means you will live forever and ever and ever and ever, without end. That's a long time, isn't it?"

The children nodded their heads.

"How many years would you say most people live on Earth?"

"Maybe eighty or ninety years if you live a really long time," answered Masumi.

"Okay, let's be generous and say people live to be one hundred years old. In the scope of eternity, one hundred years is less than a blip on the radar screen of your life, is it not?"

The children nodded their agreement.

"It is a blink, a breath, a minuscule dot on a never-ending line. Don't you think the God who made you an eternal being would want *all* of your life to have meaning? Not just the blip of one hundred earthly years—the dot on the line of time and space—but the everlasting part, too? The part that exists on the never ending line?"

"Yeah, that makes sense," said Henri, contemplating how much it truly did make sense.

"You see, your time on Earth was just the beginning, the starting point if you will, of your life with Christ. You were created with an eternal purpose—a destiny, and you will spend *all* of eternity fulfilling it. It will look different for each one of you, but I can guarantee you that you will never be bored."

"Every person is different and so each life will glorify the Father in a unique way. You will never tire of the journey, and you will never want out! God is creative by His very nature, and it will take us all of eternity to get to know Him and discover His manifold treasures."

"Do you ever get tired of serving the Lord, Abel? It seems like angels work really hard."

"Oh, absolutely not, Cristen! I, too, am discovering new treasures all the time. I never know what might happen. My life is a constant adventure. I always have new and exciting assignments, and how happy I am that one of my assignments is to be with you children! I have joy and blessings too numerous to name; but my greatest joy is to be in His presence and watch the Master at work, witnessing His creativity, His mercy, and His faithfulness!"

"Are people working in Heaven? Like, do they have jobs they go to; you said Cristen could be a fashion designer if she wanted to when she comes back, is that a job?"

"Well, young Edgas, people definitely have responsibilities—like Joseph you met in the Room of Tears; but working in Heaven is very different from working on Earth. On Earth, people must work in order to live. Much of the time they have jobs they don't even enjoy. But in Heaven, you exist in order to live! You use your gifts to bless others, and you do what you love. Best of all, your labors are never resisted but are blessed in every way. And everything is done as an act of worship that honors the King.

"So what are some of the jobs like?"

"Well, if you were an artist, you might have an art studio and an art gallery as extensions of your mansion. You could paint beautiful pictures and people could come see them in your gallery, and if they liked a painting, you would give it to them to take home to hang in their own mansions."

"*Give* it? Really? Wouldn't you sell it to them?"

"Nope. Give it. Everything in Heaven is free. It didn't cost you any money to make it, so there is no charge to take it. If someone likes something you've made, you give it to them. We don't use money up here."

"Well, it comes in pretty handy down here, Bub." Cristen said, then burst out laughing.

"Oh, it seems we have a fan of *It's a Wonderful Life*!" replied the angel.

"Yes!" Cristen's surprised eyes darted to the angel. "You know *that* movie, too? My family watches it every Christmas, and I have this habit of blurting out movie lines! Sorry I interrupted you, Abel, but you set me up for that one."

"Don't apologize—it's one of my favorite movies. Only, you do know that angel's don't earn wings every time a bell rings, right?"

"I do now!" Cristen giggled.

"What are you two talking about? What do bells and angel wings have to do with money in Heaven?" Edgas asked, perplexed.

"Nothing. That's the point." Abel winked at Cristen. "She was quoting a funny line from a favorite movie. You'll have to watch it some time."

Cristen winked back at Abel and added, "Although, if you do happen to see Clarence flying around with his new set of wings, be sure to let me know. I'd love to ask him about his time with George Bailey."

Abel laughed out loud, "You bet I will! If I see him, you'll be the first to know."

"Look there!" Henri pointed excitedly down to a broad meadow below where the group now stood. "Are those diamonds?"

TOKYO, JAPAN
UNSEEN REALM

Failure continued his nonstop assault against Michi. "It's all my fault; I killed Masumi. I'm the one who killed her; it's all my fault. I'm such an idiot. If I had only paid attention, she'd still be alive. What was I thinking? How could I be so stupid? Masumi is dead, and it's all my fault." On and on, unrelenting, the putrid lies spouted, hitting their bull's-eye every time.

When the boy moved, quite mechanically, into the squad car to be transported to the hospital, Failure leaped onto the hood shouting more curses and accusations and lies. Out of the corner of his eye, he caught sight of Shame glaring at him as the car pulled away. He gave no indication that he saw him but turned his anger towards the boy and screamed, "You're dead, Michi! You hear me? DEAD!"

Shame exhaled through gnarled teeth, unimpressed with the show. He was seething mad at the idiot for blowing his well thought out plan. "Make it right—or else," he hissed, teeth gnashing.

Failure didn't hear him but knew exactly what his superior was thinking; he'd make it right or suffer the consequences. He'd faced Shame's punishments before and had only recently regained the use of his left arm. Make it right he would. The boy would die, or else. He didn't want to think about the "or else."

Crawling to the roof of the car, he stepped inside and sat on Michi's chest. The pressure was suffocating to Michi, but the barrage of accusations stopped momentarily while the demon tried to think of a new plan. So preoccupied was he with his own problematic situation that he paid no attention to the older gentleman sitting in the car beside Michi.

Raphia had a plan of his own. He hated being this close to the odorous vermin without being able to wring his scrawny neck. Oh, he was such easy pickings right now, and to shut him up would be glorious. But, he had to lay low if his plan was going to work. Besides, angels followed orders, stayed in rank, and never acted impulsively or out of anger. He had served his Creator well for many a millennia, and he wasn't about to change that now. Keeping his own light dimmed, he carefully watched over Michi, glad for a break from the rapid-fire verbal barrage of garbage, and patiently waited for his opportunity.

Ah, but now it started up again, and the pressure was turned up a notch. *I killed Masumi. I don't deserve to live. I should have been the one to die not her. I'll make it right. I'll make it right, somehow. I'm the one that should have died. I'm the one. I can't go on living knowing that I killed my sister. I can't live like this. My life is over; I might as well end it. My life is over. My life's not worth living. I should kill myself. Besides, everyone would be better off without me.*

Well, how original, Raphia thought disgustedly. *Suicide is his plan of attack.* The angel, disguised as an elderly man, was way ahead of the parasite. *Two can play this game, Failure, two can play this game.*

And Raphia closed his ears while biding his time.

SIXTEEN

Those who are wise will shine like the brightness of the heavens, and those who lead many to righteousness, like the stars forever and ever. — Daniel 12:3 (NIV)

Diamonds! Magnificent diamonds! Thousands upon thousands of glistening, glimmering, cut and faceted, fiery diamonds ranging in size from a single carat to that of a concrete block were gathered in the heart of a bountiful and very lovely vale. Explosions of color-filled light burst from their prisms and the effect was extraordinary. It was simultaneously similar to and completely unique from the fiery display of the River of Life. Tall, graceful trees, whose delicate golden leaves shimmered ardently, encircled the diamonds like a golden ring.

"Wow!" Masumi exhaled slowly, unaware that she had been holding her breath.

"Yeah, wow!" echoed Edgas.

The children could not take their eyes off the spectacle of bursting rainbow light.

Abel took the lead down the knoll along a grassy path that led through the golden trees, right into the field of brilliant diamonds. There, a small company of saints and angels working diligently together warmly welcomed them.

How happy are the citizens of Heaven, thought Masumi.

The children meandered through the grove of diamonds captivated by the dispersing of refracted rainbows. They stroked the crystals and found them to be cool and glassy smooth. Twisting and turning the smaller ones in the ever-present light, they marveled as rainbows flashed from their hands across the sky.

Presently, an immense angel appeared flying swiftly from the far side of the vale. He landed lightly at the edge of the grove and began to walk toward the trees. He had a head full of glowing brunette hair, wavy and soft looking, and his whole being shone with light; in his hand he held a large scroll edged in gold. He stopped beneath a shimmering golden tree and held out his arms. Immediately, out of the ground, rose a silvery-looking, oblong table, as if by magic.

Abel grinned at the children's stunned faces, "It's supernatural, not magic," he reminded.

The silvery table gleamed in the light and reflected the colors of the flashing rainbows. Intricately designed, it was truly a work of fine artistry.

I guess some really talented craftsman used their gift to make that table, thought Henri. *I wonder if they gave it away for free? I wonder if these diamonds are free?*

The angel unfurled his scroll upon the silvery table.

Without being summoned, everyone in the diamond grove stopped whatever it was they were doing—of which the children had no idea what it was—and assembled by the table. The chocolate-headed angel began to read aloud from the scroll. The children could not follow all he said, but the gist of it was that So-and-so, the Soul-winner, was to get such-and-such carat diamond delivered to his mansion. When he finished, he rolled up the scroll and handed it to a strawberry-blonde, curly-headed angel slightly smaller than he. This one drew his fist across his chest and bowed slightly, sending curls bobbing every which way, and then he returned to the grove to survey the assortment of diamonds.

Like a child in a candy store, his eyes roved to and fro before selecting just the right diamond—which happened to be a very large one! He carefully tucked it under his massive arm, spread his wings, and launched himself among the fiery bursts into the bluest of skies.

A portion of the diamond shown from its nesting place and flashed like a beacon as the angel flew away.

The gathered group of diamond workers joyfully went back to their tasks; happy songs and laughter rung throughout the grove.

"What was that all about?" asked Henri, reluctantly pulling his eyes away from the flying beacon.

"The angel brought a report from Earth of a person who has done great things for God."

"I didn't exactly understand, but it sounded like he was talking about a construction project. Are they still building things, Abel? I thought everything here was finished," said Cristen.

"Yes, Cristen. Heaven is always expanding, always building, and always growing. People with architecture, design, and decorating gifts will continue to use their talents; and your Father, the Chief Architect, greatly enjoys the building of His Great City; but this particular assignment was for something a little bit different."

"What do you mean?" asked Henri.

"Come, I'll show you."

As soon as Abel said the word "come," a path of light *supernaturally* appeared. They hopped aboard like old pros this time, and the moving walkway carried them quite rapidly across miles of astounding beauty.

"Mansions!" Cristen cried with a start.

"It's a whole neighborhood of mansions!" exclaimed Edgas.

Until this tour, Edgas had never seen a mansion, much less a whole neighborhood of them. And these were some kind of mansions to be sure!

"Well, I guess Jesus meant what he said."

"What do you mean, Edgas?" Masumi turned to face the boy.

"You know, He said He was going to prepare a place for us, that in His Father's house were many mansions. Well, here you go," he spread his arms out, "...many, many mansions."

"I always thought that verse meant that He had a lot of bedrooms in His house," remarked Cristen. "Of course," she snickered, "that would have been a really, really, *really* big house!"

"Children, you are in His house right now. His house encompasses the whole world called Heaven," explained Abel. "So, in His house, or His world called Heaven, there are many, many, many mansions—enough for all His kids."

Spaciously lined on both sides of the street was one stately, sprawling mansion after another. Neighbors were close enough to come for a visit but not so close as to even see each other's homes. Each mansion sat prominently back from the street, on slight to quite steep gradients, overlooking its fine estate in royal fashion; and each mansion had spectacular landscaping which bordered and punctuated the manicured lawns of velvety green grass. Lovely paths led to impressive front doors that were arched and opened wide.

The mansions were uniquely different from each other in both architecture and personality. The children noticed one that was unusually, but very prettily, bedecked in bright colored jewels. Henri thought it looked as though an angel had flown over and flung them, quite generously, into wet stucco as a farmer throwing out feed for his chickens. The thought made him chuckle. The children gawked as they continued down the street.

"Look up there," shouted a pointing Edgas, "on that roof!"

There, on the roof of a mansion they were passing, was the strawberry haired angel who had flown off on assignment, his precious cargo still tucked under his arm, talking to two men.

"That just happens to be the home of a soul-winner," explained Abel.

"How do you know that?" asked Edgas, turning his attention to the angel in their midst.

"It is written in Daniel 12 verse 3, 'Those who are wise will shine like the brightness of the heavens, and those who lead many to righteousness, like the stars for ever and ever.' Every time a person leads someone to faith in Jesus, a diamond is placed into their home. Do you see the vast numbers of diamonds sparkling on this street? The precious saints who live, or will live, in this neighborhood have led many to belief in Him."

"So that's what the angel was doing," said Masumi excitedly.

"How cool is that!" exclaimed Henri.

"Did you know, children, that each sacrifice you make on Earth will have its reward in Heaven? Every time you feed the poor, clothe the naked, or help the hurting, God not only sees, but He remembers; and He not only remembers, but He rewards. When you are loving and kind, especially to those to whom it is difficult to be loving and kind, or to those who cannot repay you, God takes note. When you put the needs of others before your own, God takes note of that, too. No sacrifice, no matter how big or how small, has ever gone, or will ever go, unnoticed. God sees it all. His scribe angels are recording it all, and your Father promises great treasure in Heaven."

"Are there other kinds of treasure besides diamonds?"

"Certainly! There are many different rewards: the diamonds are for the soul-winners; you've seen the jewels on the white gowns, they're certainly reward for a life well lived; and although every home is wonderful, some homes are truly breathtaking and have been prepared as a reward for great earthly sacrifice. There are many, many ways that God will reward his diligent children, and some of them won't happen until the Resurrection of the Dead; but God is preparing for that day, even now."

"So, if I obey my mom, like without fussing, is there a reward for that, too?"

"Yes, Henri, absolutely. Both here in Heaven and while you're on Earth. When you honor your father and mother, doors will swing wide open for you, opportunities will come your way, and blessings will fall upon you."

"When we go back, I think remembering this will really change the way we live our lives and treat people."

"Blessed are you, Masumi, Henri, Cristen, and Edgas, for the Lord has revealed his treasure principle to you. People make all kinds of plans, but they forget to make eternal plans; you children have the unusual opportunity to change your priorities. The faithful will rule and reign with the Holy One, the others will serve those ruling and reigning. All His children will be happy to be here, but you can make plans now to be one of the faithful!"

"Oh, we will!" they promised faithfully.

"Now, who would like to peek inside one of these homes?"

"Can we?" Cristen clapped her hands with joy.

"Oh, yes!" the others agreed.

"Then follow me."

The path of light immediately stopped moving, and when the group stepped down, it disappeared. Abel led them up a path made of gorgeous, shiny stones towards a charming-looking mansion. "It's presently unoccupied, but her family and friends are preparing it for her, and it will be completely furnished by the time she arrives. The Father knows the day each of His children will come home, and their abodes are always ready for them, even if it was the enemy who took their life."

"This one's a bit smaller than some of the others," commented Edgas.

"She only wanted a cottage," explained the angel, matter of factly.

They crossed the lush lawn, and before entering the cottage, Masumi squealed. "Look at that! Gemstones are the mulch in the flower beds!"

Once again their minds were set a-spinning as they gawked at the gemstones piled liberally on top of each other and, by all appearances, just *dumped* into the flowerbeds.

"I don't think there's a money problem in Heaven," chuckled Henri, fingering the stone in his pocket.

Shaking their heads, they crossed the threshold and found the "cottage" to be strikingly simple, yet exorbitantly lavish. The children loved it and immediately felt right at home. They knew without doubt that they, too, would be content and happy to live here.

"Oh, I'm not sure I would call this a cottage, Abel," Cristen remarked. "It does have a charming feel about it, but it's bigger than any house I've ever been in."

"Well, here's a news flash for you Cristen: some people's homes are so big that they need a map to get around them!"

"Seriously?" The kids' eyes popped incredulously.

"Seriously."

"That sounds like a museum," said Henri, shaking his head.

"Yes, it does. Only the things in it are meant for enjoyment and not for display. Now off you go. Explore!"

The children took off running in all directions.

The "cottage" was charming, indeed. A warm and inviting living room with comfy furniture and a huge stone fireplace welcomed them home. The detailed woodwork of flooring and molding was absolutely exquisite. The kitchen was open to the living room and fitted with all sorts of marvelous appliances—most of which the children had never seen before. Adjacent to the kitchen, in a windowed area too big to be called a nook, was a gorgeous table large enough to seat several dozen guests.

There were a half dozen bedrooms, some upstairs and some down, all of which were exquisitely decorated and afforded wonderful views of the surrounding countryside. In the largest of the bedrooms, which was upstairs, there was a large mahogany bed covered with the softest of creamy colored linens and a thick, plush creamy colored comforter with golden silk threads woven throughout. The bed was piled high with downy soft pillows and decorated with accent pillows of rich brocade. It looked so inviting; it was all the children could do to refrain from leaping onto it.

"I didn't think people slept in Heaven, Abel," said Edgas, imagining what it might feel like to sleep in a bed such as this. He had slept on a hard floor as a very young child, and thought he had found luxury when at the orphanage he had slept on a lumpy cot.

Abel let the children sit on the bed, or more accurately, flop on the bed; they just couldn't help themselves. They sighed with pure pleasure as they melted into the downy softness.

"You will not have need of sleep in Heaven, Edgas, but you will have a fine place to rest and read whenever you want," answered the angel.

"So, everyone's home is different?"

"Yes, Henri, one of the greatest joys of living in Heaven is that everyone's home is built in a way that satisfies and ministers perfectly to them. And of utmost importance, everyone's home is built around their own special gift, for they will be using that gift to bless others and to glorify God.

"What's this woman's gift?" asked Masumi.

"I believe she's a writer."

"I think you're right," agreed Cristen, who had left the comfy bed and wandered into the adjoining room. "Look at this!"

She called her friends over to see a beautiful home library. They jumped off the bed and ran to join her.

A large wall of windows and an elegantly carved writing desk, overlooking a broad green lawn sloping down to a little brook which ran through tall flowering trees as it meandered across the property, was the focal point of the room. The view was simply delightful, and one could have sat in that desk chair and studied it for hours. Three entire walls were lined floor to very high ceiling with books and a golden, rolling library ladder encircled the room via a golden track.

"I've wanted one of those ever since I saw the movie, *Beauty and The Beast*," cooed Cristen, admiringly.

"Then perhaps there'll be one in your mansion," replied Abel.

Cristen sighed, "Oh, I sure hope so."

"Look at that view," said Henri. "Even I could get inspired to write in here." He held his chin high and cleared his throat,

"Roses change colors

And sing to you, too.

Heaven's amazing

And so is this view."

His friends groaned.

"That was terrible, Henri," laughed Cristen.

"But true!" Edgas piped in, always the encourager.

"I want to show you something; come here, children," Abel called them over to the writing table. He pointed to a small cross engraved in the corner of the beautiful desktop. "Even Jesus uses his gifts in Heaven."

The children looked at him, bewildered.

"He is a Master Carpenter, you know, and if you like, He will make something special for you, too."

"Oh, my goodness!" exclaimed Cristen. "Did Jesus make this table? Himself?"

"Yes, my dear. He marks all His work with His very own trademark. Whenever you see this cross engraved, you can be assured, Jesus made it Himself."

That little tidbit floored the children, and they pondered the implications as they continued exploring.

Edgas found a room filled with all sorts of musical instruments, many of them made from pure gold. Shouting, he called them all in to see. It was easy to guess that this woman was also either a musician, or a-wanna-be, and that she would be thrilled with this surprise. Among others, a small harp, trumpet, and guitar hung from decorative brackets on the wall.

The girls went back to the large bedroom and discovered a humongous closet filled with an assortment of wondrous clothes. An entire wardrobe awaited this woman—dresses, gowns, tunic pants, tops, shoes, and accessories—all hanging or neatly lined up on the many shelves.

Cristen turned to Masumi, "Boy, when Abel said people have a whole wardrobe, he really meant it!"

"You aren't kiddin'!" Masumi's eyes roved up and down the shelves as she admired the beautiful apparel. "It's like she has her own dress shop!"

The girls could not help but caress the soft and luxurious fabrics as they browsed through the racks of clothes.

At the back of the oversized closet, Cristen discovered a door, and as she opened it she let out a squeal of delight. As soon as the boys heard her, they came running. Reaching the girls, Henri and Edgas discovered them standing with open mouths. Cristen had found an amazing, circular room filled with hundreds and hundreds of stunning jewelry pieces: earrings, bracelets, necklaces, chokers, pins, brooches, and three tiaras. In the center of the little room stood a golden pedestal with a royal blue velvety pillow on top. And perched on the pillow was the focal point of the room—a jewel-studded diadem. This was the woman's Crown of Life! It shone and sparkled with radiant glory. And most amazing of all was the wonderful aroma flowing from it. The children had never smelled such a delightful fragrance. Once again, they gawked in stunned silence.

"Oh, my! Oh, my! Oh, my!" Masumi finally managed to say.

"Well, this is a girl's dream," chortled Henri.

"Even the men have crowns," Abel said, joining them. The ceilings were so high that his wings passed easily through the doorframe.

"Does everyone have a room like this, Abel, or is this her reward?"

"Yes, Cristen, everyone has a separate room to display their crown. One of the joys of Heaven is to visit people and see their crowns. Just like a snowflake, no two are the same."

"And what about all the beautiful jewelry?" asked a curious Masumi.

"There are many jewelers here—remember, everyone uses their gifts—jewelers design and give away amazing pieces of jewelry. As you have discovered, gemstones are readily available to artisans; and best of all, it's all free for the taking. Most of these jewels were placed in here by this woman's friends and family. They have collected things they know she'll love and have them waiting for her homecoming."

"I found something else you guys need to see, com'on!" Edgas tore out of the crown-room, through the closet, with the others right behind.

"Wait a second, Edgas," Henri called. "Come back, and look at this first."

Edgas' smiling face popped back through the bedroom door, and his bright eyes looked around the room to see what had caught Henri's attention.

A mahogany dresser matching the bed stood on the opposite side of the room from the adjoining library. Nestled in a cozy nook, with another lovely view, was a gorgeous wingback chair. Edgas supposed it was another reading area. He sat down in it and felt he would melt in its comfort.

A mahogany nightstand, inlaid with gold and beautifully designed—ornate but in no way gaudy—stood beside the bed. On it were a lovely crystal flower vase, a Bible, a pen, and a little book.

It was the Bible that had stopped Henri in his tracks; it was extremely beautiful—bound in gold and made from a kind of paper the children had never seen before, but also, it was supernatural! Light and glory poured forth from within illuminating the entire room. There was no need for any other light fixture or lamp.

"Your word is a lamp for my feet, a light on my path," quoted Abel from Psalms 119 verse 105.

"That is *so* cool!" shouted Edgas.

"Is that vase for flowers, Abel?"

"Yes, Masumi, when you come back to stay," he added, "you may go out anytime and pick any flower you want to place in vases throughout your homes; or you can order a lovely bouquet from the florist; people still use that gift, too."

Masumi thought of the wide variety of beautiful flowers she had seen, and knew she would have a difficult time choosing which ones to bring into her room. *Well,* she declared to herself, *I just might need to pick new flowers every day."*

"When you are finished enjoying your flowers," he smiled at Masumi, as if reading her mind, again, "you can place them in your garden, and they will take root."

"Oh, yeah! Remember the grass and flowers back at the wall when we first arrived?" Henri recounted, "That's exactly what they did; they rerooted themselves!"

"Remember, *nothing* dies in Heaven!" Then Abel leaned in and whispered, as if telling the children a great secret, "Inside some mansions lovely *gardens* of flowers grow right out of the floors or the walls, and they sing you a welcome song every time you come home!"

The children looked at Abel as if he were pulling their legs.

"Are you teasing us?" asked Edgas.

"Nope."

Oh, no, these children would never get used to the glories of Heaven!

Masumi, with great care and reverence, opened the luminous Bible and propped up on the bed to read from it. Edgas ran back to the music room and grabbed the trumpet, blowing it loudly, which got a great laugh out of the surprised group. Cristen went over to try out the chair. "Oh! It's just right!" she giggled, thinking she sounded a bit like Goldilocks.

"It's time to go, children, more glories await," Abel said smiling.

Cristen took one last, lingering look around the luxurious room, as Edgas hurried to return the trumpet he had taken from the music room.

"Where's Henri?" Masumi asked the boy when he ran back into the room, as she tenderly closed the Bible and slid off the bed.

"Try the crown room," Abel answered, smiling again, "and tiptoe."

"The cluster of friends quietly peeked in and found Henri placing the Crown of Life on his head.

The group burst out in peals of laugher.

A surprised Henri grinned sheepishly and then carefully returned the crown to its royal pillow. Thankfully, no fingerprints or smudge marks were left behind—another miracle of Heaven.

Leaving the bedroom, Cristen exclaimed, "Oh, Edgas! What was it you wanted to show us?" She turned her attention to the boy.

"Oh, yeah, I forgot! Come and see!"

Edgas led the group downstairs, but before they reached his destination Henri asked, "Where are the bathrooms?"

"There aren't any," said the angel.

"What?" Cristen exclaimed. "I've never seen a house with no bathrooms!"

"Some mansions have rooms with bathtubs for people who simply love to take baths for pleasure, but no one ever gets dirty here, nor is there any waste, so there is no need for bathrooms."

"No waste? But people eat," remarked Henri. "We know, cuz we ate that fruit earlier."

"Yes, of course! There are all kinds of foods in Heaven. Remember, some people have the gift of cooking or baking, and they will delight in sharing their gifts with you forever. And although it will certainly taste like the best food you have ever eaten in your life—pizza, pasta, steak, sushi, bar-b-cue, fried chicken, endless desserts, and baked goods—all of it is entirely made of light. And, best of all, there are no allergies, no intolerances, no bad foods or dieting, and no weight gain! And because the light is completely absorbed into your body, there is no waste."

It made total sense to the kids but was another unexpected surprise.

"Well, I guess I'll have to find another spot to catch up on my reading," chuckled Henri.

Edgas laughed so hard he collapsed on the floor. Even in Heaven, young boys still love potty jokes.

The girls rolled their eyes, teasingly.

Curiously, Masumi turned the handle of yet one more room they had not explored. When she gasped, her friends quickly followed her inside a very large room displaying framed and beautiful pieces of unusual artwork on canvases of all different sizes.

"Is she an artist, too?" Cristen turned to ask Abel.

"I guess you could say that," Abel chuckled. "This is her Praise Gallery."

"Praise Gallery?" the children echoed, questioningly.

"Yes, everyone has an opportunity to have a Praise Gallery in their mansion. It is a collection of all the praises they offered to God while living on Earth. Every time you sing or offer praises on Earth, you paint a beautiful picture in the spiritual realm. Every time you dance before the Lord, angels hold a canvas under your feet, and you paint a masterpiece of praise. And every stroke of an artist's brush releases a beautiful note in the spiritual realm. Any painting done for the Lord creates a lovely song which plays throughout eternity in their Praise Gallery."

"I had no idea," whispered Masumi.

"Man, this makes me wanna go home and dance!" shouted Edgas, breaking out in his familiar jig.

The children laughed, then took some time to examine the beautiful art.

"I think this room will be etched in my memory forever," sighed Cristen.

"Okay, Edgas. Wasn't there something you wanted to show your friends?" Abel spread his arms to herd his lambs out of the Praise Gallery.

"Ha! Yes, but there are so many cool things that I just keep on forgetting. Follow me, guys."

Edgas led his friends to a stunning sunroom he had found near the kitchen; it, too, had a wall of windows, and these overlooked the little hollow at the back of the cottage where several deer were now grazing.

"Look, look!" he shouted, jumping up and down with glee. "Presents! Gobs and gobs of them."

When the others looked, they saw hundreds of wrapped gifts stacked all over the bright sunroom.

"Is it the lady's birthday?" bright-eyed Edgas asked Abel.

"No, it's not her birthday. These are gifts that her family and friends have gotten for her. Whenever they see something they know she'll love, they get it for her and either place it somewhere in her home or wrap it in pretty paper and bring it in here. All of these gifts are collecting here for her Homecoming Party."

"Goodness gracious, I've never seen so many gifts for one person," agreed Masumi, staring at the floor to ceiling stacks.

"She must really be loved!" Cristen said, laughing.

"Yes, she is, and so are all of you!"

"So, do we have gifts waiting for us in our mansions, too?" Edgas' asked with twinkling eyes.

"I bet you do, Edgas! I bet you do. There certainly were a lot of people who came to welcome you to Heaven! I would think that many of them are collecting gifts for you."

"When we get to live here, will we collect gifts for our friends and family?" Masumi asked, smiling at her friends, for she was already thinking of some things she would have waiting for each of them if she made it back to Heaven first.

"Absolutely. It is more blessed to give than to receive! You will enjoy giving gifts forever because you are made in the likeness of your Heavenly Father, and He, my children, is the ultimate Gift Giver!"

The group grinned excitedly.

"Well, my young friends, are you ready for more exploring? Much adventure still awaits us."

PARIS, FRANCE
12:31 p.m.

Dazed, Celeste somehow managed to find her shoes and grab her purse. Mom and daughter ran out the door, down the front steps, and miraculously were able to hail a taxi right away. Within minutes—long, agonizing minutes—they were at the hospital.

The adrenalin rush of the past half hour was now replaced with a blinding headache. Feeling drained and weary, Celeste paid the driver and forced herself out of the cab. Her body on autopilot, she mechanically made her way to the information desk with Alison close at her side. She numbly told the woman behind the desk her name and that an ambulance had recently arrived with her son. She only half heard what the woman in the black-rimmed glasses said back to her. "Wait," was the gist of it; that's all she needed to know. Alison linked her arm in her mother's and led her to a chair in the waiting room. The two sat despondently side by side, staring at nothing, neither one speaking.

Alison's thoughts were tossed around like a small boat on an angry sea. She had trouble focusing as her mind swirled, unable to make landfall. Her faith was being shaken, shaken to the very core.

"Jesus, help us." It was the only prayer she could come up with; however, it was truly the best one she could have uttered.

Suddenly, out of the confusion, Alison's mother's words replayed sharply in her mind. "What took you so long to get here? He'd still be alive if you had come!" She stopped abruptly. *Where have I heard that before?* It sounded so familiar. *A movie maybe?* "He'd still be alive if you had come. He'd still be alive if you had come."

"Martha!" Alison practically shouted as the revelation hit her with full force. Mary and Martha had said something similar to Jesus when their brother Lazarus died. He had been dead for four days, and the sisters were so disappointed that Jesus hadn't come quickly to heal him. They had seen Jesus heal hundreds of sick people—people He didn't even know! They had no doubts, none whatsoever, that He could have, and would have, healed their brother, Lazarus—whom He loved—if He had only shown up sooner. But Jesus had a greater miracle for them. He was planning to show off God's glory. He was not late, for He had planned from the beginning of time to raise Lazarus from the dead!

Oh Jesus, I believe you can raise Henri from the dead! Do you have a greater miracle for us, Lord? Alison felt hope begin to rise in her heart. *You can do anything, Lord. Nothing is impossible with you. You are never too late, NEVER!*

SEVENTEEN

Do not store up for yourselves treasures on Earth, where moth and rust destroy, and where thieves break in and steal. But store up for yourselves treasures in Heaven, where neither moth nor rust destroys, and where thieves do not break in or steal; for where your treasure is, there your heart will be also. — Matthew 6:19-21 (NASB)

Abel led his little group of sojourners onto another path of light. However, instead of going forward as it had in the past, the light rose up, encircled them in tube-like fashion, and stretched high over their heads. As they looked up in surprise, they were drawn up into the tube of light and were carried along as in an ocean current.

"What's happening?" shouted Edgas, after the collective scream of surprise.

"It's a tube transport," replied the angel, matter of factly.

Cristen shouted with a grin, "Beam me up, Scotty!"

"This is so weird! Are we flying?" Henri couldn't tell. It was such an unusual sensation.

"It's called The Tube; it's another kind of light transport," Abel shouted, "and it gets you where you want to go, fast!"

Instantly, The Tube vanished, and the children found themselves standing in front of an enormous barn-like structure, shining as bright as any star.

"What do you think of it?"

"Of that," Edgas pointed to the building, "or of that ride?"

"Well, both," laughed the angel.

"I don't know what *that* is," a still pointing Edgas answered, "but that ride was awesomely weird, wasn't it Henri?"

"Oh, I dunno, it might have been weirdly awesome!" The group shared a laugh at the running joke.

"So, what *are* we looking at, Abel?" Masumi asked, admiring the massive structure before her.

It was made entirely of a lustrous, silvery-white platinum, not at all translucent like the golden streets or faceted like some of the buildings in the city but of such high quality as to reflect the glory of God with an awe-striking brightness.

"This is the storehouse where the Lord keeps some of the treasures that He has promised His children. Remember what I said that nothing done in His name, no matter how big or how small, will go unrewarded?"

All heads nodded.

"You are not allowed to enter this building, for these gifts are meant to be a surprise, but I can let you have a quick look. Are you ready?"

"Yes!" they replied with enthusiasm.

"Okay, on the count of three. One, two, three!" Abel opened the door and moved out of the way. The children stepped to the entrance, and their jaws fell slack in what was becoming typical Heaven-like fashion. The inside was vast and bustling with activity. Acres and acres of long platinum shelves were generously filled to overflowing with beautifully wrapped gifts and packages of all shapes and sizes, in the prettiest papers, ribbons, and bows that you have ever seen! Gemstones glittered from the ribbons and bows. Oh, how the children would love to know what wonderful things were hidden in these gorgeous wrappings.

Angels with scrolls were flying in and out of the structure through an open roof while some of the men and women were moving up and down the rows and the aisles with packages, others were busily wrapping, and still others appeared to be cataloging information. Perhaps they were keeping a record of the gifts, whom they belonged to, and where they were located. The entire storehouse was a bevy of activity.

All too soon, Abel stepped in front of them, spread his wings, and pulled the door closed with a smile.

"Did you know that every time you give your money or your time to the work of Kingdom ministry or to someone in need, God adds to your treasure in Heaven?"

"Really?" Cristen's eyes revealed her surprise.

"It all belongs to the Lord anyway, for everything you have, have had, or will have comes from Him. You are only a steward of His gifts, children; so as God gives to you, He expects you to use those gifts wisely, as a good steward. He wants you to be vessels He can use to help others who have need."

"How can I help others, Abel? I don't have very much money." Masumi wanted to be sure she understood.

"Think of your life as a water pipe. If you will turn the faucet on and share your water, so to speak, with those in need and in giving to the work of God's Kingdom, then your Heavenly Father will keep sending water to fill your pipe. In this way, you partner with God."

"So, God needs my water, I mean, my money?" asked Edgas.

"Don't misunderstand, children, the Lord doesn't *need* anything. He certainly doesn't need your money! He is not a beggar holding a cup for you to toss alms into so that He can help the needy. Quite the contrary, He has sovereignly chosen to allow you to partner with Him so that you may receive a blessing, both while living on Earth and, most extravagantly, in Heaven.

"Sadly, many of His children keep a tight fist, forgetting that their time, talents, and money come from the Lord, and when they get to Heaven, they will have no reward."

"But it *is* their money, if they've worked for it...isn't it?" asked a confused Henri.

"Yes, it is the money they are steward over, but who gave them the ability to work? Who gave them the talent and the brains to know how to get the job done? Who gave them life and breath? Who created money and gave it value in the first place?"

"Oh, I get it!" Henri's face lit up with understanding. "*Everything* is the Lord's — that really means everything!"

"I think most of us don't act like we know that," Cristen confessed.

"Why is it so hard for us to be a water faucet, like you said?" asked Masumi earnestly.

"It's easy to see the foolishness of it from this vantage point, isn't it? But remember, on Earth, it takes faith. You've been given a real gift, children, only a very few have ever seen this Treasure House; most people must believe by faith, not by sight, that what God says in His word is true."

"Now, as this one Treasure House gives evidence, there are many who have embraced this truth and have given generously of their time, gifts, and talents, and you have just seen that great treasure awaits them. For you can never, ever, out-give God!"

"And what about the people that haven't been generous? Is it just cuz they don't know any better?" Edgas hated the fact that there were people who have no rewards waiting for them.

"Oh, there are so many reasons, Edgas, as many reasons as there are people. Many do not know any better, as you have said, and most of them are just trying to make it through the day. They've never even considered that what they do today could affect their eternity. Most people have no idea what great treasure God has in store for them; if they truly understood this, they might make some changes and some different decisions.

"Then there are those folks who are just plain selfish and stingy. These don't want to share any of their blessings. But I'd say most people don't give generously because of fear. They have believed the lie that they are securing their future by holding on.

"And there is another sad reality at work here," Abel continued. "Some of those who *do* give of their time, talents, and money, do so in vain. Much of what they support has no Kingdom value. They may have helped an organization on Earth, but they have not sown any seeds for their eternity. Their so-called good deeds will be burned up as wood, hay, and stubble.

"And lastly, there are the ones who give with selfish motives; they want to puff themselves up so that others will honor them and think they are good and righteous. But I tell you the truth, these people have already received their reward, in full. There will not be anything waiting for them here.

"Jesus said not to let your left hand know what your right hand is doing, but when you give, when you fast, and when you pray, do so in secret; then your Heavenly Father, who sees in secret, will openly reward you in Heaven.

"Many will die empty handed, leaving their treasures behind. You, children, have the opportunity to put this truth into action and store up great treasure here in Heaven."

"You mean, 'you can't take it with you,' right?" asked Henri, repeating an expression he had heard before.

"That saying is quite true, Henri, but guess what? Although you cannot take it with you, you *can* send it on ahead."

"What do you mean?" Cristen turned a confused face towards the angel.

"Every time you give your money to the work of God's Kingdom, or help the needy, or give unselfishly of your time and talents to those in need, you are making a deposit in your heavenly bank account. The Lord is storing up riches untold, and treasures beyond man's imagination for those who trust Him and love Him enough to give to the work of His Kingdom on Earth.

"Therefore, be cheerful givers, young ones. Develop a heart to help others and put their needs before your own, knowing that you can never out-give God who sees your every deed. If you will do this, I know that you will be eternally glad of heart when you receive your heavenly treasure!

"By the way, you do know, do you not, that it is not the amount you give?"

"What do you mean?" asked Cristen.

"Do you remember the story Jesus told about the widow's mite?"

The children nodded their heads as Abel continued.

"The Lord honored her, saying she gave more than the others, yet all she put in the offering was a single mite, less than a penny. But it was all that she had. It was the amount of her *sacrifice* that captured the Lord's heart, not the amount of her gift."

"So, there is a reward for only giving a penny?" asked Henri.

"God looks at the heart, Henri, man looks at the outward appearance. It's not the amount you give; it's your heart. I tell you the truth, it is easier for a poor man to give what little he has, than for a wealthy man to give from his excess. Don't ever let yourselves be like that, my young friends. Trust the Lord! Open your hands, and be the water pipe! Let your Heavenly Father pour through you into His Kingdom. He has entrusted you with an overflowing abundance, not so that you can hoard it, but so you can release it where there is need."

"And, Edgas," Abel cast his eyes on the boy. "I want you to know that God sees you very much like the widow."

"He does?" Edgas felt his face flush.

"You haven't had much, yet all you had you willingly shared with the other children at the orphanage. God sees, and He says, 'Well done, my son!'"

Edgas dropped his eyes, shyly, and a wide grin covered his face. What joy to know that the Lord was pleased with him. When he looked back up, Abel's warm smile flooded his body with joy.

Henri, taking the angel's words to heart said, "More than anything, Abel, when I come back, I want the Lord to be pleased with my life." The others nodded their agreement.

"He will be, Henri," Abel looked at all the children and smiled. He loved their soft and pliable hearts. "I'm quite sure He will be."

PARIS, FRANCE
UNSEEN REALM

Heston and Capri stayed right on the heels of their human charges as the women rushed outside to hail a cab. The revolting den of hate-filled liars followed and then charged the taxi before the women could climb inside. The guardians plucked and pulled the demons away, making sure they themselves were the ones beside the women. The repugnant spirits were resigned to ride on top of the cab or fly overhead, but they were used to that. It would not hinder their ability to lob their wretched lies.

The mother was weakening, and all would watch her carefully. Both kingdoms knew well that the death of a child made easy target of a grieving parent and always created a feeding frenzy among demons.

The hospital was not far, but traffic was heavy. At last the taxi arrived, and the driver dropped the women, the guardians, and the demons off near the Emergency Room entrance. Celeste paid the fare but later had no recollection of it or even of the ride itself.

Heston knew Celeste was struggling. He kept his arm around her as she dragged herself into the hospital.

The waiting room was a dark place filled with spiritual beings intent on their evil and vindictive assignments. There were angels there, too, but they were far outnumbered by the spirits of darkness. Capri and Heston were not intimidated, but they despised the darkness.

The guardians helped the women get to their seats and stood protectively behind them. Capri and Heston knew this story was going to have a very happy ending, but they hated to see the demons tormenting Alison and Celeste this way. The attack against Celeste was intensifying, and now other sharks were joining the fray.

A very tiny demon jumped on Celeste's head and began to squeeze. Celeste moaned. Heston then saw him and immediately reached to pluck him off, but the demon had already dug his talons into her spirit.

Demons, hideously grotesque and foaming at the mouth with rabid anticipation, rushed at Celeste—more than Heston could fight off at once—grabbing at her and screeching obscenities. While Heston put one defender to flight, several more came at her. They jumped on her chest, pressing down, making it difficult for her to breathe. Some of the demons went after Heston; they plucked out feathers and pulled his hair, trying to distract him from his charge.

Capri, while beating off demons with his powerful wings, spoke peacefully in the midst of the chaos, "Come on, Alison. Call out to Jesus."

Then the girl spoke the powerful name of Jesus which is above every name and at which every knee must bow. And at the name of Jesus, the darkness over Alison was instantly repelled. A liquid stream of light came from nowhere and poured over the girl. A slight breeze began to blow, and as it covered her, it fanned the flame of the Holy Spirit, and He grew brighter within her.

Alison began to have a dialogue. She thought at first it was with herself, but in actuality, it was with the Holy Spirit. No demon dared speak, but every demonic face turned away and hid from the Light. The Holy Spirit began reminding Alison of her mother's words. He spoke quietly to her, imparting revelation deep into her mind, soul, and spirit. And as He did, a resurrection hope sprang to life inside her—and every spiritual being in the room knew it at once.

Capri and Heston turned their faces upward, soaking in the Light.

EIGHTEEN

I saw Heaven standing open and there before me was a white horse, whose rider is called Faithful and True. With justice he judges and wages war.
— *Revelation 19:11 (NIV)*

Leaving the Storehouse of Treasures, the joyful friends followed Abel with a child-like bounce in their step. The emotion and energy the group had expended on this journey would have fatigued anyone back home, especially considering how many shocks the children had had, how much they had laughed and learned, and how far they had traveled, by foot no less. They should have been exhausted, plumb worn out, but being tired never even crossed their minds. In fact, their energy level may have actually increased since arriving. Was it possible that they felt stronger and more alive than when they first arrived?

Below the Storehouse, a verdant lawn sloped to where the mighty River of Life ran through a hollow, and just beyond the river was another one of those gate-markers. This one, just like the one that marked the entrance to Expedition Park, had two alabaster white columns supporting a white iron-like gate, and it, too, seemed out of place.

"What does it say?" asked Edgas when they had reached it.

"The Golden Corral," said a puzzled Cristen. "It doesn't look like a corral; it looks like a garden.

"Looks can be deceiving," said Abel, passing through the gate. All but Edgas followed behind. He decided to skirt around the outside, like he did before.

"Hey! Where'd everybody go?"

His friends did not come out of the gate. He glanced around. Confused, he ran back around to the front. No one was there. He rushed around back, circled the entire gate-marker, and then ran through the gate from back to front. Poof! His friends had vanished into thin air!

"Not funny, you guys. Where are you?"

Edgas circled one more time, stopping at the front where he had last seen his friends. There was no way all four of them could be hiding behind these columns. He put his hands on his hips and looked around one more time; just a garden on one side and a river on the other.

"Masumi? Henri? Cristen? Okay, Abel, jokes on me! Where'd y'all go?"

Presently, Abel's large head appeared through the gate. "Aren't you coming, Edgas?" His eyes twinkled with humor. Reaching out, he pulled the boy through the open doors, and instantly, Edgas was standing with his friends in front of a large pasture that was encircled by a cowboy-style fence made out of gold. No garden, no river, no joke.

"There you are, Edgas!" His friends greeted. "Where ya been?"

Unbeknownst to Edgas, they had also circled 'round the gate—looking for him. They were just as surprised to find the river and garden missing as Edgas was to discover his friends missing.

"Weird," breathed Edgas, in very Henri-like fashion. "How'd we do that?"

"We entered a new dimension," the angel explained, like it was something you do every day.

"Oh!" Edgas snorted. "Is that what we did?"

Scattered around the circular pasture, amongst brightly flowering clover buoyed on a sea of emerald grass, grazed dozens of pure white horses. Grand horses. Muscular and quite large, they looked like they'd been chiseled out of marble, not unlike a sculpture by the artist Michelangelo. These beauties weren't sculptures, however, they were very real and very much alive.

"Oh!" breathed Cristen. "What magnificent creatures!"

"Yes! Aren't they wonderful!" Abel's statement was not a question.

There were wide bleachers for spectators to sit and watch, but Abel moved to the golden fence and encouraged the children to get comfortable there.

"So this is the golden corral, huh?" Edgas said, climbing to sit on the top rail while the others stepped on the first rail and rested their elbows on the top one.

"Yep," Abel easily hopped the fence. Careful to lift his wings out of the way, he leaned back casually against it.

"Oh! Here we go again," laughed Henri, pointing to a flower petal floating off of Masumi's shirt.

"My shirt's orange!" Edgas squealed.

The children laughed together as they examined each others' shirts, clearly enjoying the mysterious T-shirt surprise. Henri had what looked like a rodeo cowboy riding a bucking bronco on his shirt, Cristen's feathers were ruffling again, and Masumi had lost almost half of the flower petals on her back, yet the flower on the front of her shirt was still unchanged.

Suddenly, their attention was drawn to a young woman with long, brown hair pulled back in a loose braid. Stepping out of a quaint, stable-like structure just about a stone's throw away, she immediately noticed the visitors.

"You can't sneak up on anyone, can ya, Able?" Henri said, suspecting that Abel's glow was what drew her attention to the group so rapidly.

"You're right, Henri," the angel winked, "not in this form."

Henri wasn't sure what he meant by that remark and made a mental note to ask him later.

The young woman smiled joyously when she saw Abel and waved enthusiastically to the children.

"Boy, it's too bad people aren't more joyful around here," Cristen teased, returning an enthusiastic wave back to the lovely girl.

"Yes," laughed Masumi, "or more friendly."

"Hello, Gracie!" Abel called. "Mind if we watch?"

"Not at all, Abel! You've arrived at the perfect time!"

"Ha! Well that's not at all surprising," chortled Edgas, thinking back to the timing at the Room of Tears.

Gracie smiled at the children and then turning, she took about fifteen or twenty steps towards the center of the corral. She then held up her right arm, pointed her finger towards the sky, and began to move her hand and forearm in a large circle above her head—as if she had an invisible lasso. Immediately, every horse in the pasture began to trot over to her. Then, to the sheer amazement of the children, the horses lined up side by side in a perfectly straight line, facing Gracie.

Gracie had the most stunning, embroidered bag slung over her shoulder and across her chest. It appeared to be made out of linen with colorful satin ribbons. She reached inside and pulled something out of it which she offered to the first horse in line. He eagerly took the treat from her hand, and she rubbed him on his long velvety nose, then patted his neck. She again reached into her bag and offered a treat to the next horse in line which also took and ate eagerly. She repeated the giving of treats, rubbing of noses, and patting of necks as she continued down the long row of horses. The children could tell that Gracie was speaking softly to each horse as she greeted them.

"Oh, Cristen you're so right, they *are* magnificent!" Masumi leaned close to her friend and whispered so not to disturb Gracie as she moved down the line of noble steeds.

"I bet they understand everything she is saying to them," whispered Edgas, "just like the animals we saw in Expedition Park."

Each horse remained steady, patiently keeping its place in line. The only part of the horses that moved was the occasional swooshing of tails and turning of ears. That, in and of itself, was a wonder to behold.

When Gracie had finished going down the row and greeting each exquisite horse, she stepped back and stood front and center.

Abel whispered, "Now watch this." A wide smile and knowing look came over his handsome features. The children turned to him, and he raised his eyebrows slightly and nodded his head back towards the horses, excitement evident on his face. The children turned back with increased interest just as Gracie held up her left arm, straight as an arrow, beside her head.

The horses moved ever so slightly, gently stamping the ground with their gigantic hooves. Their large, sweet, brown eyes were all steady on Gracie.

She held her arm up for several moments and then quickly brought it down to her side, slicing the air. With that one swift movement, every horse simultaneously bowed its right knee to the ground.

"Oh!" the surprised friends exclaimed in unison.

"What are they doing?" whispered Edgas.

"Why they are worshipping God, of course!" Abel's eyes laughed.

"Oh, of course!" said the children, as they looked at each other and shrugged.

Then as they watched, Gracie turned both palms upward and raised her hands towards the sky; the horses immediately stood back to their feet, every pair of brown eyes steady on the lovely young woman. She slowly placed her hands straight down by her side. Waited, waited, then with a quick, sharp motion, she raised both arms straight up. Every horse immediately reared up on its hind legs, whinnied, and shook its strong head. Those silky white manes swirled around their necks while their front hooves punched the air.

The children broke into spontaneous applause.

"Are they praising God?" Cristen raised her voice over the clapping.

"Of course!" Abel said, grinning.

"I didn't know animals praised and worshipped God!" remarked Henri.

"Have you never read Revelation chapter five? In verse thirteen it states that *every* creature in Heaven, and on the Earth, and under the Earth, and in the sea will bless the Lord and praise Him!"

"Oh, sure. I guess I just didn't know it really meant it," admitted Henri.

Abel, chuckling, reached over and put his arm around Henri's shoulder, hugging him tightly, "I love your honesty, Henri," he said. "You bless me!"

"Thanks," said Henri, rather sheepishly. He had thought a rebuke was coming and was surprised by the angel's warm gesture. He smiled at Abel and added, "I guess what I meant to say is that I didn't know they would do it like that."

Edgas pointed at Gracie who was now placing both hands on her hips. As soon as she did, the horses obediently dropped down to all fours and waited for her next command.

Oh, how the children wished they could see her face. Cristen was sure Gracie knew each horse by name and was smiling at her equine friends. In finishing, Gracie spread her arms out wide, and those large beasts turned and trotted off, scattering back across the pasture.

Gracie came straight over to meet her audience. Her face glowed with pleasure. She smiled warmly as she introduced herself.

"That was awesome!" Cristen reached over the golden fence and hugged Gracie.

"It sure was!" Masumi agreed, hugging her, too.

"Are you an angel?" asked Edgas.

"No!" Gracie laughed. "I'm just a country girl who loves horses. I can't believe these beautiful animals are mine! How awesome is that? It's the most fun I've ever had."

"They're *yours?*" asked Masumi, incredulously.

"They sure are."

"How did you get them?" asked Edgas.

"I don't know. They were just here with the stables when I arrived. My mansion is right over there behind that grove of trees. The horses and the stable and the Golden Corral and all this pasture came with it."

"That's so cool!" Cristen was glad for Gracie and excited about the implications.

"Your horses look so powerful," said Henri.

"I know! Don't they? Aren't they the biggest things you've ever seen? You can feel their power when you touch them!"

The children could feel Gracie's enthusiasm.

"Won't it be incredible when Jesus rides to Earth on one of these white horses? I just can't wait!"

"Are these *those* horses? The ones that the Bible speaks of?" asked Masumi, looking back and forth from Gracie to Abel.

It was Gracie who answered, "Yes! There are thousands more, scattered in fields all across Heaven, but yep, these are them."

"Is every horse in Heaven white like these are?" asked Edgas.

"Oh, no. There are all kinds of horses, just like back on Earth," said Gracie. "I've even seen horses with rainbow colored manes, but I think these are the grandest of them all."

"They're so," Cristen searched for a word, "so, majestic!"

"Yes, aren't they?" Gracie agreed. "They're fit for a King! The King of Kings, that is! Oh, can't you just picture the King of Kings riding on one of these beauties?"

"Oh my, Yes!" exclaimed Cristen.

"When will Jesus ride one of these beau—" Henri smiled, then changed his word to, "horses?"

"Only the Father knows exactly, but the word around here is *soon*!"

The children looked at Abel with wide, excited eyes; he nodded his head, "Very soon! Very soon, indeed!"

"How would you like to ride?" asked Gracie.

"As in ride one of these beaut—horses?" said Henri with a laugh.

"Really?" said Cristen.

"Oh, yes! May we?" Masumi clasped her hands, and turned pleading eyes towards Abel.

He looked thoughtful and rubbed his chin. Leaning over, he whispered something in Gracie's ear to which she enthusiastically nodded her head. He smiled and said, "I guess our journey can be delayed."

"HURRA!" yelled Edgas.

The others squealed and clapped their hands, faces shining with delight.

Gracie turned and clapped her hands together. Then she called six horses over by name: Come Snowy! August! Come Jazeel! Come Nacre! Come Dominion! Come Mettle! Directly, the magnificent creatures came to the golden fence where the children spent a minute getting to know them by petting and talking to them. In no time, Gracie had decided who should ride on whom and included herself and Abel in the mix. She chose Dominion for Abel, for it was as enormous as he and bore his weight easily.

The children hopped down from the fence and looked up at the horses.

Henri laughed, "Maybe we should mount from the fence."

"I'll give you a lift," Abel offered and was just about to lift Edgas when Cristen asked, "Don't we need saddles?"

"There are saddles in Heaven," answered Gracie, "but you won't need them for these horses." With no further explanation, Abel plopped each rider onto the appropriate horse.

"Now there is nothing to fear, you guys," encouraged Gracie. "You had to die to get here, so don't worry about falling off. Nothing can hurt you now!" Gracie giggled at her joke, but the children found it comforting as they balanced atop these massive stallions.

Before long, the mounted six were trotting, galloping, and cantering all over the pastoral corral. The children looked like they had been riding all their lives, bareback to boot! The horses seemed to be enjoying themselves as much as the children; but the one enjoying himself most of all was Abel. He was swinging an imaginary rope and rustling imaginary cattle. He tipped his imaginary cowboy hat and said, "Howdy do!" every time he passed one of the children.

Unexpectedly, to the children anyway, Abel's horse leaped over the fence with one, swift, fluid movement.

"Come on!" he shouted. The surprised children held fast to a fistful of mane as each of their horses followed Dominion and bounded over the fence, with Gracie and her horse jumping last. You would have thought the children were experienced equestrians the way horse and rider glided effortlessly over the fence.

To their delight, Abel's secret discussion with Gracie had been about leaving the pasture and taking the horses as the transport of choice to their next destination.

They rode through miles and miles of breathtaking countryside and were surprised when they passed sprawling ranch-like mansions situated on fabulous ranch land.

"Do people live out here, too?" Edgas asked as they passed the second ranch-style mansion. "Cuz I'm seeing a lot of big houses, but we're not in a neighborhood anymore."

"Yes, that's true, Edgas; not everyone enjoys city living. These citizens love horses and cattle and wide open spaces."

"That's really awesome," replied Henri.

"There are homes in Heaven to fit every taste and personality. Some folks like the beach—"

"Oh, that would be me!" interrupted Cristen.

Abel smiled, "and some folks like the mountains—"

"Me!" Henri grinned.

"Me, too!" said Edgas.

"Some folks like the jungle—"

"Me, too!" repeated Edgas.

"Not me," laughed Masumi.

"and some like horse ranches."

They all turned and looked at Gracie. She laughed and said, "Me, for sure!"

"Some people like waterfalls, and some like the Savannah—"

"Oh, I change my mind," Edgas laughed, "that's what I like!"

"Can we have more than one mansion?" Cristen smiled. "All of those sound wonderful!"

"Or maybe we can visit each other!" Edgas' eyes brightened. "That way we can stay in all those places. Wouldn't that be fun?"

His friends nodded.

"Did you know that not everyone likes living in a sprawling mansion?"

They shook their heads, no.

"Some people live in sprawling tree houses!"

"Okay, changed my mind, that's me for sure," said Henri.

"Some people live under the water in aqua mansions."

Henri burst out with a laugh, "Me, again!"

"And there are even people from tribal communities who would much rather live in a hut! Of course, their hut would be quite spectacular—made of the finest materials—but these people would rather swing from a hammock than lie in a bed."

"But don't they feel bad when they see someone else's fancy mansion?" asked Edgas, concerned about the fairness of what he was hearing.

"If they want a fancy mansion, Edgas, they will certainly have one. God is not leaving anyone out, neither is he favoring one people group over another. The only favoring done in Heaven is the doling out of lavish rewards to those who faithfully served their Lord on Earth. And that is the Father's good pleasure. Whenever Jesus said, *Great will be your reward*—he meant it."

"I would think some of the things we've seen would freak out someone from an undeveloped, tribal community," said Masumi thoughtfully.

"Yes, indeed it would," Abel chuckled. "It's freaking you children out, and you are all from big cities. Imagine the shock of someone who has never even seen a light bulb."

The children thought about that for a moment.

"Yeah, you're right," said Henri reflectively, "it would totally blow their minds."

"It's blowing my mind, too, but I love it!" laughed Edgas.

"Your Father is gentle. He doesn't just throw His kids headlong into this amazing, supernatural world if they are not quite ready for it. He has places all over Heaven that look like the most perfect version of what some people are used to, and he gradually introduces them to the full measure of His splendor. In fact, He's done the same for you. He's unfolding things to you as you can perceive them, which means, there are still more glories for you to discover on your tour."

The children smiled as they contemplated that.

"And it will take all of eternity for you to discover the things the King has in store for His royal children. And believe me, those things will really blow your mind!"

The children laughed as Abel wiggled his eyebrows.

Reaching a pleasant spot overlooking a fertile plain, Abel announced that it was time to dismount and say goodbye to Gracie and the horses.

"Thank you, Gracie, we've had a wonderful time," Masumi hugged the girl again and then rubbed Snowy on the nose, "and goodbye to you, too! Thank you for the awesome ride." Snowy whinnied, and the group laughed.

"Yes, thank you, Gracie," the others echoed as they, too, patted their horses and hugged Gracie goodbye.

"This was the best day of my life!" Edgas said when he hugged Gracie. "Thank you for letting us ride your horses."

Gracie returned the hug saying, "It was wonderful to meet you all! Come back and ride anytime."

"Thank you, Gracie." Abel said kindly, as she turned to leave.

She grabbed a hold of mane and easily and gracefully swung herself up on top of the horse. *She's aptly named*, thought Cristen, watching the lovely rider with perfect posture hail the other horses and start back for the stables.

"Goodbye! Goodbye!" the children called to Gracie as she rode away with five horses trailing obediently behind. Gracie gave the children a final wave before disappearing around a bend.

Abel turned to face the children. He looked hard into each of their eyes, studying each precious face. He had grown to love them so much. The children, bright-eyed from the fun horseback adventure, stared back into his eyes. It sort of reminded Henri of the stare-games he had played with his friends at school when they stared at each other until someone would blink or turn away. But this time, he was not the least bit uncomfortable and never felt the urge to turn away. The angel's stare was penetrating, like he was reading their minds or even their souls. The children didn't mind, however, for they had nothing to hide, no shame or embarrassment to cover, no secret sin lurking. They were completely free.

Abel's steady gaze filled them with warmth and a deep knowing that they were loved. They were certain he was about to say something profound, they had learned to listen carefully when he had something to say. So, when a twinkle suddenly came into his eyes, and he flashed that row of perfect, pearly whites, they were taken by surprise, but they knew instantly he had another fun surprise in store.

MAPUTO, MOZAMBIQUE
12:32 p.m.

Each time Isabel looked down at the boy in her lap, she could picture his glowing face, and she felt joy rise in her heart. His encounter with the angel was truly the most amazing thing she had ever seen. Part of her wanted to get up and dance a jig, but part of her mourned for the loss of life at such a young age. Her emotions tangled into a mess. She teetered-tottered back and forth from triumphant joy to unbearable grief, but each time the pendulum swung back to grief, it lasted longer until the grief finally overtook and swallowed up the joy. She felt a heaviness press in on her that she had never known and couldn't explain.

"I know he's with you, Lord, so why do I feel so blue?" Her joy had vanished, leaving behind an unbearable ache. She heard herself moaning as she continued to rock the dead child. She clung tightly to Edgas, unready and unwilling to let him go.

NINETEEN

Now to Him who is able to do immeasurably more than all we ask or imagine, according to His power that is at work within us, to Him be glory in the church and in Christ Jesus throughout all generations, forever and ever! Amen. — *Ephesians 3:20-21 (NIV)*

Abel reached over and took Edgas by the hand, sending a powerful, yet painless, electric-like wave through the boy's body.

"Hold hands," he commanded, dwarfing Masumi's petite hand in his other.

Masumi and Cristen joined hands while Edgas grabbed a hold of Henri. The others felt the surge of energy pass through them, as well.

Abel, beaming with a secret, spread his enormous wings behind the children and began to flap them. The four drew a sharp breath of surprise. Off the ground they lifted, rising higher and higher into the crystal sky as their forward motion and speed increased.

They were FLYING! They were flying like a giant bird in the sky. Albeit a very strange looking giant bird but a giant bird nonetheless!

"Ohhh!" Henri yelled, gripping Edgas' hand tightly.

Cristen couldn't speak. She grabbed Masumi's whole arm and squeezed with all her might.

"I had to die to get here, I had to die to get here, I had to die to get here..." Henri repeated, easing himself with Gracie's wisdom.

Cristen thought she might plunge to the ground below if she lost her grip, but then she got tickled listening to Henri and found herself relaxing. None of the children truly felt afraid or even anxious—an impossibility since there's absolutely no fear in Heaven— it was just that their minds had to adjust to the new reality of Heaven-life.

Abel laughed, delightedly. He had a firm grip on Edgas and Masumi, and was very calm about the whole thing. "Cristen and Henri, trust me. You are completely safe. Hold hands just as if you were walking down the street. I promise, I won't let you fall. But even if you did fall, your spiritual bodies can not get hurt."

"I'll try," responded Cristen, loosening her strangle hold on Masumi's arm. "But can I keep my arm linked in hers? Even if I had to die to get here, I'd just feel better out here on the end if I could."

"If it makes you happy."

"Yeah, it totally makes me happy."

Abel grinned.

Henri decided to put Abel's words to the test, quickly discovering that he loved the feeling of flying. "This is so weird!" he yelled to his friends.

"Awesomely weird or weirdly awesome?" Edgas yelled beside him.

"YES!" The group replied with a laugh, including Abel.

Whoosh! Zip! Whoosh! Zip!

Angels traveling at light speed rushed past them in a blur. Several times the group heard the buzz of wings coming from behind, but by the time they realized it, the angels were just a blip of glowing light in the distance.

"Wow!" yelled Henri. "They're so fast!"

The flying group, with Abel at center, continued on hand in hand and arms in arm. By now, Henri was so relaxed that he held his free hand straight out to the side pretending he really was a bird. The wind played with the girls' long hair like kite's tails whipping in a breeze.

They were *flying*—flying with the angels! It was the most exhilarating thing any of them had ever done.

The Eternal City sprawled beneath them as far as they could see in every direction, and their perception of it changed dramatically. The gorgeousness of this dazzling city simply cannot be described. Starbursts of color shot into the atmosphere from the river, and the buildings, and everything else that reflected God's glory.

Everything looked so green from this vantage. Sprawling meadows, pastures, valleys, and lawns were hemmed and bordered by large trees of varying green shades. The golden streets were lined with an endless variety of beautiful trees. The most fascinating of them all were the golden ones, like they had seen in the diamond field. They could now see that large, golden trees were sprinkled throughout the Eternal City. Patches of open fields were splattered with vivid colors. They saw lovely gardens, velvety lawns, beautiful mansions, and everywhere flowering trees, shrubs, and bushes. The city looked alive, and the children believed that somehow it was.

The River of Life was easy to spot as it sparkled and reflected with every twist and turn through the whole land. They could tell from this height that it split into many smaller rivers, streams, tributaries, lakes, and ponds as it brought life giving nourishment to all of Heaven. And over the river, they saw dozens of beautiful, golden footbridges just begging to be crossed.

The River of Life flows straight from the Throne of God recalled Cristen as she gazed upon the sparkling, winding, ribbon. She strained to find its source but did not.

Off in the distance, they noticed a new wonder that covered the entire horizon. It appeared to have movement, like that of water, and it gave off a sparkling rainbow display of such magnitude that it dwarfed the River of Life by comparison.

"What's that over there?" Masumi pointed to the horizon.

"The Crystal Sea," replied Abel.

"The Crystal Sea?" repeated Henri. "What's that?"

"Is it like an ocean?" Cristen turned her gaze to the angel.

"Yes, Cristen, it is exactly like that. The River of Life empties into the Crystal Sea." Masumi gazed at the wonder. "It looks like it's made of a billion diamonds,"

Abel smiled and answered, "You're close. Try multiplying your billions by a few trillions!"

"That's a whole lot of diamonds!" Edgas knew it was a whole lot of diamonds not by the math equation but by the intensity of the flashing.

"Music sounds different up here, Abel. It's like it's traveling with us." Masumi closed her eyes and enjoyed the melodies.

"Or, maybe we're traveling with it!" Edgas offered.

"All worship flows on air currents directly to the Father in His Throne Room," Abel explained. "As a matter of fact," he added with a sly grin, "you don't even need me in order to fly! You can ride across the skies of Heaven on your own worship. It's another heavenly transport, and no matter where you are, it can take you straight to the Throne Room."

"How in the world is that possible?" It made no sense to Henri.

"Henri, you keep forgetting we're not in the world!" laughed Edgas.

"It's supernatural, right Abel?" Masumi thought it one of the most marvelous things she'd heard since coming to Heaven.

Abel winked at Masumi and nodded affirmatively.

"Is it like traveling on light beams?" asked Cristen. "That doesn't make sense to me either, but that didn't stop us from doing it!"

"Almost exactly like that."

"Well, should we let go of each other, then?" Henri suddenly felt brave.

"You can if you want to. You're perfectly safe."

Masumi and Cristen's eyes grew wide.

"Although, you might want to worship first. Remember it's the worship that carries you. It doesn't have to be a song, but that's generally a good place to start."

Henri began to sing with the chorus of music that filled the atmosphere. As soon as he did, a cloud-like misty ribbon flowed out from his being and floated under him.

The group gasped. That had not happened before. Perhaps it was the new unfolding of glories that Abel had just told them about.

Excitedly, the others burst into songs and watched as three more wispy ribbons swirled from within them and drifted below.

With the faith of a child, Henri said, "Well, we had to die to get here," and immediately let go of Edgas' hand. He dropped a little, and his speed slowed considerably, but he remained suspended in the air, buoyed on the wispy worship ribbon.

"Look! I'm flying!"

The group quickly turned to watch Henri. He was hovering behind them flapping his arms with all his might. "This is *way* cool!" he shouted. "You guys should try it!"

"You don't need to flap, Henri. It makes you look weird. And no, Edgas, not awesomely weird." Abel laughed with the children at his own joke.

Henri quit flapping and found that he still floated in the air. It took him a moment to figure out his balance, but before long, he got the hang of hanging out in the sky. He realized that he only needed to sit back and relax, but it was much more fun to pretend to fly.

Abel turned the group around and flew them back to Henri. "All right, who's joining Henri? Now is as good a time to learn to fly as any."

Edgas was next. He stretched out his toe, trying to feel for a solid footing. Finding the wispy cloud to be just that, wispy, he closed his eyes, took a deep breath, and dropped Abel's hand.

"HURRA!" He dropped into the wisp and it caught him. He knew not to flap his arms and quickly figured out how to stay balanced. The wisp of worship carried him along on invisible air currents, just like it did Henri.

"I don't believe it! I'm flying!" Edgas shouted.

"Believe it!" replied Abel.

"I can't believe I'm going to do this," laughed Cristen, closing her eyes.

"Let's do it together," Masumi suggested.

"Great idea! On the count of three. Ready?" Masumi nodded, and the girls counted together, "One, two, three!"

"WHEEEEE!" they shrieked, dropping hands. The wispy ribbons caught them, too, and, wonder of wonders, they hung in the air with the angel and the boys.

"How is this possible?" asked Cristen, bright eyes replacing her shocked look.

"I should be scared silly, but I love it!" Masumi smiled as the suspended group leisurely moved along with the air currents.

"I feel like Superman!" Henri stretched out in a Superman pose.

"I feel like Superwoman!" Cristen copied his pose.

"I feel like a bird!" Edgas flapped imaginary wings, then quickly turned to Abel and added, "I'm just flappin' to be a bird."

"I'm an angel." Masumi flapped her arms then whispered to Edgas, "Don't worry, Buddy, we don't look weird!"

"Look at me; I'm a fish," Henri puckered his lips and "swam" around the group. There was an eruption of laughter.

The group, with Abel as teacher, quickly learned how to float on invisible air currents—buoyed by worship—like a sailboat crossing the sea.

"This is by far the coolest thing I have ever done." Henri's smile could not have been any wider.

When the children passed over some people out walking, Edgas shouted down to them, "Look, everybody, I'm a bird!" The people broke into smiles and waved up at the children. "Oh, Abel," he squealed, "this is the most fun I have ever had!"

"I thought it was riding the horses," he teased.

"Yes, well, no, what I said then was that this was the best *day* of my life, and it still is, cuz it just keeps on getting better and better!"

"Yeah, it does," Henri agreed.

Drifting along, they continued to observe the busy city below, waving and calling to everyone within earshot until at last Abel spread his wings and said, "All right, kiddos, hold hands again; we're picking up the pace."

The children grabbed hands as they had done before, and with a few quick thrusts of those mighty wings, the strange-looking bird was soaring once more across the electric-blue sky.

In no time, they flew to the top of a large grassy hill and landed softly. Abel quietly folded his wings behind him and walked towards the crest of the hill. The very exhilarated kids bounded after him like happy little ducklings. Near the top of the hill, they discovered another beautiful, columned, marker-gate. Edgas grinned at the sight of it. He decided he better follow his leader through it this time, just in case it, too, was the entrance to a new dimension.

"Look, it says Valley of Forgiveness" noticed Masumi. "I wonder what this place is going to be?" The others nodded, all curiosities peaked.

They quietly passed through the gate, saw that they were in the same dimension, and then took the last few steps to the top of the hill. Looking down the grassy slope, they saw a very large valley situated between two hills. There was a blur of activity below, and as was becoming customary, their mouths dropped open. They watched the activity in stunned amazement.

Abel loved their surprised faces and threw his head back and shook with laughter.

"You're kidding us, right?" Henri said, as he and the others took in the surprising sight with wide eyes.

MAPUTO, MOZAMBIQUE
UNSEEN REALM

The impish demon did not buzz off but continued his poisonous rant. But even under this attack, Isabel worshipped, her song ascending to the heavenlies.

The missionary felt old and weary, wondering if she was doing any good here in Mozambique. Wondering if she should go home. Wondering if she did anything that mattered, anything that made a difference.

Michale knew those were her thoughts because those were the lies spewing out of the foul demon's mouth.

"I can't go on like this," belched the demon. "I'm so tired. I'm so very tired. This is just too hard. What's the point? I need to go home. They all die anyway. My heart can't take anymore. My heart is breaking. I'm done. It's too hard."

Suddenly, there was a rift in the room, and it was flooded with a bright Light, chock full of dazzling, colorful, glitter-like bits. The Light poured over Isabel, and although she could not see it, she felt its presence. God Himself, the One Who is Light, was answering Isabel's prayers from His throne!

Oh good, her tears have reached The Great One. Michale could not stop his grin.

The hideous demon shrieked in fear and agony, as though in great pain, and fled from the Almighty's presence. The pompous pest was gone, at least for the moment.

The Light of the World began to minister hope and truth to Isabel's spirit.

Michale stood with Isabel in the river of Light, face upward, drinking it in. Oh, how he missed being in the Throne Room! He raised his hands in worship, glad of heart for the refreshment.

Suddenly, the Fire of the Holy Spirit within Isabel began to burn many times brighter. The Fire expanded until it filled every square inch of her being, from the top of her head to the tips of her toes. He surged from her and joined the Light, intertwining into an inseparable dance. Michale watched the Light and Fire merge as One in perfect unity, as he had so many times in eternity past. The Holy presence of the God-Head filled the atmosphere with electrifying power. Michale bowed His head and went down on one knee.

Then the dance of Light and Fire circled the guardian, wrapping around him once. Michale felt a surge of energy, and instantly his strength was renewed.

"Thank you, your Majesty. Thank you, Holy Spirit," he whispered. "All honor and glory and praise belong to You!"

Michale worships with Isabel

TWENTY

But Stephen, full of the Holy Spirit, looked up to Heaven and saw the glory of God, and Jesus standing at the right hand of God. "Look," he said, "I see Heaven open and the Son of Man standing at the right hand of God." While they were stoning him, Stephen prayed, "Lord Jesus, receive my spirit." Then he fell on his knees and cried out, "Lord, do not hold this sin against them." When he had said this, he fell asleep. — Acts 7: 55-56, 59-60 (NIV)

A sparkling brook wriggled its way through the entire valley spilling into a shimmering pond. Wide paths and little trails wound their way through beautiful tall trees. Benches and picnic tables were dotted along the babbling brook while little footbridges crossed it here and there, and, as always, flowers of every color adorned the whole scene.

This stunning valley was home to the most state-of-the-art playground ever fashioned, abounding with the tallest slides which twisted and turned down the sides of the hills; the highest swings which could flip completely over the top if the rider desired; the fastest merry-go-rounds and spinners; the biggest jungle gyms complete with trapezes, monkey bars, platforms, bridges, curlicue slides, and shiny "firefighter" poles to slide down; and seesaws, which could catapult the rider high into the air if they chose to do so. The playground was constructed in bright colors and creative designs, and each piece represented a different Bible story.

Besides the *usual* playground equipment, there were many *unusual* and quite supernatural apparatuses to climb, ride, and play on, and they, too, were done in a Bible motif.

In the heart of the valley, an enormous, old-fashioned but extremely high-tech, carousel with intricately carved animals riding two-by-two in a Noah's Ark theme took center stage beckoning the younger children to come and play. These carousel animals did more than slide up and down a pole while ever circling on a platform. In fact, there was no pole at all! They were untethered to buck and hop and fly and spin. The playing children squealed with delight and held on tightly for they never knew which way their mount would go.

In the pond was a whale which opened its large mouth to "swallow" children, and then it blasted them high into the air through its waterspout, Jonah style. The water fount kept them aloft, tossing them up and down in the air like a cartoon character, until at last it would drop them on its back where they would slide down the tail and splash into the pond. The squeals were hard evidence that the children absolutely loved it.

The park was also home to plenty of fun activities for teenagers. There was an enormous rock-climbing wall, high and quite treacherous, erected up the side of a hill. There were large trees just right for climbing, with fabulous tree houses in some of them. High suspension bridges connected paths from tree to tree. There were tunnels and caves to explore. A challenge ropes-style course was suspended high above the park in some of the tallest trees, and zip lines which soared overhead were at least a mile long each. There were bouncing areas where the ground itself was springy like a trampoline, and a giant maze made of beautiful lush green hedges sprawled for acres. There were giant puzzles and life-size games that used children as game pieces. There were kick ball games, dodge ball games, T-ball games, soccer games, and football games all being played on different fields. There were basketball courts, tennis courts, volleyball courts, racquetball courts, handball courts, and badminton courts. Over near the forest was the largest skatepark ever constructed where impossible skateboard tricks were possible. And best of all—no safety equipment was required for anything! The children were perfectly safe and able to run and jump and climb and play without fear.

And children there were! This wonderful playground was filled with running, skipping, laughing, giggling, playing, climbing, happy, squealing children. There were thousands of them, yet so large was this park that it didn't seem crowded or chaotic. The happiness was palpable and electrified the air.

Surprised expressions slid into ginormous smiles as Henri, Cristen, Edgas, and Masumi watched from their perch in amazement. They turned to Abel for an explanation.

"Behold," Abel opened his arms out wide in a dramatic gesture, "the *Valley of Forgiveness*."

"Valley of Forgiveness? That's a weird name for a playground!"

Edgas snickered at Henri's continued use of the word weird.

"There are many other wonderful playgrounds in Heaven, Henri. This one has a special name for a special reason."

The children turned and looked at Abel, waiting to hear the reason.

"All of these children are experiencing the joy of forgiving someone."

"Where did all these children come from, Abel?"

"From all over the Earth, Masumi. Most of these children never had a chance to play before coming to Heaven. Some came before they were even born."

"What?" Cristen said, surprised. "Really? Some of these children were never born?"

"Yes, really," answered Abel. "Some of these were aborted, some were miscarried, and some of them died by accident, illness, or evil intent."

Abel's troop looked shocked.

"Did you know that the very instant a baby is conceived, the Lord knits a spirit to that itty-bitty dot of flesh?"

The children shook their heads, no.

"That is the reason life begins at conception. There is no debate here in Heaven."

"But I don't see any itty-bitty babies down there," said Edgas.

"You're right, Edgas. Infants are not playing in this park, not yet anyway. Immediately upon an infant's earthly death, whether it's by abortion, miscarriage, or other health reason, the infant's spirit is carried to Heaven by his or her guardian angel. Whatever size the baby is at the moment of earthly death, so is the spirit. Many times the baby is unimaginably tiny—the fashioning of its physical body has not yet been completed, but the baby's spiritual body is perfect and perfectly complete! It's a wonder to behold such a teeny person." Abel held his hand out as if holding a baby in his palm.

"It's hard for me to picture such a tiny, fully developed child," Masumi said, looking at her own opened palm. The others nodded their agreement.

Abel continued with eyes that spoke of the pleasure he felt at what he was describing. "Upon arriving in Heaven, the infant spirits are taken to one of Heaven's many nurseries where they are loved and nurtured by special angels who cuddle them and sing to them and love them just like a parent would. These delightful nurseries are filled with the peace and joy of God. Bathed in a peachy glow, they are shaped much like a bee-hive with high, opened roofs. Fragrant flowers grow on the walls, and songbirds fly in and out, perch on the floral branches, and sing sweet melodies to the happy babies. Little fawns come in from the meadow and take groups of babies for rides on their backs, and—you'll think this is funny—kangaroos will come in and take groups of babies for rides, too."

"Like in their pouches?" asked Henri, with questioning eyes.

Abel smiled and nodded as his charges laughed at the picture in their minds. "The babies love it, and it's kind of adorable to see those little faces peeking out of the pouches."

"Where do they sleep? Are there cribs in there?"

"These babies don't need to sleep, Masumi, but they do rest when they're not playing or being rocked or cuddled. Their tiny beds are made from beautiful seashells lined with mother-of-pearl, and they're soft and luxurious. The shells are situated all over the walls, in little niches, and the baby's name hangs over each bed embellished on lovely ribbons for girls and on stately shields for boys."

"Oh, what a special place. I would *love* to see one of those nurseries," cooed Cristen.

"Indeed you would! They are one of the most beautiful, special places in all of Heaven. And sadly, they are also one of the most populated places in all of Heaven." The angel's face reflected great sorrow. "Every discarded child is there; Heaven never loses or forgets even one of them."

Brightening, Abel continued, "But the wonderful news is that Jesus heals the babies' wounded hearts. They know exactly who their parents are, they forgive them wholeheartedly, and all they want is for their parents to join them here one day. And amazingly, if the parent is a follower of Jesus, they will not only come to live in Heaven, but they will also get to raise their baby because God will let that baby grow ever so slowly. If the parent wanted to raise a newborn, they will be handed a newborn. If the parent envisions a toddler, there will be a toddler awaiting them."

The children were stunned.

"Your God is unfathomably gracious, loving, and merciful. He wants the restoration and healing of families. He is ready and willing to forgive, and He gives the parents a second chance to raise their baby! How's that for unmerited forgiveness? God is not sitting on His throne with a big stick, ready to strike. No, quite the contrary, His arms are wide-opened, ready to embrace the humble."

"Who names the babies?"

"Good question, Edgas. No child is ever just a number in Heaven, so if the parent hasn't named their baby, the angels give them a nickname. But, if a parent does name their baby, even if it's thirty, forty, fifty years later, there is joyous celebration in Heaven when that baby is presented its name!"

"Do the angels have to change diapers?" Henri pinched his nose.

His friends laughed, and Abel laughed with them. "No, Henri. Heaven's babies don't need diapers! No waste, remember?"

"So, the babies aren't ever alone or lonely?" asked Masumi.

"Never! Sometimes a grandparent or close relative will watch over the child until the parent arrives in Heaven. And what a joyous reunion that day is! Some women have lost babies and didn't even know they were pregnant. Imagine their surprise and great joy when they get to Heaven and meet children they never knew existed. Like I said, the Lord allows these baby spirits to remain very young so that the parent can raise the child here in Heaven. You see, the enemies of God can never steal those very precious destinies."

"What if the parents don't follow Jesus?" A concerned Edgas asked.

"The Omniscient One knows if the child's parents will join him or her here. You need to know that it is His desire that all would come here, but if those parents choose to turn from Him, He will let that little spirit go ahead and mature into a young man or woman."

"But if they were aborted, aren't they mad at their parents? Do they really want to see them?" asked Masumi.

"Yes," added Cristen. "What if they were murdered or abused?"

"That is a very good question, girls. Look down there; do those children look mad?"

"No! They sure don't!" laughed Masumi.

"They're the happiest children I've ever seen!" said Edgas.

"That's right, Edgas. When the infants reach a certain maturity, they go through a ceremony to forgive their parents or the one that mistreated or abused them, and then they invite Jesus into their hearts just like you do on Earth. From that point on, they begin declaring over their parents to know Jesus so that they will be reunited with them forever."

"Oh, I get it! That's why this is called the Valley of Forgiveness!" exclaimed Cristen.

"Yes, Cristen; all the children you see down there have forgiven those who harmed them on Earth. Some of these you see were not abused in any way but died of sickness or disease. They, too, have learned to walk in forgiveness."

"What do you mean?"

"Well, Henri, sometimes we need to extend forgiveness to our situations and to those who weren't able to prevent those situations from happening. For instance, some of these children were crippled or sick on Earth,"

"Like me?" interrupted Edgas.

"Yes, dear Edgas, just like you." The angel smiled warmly at the boy.

"And there are others who never had the chance to play. Many, because of tragic situations, are forced to grow up way too soon, and they miss their childhood. Here, they can spend the day running and leaping and playing and just being children! They never think about the past, either the pain of how they lived or the pain of how they died; they just enjoy their new life to the fullest. Oh, if you only knew how much the Father loves His children and what pleasure He takes in them! Life is not fair, but be assured—God is!"

"I never even imagined that there would be such a playground in Heaven." said Masumi.

"Me neither," said Cristen, "but I think it's wonderful, absolutely wonderful!"

"Well, are we just gonna stand here and talk about it, or do we wanna go play?" Abel's playful eyes sparkled.

The children looked at him, surprised.

"Really?" asked Henri.

"Do you *really* need to keep asking me 'really'?" answered the laughing angel.

"HURRA!" cried Edgas, as the ecstatic group took off running down the hill.

Quickly reaching one of the hilltop slides, they jumped on, even Abel, and went twisting, turning, and squealing with delight all the way down to the Valley of Forgiveness.

TOKYO, JAPAN
7:45 p.m.

The policeman, carrying both backpacks, led Michi and Mr. Ninomiya to the only empty seats in the ER waiting room and bid them sit while he went over and spoke to the woman at the reception desk. So despondent was Michi that he didn't see her glance at a chart and shake her head sadly. The officer handed the woman what little information he had on the girl, found in her backpack: namely her name and telephone number. They discussed the fact that the young girl's brother would be waiting here for the parents to arrive. She looked with pity at the distraught young boy covered in blood.

Officer Tsukahira lumbered back feeling very uncomfortable. He awkwardly patted the boy on the shoulder. "I'm sorry," he said. When the boy didn't respond he looked over at Mr. Ninomiya and shook his head to indicate that the receptionist had not given good news, and then he sat down beside him.

The three sat silently together; the tension could be cut with a knife. After a few more awkward minutes of silence, the officer slapped his knees then stood quickly to his feet, saying, "I've got to go now."

Mr. Ninomiya immediately stood to his feet, and the two men bowed to each other. "Thank you for coming, Mr. Ninomiya."

"I am happy to do it, Officer Tsukahira."

"I found his identification in his backpack; his name is Michitaka. The police department has contacted his parents, and they should be here shortly."

Michi, for the first time, tuned in to what the officer was saying. He needed his parents more than anything in the world, and yet he could not bear to face them. How could he, knowing that Masumi's death was his fault? *They will never forgive me.* He would never forgive himself for that matter. He wanted to get up and run but where? There was nowhere to go. He would sit and wait—helplessly, shamefully—for them to come.

"I must go now, Michitaka," said the officer, interrupting his thoughts. "Here is my card; please let me know if there is anything I can do for you."

Michi looked at the officer, albeit with a blank face, but he reached up and took the card. The officer hesitated, then he bowed deeply, turned, and made a beeline for the exit, leaving Michi alone to wait for his parents. Well, not completely alone. For some unknown reason, there was a complete stranger sitting next to him, keeping him company, or perhaps just watching him wallow in his grief and sorrow; and there was an entire roomful of people, waiting and watching. But he had never felt so alone in his life; he was alone with his dread, alone with his shame, and alone with his grief, as he waited to face his parents.

TWENTY-ONE

I tell you the truth, anyone who will not receive the kingdom of God like a little child will never enter it. — Mark 10:15 (NIV)

Edgas, Henri, Cristen, Masumi, and Abel spilled from the slides and were immediately accosted by enthusiastic welcomes from dozens of happy children dressed in colorful play-clothes; many of whom stopped their play to welcome the new faces.

The children stayed close to Abel at first, walking with him towards a large pond where little toddlers were at play. Ducks paddled in and out of the splashing children, and the clear water afforded delightful views of brightly colored fish swimming around little legs and ankles.

It was almost humorous to watch these little ones play because they were as coordinated and able as children much older. It was impossible for them to get hurt, so their fearlessness took some getting used to. The girls' instincts were to run protect them or scoop them up when they went under the water, but the little ones would pop right back up laughing and squealing with glee.

Two small turtles swam by with toddlers riding on their backs.

"I'm not believing what I'm seeing," Masumi shook her head.

"Yeah, it's so weird," murmured Henri, and then quickly added, "and cool."

Several toddlers jumped out of the pond and stepped on a small circle of light. Instantly, a small rainbow appeared and arced right into the pond. The little ones shimmied up the rainbow, and then slid down it like a slide.

The four visitors were speechless.

It was apparently a favorite activity, for more joined them and the group of squealing toddlers slid down that rainbow, into the pond, over and over and over again.

Abel found a spot at the pond's edge under a lovely tree and sat back to watch the playful tots. Taking off his sandals, he dangled his large feet in the water and laughed at the little one's antics.

Not interested in sitting, this was the group's cue to part from their tour guide.

"Where do we even start?" Cristen wondered, as she and the others goggled at all the fun things to do.

"I think this is our first problem in Heaven," chortled Henri.

A group of lively children, seeing the new arrivals just standing there, ran over and began pulling them around by the hand, excited to show the visitors their park.

Some boys about Edgas' age invited him to play; he looked at his friends for permission to abandon them. "Go!" they said enthusiastically.

"HURRA!" He trotted backwards and called to his friends, "I've never seen so many wonderful things to do!" Then he turned and ran off with the other boys; he was both literally and figuratively—in Heaven!

Baby animals roamed the valley just waiting to be petted. It seemed their sole purpose was to bring pleasure to these children. Romping here, there, and everywhere were puppies, kittens, lambs, goats, piglets, chicks, ducklings, bunnies, bear cubs, lion cubs, calves, ponies, and even baby elephants! The girls would have stopped to snuggle each one of them but for the tugging of eager children on their arms.

Angels were everywhere, playing and interacting with the multitude of children. Many of the angels were without wings and looked just like children themselves. The visitors only guessed they were angels because of the way they glowed, and their new friends confirmed it. What happy playmates they were for the little ones, much less intimidating than the nine-foot-tall variety. It amazed the sojourners to think of how kind God must be to care so tenderly for even the youngest of heavenly residents.

Angels were pushing swings and playing games like hopscotch, catch, and kickball; angels were playing hide and seek and chasing giggling children; and angels were sliding down slides and climbing in trees and on jungle gyms. Scores of children and scores of angels skipped rope, rode bikes and scooters, played tag, ran through mazes, and played dodge ball. Giggles and laughs intermixed with squeals of delight, and the happy sounds resounded through the park.

In the midst of all the activity, Edgas felt certain he saw that angel from before, watching him. Again, he was peeking at him from behind a tree. Edgas ran over to investigate and found nothing but playful children. *Hmmm, that's weird*, he thought, in his best Henri fashion.

Soon the shouts and giggles of the four visitors blended with the shouts and giggles of the residents as they, too, ran and climbed and tossed and hid and explored and played all over the Valley Of Forgiveness. They soon discovered that some of the ways children play in Heaven is, plainly put, supernatural. One of these supernatural games was inside a large glass atrium. When children entered the atrium, a giant bubble, twice the size of the children, enveloped them and carried them up high in the air. The children could run inside their bubbles and bump into each other, all the while giggling with glee; and when they tired of this game, they would simply pop their bubble and float back down to the floor.

Abel's guests were having a blast going from one thing to another. Masumi wanted to explore the tree houses while Cristen wanted to go to the rock-climbing wall. The girls agreed to do both of these fun things together. When they skipped off to climb the trees, Henri decided it was a good time to check out the skatepark. It was over 300,000 square feet of white marble-like material. There were four different areas for four different levels of skill—a practice course for warming up or getting your skate legs; a beginner street course with small technical obstacles like ledges, flatbars, and stairs; an intermediate course with a perimeter track of bigger stairs, rails and ledges and a twelve-foot-deep bowl that weaved its way through the center like a winding river; and an advanced obstacle course which included a giant cloverleaf bowl, a street course, and a massive fullpipe. The cohesive design of the park allowed skaters to flow from obstacle to obstacle without having to step off their boards.

Henri loved to skateboard but never felt very proficient. He watched the other boys and girls and couldn't get over the tricks they could do. One boy flew by and landed a perfect 360-flip—he kicked the board horizontally 360 degrees, it rolled over itself once, and then the boy landed right back on it and kept going. Henri applauded.

"Come carve with us!" shouted one of the boys. "It's fun!"

The boy brought a skateboard over to Henri, "Here, you can use mine."

"Really? Gee, thanks!" said Henri. "This is a really cool design on your board."

"Thanks! I made it myself!"

"That's impressive."

"Oh, it was easy! You can make one, too. I'll help."

"Well, that would be awesome, but I'm just visiting. Thanks though."

"No problemo, I'll be glad to help you whenever you come back."

"Even if I'm not a kid anymore?"

"Hey, everyone gets to be a kid in Heaven! Anyway, you ready to carve?"

"I guess now that I have a board, I don't have an excuse! Let's go." He smiled at the boy, took the proffered skateboard, and carried it to the practice area; gingerly he stepped on the board and quickly discovered that he could keep his balance quite easily. He pushed with one foot and picked up some speed; then placing both feet on the board he began to move his body in a front to back motion to build his momentum and keep it up. Other boys came over to offer him some tips and pointers.

Henri stayed on the practice course until his confidence was buoyed, then he headed out to the beginner course, helmet*less* and knee and elbow pad*less,* just like the other children. He soon found he could do ollies, kickflips, and heelflips, all with very little bailing. He did fall a couple of times, but it never hurt, and it never left even so much as a scratch on him. He was sure his brain would eventually register the fact that he could not get hurt, but it would take some getting used to.

Moving on to the intermediate course, Henri quickly realized he had lots more learning to do. Others were zipping and carving all around him, doing railstands, fakies, rock and rolls, 180s, 360s, and grinds—they twisted and turned, flipped and jumped, and seemed to fly as they easily maneuvered many amazing tricks. Henri felt sure that if he could come back here every day, he would quickly learn to do them, too.

A hint of sadness fell over him thinking about leaving Heaven. He looked around, drew in a big breath, and in his best Arnold Schwarzenegger voice thought, *I'll be back.* He let out a contented sigh and joyfully took off for another run.

TOKYO, JAPAN
UNSEEN REALM

Darkness covered the ER waiting room like a shroud. A repulsive spirit of Fear was pacing above the waiting room, his sharp, evil eyes overseeing everything. Despair, Pain, Hopelessness, Infirmity, and a host of others were all whispering lies and inflicting pain into the minds and bodies of the men and women in that room. The smell was rancid, a vile mixture of feces, blood, and death.

Some of the people in the room were covered in green slime, a sign to those in the spiritual realm that the person had fallen into a sin. The person had either gone somewhere they shouldn't have been, or watched something they shouldn't have watched, and when they did, a demon had vomited on them, coating their spiritual bodies with a nasty, foul-smelling, slime. No matter where they went, every demon within eyesight would know that this person had fallen and that they were vulnerable to temptation. The mark was an open invitation for more demons to harass the person—easy prey—as they saw it. Sadly, with enough slime hardening over a human spirit, the heart grows stony and cold to the things of God. But every angel knew that a simple prayer of repentance would wash away every trace of that nasty slime, and the King of Heaven could turn a stony heart back into a heart of flesh.

Failure entered the room, clinging to his human assignment and intent on his mission. Fuming with rage, born of his own fear of torture, he turned up the heat and bombarded Michi with accusations. He was so focused on destroying Michi that he took little notice of the other demons tormenting their own human assignments. But they took note of him. He came barreling into their domain with a loud voice both irritating and grating.

They bristled at the sight of him, annoyed before he had been there fifteen seconds. Failure's determination, however, as disagreeable as it was, raised the intensity level in the entire waiting room as demon began to compete against demon. Before long, the room was frenzied with the wretched rantings and ravings of the Kingdom of Darkness.

The angel of light sat quietly, hidden from the view of the demons, waiting for his opportunity to minister truth. If the demons had been paying any attention, they would have seen that this lone man had no spiritual being assigned to him, angel or demon, in stark contrast to every other human in the room. But they were too absorbed in their own work and too interested in impressing their neighbor to notice.

Failure continued his relentless barrage of lies to convince Michi to kill himself. It was sickening. And Raphia hated listening to the putrid poison. He knew that Michi was listening, though. He'd believed he was an idiot for a long time, and Failure was expertly twisting the lies to sound like valid reasons for Michi to give up, to quit, to throw in the towel. Raphia patiently waited, though. He knew he would be victorious for, Glory To God, the victory had already been won.

TWENTY-TWO

However, as it is written: "No eye has seen, no ear has heard, no mind has conceived what God has prepared for those who love him," but God has revealed it to us by His spirit. The spirit searches all things, even the deep things of God. — 1 Corinthians 2:9-10 (NIV)

Bursting with fun facts, Edgas, Cristen, Masumi and Henri bombarded Abel with elated accounts they had gleaned about Heaven from the other children.

"Fletcher said you can swim with dolphins in the Crystal Sea and that some people's homes have portals in them where they can jump in and out of the sea whenever they want to and swim with the dolphins and the whales and the sharks and when you get out of the water," Edgas' eyes widened for emphasis, "you're already dry, even your clothes! And, I almost forgot, he said you can breathe underwater, too!"

"The kids at the skatepark were talking about the sea, too. Zac said people wake board and water ski in it all the time. And, oh yeah, he said there's an awesome place to go surfing where the waves are unbelievably high. It's called, get this, 'Wipe Out!'"

"Wipe Out? That sounds dangerous." Masumi looked at Abel to corroborate this story; she couldn't imagine surfing in a place with that name.

Abel nodded his head affirmatively while Henri answered, "I know, but he said it's not, 'cause you can't get hurt, but you still feel the excitement like in the skatepark."

"Yeah, remember what Gracie said!" Edgas chimed in. "We had to die to get here. And, oh! Alden told me he rode on a huge sailing ship to a *real* island and went on a *real* treasure hunt with a *real* treasure map and a *real* pirate, but the pirate loves Jesus and everything just like you said, Abel!" Abel smiled and winked at Edgas.

"Some kids were talking about the Safari in Expedition Park but instead of riding on elephants, like we did, they rode on the lions and giraffes." Masumi said, thinking it might be kinda scary.

"Hey, do you think I could ride on Aslan?" Edgas turned an excited face to Abel. "He was a friendly lion, wasn't he Henri? I would ride him, wouldn't you, Henri?"

Henri nodded, "I sure would, Edgas."

"Well, get this," Cristen offered, "I heard there's an amusement park with huge rides! Lindsay said she rode on a ginormous roller coaster with her brother, and the cars leap from track to track in the middle of the ride!"

She had their full attentions.

"What? There're roller coasters here? You gotta be kiddin' me! That is totally awesome!" Henri was floored.

"Really, Abel, roller coasters?" Masumi turned to the angel again, and again he corroborated the story with a nod.

"It's true, Masumi, and angels like to ride it, too! You should see them raise their hands and scream, just like the people do!"

"I can't get over this place. I just had no idea," Masumi shook her head, "no idea at all. I still can't believe that I thought Heaven would be boring."

"Where does creativity come from, Masumi?" asked Abel.

"That's easy—from God."

"He is the Creator of all things, is He not?" The children nodded.

"Therefore, everything you have on Earth had to have its origin from the Creator, right?"

"I see where this is going," laughed Cristen. "So, if we have roller coasters and other fun things on Earth, why wouldn't those things be in Heaven where the Creator Himself lives. Is that what you're driving at?"

"Yes, dear student. That is *exactly* what I'm driving at." He smiled at Cristen. "Always remember, kiddos, Earth is a shadow of Heaven not the other way around. If you have it there, it was surely here first."

"And it's much better in Heaven cuz you can't get hurt," Edgas added with a definitive nod.

The children were almost giddy with happiness.

"Anything else you learned about Heaven from your friends?"

"Oh, tons!" Masumi smiled. "Jordan said her dad has an ice cream shop, and you can go anytime you want. There are no 'after you eat your dinner' rules. And she said there are all kinds of restaurants with all kinds of delicious food to eat."

"Ohhh, can we get some ice cream, Abel?" Edgas' eyes lit up like stars.

"A boy named Tucker told me about the movie theaters that you mentioned earlier, Abel, where people can be the actors in the movie if they want." Henri wiggled his eyebrows, "And best of all, he said you don't even have to rehearse because as soon as your foot hits the set, you automatically know your lines. He said there are many things in Heaven that you just know."

"I think it would be fun to be a real actress," Cristen smiled. "Maybe when we all come back, we should be in a movie together!"

"That's a great idea, Cristen!" Masumi smiled approvingly while the others nodded their agreement.

"Hey, did you know they play all kinds of sports here, too?" Henri said. "My new friend, Barrett, was leaving the skatepark to go play in a basketball tournament. He said that the teams are competing to see who can stack up the most points for Jesus! Barrett said he's the captain of a championship team, and I can play with them if I want when I come back! I liked him a lot; he was cool."

"Boy, that ice cream sure sounds good!" Edgas licked his lips dramatically.

"Oh, Abel," Cristen spoke up, "I also heard that there are places where it snows all the time, and you can go skiing and sledding and snowboarding! I'm sure it is, but— is it true?"

"But of course! And you can drink hot chocolate and ice skate there, too."

"And eat ice cream?" said the child who had only tasted ice cream once in his whole life.

"Here's something else you may not know, children. There are many, many beautiful places all over Heaven, and when God made Earth, He chose four of His favorites and put them on Earth as a season. But in Heaven, those places are not a season; they exist all the time."

"You mean there's a place where it's always winter?" asked Cristen and then to be funny added, "and never Christmas?"

"Oh, that's from *Narnia*!" laughed Henri.

"Yes, Cristen. But believe me, we certainly celebrate Christmas here! You just wait and see how many gifts are given in celebration of the greatest gift ever given!"

The children grinned.

"And," continued Abel, "there're places where it's always fall, always spring, and always summer."

"I love that!"

"So, if you want to enjoy a ski vacation, you could go to the winter place any time?" Henri asked.

"That's exactly right," Abel answered. "And families go there to have fun together all the time."

"I heard there are concerts all over Heaven," Masumi added, excitedly. "Aidi told me that if you always wanted to be in a band and play the guitar or drums or sing or something, you can be in a band and even perform on a stage, and people rock out if they want, and the old people—who don't look old—don't mind it because they're young now, but they can be in a band, too, if they want, and the bands can play whatever kind of music they like."

"Did someone say ice cream?" Edgas had a hard time keeping a straight face. He really was listening to the others, but he couldn't get the thought of eating delicious ice cream off his mind.

"Erica's mother loves to garden, so she's making a beautiful secret garden just for her and her mother." Cristen's eyes grew misty as she thought of the darling little girl she met. "It's the gift she'll give her mom when she comes to live here. She said she planted her mother's favorite flowers and one of the varieties in her garden actually sings."

"Oh, I would love to do that for my mother," Henri said. She loves flowers, too. Maybe not a secret place for her and me, but maybe a secret place for her and Alison. Hmm, if I get back before they do, I just might do that for them."

"Then you'll like this tidbit, Henri. Erica also said that if you dig in the ground to plant flowers and stuff, your hands won't even get dirty because as soon as you pull your hands out, they're perfectly clean!"

"I heard that, too," added Masumi, "and just like Abel told us in the cottage, you *never* have to take a bath or shower unless you want to, just for pleasure!"

"It seems like you can do just about anything you want in Heaven," Henri commented.

"What *can't* you do here, Abel?" Cristen asked, curiously.

"Oh, there's lots you can't do!"

The group looked at Abel, surprised. He grinned and added, "You can't feel pain, get hurt, or hurt others; you can't be sad or mad or in a bad mood; you can't give in to temptation or entertain evil thoughts; and you can't be selfish, critical, judgmental, argumentative, or just plain mean."

The kids chuckled.

He winked at them, adding, "Not a bad trade, wouldn't you agree?"

Agreed!" they shouted together.

"I know another thing you can't do here," Cristen smiled at the group. "You can't get bored!"

"Jeepers, I'm with you, Masumi, I still can't believe I thought Heaven would be boring!" Henri shook his head. "This is anything *but* boring!"

"There are many differences between Heaven and Earth, dear ones, but remember what I told you before? On Earth you make a living in order to exist—in Heaven you exist *to live*! This is why you were created—to enjoy your God! Your Heavenly Father created this place for you to enjoy, and you enjoy His gifts, not *instead* of Him, but *because* of Him!

"Heaven is not only God's gift to you, but He has also given you gifts and talents so that you can be a blessing to others. In this way, you are acting like Him. These gifts have been given to you while you are living on Earth, but not everyone recognizes their gifts or has the chance to develop them. Some people, not all, but some, waste their gifts. But here, everyone knows what their gifts are and uses them to the fullest. There are no untapped or underdeveloped gifts in Heaven."

"How do we know what our gifts are, Abel?" Masumi wondered.

"First, you ask the Father to show you, and then you think about the things you enjoy doing. Very often it is the thing you enjoy doing the most, like your hobby or passion. Do you like playing an instrument? Perhaps you'll be a musician or music teacher. Do you enjoy cooking or baking? Perhaps you'll have a restaurant. Are you good at hospitality and making people feel welcomed? Perhaps you'll have a Bed-and-Breakfast. You could be a designer, a decorator, a jeweler, an artist, a gardener, a comedian, a pilot, an actor, a singer, a safari guide, and the list goes on and on.

"The Father loves to give good gifts to His children, and here his children love to give good gifts to each other," Abel's eyes were twinkling again.

"Like ice cream?" asked a persistent Edgas.

"Are we going to meet the Father on our journey?"

"Yes, Cristen. You will not leave Heaven until you have met your Maker."

"Oh, I'm so glad, I want to thank Him for this wonderful adventure."

"Oh, me too!" said Edgas.

"Me, three!" said Masumi.

"Ha! Well, me, four, I guess!" laughed Henri.

Cristen thought her heart would burst from the appreciation she felt toward her Heavenly Father for creating such an amazing, fun, and beautiful place for her to enjoy. She felt a song rising in her heart. She closed her eyes and began to sing with the chorus filling the air. Worship poured out of her. As she sang, she felt her spirit rising, and without knowing it, she lifted up off the ground and began to float away on the wispy ribbon that her worship created.

Stunned, the group of friends watched her float up in the air with opened mouths and wide eyes. But they were not nearly as stunned as Cristen was when she reopened her eyes!

"It's okay, Cristen!" Abel called out. "Just keep worshipping!"

He then looked at the others, "Shall we join her?"

Soon the five voyagers were adrift on worship, waving goodbye to their new friends. Shouts of farewell quickly abated as they rose high above the lovely park and playground.

Abel turned to his flying brood, "Now, about that ice cream..."

MAPUTO, MOZAMBIQUE
12:46 p.m.

Isabel was experiencing profound grief, to be sure, but still her grief was not as those who have no hope; she knew that Edgas was in a much better place and that her ultimate goal was to join him there. No, her grief was more over the situation in which she found herself. She had had no idea that she would love these children so much when she volunteered to come to Mozambique so many years ago. This was her home now, and she was grieving for her children. So many still suffered.

And she was grieving for her own heart. How many more times could it stand to be broken?

And she was tired. So very, very tired.

With an anguished heart she cried out, "I can't go on like this, Father! Yet, I know I can do all things through Christ Who gives me the strength and power. Lord Jesus, please, please, help me. Strengthen me. I am in desperate need, Lord. I need your strength and your power if I am to get through another day. I need you, Lord. Oh, how I need you."

TWENTY-THREE

Death and life are in the power of the tongue, And those who love it will eat its fruit. — Proverbs 18:21 (NKJV)

"Yum!" Cristen licked her lips. "This is delicious!"

"Uh, huh!" remarked Edgas, his mouth full of the creamy treat.

"So good," Masumi agreed, taking another lick.

"Uh Huh!" Edgas said again, opening his mouth for another bite.

Abel, in response to Edgas' ice cream enthusiasm, had taken the kids directly to an old-fashioned ice cream parlor—a fun, color-splashed building with several big archways and a large wraparound porch filled with spacious groupings of tables and chairs. A row of rockers along the second-floor railing invited guest to enjoy a relaxing panorama overlooking a sublime park. The whole shop was abuzz with happy folks ordering their favorite ice cream desserts and then sitting with friends to enjoy them both.

"Who's paying?" Henri had asked, to which Abel had patted himself, pretending to search for a wallet. A little girl giggled, "We don't need money in Heaven, silly. Everything's free!"

"Oh, yeah!" laughed Henri. "I already forgot!"

"It's ingrained in you, Henri, but it won't take long to unlearn," the angel winked at the little girl who was still giggling, and he leaned down and whispered, "Newbies."

She nodded understandingly and smiled widely at the group.

When the ice cream man handed Masumi her cone, she asked him if he was Jordan's father. "I am!" he exclaimed, "Did you meet my little darling today?"

"Yes, I did! In the Valley of Forgiveness. We played together."

"Well, how very nice. What's your name? I'll tell her you came by."

"Oh, please do! I'm Masumi. We were climbing the tree houses together."

"Nice to meet you, Masumi. Now that you know where we live, come back and see us anytime."

"This is where you live?"

"Absolutely! This is my mansion. Isn't it wonderful?"

"Oh, yes! It's fantastic."

"Can I come visit, too? Whenever I come back to Heaven, that is." Edgas smiled at the ice cream man.

"Oh! These are my friends," Masumi quickly introduced the group to Jordan's father. "We're only here for a visit." Her face fell slightly.

"It's so nice to meet you children; my name's Tanner. Yes, of course, you are all welcome to come back for ice cream or just to visit whenever you move home. It will be my pleasure.

After receiving their cones, the group headed out towards the park, waving goodbye to their new friend, Tanner the Ice Cream Man.

"Thank you!" Edgas turned and trotted backwards. "Thanks again for the free ice cream cone."

"You're more than welcome!" Tanner said, waving back to the children.

Strolling along a lovely tree-lined path, enjoying a light but scintillating breeze, the children licked their free, triple scooped, ice cream cones. The hardest part had been choosing the flavors.

"Mmm, I *love* chocolate! One scoop of dark chocolate between a scoop of rocky road and chocolate chip cookie dough—Mmm, mmm, mmm! I must be in Heaven." Henri chuckled at his own joke as he crunched the last bite of his waffle cone and licked his fingers. "My mother would have never let me have this! Can this day get any better?"

"Ah, but she would in Heaven! Isn't light wonderful? No sugar highs, no sugar lows, never filling, and zero calories." Abel sounded like a television commercial.

"I'm beginning to understand why light is so wonderful. Everything here is made of it, and everything sparkles and dazzles because of it—even you, Abel. You're like a living glow stick!" Cristen exclaimed with a smile. "I really do love the way light reflects off of everything. Even the grass is filled with light."

"Just the grass alone is amazing, I mean, just look at it," Masumi walked along licking her triple-decker, raspberry swirl, mocha, and butter pecan cone. "I could just sit down, here and now, and stare at these blades; each one is so perfect. Then after I finish staring at the grass, I'll stare at these flowers. And then after I finish staring at the flowers, I'll stare at these trees. It might take me half of eternity just to examine this one park!"

The happy group agreed with Masumi as they meandered through the amiable park.

"Time is weird here, isn't it?"

"Yes, Henri, I guess time is weird here," Abel looked at Henri and laughed. "You and that word are fast friends aren't you?"

Henri laughed at himself, then added, "What I mean is, we keep using the word *day*, but I don't think that's right. I can't explain it; it's like, if this is a day, it's been a really, really long day! Yet, I don't feel like any time has passed even though we have done so many things since we arrived. I can't tell if we've been here years or minutes."

The others nodded, completely agreeing with Henri's account.

"Heaven exists outside of time, Henri." the angel explained. "We progress through events but not by way of a clock."

"Listen!" shouted Masumi suddenly pointing excitedly at the blossoms hemming the path. The group stopped. "Those flowers are singing! Just like Erica said."

Jaws dropped opened.

"How do they do that?" asked Henri.

"I JUST LOVE HEAVEN!" shouted Edgas, licking strawberry off his chin before it could evaporate, and he might miss a drop of the sweet goodness.

Abel smiled. He truly loved this assignment.

"Remember, I told you before that flowers sing—some welcome you into your home. Everything in Heaven worships the Lord."

"I know you said that people sometimes confuse acts of religion with worship," commented Masumi, "but I'm still kinda surprised that we haven't gone to a worship service yet. It's just strange since I used to think that's all that Heaven was."

"Well, Masumi, what do you feel in your heart right now?"

"I feel happy. I feel overwhelmed by the goodness of the Lord. I feel thankful that God has prepared this wonderful amazing place for us."

"Don't you think that is worship?"

"I guess."

"What does worship look like to you?"

"Well, it's when you sing slow songs to Jesus or when you bow down or raise your hands."

"Yes, it can look like that, but it's more. True worship is a heart response to the love of your Father. It's an expression of your love, your appreciation, and reverence—out of your heart—back to the One who first loved you; the One who cherishes you beyond what you can even begin to comprehend; the One who lived and died so that you could live here with Him and enjoy all that He made for you. Worship is an expression that comes from your heart; it needs no words. Therefore, it can manifest itself in many different ways. Yes, it's singing and dancing; yes, it's lying prostrate before the Lord; yes, it's raising your hands in a symbolic gesture of surrender; and yes, it can even be living and enjoying your life with an attitude of thankfulness."

"That makes sense!" Cristen said, her face lighting up with understanding. "So in Heaven, everything you do is an act of worship!"

Abel gave Cristen one of his trademark smiles sending a warm sensation surging through her.

"But you said that we were floating on worship," commented Henri.

"You are right, Henri. All worship travels directly to the Throne Room of God. And words of worship are powerful, as you have seen, they can carry you across the skies of Heaven! Even on Earth, words have power. Once a word has been spoken, it releases power into the air, either to build up or to tear down."

"We saw the worship cloud ribbons, but we didn't see any words."

"You saw the evidence of the words flowing right out of your heart, and it looked to you like wispy cloud ribbons. Remember, you couldn't see Heaven before you came here, but that didn't mean it didn't exist. There is a very real spiritual realm operating on Earth; just because it is invisible to the human eye in no way means that it isn't there. What is seen was created by what is unseen, therefore it is the greater reality."

"So, our words are alive?"

"Yes, it is somewhat like that. You have been made in the image of God. He created all that is seen and unseen by His word! His words are alive, they are active, and they *will* accomplish that which He sends them forth to do. God's word will never return to Him void. This means they will never come back to Him without fulfilling their intent; what God wills, He gets.

"And although you are not, nor ever will be, God, you *are* created in His image. Your words have creative power. The Bible says that the power of life and death is in the tongue; therefore, it would serve man well to keep a guard over his tongue. It is important that you choose your words carefully and say only those things that line up with the will of the Father so that your words bring life and not death, so that they encourage and don't discourage, so that they build up and don't tear down, so that they enlighten and don't confuse, so that they bring comfort and not grief. You want your tongue to be an instrument of the Holy Spirit not an instrument of Satan."

"That's so easy to do here but much harder to do on Earth, isn't it, Abel?" Masumi observed.

"Yes, my dear; but God is with you, and His Spirit will always remind you. Ask Him to put a guard over your tongue so that you may control it. Ask Him to give you the words to speak. Ask Him to mold you into His image. Ask Him to make you His ambassador of mercy. Ask Him for His love for others.

"Oh, do not fret, children; you will not be the same as you were before you arrived here. You have been given a great gift, to experience and know God's great love for you. You will not be perfect when you go back to your earthly home, you will make mistakes, but you will have an immense love for the Father, and a great desire to please Him."

"I wish I could be perfect," said Edgas. "I will try my hardest." He looked at the angel with big, brown eyes full of hope. Abel tousled the boy's curly head and smiled warmly.

"I know you will, Edgas, but remember, it's your heart that your Father wants."

"What are those colors we keep seeing floating by in the sky?" Cristen asked, looking out across the sweeping lawn. "There are a lot of them in this park, maybe more than anywhere else we've been."

"Yes, I was going to ask you about those earlier; they kinda look like the wispy cloud ribbons, only made with rainbow colors." Masumi turned to Abel for his answer.

Edgas looked in the direction of Cristen's gaze. "I wondered, too, but there's been so much to see and do I can't keep up with all my questions," he laughed. "So, what are they anyway?"

"*It's music.*"

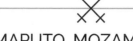

MAPUTO, MOZAMBIQUE
UNSEEN REALM

All was quiet except for the sound of Isabel worshipping.

The Holy Spirit had retreated to His home within Isabel, and the Portal, revealing the glorious Light from the Highest Heavens, had shut. Yet, the presence of the Lord still permeated the atmosphere.

Isabel was breathing easier now. As soon as the Portal closed, Michale glanced around the room. He knew the demon was still around because he still smelled his foul stench.

The beast, knowing full well that his opportunity was limited, waited only a minute before launching an all-out verbal assault.

Michale shielded Isabel with his wings, but too many of the venomous lies hit their intended target. Isabel was listening, and both demon and angel knew that once someone started listening, it wasn't long before they were accepting the lies as truth. And why not? They certainly felt like truth. She *was* tired. It *was* hard. So many of these children *did* die.

But Michale knew the difference between thoughts that *feel* like truth and thoughts that *are* truth. The truth is that Isabel can do all things through Christ Who strengthens her. The truth is that those who wait on the Lord will mount up on wings as eagles, they shall run and not be weary, they shall walk and not faint. The truth is that to be absent from the body is to be present with the Lord. The truth is that Isabel's life was making a difference, and God was using her mightily to bring about change in this community.

"Help me out, Isabel; it's time to get out your shield of faith. Work with me, sweetheart; we can quench these fiery darts together."

Self Pity left his place in the shadows and started circling Isabel.

"Nobody understands what's it's like to live here. I've sacrificed everything for these children, given up everything, and nobody even knows. Nobody even cares. I'm not appreciated. I gave up marriage and having my own family for what? Heartache? Few people have ever sacrificed what I have. It's so hard. I miss my family back home. I just want to have a normal life."

On and on Self Pity whined and whined, throwing out ridiculous lies in an effort to wear down Isabel. He once tried to climb on Isabel's chest, to press her down in sorrow, but Michale would have none of that. He shoved him back on his haunches. There was no way under the sun that Michale would let the little tormentor touch her. He could not stop the wretched lies; she would have to do that herself, but she belonged to the King and lived a life of holiness. The vermin had no authority to touch her.

Michale could have destroyed the gnarly demon with one blow, but that's not how guardians operate. It's the Host of Heaven, the warring angels under the leadership of Michael, who are sent to fight and destroy demons. A guardian's assignment is to guard, to shield, and to comfort their charge. Their constant presence keeps the Kingdom of Darkness at bay, especially in the life of a believer. However, a guardian will eagerly intervene when commanded by a superior to do so and will most certainly intervene if it is not their human charge's appointed time to pass from this life to the next; they do not need a special order for this type of intervention.

Michale knew that he couldn't prevent any demon from reaching Isabel if she had opened any doors to them, either knowingly or unknowingly. Demons don't care if a door is opened on purpose or not; if a door is opened, they will come in, and if a door is not opened, they will try to break it down with trickery, lies, and deceit. They have come to steal, to kill, and to destroy—period.

But thankfully, Isabel avoided all forms of darkness, and she repented quickly whenever she was convicted of sin. There were no open doors in this woman of God, and both Michale and the demons knew it.

"Come on, girl. Stop listening, and start speaking the truth of God."

Michale understood that if a person would declare what God says and stand on His promises and the truth of His word, repenting when necessary, binding and loosing when necessary, *then* the demonic forces lose their authority and power over the human, and the guardians are free to actively participate in the removal of evil spirits from their charge's life. Guardians wait and watch for these things, and as soon as they happen, they go right to work on behalf of their charge.

Self Pity circled dizzily, "God doesn't care about me or these kids. He never answers my prayers."

Isabel's spiritual ears pricked at that one—*Now wait a minute, that is not true! Where did that thought come from?*

She lifted her tear stained face to the ceiling, "Oh, I'm sorry, Father. I know you care. For Goodness sake, I just witnessed the most incredible answer to my prayer. I know you hear me. I'm so sorry for listening to those lies! Father, in Jesus' name, I take that thought captive to the obedience of Christ, and I cast it down. I declare that you do care. You do hear my cry! I will not listen to these lies. Oh, please forgive me. Help my unbelief, Lord."

Now he'd done it. Self Pity had gone too far with that last lie and thereby pushed Isabel right into a prayer of faith. He cursed vehemently and foul smelling saliva spewed across the room. He knew that faith is the shield that stops his lies cold and keeps them from penetrating his victim. He also knew without doubt that he would be severely beaten for his defeat. More profanity flew from his cracked lips. *Why was I assigned to this stupid Christian anyway? It's not my fault she believes God's word, yet I'll take the punishment for it.*

A smile burst across Michale's face which lit up the room like a sunrise. "That's my girl!"

The guardian snatched up the evil menace by the scruff of his scrawny neck and slung him with all his might into the atmosphere.

Every demon within a hundred miles heard the shriek as Self Pity went spiraling away from the little hospital room.

"And stay out!" Michale commanded.

TWENTY-FOUR

From the lips of children and infants you have ordained praise...
— Psalm 8:2 (NIV)

"Music?" they chorused.

"Yes, my friends. Music is alive, too!"

"All the rainbows are floating away. Where are they going?" asked Edgas.

"To the Throne Room, of course!" Abel's chuckle rumbled right through the children. "Remember, kiddos, the spiritual realm does not operate by the same laws as Earth. The natural realm, the human mind, the human body, time and space, the laws of nature, the laws of the universe all have their set limits and boundaries, but life in the spiritual realm is unlimited and unhindered. Sound, taste, touch, sight, smell, and knowledge are distinct yet inseparable from each other; they are intertwined together like an intricate and great tapestry. All are experienced as a whole. Here, thoughts burst within you in explosions of color and sound. Waves of love roll through you with bursts of heat and beauty. It is impossible for your earthly minds to comprehend, or your earthly body to experience the unquenchable, unending, unreachable depths of the Great I Am!

"You have only tasted—and a very, very small taste, I might add—what it is like to live in this immeasurable world. You, being visitors, still have some limits for He has not yet opened all things in this realm to you. The multidimensional aspects of the spiritual realm are innumerous, the depths of the Holy One are unfathomable, the riches of His Glory are unending. His universe is truly a place of wonder where time and space do not exist, where your thoughts are answered by waves of understanding and knowledge, where His unconditional love washes over you in waves of glory. Concepts that you could never grasp on Earth will be unfolded to you, and you will spend all of eternity exploring the never-ending depths of His knowledge and love."

When Abel finished speaking, there were four open mouths and four sets of wide eyes staring at him.

"I'm not sure I caught all that, Abel," Henri said, when he regained speech, "but I think you just blew our brains!"

Abel couldn't help himself; he threw his head back and roared with laughter.

"I think you said that God is more amazing and more wonderful than we will ever know and that it will take us forever and ever and ever to discover just how great He is," Cristen said, her eyes still wide with the wonder of all that Abel just shared.

"*I* think you said that we can hear colors and see music and right now, we're seeing music, and it looks like rainbow ribbons floating right to the Throne Room from over there by that fountain." Edgas smiled, feeling proud that he had figured that much out from what Abel had said.

Abel laughed again and snatched them up in a group hug.

"Let's go see what's making your rainbow, Edgas."

Enthralled by the delightful music, the children ran across the park towards the rainbow ribbons. On closer inspection, they saw that the music rainbows were coming from a group of children who were gathered just beyond a very large fountain. But as they approached the fountain, they discovered that passing it by would prove to be a difficult task, for they were completely captivated by the wonder of it. The fountain was made entirely of iridescent mother-of-pearl. It's own rainbow-whiteness stood out sharply against the backdrop of the different tints and shades of forest green trees, azure blue sky, and rainbow ribbons.

"They're alive!" cried Edgas, pointing at the fountain with one hand and covering his mouth from the shock of it with the other.

Water flowed peacefully over the mother-of-pearl as it rained down in a myriad of cascading waterfalls; the effect was breathtaking. But that is not what stunned the visitors. A mural, sculpted into the walls of the mother-of-pearl fountain, which captured the joy of children at play, was alive. At least it was so lifelike that the visiting children expected the little ones to dance right out of the fountain and into the park. The mural-children ran and jumped and hopped and skipped in a circle of activity around the fountain. There were mural-children sliding down the waterfalls and mural-children splashing in them. It was unreal how real it was.

"Will wonders never cease?" whispered an amazed Cristen.

Abel laughed, "Nope, never!"

"Kansas City doesn't have any fountains like this," she added.

"No joke, Paris either!" Henri said, barely breathing. "Okay, you guys have to admit that this is weird—I mean, really, really, weird."

"But isn't it beautiful?" Masumi couldn't take her eyes off of it. "How is this happening, Abel?"

The angel's blue eyes sparkled, "I told you, everything in Heaven is alive."

"Then are those real kids?" asked a shocked Edgas.

"No, those are not real children; it's only a fountain. But, isn't it fun? This particular fountain is here as an everlasting memorial to a man on Earth who was very kind and generous to orphan children. A memorial is another way God loves to honor someone for an unselfish life of service and sacrifice. There are memorials all over Heaven; not all are fountains, but quite a few are, and they are all fantastic. Every time someone sees this fountain, the memory of what that one man did is being honored. As we've already discussed, what you do with your life on Earth really does matter to God. He notices, so you remember that next time you see a fountain.

When the visitors were able to tear themselves away from the dancing, playing, splashing, mural-children fountain-memorial, they remembered their quest to find the musical source of the rainbow ribbons.

Just beyond the fountain, small groups of children and angels were scattered about here and there on the luxurious lawn playing all sorts of musical instruments. Every child had an instrument of some kind, and it appeared that this was a music class. With every puff on an instrument, every stroke of strings, and every beat of a drum, bright colored ribbons of light poofed into the air and floated off. Every action had an opposite and equal reaction!

"Crazy cool!" said Henri, watching the phenomenon take place.

"Don't you think it's weird?" Edgas, tickled by his own joke, giggled off and on for a full minute.

"Yeah, crazy cool and weird," Henri smiled at Edgas and wiggled his eyebrows.

Angels held up music sheets, embossed in gold, while children expertly played golden trumpets, flutes, harps, cymbals, bells, and drums. There were guitars, ukuleles, banjos, sitars, and even some instruments the kids had never seen before.

Many of the children were singing while they played their instruments, and all of them were enjoying these lessons immensely. Some of the bystanders were even dancing along in rhythm to the music.

Masumi, having studied the violin since the age of three, was amazed at how well the children were playing their individual instruments. Not once did she hear a missed note or a sound that was off-key or even a little squeaky. These children, of varying ages, were playing like professional musicians.

A fascinated Edgas skipped over to one of the groups and stood on the outskirts, watching. When the angel-instructor noticed him, he smiled widely and motioned for Edgas to come join them. Edgas eagerly plopped down on the soft grass with the other children who welcomed him warmly. The teacher handed Edgas a golden trumpet. After a brief instruction, Edgas put the trumpet up to his lips, puckered just like the angel had demonstrated, and began to blow. The group of friends, along with Edgas himself, were shocked when, not just a loud sound, but actual music came out of the trumpet! Before today, he had never even seen a trumpet; now he was making wonderful music and sending colorful ribbons of light to the Throne Room.

That was all it took; the others rushed over to join Edgas. The angel-instructor greeted them warmly and then handed them each a different instrument.

Masumi tenderly took the golden violin with its golden bow and gently placed it under her chin as she had a thousand times before. She began to draw the bow, slowly, back and forth and was thrilled to discover how easily and deftly her fingers danced over the strings. She thought that she and the beautiful golden bow, together, made that violin sing more sweetly than the violin under the acclaimed First Violinist in the Tokyo

Philharmonic Orchestra. She was thrilled from the inside out. Imagine, her, a virtuosi! And producing rainbow ribbons to waft away on a breeze was a crazy cool bonus. *Crazy cool and weird*, she thought with a grin.

Henri was handed a beautifully carved djembe—a wooden African drum covered in a sheepskin-like fabric. He began to slap his hands over the taut canvas in beat to the music swirling around him. He found it fun to tap out a rhythm and absolutely loved it!

I'm a natural at this. Maybe playing the drums is my gift, and I never knew it! Henri glanced around at the young musicians in the park and decided that if these children were any indication, musical ability might be a gift everyone gets when they come to Heaven. He had certainly heard beautiful music, harmonious singing, and mind-blowing symphonic sounds since the moment he had first arrived. A new appreciation for the extravagant goodness of God swelled within him. Praises gushed forth from his innermost being and expressed itself in his newly discovered passion. Henri rum-a-tummed and rat-a-tatted in complete abandonment.

Meanwhile, the angel-instructor pointed Cristen to a lovely golden harp. Not a little one like one she'd seen hanging in the music room of the mansion she went in. No, this one was quite large. She had seen a harpist at the mall once and knew that she was supposed to straddle the harp and play the strings with both hands, one on each side. She sat down on a marble bench—which she expected to be hard but found surprisingly comfortable as it conformed to her body—and placed one leg on each side of the instrument.

Now what? Bewildered, she looked somewhat like a cow staring at a new gate. She hadn't a clue how to begin. When she looked questioningly at the angelic instructor, the joyous angel threw his head back and laughed very Abel-like. Unusual, but not too surprising, this angel's laugh sounded almost musical.

"Here, let me show you," he came right over to help her. "Place one hand here," he said, "and the other one here, like so. Now pluck the strings gently, like this." Cristen did just as the angel instructed and was delighted to discover that her fingers obeyed her brain! She plucked until she became familiar with the large instrument.

"Jeanette, would you like to play the harp with Cristen?"

Why I am still amazed that everyone knows our names?

A darling girl, who didn't seem any older to Cristen than seven or eight years, jumped to her feet and joined Cristen at the harp. Jeanette, with a wide grin, squeezed right in between Cristen and the harp and began to play. Cristen watched the girl's little hands with intensity, and after a moment, began to mimic her fingers as they expertly plucked and strummed the strings. In no time at all, and to her sheer and utter amazement, Cristen played with ease, causing the harp to resonate melodically across the park.

"You're a very fast learner," complimented Jeanette, as she unstraddled herself and stood up beside Cristen.

"You're a very good teacher," replied Cristen. The two girls smiled at each other, and then Jeanette gave Cristen a great big hug before skipping back to her lesson.

The visiting children loved playing their instruments and felt just a smidgen of disappointment when Abel said it was time to go.

"There are many more glories to see." He had that mysterious look again. "Say goodbye to your new friends. Thank you, Simeon, for the lessons," he nodded his head, acknowledging the angel-instructor.

"Yes, thank you!" the children echoed standing to their feet.

"You are more than welcome. The pleasure was ours, wasn't it children?"

"Oh, yes!" came the happy reply. "We will see you again!"

The four weren't quite ready to leave this joyous, musical place with its living fountain, musical puffs of rainbow ribbons, singing flowers, and more new friends. They would have been glad to stay here and continue their music lessons indefinitely. Nevertheless, they waved goodbye and followed Abel along the path leading out of the park. It was quite astonishing, even to them, how quickly, readily, and willingly they obeyed their leader, without any grumbling or complaining.

"That was really fun," said Masumi. "I've taken violin lessons since I can remember, and I was always glad when my lesson was over, but I didn't want this one to end."

"I can keep a beat," Henri tapped his pant legs and then remembered his living stone in his pocket and smiled.

"Did you hear me on the trumpet?" Edgas asked.

"You were a natural!" Abel answered.

"Does everyone in Heaven have musical ability?"

"Yes, Cristen, everyone has the ability to learn any instrument they want to learn; however, some people will enjoy it more than others. Those on Earth who always wanted musical talent, and those who were gifted with it, will all enjoy using their musical gifts in Heaven. There are studios here where you can take lessons from some of the finest musicians and composers of all time."

"I always wanted to learn how to play the piano," remarked Cristen. "My Aunt Leigh was a piano teacher, but she died when I was little, so I couldn't take lessons from her. I have a fond memory of a time when she played the piano, and we all sang Christmas carols."

"She probably has a music studio as an extension of her mansion, Cristen," Abel said with that knowing smile of his. "When you come back home, you can certainly take lessons from her. We'll even come to your concert, won't we kids?"

"You bet!" Henri grinned at his friend.

"Who knows, maybe I'll be in it with you!" Masumi squeezed her best friend's hand, never ever wanting to be apart from her. "Where you go, I'll go."

Cristen hugged her friend, "It's a deal."

"Okay, you two maestros," Henri laughed, "just be sure to send the rest of us an invitation! Or better yet, perhaps I'll be your rhythm section."

PARIS, FRANCE
12:50 p.m.

Alison was roused out of her thoughts by a tall, slender woman approaching her mother. A quick glance at her mother revealed heavy eyes shut tightly along with a heavy heart. Looking up at the woman's grave face, Alison gently nudged her mother with her elbow. A rush of panic jolted Celeste; her eyes sprung open, and her heart pounded madly, matching her pounding headache beat for beat.

"It's okay, Maman," Alison whispered sweetly, giving her mother's hand a slight squeeze and nodding in the direction of the woman standing before them. Taking a deep breath of relief, Celeste turned her gaze to the woman.

"Ms. Leonard?"

Celeste stared blankly.

"Ms. Leonard, I need you to come with me. There are some papers you'll need to sign before the coroner can examine your son's body."

SLAM! Celeste felt like the woman had taken a sledgehammer to her stomach. She grabbed her sides and doubled over in her chair, a torrent of nausea threatening to explode.

The woman loomed before them, waiting, waiting. She quickly became impatient. "Ms. Leonard? Could you follow me please?" She turned on her heels and walked briskly across the waiting room. Opening the door, she turned to discover that Celeste had not budged. With a loud sigh of frustration, she dropped the door and crossed back to the two Leonard women.

"Ms. Leonard, I really need you to follow me." She smiled down at Celeste, but there was little compassion in her eyes.

Alison's blood began to boil. *How heartless can you be, you sour pickle? My brother is dead, and you can't wait one minute for us to follow you?* She wished she had enough nerve to say that to this woman's face.

"Please, Ms. Leonard." Her now terse voice went down an octave.

Alison stood slowly, glaring at the insensitive woman, and began to help her mother to her feet. Celeste felt one hundred years old, two hundred maybe. She could not make her legs move; they felt like they had been cast in heavy cement. Her head knew she was to follow this woman; her body, however, was unable to comply. She finally managed to shuffle across the large waiting room, with Alison's patient help, and follow the impatient woman through the door.

The Leonard women made their way down a long, stark corridor to a small office. Sour Pickle motioned for the women to take a seat. There were two stiff, wooden chairs facing a large office desk. The desk was cluttered with stacks of papers, several large, thick books, a couple of pens, a stapler, some paper clips, and an old landline style telephone.

"You'll need to present your insurance card," said the woman, and then she excused herself saying someone would be with them shortly, quite obviously relieved that her duty was over.

"I can't believe this is happening," muttered Celeste. "I just can't believe this is really happening."

"I know, Maman, I know." Alison squeezed Celeste's hand again. Her mother was falling apart, and she knew she had to stay strong for her mother's sake. *Jesus, help me.*

The clock on the wall ticked loudly as the minutes slowly passed. With every tick, tock, tick, tock Celeste's head pounded. All she wanted to do was crawl into her bed, pull the covers up over her head, and never come out again. Ever. A deep, deep sadness was creeping in and infiltrating every corner of her being. *How can I go on without my Henri? It's not fair, it's just not fair. IT'S NOT FAIR!* Her whole being silently screamed.

Errgh. That sour pickle was so mean and impatient, just to bring us in here to wait. I don't understand some people. Alison could feel annoyance and frustration building inside her. *God, what's happening? I don't understand. Why would you take Henri? Help me trust you, Lord. Help me. Please, help me.*

A suffocating heaviness filled the room. It was hard to breathe. Both of them felt it. Tick, tock, tick, tock, tick, tock...

God doesn't care. He took my Henri. He's too busy to help me. A barrage of thoughts continued crashing through the pounding of Celeste's head as an internal war waged within. *No, Alison says He's not too busy, and He does care. Well, if God cared, He wouldn't have killed Henri. He doesn't care. But Alison says you love us, God, but this doesn't look like love to me. You don't even know I exist.*

She wished she could turn her thoughts off, clear her head of everything. Feeling suddenly stiff all over, she shifted in the hard seat and glanced over at her sweet Alison, the very image, though feminine, of her Henri. She was filled with sudden remorse realizing she hadn't paid any attention to her daughter. She had been so overtaken by her own grief that she had completely ignored her.

"Oh, Alison! I'm so sorry!"

"For what?"

"I should be the one who's strong. I should be supporting you." She reached over and patted the girl's knee. She tried to smile, but she could not hide the pain in her eyes.

"Oh, Maman, don't torment yourself! We're in this together."

"But you need someone to lean on, and I'm so weak. I can't even hold myself up. I'm sorry. I'm so, so sorry." Fresh tears sprang to her eyes.

"Don't be," Alison gazed compassionately at her mother. She took a deep breath, mustering all her courage. "I'm leaning on Jesus. He is my help in time of need."

As Alison spoke, there was an ever-so-slight difference in the air. Hardly noticeable but it was easier to breathe; the suffocating heaviness loosened its grip. And somehow, though she could not explain why, Celeste felt comforted.

TWENTY-FIVE

They feast on the abundance of your house; you give them drink from your river of delights. — Psalm 36:8 (NIV)

At the edge of the park, a golden footbridge crossed over a sparkling, crystal, clear brook. It was just one of myriads of tributaries flowing from the great river. It, too, had beautiful gemstones carpeting its bed. Seeing the gemstones' refracted light shooting out in burst of color into the blue sky reminded Masumi of the one in her pocket. She pulled out her yellow treasure and rubbed it in her hand. Her friends immediately did the same, each of them admiring their own stone's striking beauty.

On the other side of the brook, the path disappeared into a lusciously green forest, denser than any they had yet seen.

"Yes, we will cross," said Abel, anticipating the question that was sure to come, "but first, who would like a drink of water?" He walked down a slight incline to where a narrow, but beautifully sculpted, marble table stood under a large tree with shimmering golden leaves. Upon the table was a lovely, long-handled, silver ladle. The curious children stuffed their gemstones back in their pockets and followed him quietly. He grasped the handle and lowered it into the brook, filling the bowl with the crystal, clear water.

"Come, if anyone is thirsty, let him come to the Lord and drink!" he said, referencing John 7:37.

He handed the ladle to Edgas who put the bowl to his lips and drank deeply. He had not noticed that he was thirsty until he began to drink, but thus realized, he drained the entire contents in one breath. "Wow!" he cooed, feeling the cool, energizing water surge through him. "That was awesome!"

Abel gave each of the children a chance to partake of the heavenly water. "By the way," he said, dipping the ladle for the next one, "don't worry about germs." He handed the ladle to Cristen, "There are no cooties in Heaven," he grinned, "and even if there were, the healing properties in this water would eradicate them completely."

The water was supernaturally refreshing! Just like before, they all felt a surge of life and energy flow through their bodies as they drank. Now fully invigorated, they were ready for their next adventure.

After drinking a ladle full of the energizing water himself, Abel placed the ladle back on the marble stand for the next sojourners and then led the children back to the bridge.

Suddenly, a group of six or so teenagers raced up and ran straight into the brook. A full-on water fight ensued. Laughing and squealing, they dunked each other and splashed about wildly, thoroughly drenching themselves in the crystal waters. Ignoring the ladle, the teens scooped handfuls of water to their mouths and drank heartily.

The visiting children stood speechless, watching the action with keen interest. When the wet teenagers noticed their audience, they smiled and waved enthusiastically. Their exuberant joy was contagious, and the children smiled and waved back to them.

But, as quickly as the teens came, they were off again, chasing each other towards the park. Cristen thought she heard one of them say, 'Let's go to Jello-land!' but figured she only imagined it.

The stunned group looked at Abel.

"They're not on a tour," was his reply. Then he laughed, adding, "You will never be lonely or bored in Heaven."

"Hey! When did our shirts change?" Edgas asked, looking down at his blue and green striped shirt.

"Look, Henri," Cristen pointed, "yours has those drums you were playing."

"And yours are flapping again, Cristen," he returned.

"And yep, looks like mine is still dropping petals," Masumi said, watching one float down. "Are there any left back there?"

Edgas checked. "Yeah, there're still a couple."

"I wonder if we have to go home when your last petal falls, Masumi," Cristen said.

"Oh, that would be sad," moaned Edgas.

"Hey, Abel, do you have any adhesive tape?" asked Henri, chuckling. "We could tape Masumi's petals on so we don't ever have to leave."

"Great idea!" the girls agreed, laughing with Henri.

"Hey, can we cross this bridge now?" Edgas had one eye on the bridge and one on the angel.

"Yes," Abel bowed with exaggerated formalities, "now you may cross."

The children laughed at his gesture.

"Come on!" shouted Edgas. "Last one over is a rotten egg! Oops, I mean, just a plain ol' egg since nothing ever rots here!" He rushed over the bridge with Henri close behind.

"I think the last one over should be a golden egg!" Cristen looped her arm through Masumi's and smiled playfully at her friend.

Masumi returned the smile, "Let's be golden eggs together!"

With locked arms, the giggling girls darted across the golden footbridge behind the boys. Abel chuckled as he watched them run. He then spread his massive wings and zipped over their heads with amazing speed and dexterity. His sandaled feet landed on the lush grass just ahead of the children.

"Didn't want to be the egg, rotten or otherwise!" He cracked himself up, laughing merrily.

The surprised children, tickled that the angel was having fun with their joke, doubled over in fits of laughter. Oh, how much they had grown to love him; it was hard to imagine that they were all new acquaintances, for it seemed as if they had known him and each other forever.

Abel left the laughing children and walked swiftly—or perhaps he floated—down the short path that led into the forest where there was another one of those beautiful arched gate-markers that signified the entrance into something new.

Walking through the gate, Abel turned and motioned for them to follow. Pulling aside a hanging curtain made entirely of leaves, the angel ducked his head slightly then glided past the drape and disappeared.

The startled children ran to catch him. Edgas again took no chances and followed his friends through the gate but not before noticing the sign overhead.

"The Emerald Cathedral" Henri said, reading the words out loud for Edgas.

"I wonder what it is?" Masumi whispered.

As they approached, they whispered back and forth that emerald was a kind of green gemstone, and cathedral was a type of big church. Were they going to a green church?

Curiously, they pulled back the curtain of leaves and stared in awe at the beauty that awaited them.

PARIS, FRANCE
UNSEEN REALM

Capri and Heston stayed right with the women as they made their way to the small office. The angels exchanged glad smiles as The Light continued to shine over Alison, for they knew that Light overcomes darkness every single time. Darkness is not the opposite of light; it is the absence of light. And when light shows up, darkness disperses. Period.

Those demons not assigned to assail the women decided it would be much wiser to stay away from The Light; they quickly abandoned the Leonard women. The ones assigned were suddenly stricken silent, knowing for certain that this was not going to end well for them. The Holy Spirit was actively at work inside the girl, and The Light of God was upon her. If The Word began to speak, His truth would shatter the lies they had so persistently deposited. They cursed under their breaths for a brutal beating was surely awaiting them when all was said and done.

The tiny demon clung fast to Celeste's head, but he kept his eyes shut tightly, trying in vain to shut out The Light that followed the women.

Gathering his courage, the scourge began a last-ditch effort to influence Celeste's heart against God. "How can I go on without my Henri? It's not fair, it's just not fair. IT'S NOT FAIR!"

This encouraged the other demons to keep up the fight. Staying as far out of The Light as possible, they polluted the atmosphere with their filthy lies and abominations.

An internal battle played out in Celeste's mind. But with every lie aimed at her, she found herself coming back with a rebuttal of truth. There was a shift happening in the atmosphere. Demons were losing their power over Celeste, and for the time being, had given up their fight over Alison completely.

The women felt the change.

As soon as Alison confessed that she was leaning on Jesus, a tangible peace settled over her, evidenced by the flame of the Holy Spirit burning many times brighter.

TWENTY-SIX

He that dwelleth in the secret place of the Most High shall abide under the shadow of the Almighty. I will say of Jehovah, He is my refuge and my fortress; My God, in whom I trust. — Psalm 91:1-2 (ASV)

A hush fell over the children as they passed through the leafy curtain and entered the magnificent rainforest. Like Alice through the looking glass, they passed into another new world, a secret garden of rainforest proportions. It was thoroughly enchanting like a page out of the grandest of fairy tales, beyond anything they could have ever imagined or dreamed up on their own.

Their leader was not in sight, so they continued deeper into this green, cavernous world. Craning their necks, they tried desperately to take it all in. Ancient, towering trees—sky high and thick with leafy green foliage—created an enormous canopy overhead while an innumerable variety of thriving plants and trees grew in lavish abundance beneath. The rich and variant hues of green were generously strewn with splashes of vivid, bright colors, and again, some of the colors were brand new to the kids.

The wide path through the forest was a carpet of soft, green moss, and ferns sprang up airily alongside it. Extraordinarily lovely, exotic flowers hemmed them in and permeated the air with a scintillating aroma; and the beauty of this forest created a lively music of its own.

Bright birds perched on branches, flew in the rafters of the tree canopy, and strutted along the ground, all while singing out praises to the One who made them.

"It looks like Hawaii threw up in here!" laughed Henri, interrupting the pensive mood.

"Gross!" said Masumi, pushing him teasingly.

Edgas laughed so hard he snorted.

"I agree with Masumi, Henri. That's gross...and a little bit funny." Cristen couldn't stop the smile that tugged at her lips.

"It *is* funny, Henri," laughed Edgas, "but, I don't think Hawaii can throw up in Heaven; it's down on Earth!"

"I don't think anything throws up in Heaven!" said Cristen, trying not to laugh.

"Might we change the subject?" Masumi pretended to be annoyed, but her laughing eyes gave her away.

"Sorry," Henri said sheepishly, "didn't mean to spoil the mood."

"Well, I can imagine that a Hawaiian rainforest could look something like this," agreed Cristen. "Well...maybe not *quite* like this."

Graceful palms followed the mossy path while kapoks and bright poinsettia trees burst with colorful blossoms. Macadamia and cashew trees grew in abundance as did banana, kiwi, and pineapple plants. Balsas, mahoganies, and rosewoods were among the thousands of tall stately trees.

Purple, yellow, pink, white, and variegated orchids by the millions held their dainty heads high as they grew anchored on the branches of other trees; and azaleas, hibiscus, bougainvillea, oleander, and hundreds more flowering trees and bushes paraded their vibrant blooms.

Everything under the canopy of trees was bathed in a soft green light. The bold and brightly colored flowers were in no way diminished by the greenness that washed over them. Indeed, it was what gave this forest its distinct beauty.

And, like everywhere else the children had been on their journey, there was nothing dead or decayed to be seen, no dangling or broken branches, nothing stripped or barren—only absolute perfect perfection in every direction as far as the eye could see.

Rounding a bend, the children spotted Abel waiting for them, and the sight of him took their breaths away. Awed, they slowed their steps, for it somehow felt as though they had entered a holy cathedral. They instantly realized how rightly the gate had been named.

Beams of brilliant green light rays slanted down across the guardian, enveloping him in an effervescent, emerald glow. Both broad and narrow shafts of light in various shades of emerald green filtered through broad leaves all the way to the mossy floor. Dense as it was, this tropical rainforest could not even begin to block the heavenly light, for even here under this rainforest canopy, everything reflected His glorious light. There is no place created in the heavenly realm that can hide from the light of Him who *is* light.

"I do feel like we're in a cathedral," Cristen whispered.

"Yeah, a big one," agreed Henri.

"With green, stained glass windows," said Masumi, in a hushed tone.

"Yeah, big ones!" added Edgas, making them all laugh and changing the quiet mood back to a jovial one.

Abel was standing among a variety of fruited trees generously laden with tropical fruits and blossoms. There were orange, papaya, guava, and mango trees, among many others. When the children reached him, he greeted them warmly and handed them each a section of a peeled, sweet and juicy, tangerine or something like a tangerine. It was absolutely delicious, whatever it was, and they gobbled it up. What they knew for sure was that it was bursting with melt-in-your-mouth, tangy-sweet flavor!

The scent of the blossoms permeated the air with its crisp and zesty fragrance. It was delightful to stand among these trees. Without even realizing it, the children began taking deep breaths of the fruity aroma.

Reaching high, Abel plucked a few more of the fruit and tossed each child a whole, bright, orange one. Eagerly, they began peeling. Abel picked another for himself. As Abel peeled his fruit, he dropped the rind and it disappeared before it hit the ground.

"Oh, yeah!" Edgas squealed. "I almost forgot!"

The excited children couldn't drop their peelings fast enough. It was like performing their own magic trick; as soon as the rinds dropped, they'd vanish into thin air. Joyous laughter resounded through the Emerald Cathedral.

"These remind me of something we call 'mikans' in Japan," said Masumi, plopping another section in her mouth. Speaking with her mouth full, she continued, "A mikan is like a Mandarin orange."

"It reminds me of a tangerine," Henri said with a mouth full of fruit, "only sweeter."

"And without seeds to worry about," added Masumi.

"That's too bad; I like spitting seeds!" chuckled Henri.

"Boys," teased Masumi, rolling her eyes in mock disdain.

Cristen took another delightful bite. "We have something similar we call clementines, but these are better,"

"Well, I don't know what it reminds me of," said Edgas. "Some kind of orange I guess, but no matter cuz I started with the best!"

"Well, that's true!" agreed Henri, swallowing another bite. "Even if you don't get to spit seeds!"

Just as they were finishing their tasty tangerine-like fruit, chattering squirrel monkeys scampered over to greet them, swinging noisily from branch to branch and limb to limb, encircling the children.

The littlest of the group scampered down a branch, right up to Henri. He stuck his face so close to Henri's that they were almost touching noses. Startled, Henri stood stock still, not even blinking while the monkey looked him square in the eyes. Unexpectedly, the little monkey reached out and patted Henri on the head, then sat back on his haunches and smiled. That's right, smiled! The surprised children burst out laughing.

"He likes you, Henri!" laughed Edgas.

"How do you know it's a he? Maybe it's a she, and she has a crush on Henri!" laughed Masumi.

"Very funny," said Henri, good-naturedly, "but I doubt it. I bet *he* just wants some of my tangerine!"

He turned his attention back to the monkey, "Hey there, little fella. Are ya hungry?" Henri opened his palm and held out his last fruit section. The smiling, squirrel monkey snatched the fruit, popped it in its mouth, and then sprung a back flip, delighting the children. They laughed again as the little monkey clapped its hands together and held them out for another piece.

"Cute little beggar," teased Henri.

"Oh, it's cute all right, but it's not really a beggar, although I agree it appears that way," Abel explained. "He can have his fill of tasty fruit; this one just knows it's a great way to meet people." Abel looked at the monkey, "Isn't that right? You're a smart one, aren't you?"

The little fella's family knew this trick, too, for suddenly several more miniature, hairy brown hands were thrust in front of the children's astonished faces.

One of the monkeys climbed down a branch and perched onto Abel's broad shoulder. Abel plucked a few more of the tasty fruit and tossed them to the children. He then looked at the monkey on his shoulder, said something the children could not discern, and laughed heartily. The monkey laughed with the angel, chattering and bouncing up and down excitedly. It seemed quite happy with its roost atop the angel and looked comically small sitting on that massive shoulder.

About twenty small pairs of adorable black eyes watched patiently as the children peeled the fruit. The monkeys bobbed up and down with eagerness as they were handed fruit sections then they squealed with delight and jumped back into the trees, continuing to scamper about without a care in the world.

Between bites of his own, Henri held up more fruit sections for his new little friend. To the surprise of everyone, especially Henri, it suddenly leaped from the branch to Henri's back and clung there. The monkey then took the proffered fruit and chattered loudly, tickling Henri's ear.

The others doubled over with giggles.

"All right kiddos, let's move along," said Abel, lifting the monkey from his shoulder, dwarfing it in his large hands. He placed it gently back on a branch and scratched its little head before leading the children deeper into the Emerald Rainforest Cathedral. The squirrel monkeys scampered along noisily beside them, running and leaping from tree to tree, all except for the little guy, now dubbed "Little Fella," who continued to ride on Henri's back.

He remained there quite happily until Edgas begged to hold him. The monkey complied willingly and immediately switched transports as if he understood the request and was now perched on Edgas with a tight grasp of the boy's curly locks.

A wonderful new fragrance filled the air as the group continued deeper into the rainforest. The colorful birds kept the entourage company and joyfully sang and chirped as they flew along. There were birds of every size and plumage. Their bold colors, melodic songs, and joyous flight enraptured the children. As they walked along, they also saw roosters with bright red and orange combs and plumage; peacocks strutting about, proudly showing off their glorious blue-green tail fans; brightly patterned butterflies, fluttering in abundance; all colors of little songbirds flitting from branch to branch; tiny green and pink hummingbirds sipping nectar from flowers; larger birds flying high just beneath the upper canopy; and even colorful parrots and toucans, sitting on tree branches, singing out praises to Jesus—with words the children could understand!

Soon the aviary was joined by larger monkeys scampering and swinging along on vines and branches like Tarzan and Cheetah.

The children spotted scurrying geckos; roaming iguanas; jumping tree frogs and croaking bull frogs. There were flying lemurs and flying squirrels gliding from tree to tree, and galagos and marmosets jumping from branch to branch; antelope, deer, hogs, and tapirs watched the children or came over to be petted when they weren't darting about between trees. And, not surprisingly, there were a number of unusual animals the visitors had never seen.

Chirping, croaking, creaking, crowing, gurgling, calling, squealing, cackling, whistling, and singing—all together created a beautiful, rhythmic melody of praise which filled the Emerald Cathedral to the very top of its rafters! These creatures were praising God with all that was within them, and it was a marvelous marvel, through and through!

"Listen!" said Masumi, coming to a sudden stop, practically tripping the others in her abruptness.

"What do you hear?" asked Cristen, curiously.

"Is it the birds singing praises to Jesus?" asked Edgas.

"Isn't that so weird?" added Henri. "What kind of birds are these anyway? I mean, not one of them said, 'Polly wants a cracker!'"

"They're heavenly birds, Henri. I think they're saying, 'Polly thanks Jesus for the cracker!'" Edgas grinned, and the others chuckled at his joke.

"No, it's not them. I mean, yes, I hear them, and they're totally amazing," said Masumi, "but I hear something else. Listen! It sounds like thunder or something."

No one breathed as they strained to hear Masumi's thunder over all the other sounds of the rainforest.

"I think I hear something, but it sounds really far off," said Cristen.

"Yeah, I hear it too. What is it, Abel?" asked Henri.

"You'll soon find out," he said, with one of his famous grins and that twinkle that says, "Something wonderful is about to happen!"

"Oh! I can tell by your face it's another surprise!" Cristen wiggled her finger up at Abel. He grabbed her finger and pulled her into a bear hug.

"Oh, you think so, do you?" he asked teasingly.

"YES!" they chorused.

"You've figured me out!"

"Let's go find Masumi's thunder!" Edgas sprinted ahead like one of the gazelles they'd seen. He looked hilarious. Little Fella had climbed to the top of his head and was bobbing up and down as if riding on a pogo stick instead of a boy.

Cristen doubled over with laughter and fell behind the group. Little Fella looked back and waved one arm wildly, gesturing for her to catch up. He looked to her like a miniature rodeo cowboy on his bucking bronco which only served to make her laugh harder.

As they made their way deep into the tropical forest, Masumi's thunder grew increasingly louder and louder. Running down the path together, they were still laughing at Edgas and jabbering excitedly when they burst upon a clearing and skidded to a halt. They had discovered the source of Masumi's thunder.

No one uttered a sound as they stared, amazed—again.

KANSAS CITY, KANSAS, USA
5:55 a.m.

About forty-five minutes after making their first phone call, the tiny hospital room was bursting at the seams. The next ones to arrive were Cristen's older brother, Scott, with Will's mother, Margaret. Margaret had awoken the next-door neighbor who came straight over to stay with the younger two Maples boys, Carter and Chad. Scott, however, would not be left behind, so he came along with his grandmother. The teen was visibly upset as he rushed to hug his mother.

"Is she gonna be okay?" he choked.

"We don't know, honey."

Margaret, or Grammy, as the kids called her, had obviously been crying. "We got here as quickly as we could." She scooted to her son and gave him the kind of hug only a mother can give, her teary eyes full of concern.

Jon and Ginger said their hellos and gave warm hugs to the newcomers, but then they stepped out to let the family have some time together.

Scott turned to his dad. Will reached out and drew him into a hug. He held him a little longer and a little tighter than would be comfortable for most fifteen year-old boys under normal circumstances. But this wasn't a normal circumstance, and they both needed the security it brought.

Grammy hugged Elaine. "I'm so worried, honey. I prayed all the way to the hospital."

Ever since Elaine's mother had passed away, Grammy had stepped into that spot and been a mother to Elaine. Right now her hug spoke where words could not, and it communicated all the love in the world. Grammy's sweet compassion caused Elaine's faucet of tears to start leaking again.

"Are you okay, sweetheart?" Grammy's voice was tender.

"Yes, I'm okay." Elaine wiped her puffy eyes while Grammy tilted her head and looked at her skeptically. "No, I'm not," Elaine breathed out heavily, "but I'm trying to be. I'm trying hard to trust the Lord. I'm just so afraid."

"What happened, Mom?" Scott's voice was thick with emotion.

Elaine looked at her son and tried to smile, but she couldn't stop the tears from flowing down her cheeks. Grammy embraced her again, and this time Elaine didn't try to stop the tears. She gave way to the emotion and her body heaved as she wept. Grammy held her all the tighter.

Will and Scott thought their hearts would break from the pain of seeing Elaine like this.

After a minute, Elaine grabbed a fresh tissue and blew her nose. "These tears are your fault," she looked at Grammy with a half-smile. "Whenever I'm upset and someone's nice to me, it always makes me cry."

Grammy smiled and embraced Elaine again, then after a long moment she whispered in her ear, "I can be mean if you think that will help."

Elaine smiled as she pulled out of the hug. *Leave it to this wonderful woman to try to lift my spirits.*

"So, mom? What happened?"

Elaine quickly relayed the horrifying events of the early morning. Scott and Grammy eyes widened, and they shook their heads in unbelief as they listened.

"All we can do now is wait and pray," said Elaine as she finished her account. Deep inside, she knew this was truly their only hope. It was the waiting part that would drive her crazy.

Scott reached out and took his mother's hand. He sincerely hoped that prayer would work; he wasn't sure, but he kept his doubts to himself.

There was a soft knock on the door. Ginger's head peeked inside. "There's someone here to see you; is it okay if we come back in?"

"Yes, please, come on," Elaine answered.

Into the little room returned Jon and Ginger followed by Pastor Mac. Sunshine entered the room with him, and that wasn't because the sun was now rising. No, the man's whole countenance exuded joy and hope and peace. His kind face conveyed his concern and compassion. Oh, his presence was such a blessing. Elaine found herself crying again as she moved to greet him.

"Thank you for coming. You didn't have to."

"Are you kidding? I wouldn't be anywhere else. This is why they pay me the big bucks." Elaine smiled at his joke, for they all knew that this man did not take a big salary and gave away much of what he did receive.

Elaine loved him dearly and always thought his eyes were as kind as anyone's she knew. At this moment, she felt like Jesus Himself was looking at her through Pastor Mac's eyes.

After greeting everyone in the room with a hug, Mac listened to Will explain the situation, and then he gathered them all in a circle and led them in a prayer for Cristen and her team of doctors.

TWENTY-SEVEN

Deep calls to deep in the roar of your waterfalls; all your waves and breakers have swept over me. — Psalm 42:7 (NIV)

"What in the world?" Henri uttered over the thunderous roar.

"We're not in the world, remember?" Edgas smiled at their old joke and elbowed Henri with a friendly jab.

"No kidding!" Henri jabbed back.

"Oh. My. Goodness." Cristen stared, astounded.

"It's beautiful!" whispered Masumi.

Crashing thunderously across from them into a large, shimmering, lagoon was a waterfall like no other; it looked like a liquid rainbow of rich and bright colors, and it cascaded from at least four-hundred feet above them.

"I think we've found the end of the rainbow!" said Henri, meaning it.

"And there's the pot o' gold!" laughed Cristen, pointing to broad golden ribbons running across the lagoon floor.

"Is that water, Abel?" Masumi could not tell if a waterfall was in the rainbow or if a rainbow was in the waterfall. Whichever it was, it was simply magnificent. The colors of Heaven's unlimited spectrum surged over a cliff and plunged into the lagoon below, sending rainbow infused spray high into the air. As the spray settled, it drifted softly, hovering over the entire lagoon as a misty, rainbow veil.

"Yes, my dear, it's water."

"I can't get over this place," said Cristen, admiring the secluded lagoon.

The cliff from which the water tumbled was high and rocky but not worn like cliffs on Earth. Instead, it seemed to have been sculpted perfectly for this purpose. Exotic trees and bushes with colorful blossoms and foliage surrounded the lagoon, peeking through large, banana shaped leaves. A white, sandy beach stretched along the side opposite the waterfall.

"I think we've found the Garden of Eden," sighed Masumi.

"Everywhere we turn there is another surprise as spectacular and glorious as the one before it," Cristen mused. "Does it never end, Abel?"

Before he answered, Masumi added, "I know what you mean, Cristen; *everything* I've seen so far is my favorite!"

"I can't begin to pick a favorite, but this has to come close!" said Henri.

"I think this is the prettiest place in the whole wide world!" The group smiled at Edgas. It was hard to take anything he said seriously with Little Fella perched comically on top of his head.

"Indeed, it *is* beautiful," Abel's eyes twinkled with mirth at the sight of Edgas and his monkey hat. "I'd have to say, this is one of my favorites, too. All right, kiddos, follow me to the shore."

Abel walked down a sloping embankment to the white sandy beach; the children followed like baby ducks in a row. Stooping his huge frame down low, he pinched several grains of sand, then sifted them in his fingers until only one remained. He held it up and rolled it back and forth between his very large thumb and forefinger.

"See this grain of sand?"

"Uh, not really," Henri's face scrunched as he strained to see the tiny grain lost between the angel's fingers.

Smiling at him, Abel placed the grain in his open palm, held it low for the children to see and then continued. "Let's say this little grain of sand represents more than what most people ever begin to discover about God. In fact, children, most people barely scratch the surface of this one grain of sand."

"There's not much surface on that little grain," observed Henri.

"Exactly," Abel leaned over and scooped up a handful of sand. "Now this represents what the Lord desires to reveal to you about Himself."

"You mean when we come to live with Him in Heaven?"

"No, Edgas, while you're still living on Earth."

The children's faces registered surprise.

"And although this is God's desire, very few have even come close to achieving this."

"Why is that, Abel?" Masumi suddenly felt something akin to sadness; the others felt it, too.

"The reasons vary from person to person, Masumi, but the most common reason is that few understand the difference between knowing God and knowing about God. God is relational. He doesn't just want you to be able to spout off facts about Him, but He desires to have a relationship with you. That's amazing if you stop to think about it. And the closer your relationship, the more of Himself He'll reveal to you.

"There is so much more available than what most have discovered. Don't settle for anything less, children! Spend time with him. Seek Him. Develop ears to hear His voice. Listen to Him. Obey Him. Follow Him. He knows your end from your beginning, and you can trust Him with your life. If you let Him, He will send the Holy Spirit to flood your life. Like this powerful waterfall, He will fill you with His life! He will empower you to live lives of purpose and beauty. He will empower you to live victorious, overcoming lives. Triumphant lives that defeat evil. And in that secret place, that place of deep fellowship with Him, He will reveal many of His mysteries to you.

"From now on, whenever you see a grain of sand, remember what I have said to you here; remember that God has so much more for you to discover about Himself. And, whenever you see a rainbow, remember this waterfall, and ask the Holy Spirit to fill you anew and empower you to live godly and effective lives."

"Oh we promise to remember!" Masumi placed her hand over her heart as a pledge; the others did too.

"Always!" Edgas added solemnly—though he did not look as solemn as he felt with that monkey on his head. Abel could not stop his grin.

"Yes, Abel," Cristen said, with Henri nodding his head in agreement beside her, "we promise to remember."

"Now children," Abel continued, "look around and see all the sand on the beach."

"That's a lot of sand," said Henri.

"Yes, it is; and it doesn't even represent a fraction of what God has in store for you to discover about Himself throughout eternity. Think of the sands on a seashore; that would be more like it. The depths of His wisdom, creativity, power, and majesty are infinite. We will need all of eternity to discover just how great He is! There will be new wonders around every bend, new favorites each moment, new joys to delight us as we get to know our marvelous Creator!"

"Oh Abel, do we really have to go back to Earth? Why can't we get started right now discovering the depths of God?" sighed Cristen, looking at the beauty around her. "This is all so wonderful, I just hate to leave it!"

"Yes, Abel, why do we have to go back? We don't want to leave this beautiful place!" echoed a monkey-crowned Edgas.

All eyes were focused intently on Abel, hoping the answer might be different this time.

"Children," Abel brushed the sand from his hands and spread his arms wide, "all of this will be waiting for you, but now there is still unfinished purpose for your lives. You must go back, for it is the Lord's will; remember that He is all wise and always knows what is best." Abel looked at each face, and then added, "Do you not trust the Lord's wisdom?"

"Oh, we trust the Lord!" they replied, brightening.

"We will just miss you and this amazing place," Cristen voiced what they all felt.

"Yes, but remember, the Lord is with you, always. He has promised that He will never leave or forsake you. On Earth, He has chosen to live inside His children, so you will not be away from Him, not ever!"

"I hadn't thought of it that way," said Henri. "We're not leaving God's presence! And," he reached down and scooped up some sand, holding it up for all to see, "we can spend the rest of our earthly lives getting to know Him more and more. If this much is possible on Earth, then I, for one, intend to do my best to discover it!"

"That a boy, Henri!" Abel reached over and slapped him on the back, "I like your attitude!"

"One day, hopefully *soon*," he added, with emphasis on the soon, "we'll be back here, for keeps, and we'll get to spend the rest of eternity exploring the depths of God!"

"By George, he's got it!" laughed Abel.

"Oh, me, too!" Cristen smiled broadly at the angel. "I got it, too!"

"Me, three!" giggled Masumi.

"Whose George?" asked Edgas.

"Oh, how I love you, Edgas!" Abel, in his trademark, angelic way, threw his head back and laughed heartily! He grabbed Edgas in a great big bear hug, and when he did, Little Fella jumped up and perched on Abel's wing.

"So, you want to fly, do ya, Little Fella?" Henri spoke to the monkey, and the group shared another laugh together.

"Well, Little Fella may want to fly," said Abel with that wonderful twinkle in his eyes, "but which of you wants to swim?"

KANSAS CITY, KANSAS, USA
UNSEEN REALM

Before long, there were more angels in the little hospital room than there were people. Two twelve-foot angels walked in with Pastor Mac. They flanked him constantly, fiercely protecting this man of God from any assignment against him. They were of a different tribe than the guardians. Their assignment was to assist Mac in his ministry to his congregation. The other guardians immediately recognized their authority and saluted them.

None of the angelic beings were the least worried about Cristen—not that angels ever worried—for they had all been alerted that she was only visiting Heaven and would return. They knew that their fight was most specifically for the faith of the mother, father, and brother.

None of the humans, however, knew that Cristen would not die, and so this was a test of their faith. A big test. Before the noonday sun, these children of God would know whether or not their faith was built on the rock or built on sinking sand. And whichever it was, rock or sand, they would be stronger by days' end. If rock, they would rejoice. If sand, they will have been given a gift—an opportunity to move their house onto the rock.

The humans were aware that James says to consider it all joy when you face trails of many kinds. They knew The Word of God promises that the testing of their faith would produce perseverance, and perseverance would finish its work, causing them to be mature, complete, lacking nothing. But knowing it and walking it out are two very different things. Today would be a lesson chalked up on the experience side of the board.

The enemy in the room had also been informed that the child was only sleeping and would return. They knew their time was short, and so they intended to make the most of the opportunity. Now was their chance to sow seeds of doubt and unbelief into the hearts of these despised believers. Why Heaven gave these pathetic creatures any mind, they not only could not understand, but it also made them hate the humans that much more. Besides, they had only been given one chance. One. They could never repent for their folly. They could never be forgiven and obtain entrance back into the Light of Heaven. Yet pitiful, pathetic, mankind mocked God, cursed Him, denied Him, worshipped themselves and other created things, raised their fist to Him, over and over and over again—and He has the audacity to forgive them! How can that be fair? How can that be just? Oh, how they despised the blood of Jesus that covers the sins of these believers. The blood, the blood, the blood. They were sick of the blood. There was no blood for them. They would never be washed clean, white as snow, forgiven. No, they went in the complete opposite direction, becoming uglier and more hideous as darkness had its way in them.

TWENTY-EIGHT

And without faith it is impossible to please God, because anyone who comes to Him must believe that He exists and that He rewards those who earnestly seek Him. — Hebrews 11:6 (NIV)

"Swim?" Cristen's face registered her surprise.

"Here, in the lagoon?" A puzzled Masumi looked at the rainbow water and then back at Abel.

"Are you kidding?" Henri had learned by now that Abel rarely kidded, but still he had to ask.

"Nope, not kidding!" Abel loved surprising them. "Now off with you; jump on in!"

"I don't believe it!" shouted Edgas with a smile that almost split his face in two.

"No unbelief allowed in Heaven, remember?" Abel teased in Edgas-like fashion, and then he shooed them off with the back of his hands.

The four friends grinned at each other, and then without hesitation, sprinted into the rainbow lagoon, delighted to discover that they could swim with ease. The water was clear and invigorating, just like the River of Life—indeed, its source was that very river—and the temperature was perfect. It was cool enough to refresh but not so cool as to cause discomfort.

"I've never gone swimming in a rainbow before!" said Masumi. She looked around at the others and began to laugh. The hovering mist painted rainbows on their faces.

Henri, realizing why she was laughing, lifted his hand to see if the rainbow water had indeed dyed his skin. He honestly couldn't tell. "I'm an Easter Egg!" He showed his hand to the others.

Giggling, they checked their own hands and then laughed good-naturedly at each other's painted faces, exceedingly happy to splash and play in the liquid rainbow.

"Hey, remember what the kids told us in the Valley Of Forgiveness?" Edgas' face lit up at the remembrance.

"Yeah, but they said a lot of stuff," Henri responded.

"Of what are you referring?" laughed Cristen.

"That we can stay underwater as long as we want."

"Oh, yeah!" Henri cried with recollection. "That's so weird."

"It's awesomely weird! Let's try it!" shouted Edgas, looking hopefully at his friends.

"This would make me so nervous on Earth," commented Masumi, "but I'm not at all afraid to try!"

"Then let's do it!" encouraged Henri.

"OK then, on the count of three," started Cristen, and they all joined in at once with a loud, 'One, two, three!'"

On the third count all four children took a big breath, out of habit, and then disappeared under the water. Opening their eyes, the very first thing they noticed was that they could see as clearly under the water as they could above it. They smiled and waved to each other, still holding their breaths. The girls' hair floated around them, and the look of it tickled Edgas. He burst out with a laugh, and that was the second thing they noticed. They could hear just as clearly under water as they could above it.

When Edgas laughed, he instinctively drew in breath afterwards and discovered the third thing: the kids in the playground were right. He could breathe easily underwater. He never sputtered or choked but continued exactly as he had above the water.

"It works!" he hollered. "It works! Do it! Do it!"

The others exhaled and then inhaled. Nothing changed. Again, they exhaled and inhaled."

"Wow! It really does work!" said a flabbergasted Masumi.

"This is SO WEIRD!" yelled Henri.

"Yes, but is it awesomely weird or weirdly awesome?" asked Cristen.

"Both!" Henri exclaimed.

Henri and Edgas pretended to be one of the many colorful tropical fish that were swimming around them, opening and closing their mouths and circling the girls with exaggerated frog-like swimming motions. The girls giggled at the silly boys.

The group stayed under the water for a long time—long enough for their skin to wrinkle and prune which it did not. They happily explored the underwater beauty and discovered that not only could they swim underwater, but they could also walk around or just sit and rest if they wanted. It was another one of the most amazing things they had ever done. It defied the laws of Earth and what their natural minds could explain; and it seemed with each "breath" they were energized and refreshed. Oh, the wonder of this heavenly fount!

The tankless scuba divers also discovered a small underwater cave behind the waterfall and had great fun exploring behind its watery curtain.

"So, this is what the back side of water looks like!" said Henri as the group climbed the rocks behind the waterfall. The others laughed heartily at his joke.

While the children discovered the lagoon and their new abilities, Abel leaned back against a large tree with long, graceful branches that stretched out effortlessly over the lagoon. Little Fella scampered up the tree. The angel laughed as he watched the children play, and then he slowly turned his gaze over to the waterfall. Lost to the world, so to speak, he seemed to be thinking of something grand. Closing his eyes, he began to sing. His deep voice united with the water that spilled into the lagoon.

The children heard him from their underwater exploration and curiously popped their heads out to check on it. Abel was radiant. He was breathtakingly beautiful as he worshipped under the tree. His glow seemed to have increased, again. Within moments, the children were so taken with the angel's song that they laid their heads back and floated quietly on the water, feeling very reverent. They let the music fill them completely and found their own hearts, too, were full of worship.

It sounded to them like the waterfall and the angel were singing a song together. The melodic sound flowed gracefully across the rainbow lagoon. The children felt the vibration of the deep tones fill their chest. Abel raised his arms in praise as he worshiped his Magnificent Creator. His angelic voice was mesmerizing. The moment was magical; it was yet another that would be ingrained in the children's memories forever.

They found they had no idea how long it was they floated around the lagoon enjoying Abel's duet with the waterfall, but some time later, Edgas opened his eyes and spied Little Fella climbing a long shiny cord hanging from a branch over the lagoon.

"Look!" he shouted abruptly, interrupting their meditation with a jolt. He immediately clapped his hand over his mouth for the shout had slipped out unbidden; but when he saw that no one seemed to mind, he unclapped his mouth and smiled. The others quickly searched for what had excited him.

"A rope swing!" shouted Henri, pointing to the shiny cord as Edgas swam off in a breaststroke towards it. Henri followed right behind, swimming with a freestyle stroke. The boys reached the swing in a jiffy, grabbed it, and then scrambled up the bank with it in hand.

"Look, Henri," said Edgas, "this isn't even made out of rope. I wonder what material it is?"

"Let me see." Henri took the knot in his hand and pretended to study the cord, all the while backing up as far as the cord would go. "Hmm, I don't know," he said with a perplexed look on his brow, "but it's something that swi-i-i-i-ings!" He ran full speed and jumped out over the lagoon.

Edgas stood grinning as Henri released the rope at the peak of its pendulum. Flying high in the air, he did a front flip and then landed straight up like a tin soldier into the water.

KERSPLASH!

Edgas quickly scooted over to grab the rope and then followed Henri's example of backing way up and running at full speed.

"H-U-R-R-AAAAA!"

He looked like he had been swinging on rope swings all his life for his lithe body sailed in the air and then sliced into the pool with hardly a ripple. His head popped up like a beach ball, exhilaration lighting up his face. "Wow! That was awesome!"

Henri scampered up the bank, grabbed the rope, and took another turn. Letting go of the cord, he grabbed his knees and yelled, "Cannonball!" He landed with a great splash, scattering rainbows across the lagoon.

Little Fella sat on an overhanging branch, bouncing up and down and squealing with excitement. Soon, his ruckus attracted a crowd of monkeys who gathered to watch and cheer the boys on.

"Come on, Masumi," said Cristen, "we can't let the boys have all the fun!" The two girls raced over to join the boys on the bank, and the four friends had a blast as they took turns swinging into the lagoon.

Cristen surprised herself as she did a backward flip off the rope landing gracefully with no splash. Oh, what good-natured fun that started as they each tried some acrobatics. They were more than a little amazed when they could easily do every dive, twist, flip, and turn that came into their minds. Their agile bodies obeyed what their brains told them to do. Unbelievable!

"Have any of you ever seen the Olympics?" Henri asked.

"Yes!" answered both Masumi and Cristen.

"I love to watch the Olympics!" added Cristen.

"Well, I don't know about you guys, but I feel like an Olympic champion!" laughed Henri.

"Me, too! I think we all earned a least one perfect ten!" said Masumi.

"You are all champions in Heaven!" Abel called out from the shore. "Gold medal champions, every one!"

The children grinned and took a bow towards Abel.

"It's probably no big deal to win gold up here; that would be like winning asphalt on Earth!" Henri chuckled.

"Not so, Henri!" Abel called out again. "Remember what I told you earlier? Gold is very valuable! Indeed, that's how much the Father loves you. He gives you the very best, even to walk on!"

The children felt loved, and their faces showed it.

"And now, my champions, one more dive each for it is time for us to go!"

Henri took the rope and handed it to Masumi. "Ladies first," he said.

"Thank you, Henri," she curtsied and then began to back up for another running start.

"I said *dive*," Abel called out, interrupting Masumi in mid-run. She stopped and turned to him, questioningly.

"That's a rope swing."

The children looked at him, a bit confused. Abel turned his head and looked up to the cliff at the top of the waterfall. The children followed his gaze and for the very first time noticed a diving platform hanging out over the falls.

"No way!" shouted Cristen.

"Way!" shouted Abel. "It's called *The Leap of Faith!*"

"Are you kidding? You want us to dive from there?" asked Masumi, incredulously, taking another look up, up, up at the precarious platform.

"Or jump! It's great fun!"

"How do we get up there?" asked Edgas, eager to try.

"Follow those steps over there," the angel pointed his long arm in the direction behind the waterfall. "Take the path and climb it all the way to the top. The path will lead you right to the platform."

The group swam over to where the angel had instructed and scurried up the path leading to the platform. They climbed quickly and were glad to discover that they were not in the least winded or tired when they finally reached their destination, four-hundred feet up.

"We had to die to get here," reminded Edgas, laughing.

The group cautiously looked over the edge. They were really high. The lagoon looked really small—really, *really* small.

"Well, let's do this," said Henri, summoning his confidence. "We had to die to get here; we cannot get hurt."

The thrill of excitement coursed through each one of their spiritual bodies, and they smiled at each other although no one budged to be the first to leap.

"Ladies first," Henri bowed to the girls.

"Um, not this time!" laughed Cristen, with Masumi nodding vigorously in agreement.

"Why don't you show us how it's done?" asked Cristen, peeking over the edge.

"Come on down," shouted Abel. "The water's fine!"

"Okay," said a determined Henri. He slowly edged his way to the end of the diving platform. Looking straight ahead, he breathed in and he breathed out; he breathed in and he breathed out. Then taking a huge breath, he gathered his courage, closed his eyes, and took *the leap of faith*. "Geronimooooooooooooooooo!" Henri shouted the entire drop until he plunged into the water far below.

His friends cheered loudly as they waited and watched for his head to pop up. "WHOA! WOW! WHOOP WHOOP WHOOP!" What an adrenaline rush. "Come on you guys! It doesn't hurt at all!" he hollered up to his nervous friends.

One after the other, they each, very bravely, took the leap of faith, screaming all of the four-hundred foot drop into the lagoon while the others cheered them on loudly, Abel loudest of all.

With the "one more dive," that was really a jump, behind them and anticipation before them, the four cheerfully scurried out of the pool to the sound of cheering monkeys and one very proud angel. "BRAVO! BRAVO!"

"Oh, that was awesome, Abel! Thank you so much for bringing us here," said Edgas. The others heartily echoed Edgas as they dripped up the bank. Rainbow skittles splattered about as they shook the excess water from their hair and clothing. But, to their surprise, by the time they reached Abel, they were completely dry.

"That's so weird," remarked Henri.

"I know, really!" laughed Masumi, "I ran into the lagoon without even thinking about my clothes getting wet; it never even crossed my mind to put on a bathing suit!"

"Me, either," agreed Cristen. "It's kinda nice not to worry about things like that. I think I tended to be a little too concerned over my clothes."

Masumi nodded, "Me, too."

"Who cares about clothes?" said Henri. "It's just so great to be here, and *that* was totally awesome!"

"I know, it seems silly now, but I used to care very much about my clothes, like *really* care. Being here is so freeing, Abel!" said Cristen.

"Speaking of clothes," Edgas pointed to himself excitedly. "Look! It's happened again!" Edgas' blue and green striped T-shirt had changed into rainbow stripes, "At least I think it's happened; maybe it's just from all the rainbows in here! I can't tell."

"I think it has changed, Edgas, 'cause look at my shirt," said Henri. "It has a diver on it. Ooh, that's a cool design. I like it."

"There goes another one of your petals, Masumi. I wonder why your flower is losing its petals?" said Edgas.

"Yeah, that's kinda weird," said you know who.

"There's got to be a reason," offered Cristen. She turned and looked at Abel, and he took his big fingers and zipped his lip and pretended to throw away the key. "You know, don't you, Abel? Oh. tell us, please," begged Cristen.

"It's for me to know and you to find out—later." Abel chuckled. "But you, Miss Angel Wings, are about to fly away!"

Her friends got behind her and saw that the wings on her shirt were not only rippling, but now they appeared to be moving just a little.

"Cool!" shouted Edgas. "I think your wings are really flapping!"

The children chattered excitedly as they walked behind Abel. They continued on a path that was now leading them out of The Emerald Cathedral, talking excitedly of the many things they had learned since arriving in Heaven.

They wondered together how that in Heaven they seem to only notice people's hearts and countenances and not so much their outward appearances. They obviously knew what people looked like and how they were dressed, and they thought all the clothes were just lovely, but even so, it had not been what stood out to them. As gorgeous as it was, clothing was just not the focus here.

They decided that what stood out the most, above all else, were the smiling, joyful faces. Everyone they had seen was simply radiant. Abel said that that was Christ-like. As they walked along, he reminded them that God looks at the heart, and man looks at the outward appearance.

Nearing the end of the dense Emerald Cathedral, they began to hear bells pealing and trumpets blasting in the distance. The new sound interested them so much that they rushed from within its leafy, cavernous canopy and burst into the wide open under a brilliant blue sky. As soon as they emerged from the tropical paradise, they spotted a mammoth structure situated on a large grassy knoll about a mile away. Abel took off in its direction, and they knew immediately this was their new destination. Soon, and still from quite a distance, the sound of shouts, cheers, and praises joined the bells and trumpets. The joyous celebration was originating from this enormous building which appeared to have no roof.

The golden streets leading to it were filled with throngs of people both coming and going. Some were walking, others were zipping in and out on a monorail system of sorts, and some were coming and going in hovercrafts. There was a group of teenagers arriving on hover boards, there were dozens of chariots about and many other types and styles of very unusual transportation.

"Where's everybody going?" asked Cristen, looking at the crowd entering the structure.

"Where's everybody been?" asked Henri, looking at the crowd leaving the structure.

"Come and see," said Abel, a hint of mystery in his smiling eyes.

TOKYO, JAPAN
7:56 p.m.

Michi squeezed his eyes tightly and shook his head, but he couldn't erase the image of his sister's face soaked with his desperate tears or her long black hair soaked with her own blood. Whether his eyes were open or shut, he saw her. Her innocent face would haunt him forever.

I don't believe in your God anymore, Masumi, Michi thought angrily. *You said He was a God of love, but this is not love to me. This isn't the way you treat your subjects if you're a God of love.* Quiet tears began to stream down Michi's cheeks again.

"Did you say something, son?" the stranger asked. He had not heard Michi's thoughts, but the Mighty One, who knows every thought and intention of every heart, had prepared him for what Michi would be thinking.

"No." Michi had forgotten the man was there.

"I'm sorry, I sure don't mean to bother you, but I thought you said that you don't believe in God anymore."

Did he really say it out loud? He was sure he had only thought it. "I didn't mean to say it out loud." He looked questioningly at the stranger who was looking intently at him. The man had a nice face and tender eyes. Michi warmed up to him immediately and was suddenly glad the man had stayed with him.

"Which god are you referring to, if you don't mind my asking?" said Mr. Ninomiya.

"Jesus."

"If you'd like to talk about it, I'm glad to listen."

For a reason that Michi couldn't explain, he began to pour out his heart to the stranger. He couldn't even remember the man's name, but he had listening ears and kind eyes that made Michi feel he was a safe person to open up to.

"Masumi taught me all about Jesus; she said that He was God's son and that He loved us so much that He died in our place. She said that He was raised from the dead and was still alive and living in Heaven and that if we believed in Him and made Him Lord of our lives, He would come and live inside of us, helping us every day."

"And did you do that? Invite Him to be the Lord of your life?"

"Yes, and see what a mess He's made of it!" Michi wagged his head and pressed his lips together. "Maybe it was just a nice fairytale. Maybe there's not really a God who cares at all."

"So, you don't believe that anymore?"

"Oh, I don't know what to believe!" he blurted. "I guess I still believe it; I just don't understand why He let this happen."

"That's a hard one, isn't it? Why bad things happen to good people?"

"I'll say."

"Well, Michi, I think God wants us to learn how to trust Him, even when things don't go like we think they should, knowing that He can see the whole picture. You know, His view is much better than ours. Just as Masumi said, now you have an opportunity to learn how to lean on Him, and let Him get you through the pain."

"So, He killed my sister so that I could learn how to trust Him? How nice of Him to care so much," he said, sarcastically.

"You are His son, Michi. He does care about you, very much. We can never understand His purposes, but we can know that He has our best in mind because He loves us with a love so deep, it's beyond any love we have on Earth. When nothing makes sense, we have to quit trying to figure it out in our heads, and cry out for grace to simply trust Him. Doesn't your Bible say that the thief comes to steal, kill, and destroy? And that Jesus came to give you life? I don't think Jesus killed your sister."

Michi sat back and breathed a deep sigh. He was glad to have someone to talk out his frustrations and confusion with.

"You know, you're not in Heaven yet, Michi. The world is at war, and there is a real enemy of your soul. He's called 'the accuser' for a reason. He accuses you to God, he accuses God to you, he accuses you to yourself, and he accuses others to you. But you must always remember that he is a liar."

What Mr. Ninomiya said made sense — the one called the accuser is the one that took Masumi's life, but what good does knowing that do? The accuser was able to do it. How could he trust a God that would let his sister die? Trusting God now, in the face of Masumi's death, seemed like an impossible request. He could not see any good coming out of her dying, only pain and heartache. And he could not imagine how he could live with the guilt that threatened to swallow him whole.

But he was breathing easier now, and he felt a glimmer of hope spark to life deep in the recesses of his grieving soul, and he knew it was mostly because of the words of the stranger. Maybe there was something to what he said. Maybe.

TWENTY-NINE

Therefore, since we are surrounded by such a great cloud of witnesses, let us throw off everything that hinders and the sin that so easily entangles. And let us run with perseverance the race marked out for us, fixing our eyes on Jesus, the pioneer and perfecter of faith. For the joy set before him he endured the cross, scorning its shame, and sat down at the right hand of the throne of God. — Hebrews 12:1-2 (NIV)

"It looks like a stadium."

"You're right, Masumi, it's very much like a stadium," Abel answered. "It's called the *Acts of the Faithful Arena*."

The children stared up at the enormous arena before them and followed Abel up the marble-like steps.

"444," said Henri when they had reached the top.

"444 what?" asked Edgas.

"Steps. I counted them."

"Oh, that's a lot!" said Edgas.

"What's the *Acts of the Faithful Arena* for, Abel," Cristen asked, as she looked around at the large crowd entering the arena, "sporting events?"

"Well, an arena is—"

"It reminds me of the Colosseum in Rome," Henri interrupted. "Well, except for the fact that it's not in ruins and way huger."

"Why? Because it's white?" asked Masumi.

"Yeah, well, I don't know, maybe."

"It kinda reminds me of the wall when we first entered Heaven," said Masumi as they came to a wide mezzanine filled with excited people, "because of the way it resonates with light. It's still amazes me how everything in Heaven looks alive!"

"That's because everything in Heaven *is* alive!" replied Edgas.

The shouts and cheers grew louder as they approached the entrance. It sounded to Cristen like a Kansas City Chief's football game she had once attended, only much louder and, truth be known, much happier. The children were very curious by now to see what everyone inside was so excited about.

"An arena," Abel began again, "is a place where multitudes can gather to watch an event. And here in this arena they gather for a very special reason."

The children stood at the top of the landing under an enormous archway, one of many, that led into the arena. They saw row after row of bench style seating cascading downward. The arena was at least ten times the size of the largest American football stadium, and it was teeming with people as a steady stream of newcomers replaced a steady stream of departers.

"There must be a million people in here!" exclaimed Henri.

"That's just about right," replied Abel.

The children were flabbergasted by the sheer number of people; no wonder the shouts and cheers were heard from so far away. It was especially notable how orderly everyone was, aside from the shouts.

Cristen gasped and pointed to the air above the arena. There must have been as many angels as there were people.

Henri looked for a field, thinking there must be a soccer game or some sporting event going on, but didn't see one.

Abel led the children to a section of seats near the top, and they quickly and quietly sat down, amazed again by the comfort of the seats. It seems that comfort is of highest priority in Heaven. Surprisingly, the visiting group of laughing chatterers were probably the only quiet ones in the entire arena.

The most unusual feature in this arena was a ginormous cloud of mist that hung in the air about twelve feet above the ground and rose up as high as, or higher than, the highest seats in the arena. This misty cloud permeated the entire center area of the arena.

Shouts and cheers continued to ring out with bells and trumpet blasts. The air was electric. And even as incredibly loud as it was in this place, it was not the kind of loud that hurts your ears. It was the kind of loud that sent goose bumps down your arm. The four friends were incredibly excited, and they were yet to know why.

The children couldn't keep their eyes off the cheering crowd, and the crowd it seemed, couldn't keep their eyes off the hovering mist. As the children began to focus on what was causing all these people to yell and cheer, they were blown away.

There in the misty cloud were thousands and thousands of perfect 4-D color images. These images, both simultaneous and different, were popping right out of the mist on every side, similar to a hologram, only much clearer. No matter where one was seated in the arena, they had a perfect view of the action as it sprang to life. Scene upon scene, all over the arena, unfolded before the crowd. It was as if the mist was a giant movie screen showing the latest blockbuster hits, only it was so real that the children were not convinced that people weren't actually suspended in the mist.

"They've all come here to watch movies?" asked Masumi.

"Oh, no, not just a movie; take a closer look, Masumi," said Abel.

Masumi turned back and began to watch one of the images. It was so true to life that she felt she could touch it, even enter it. As she watched, she suddenly realized she was witnessing an event happening on Earth.

"Oh my!" she gasped. "I get it now! What did you say the name of this arena was again?"

"The *Acts of the Faithful Arena,*" answered Abel, with a knowing smile.

"Is this stuff happening on Earth right now?" questioned Henri, excitedly, as he too was grasping the realization.

"Yes, Henri. Indeed it is!"

"So, 'Acts of the Faithful,' what exactly are we watching, Abel?" Cristen was still a bit confused.

"You are witnessing acts of faith taking place, right now, all over the Earth, both great and small."

"It's almost like we're there, the picture is so real looking!" said Edgas.

"Perhaps it's not a picture," replied the angel.

At that moment a cheer erupted in the section of seats right below them, causing them to jump a little.

"Why is everyone cheering, Abel?" asked Masumi.

"This is one of the great cloud of witnesses," explained Abel, spreading his arms out wide. "People are rejoicing with the Heavenly Hosts as they watch and witness God's children exercising faith. No amount of faith ever goes unnoticed in Heaven. Every act of faith, no matter how big or how small, rings bells in Heaven. We get to come here and witness it! There are many people on Earth, right now, running the race, and many who are finishing strong. And we are cheering them on. Not one child of God ever runs his race alone."

"So, this place is like a twenty-four hour movie theater!" said Henri.

"Well, I guess you could think of it like that," chuckled the angel. "Citizens of Heaven constantly come and go as scenes from Earth are revealed continuously in this arena."

What was also amazing to the children was that they could easily hear the thoughts and conversations of these faithful on Earth over the loudness in the arena. It was like waves washing into their consciousness. And not only that, they were able to watch several different scenes at once while not missing a thing. They weren't sure how their minds were able to take in so much information at once, but they quickly got over the surprise of it and simply enjoyed it.

It wasn't long before they found themselves shouting, cheering, high-fiving, and rejoicing over the faithful acts of the saints along with the multitude of others. It was thrilling to witness scene after scene, in rapid procession, of people believing God. Person after person, family after family, group after group, church after church, from country after country, were trusting and believing God in hard and even impossible circumstances.

Each time a scene was shown, great shouts of joy and exclamations of praise went up from those watching. Cristen had been a part of "the wave" when she had gone to that Kansas City football game. The way shouts went up and people jumped to their feet all around the arena, at different times, reminded her of how the wave had swept across the stadium. It was such a joy to be a part of this, to be a part of the great cloud of witnesses.

As the captivated foursome, along with their angel friend, watched events unfold on Earth, a group of participants several rows down stood to their feet and turned to exit the arena. Cristen drew in a sharp breath when she saw them and squeezed Masumi's hand.

"What is it?" Masumi whispered, seeing the look of surprise on Cristen's face. Cristen just stared at the group with her mouth wide open. Masumi turned to see what had taken Cristen's breath away.

"What is it?" Masumi asked again.

"Not what, who!" said Cristen, not taking her eyes off of one individual. "Do you know who that is?" she asked, excitedly.

"He looks familiar, but I'm not sure. Who is he?"

"He's George Washington, the first president of the United States of America!"

TOKYO, JAPAN
UNSEEN REALM

The instant Raphia began to minister truth to Michi's spirit, a seam, if ever so slight, began to split in the cloak of darkness suffocating Michi's body, soul, and spirit.

Failure never noticed that he was being repelled, pushed back, or that he was having to beat his leathery wings hard to stay in place over Michi. In his fury, he continued his vicious attack, but Michi began to breathe a little easier, and soon, truth would overtake emotion.

Nevertheless, a battle was raging for the heart and mind of the boy. The Lord had a great plan in place, but, for a short while it would look like the enemy had won. Raphia obediently carried out the plan to the letter, knowing well that Hope was on its way. And Hope has a name. And its name is Jesus.

THIRTY

Now we see but a poor reflection as in a mirror; then we shall see face to face. Now I know in part; then I shall know fully, even as I am fully known.
— *1 Corinthians 13:12 (NIV)*

"Abel?" Cristen leaned over and whispered excitedly to the angel sitting next to her. "Is that who I think it is?"

"Yes, Cristen. That is George Washington."

"Oh. My. Goodness. I can't believe it! I never thought I would see *him* in Heaven."

"Oh, but of course! Every one who loved the Lord Jesus Christ is a resident here, even famous historical figures," Abel said as the first president of the United States walked past their row. Smiling widely, he looked over at Cristen and her friends, slowed his step, and nodded his head in acknowledgment. Cristen could easily imagine him tipping a tri-cornered hat, if he had been wearing one. Her face beamed as she returned his smile and nodded her own head in return.

"He's dressed in different clothes, but he looks just like his pictures only younger and much more handsome," whispered Cristen to Masumi after the former president had passed their row. "And I bet he was glad to leave his wig and false teeth behind on Earth."

"What?" said Masumi, bewildered.

"He has such a lovely smile," Christen snickered. "I was just remembering that he had false teeth; for some reason that silly fact was in my history books."

Cristen twisted in her seat and watched George Washington as he exited the arena. She thought he looked very regal and that he carried himself with grace and elegance. It was just what she would have expected of a General and a President who walked in authority and position. But as she turned back in her seat, she realized that everyone she saw carried themselves in the same regal way. Every person in the arena could have been a king or queen, prince or princess, president, prime minister, or dignitary. They certainly dressed like one when they wore those royal robes. It seemed that everyone she had seen in Heaven had a dignified quality about them. Not in a snobby or stuffy way; she couldn't put her finger on it exactly, but she suspected it had to do with confidence in who they were in Jesus.

Abel leaned over and whispered in her ear as if he knew her thoughts, "They *are* royalty, Cristen, as are you!"

She turned and looked at him in surprise. *He really can read my mind!* He laughed at her shocked expression. "Remember, your father is the King of Kings, dear one. That makes you royalty!" With that Abel stood up and began to exit the row.

The children followed him without question as he led them back to the landing and then down the four hundred forty-four steps. Immediately upon reaching the lush, sprawling lawn, a beam of light appeared and stretched out before them, and the experienced group hopped up on it and began to coast away from the arena.

Cristen suddenly giggled, "If I'm a princess, Abel, will I get to wear a tiara, like one of the ones we saw in that cottage?"

A smiled flashed across his face. "Indeed you will, Princess Cristen, and so will you, Princess Masumi! And not only a tiara, but the day will come when all God's children will be given a crown, similar to the one you saw displayed on the pedestal." Abel looked at Henri, and his eyes danced at the memory of the boy trying on the crown. His friends could not help but turn to him and smile.

"As you know," Abel continued, "a crown is a universal symbol of royalty and authority, and one will be placed on every humble head. This bestowed crown will be a gift from your Father, the King. All His children—every prince and princess of this heavenly Kingdom—will joyfully receive this exquisite gift.

"And then, without second thought, in a corporate act of love, appreciation, and worship, every crown will be taken off and cast at the feet of the One, the only One, Who is truly worthy to wear a crown. There will be great rejoicing in Heaven, such as there has never been before, as shouts of acclamations rise before the glorious King in all His splendor. He alone is worthy, children! He alone!"

The children listened attentively to Abel.

Masumi replied, "I think I get it, Abel. We come to Heaven empty handed with nothing at all to give the King. Even the crowns are a gift from Him, but they represent the only thing we can offer the Lord: the greatest reward we get for our lives lived on Earth!"

"You're absolutely right, Masumi," he said.

"I think I understand," interjected Henri, "but if it's a gift, why can't we keep it?"

"Perhaps He will give them back, Henri. I don't know. But I do know that you will be so happy to have something of value to offer back to Him. You won't want or need to keep the crown for you will be completely satisfied in Jesus."

"Will it be hard to give back the crown?" asked Edgas.

"Oh, no, Edgas. Extravagant giving is one of the great joys you experience in Heaven. Only on Earth is it difficult to give freely."

"I love to give gifts!" exclaimed Masumi.

"Indeed you do," replied the angel with a grin. "You have already begun to taste on Earth what you will fully realize here in Heaven, that it is more blessed to give than to receive."

"That's in the Bible, isn't it?" asked Edgas.

"Yes," answered the angel. "Children, you don't need to worry; you will have everything that your heart could desire. You will be completely and totally satisfied. Your bodies will have no cravings, and everything you need will be readily available to you. There is no lust of the flesh, no evil desires, no pride, nor will anyone be trying to outdo his neighbor. Complete and utter satisfaction and fulfillment will be yours throughout eternity."

"I think I can imagine what that will be like because I feel completely happy and satisfied right now," offered Cristen. "I haven't even thought about stuff since we arrived, and that's not like me at all. I'm usually thinking that I *need* something, just about all the time! I guess I used to think that things would make me happy, but stuff doesn't make us happy, does it? I'm so happy right now, and I don't have any stuff at all!"

"Yeah, me, too," agreed Henri. "Well, I don't think so much about stuff, but I'm almost always thinking about food: like when's my next meal or what can I eat for a snack! It's pretty unbelievable that food hasn't crossed my mind. I mean, now that I think about it, it's more like a miracle!"

Abel threw back his head and that marvelous deep laugh resonated from him again. His golden hair flowed freely around his bronzed and chiseled face.

Cristen thought he was the most handsome person she had ever seen. Then she remembered he wasn't a person at all. "Well, he may not be a prince," she thought, "but he is very, very regal."

Cristen admired the glow from Abel's garment and the shimmer of his large wings as they traveled on the path of light. She thought him simply beautiful, and so powerful, and so graceful.

"Your wings just flapped in the air, Cristen!" Masumi squealed from behind her friend. "It's like they became real and flapped right off your shirt!"

"What?" Cristen cried. "How is that possible?"

"This is Heaven," laughed Edgas. "Nothing is impossible here!"

The children took a minute to examine each other's shirts. Edgas' shirt was now a bold red, Masumi's dropped another petal, and Henri's shirt had a strange red, blue, and white gemstone on it.

That they were now accustomed to the changing shirts did not dampen their enthusiasm over the mystery. All smiles, they shrugged as the light walkway carried them over delightful landscapes.

"Where to now?" asked an enthusiastic Henri. "I can't wait to see what's next 'cause I have no idea what this thing on my shirt is!"

"We are following the great American president to an assembly. There are many like it all over Heaven, but since we have seen George Washington, I believe it is fitting that we attend his assembly."

"What kind of assembly?" asked Masumi.

"A prayer assembly."

"What's an assembly?" Edgas wanted to know.

"A large gathering for a common purpose."

As the children followed Abel to the assembly, Cristen commented, "Will we ever learn our way around Heaven? I have felt completely lost since our first moment here."

"Oh, yes, children. When you come back, there will be many things that you will just know. You will not need an angel to guide you, but for now, since you are just visiting, God has not given you that ability. However, when you return, you will quickly learn your way around; that is, after your family members drag you to all the places they want you to see first."

Then as if an after thought, he added, "You will also know everyone you see. You will know their names, and you will know where and how to find them. You will know both where to go and when to be there. God has set up some wonderful systems of communication. So, don't you worry one bit; you will never get lost or be lonely or miss anything important."

"So, even though we're here now, it won't be like this when we come back?" asked Edgas.

"Oh, Heaven will be the same," answered Abel, "but you will be different."

Just then, they came upon a beautifully manicured park with large grassy areas, lovely trees, hedges, and gorgeous flowers. The park had benches scattered about, several sparkling fountains, and right in the center like a gigantic gazebo was a crystal building filled with people. The building was made out of a faceted gemstone; and the gemstone was made of three different colors and had an unusual shape with several pointed corners. The colors were set one on top of the other: sapphire blue was closest to the ground, ruby red was the topmost color, and a clear crystal was in-between. The children could not tell if it was one stone of three colors or three different stones, for they could not discern any seams or mortar where the colors joined.

"It's your shirt, Henri!" Edgas was the first to make the connection.

"Is this the prayer assembly?" Masumi asked.

"This is it."

"Why do people need to pray in Heaven? Isn't it too late to pray for things after you die?" wondered Henri.

"They are praying for you, Henri, and for those who are still living on Earth. They are praying for nations to come to the knowledge of the Lord. They are praying that the Lord will receive the honor and glory that is due Him. They are praying that the will of God will be done on Earth as it is in Heaven."

The children walked up to one of the large open windows and peeked inside. It was a vast room with row upon row of intricately carved kneeling benches covered in a thick padded velvety blue material. Each row faced the center of the room, completely encircling it, except for an occasional aisle break. In front of the kneeling benches was a matching intricately carved railing at just the right height to make a comfortable elbow and forearm rest. The room was filled with intercessors.

To Cristen's surprise, George Washington was in the center of the large room on a small crystal platform supernaturally suspended in the air slightly above the other intercessors. He was not on a kneeling bench but rather was down on one knee, with head bowed, praying fervently. Everyone seemed to be praying along with the first president.

Abel stepped through the arched doorway and motioned for the children to follow. They stepped inside and quietly and reverently watched the assembly. Now inside, the children could tell that the room was shaped like a five-pronged star, and the colors of the gem radiated inside the room, instead of flashing outside like most of the other gemstone buildings they had seen.

Still standing near the doorway, Cristen's eyes grew as big as saucers as she began to recognize person after person. *This room is full of Americans*, she thought excitedly, *and they're praying for the church in America!* She looked over at Abel who gave her a nod and a knowing smile. It only took Cristen a few seconds more to grasp that the colors radiating from the faceted walls were red, white, and blue. The star! The colors! The prayer room itself was made to represent her country. She was blown away, again, at the intricate details of the heavenly city!

At that moment, a great desire came over her to pray that her nation would come to know Jesus, the One and Only true God. She immediately found a place on the kneeling bench and dropped to her knees alongside her American brothers and sisters in Christ and joined her heart with theirs. She prayed fervently and in agreement with the prayers offered by George Washington and the others.

She didn't know whether or not she prayed aloud; it never even crossed her mind. She probably did, but her thoughts were not on herself at all but on the prayers around her. Just as she could hear and understand a thousand melodies simultaneously, she could hear and understand each prayer uttered from each mouth. She squeezed her eyes shut and interceded with all her heart.

When Cristen opened her eyes, she was surprised and totally blessed to find that Masumi, Henri, Edgas, and Abel had all dropped to their knees beside her to intercede on behalf of the American church as well.

A little later, well, it could have been a lot later, they simply had no concept of time, the little group got up from their knees and quietly slipped outside.

"That was amazing, Abel!" said Cristen, practically shouting with joy. "To think that so many of the faithful American believers were gathered in that assembly to pray for our country. I'm just astounded!"

"As I said before," said Abel, "there are prayer assemblies all over Heaven. At any given moment, there are groups gathered together to pray for every nation on the Earth. There are assemblies praying for each of your countries."

"I still don't understand why they need to pray in Heaven, can't they just go talk to God?" asked Henri. "Isn't that what prayer is—talking to God? If He lives here, somewhere in Heaven I mean, why don't they just go to where He is and talk to Him? Why is a prayer assembly necessary?"

"That's a very valid question, Henri," replied Abel. "Each person in that room can, and does, go and talk to the Father in the Throne Room; and each and every one of them can, and does, ask the Lord face to face, to save their families and their nations. But there is something about coming together in agreement that is special to the Lord."

The angel looked at each of the children, then continued, "The Holy Spirit of God was present in that assembly. I'm sure you felt Him, didn't you?"

The children nodded.

"Every soul in that room *was* in His presence, just as much as they are in the Throne Room. You see, they *were* talking to Him. He heard and received every utterance out of every mouth, every thought in every mind, and every prayer from every heart. To the Lord, there was no difference than if they had come and stood face to face before His Throne. But this kind of prayer, however, which we call intercession, is more than just visiting with Jesus. Those gathered in that room were joined together with one mind and one heart, in complete agreement, standing in the gap for the church in America. God has invited His children to join Him through intercession. These believers were partnering with God to see His will come to Earth as it is in Heaven."

"What about after that happens?" asked Edgas.

"What do you mean, Edgas? After the Kingdoms of this world become the Kingdom of our Lord?"

"Yeah, I guess so. I mean, after Jesus comes back, and Heaven is on the New Earth, and there is no more sin or sickness, and no more evil. Will we still have prayer assemblies?"

"Well, let me ask you a question. Do you think intercession will be necessary then?"

"I don't know, but I guess not. I think that intercession is very important now because of sin and evil and bad stuff, but once those are gone, then I guess there will be no need for it. We can still talk to God, but will that still be called prayer?"

"Well, Edgas, you are right that intercession plays a critical role in the purposes of God in this present age and that prayer is talking to God. But as to the future role of intercession, I guess you will have to wait and see," replied the angel.

"Aw, why can't you tell us now?" asked Edgas.

Abel's eyes twinkled with delight as he looked at each eager face. He loved these children and thoroughly enjoyed being with them. Masumi wasn't sure, but it seemed that his garment of light increased in intensity after being in the prayer assembly. He smiled lovingly at them as he answered Edgas' question. "You have been given a special gift children; a glimpse into eternity. But it is only a glimpse. It is not time for you to know these things. But one thing is for certain: a day is coming when you will know the answer to these and all of your questions. Until then, trust the Lord, and seek Him. For it is the glory of God to conceal a matter, and the glory of kings to seek and to search it out."

MAPUTO, MOZAMBIQUE
UNSEEN REALM

As it had before, the atmosphere ruptured and light came rushing down upon Isabel. And accompanying the light this time was a sweet aroma that filled the room.

Jesus.

Michale immediately dropped to one knee, slapped his fist against his chest, and bowed his head.

Jesus smiled at the guardian and nodded approvingly.

He leaned over and gazed at his sweet daughter. He loved her deeply. He put his hands on her hands and spoke directly to her spirit. Truth and encouragement flowed from the One who is Truth.

Michale could feel excitement course through his veins for he knew well that when a person embraces Truth, it most certainly will make them free.

Keep loving them, Isabel. You're making a difference in their lives. I'll watch over your heart to heal and protect it.

I know, daughter. You have generously opened up your heart to these children of mine. You have loved them well, and that makes your heart vulnerable to hurt. Don't close your heart; many still need your love and your prayers. I'm proud of you, Isabel.

Isabel wept.

You've given your life for these young ones and for the building of my Kingdom; it has not gone unnoticed, my daughter, nor will it go unrewarded. I've come to heal your broken heart.

MAPUTO, MOZAMBIQUE
12:56 p.m.

Despite the tears, Isabel suddenly felt peace fill the room. Then that voice. It was as clear as her own thoughts, but she knew it was not her own thoughts she heard. She had learned over the years to recognize the voice of her Savior, and this was Him. She gave her full attention to His whisper.

Keep loving them, Isabel. You're making a difference in their lives. I'll watch over your heart to heal and protect it. The thought came quietly into her mind. She knew it was her Lord speaking.

"It hurts so badly, Lord. I don't think I can bare to loose another one." Rivulets of tears dripped off her chin.

I know, daughter. You have generously opened up your heart to these children of mine. You have loved them well, and that makes your heart vulnerable to hurt. Don't close your heart; many still need your love and your prayers.

"I don't want to stop loving them; they've brought me more joy than I could ever have imagined. I just wonder if it's time to go back home."

I'm proud of you, Isabel.

The weeping started afresh. "Thank you, Lord," she whispered.

You've given your life for these young ones and for the building of my Kingdom; it has not gone unnoticed, my daughter, nor will it go unrewarded.

"I just want the hurt to go away, Lord. I know I can make it through anything with your help."

I've come to heal your broken heart.

At that moment Isabel felt a warm salve-like sensation flow from the top of her head, down her spine, all the way to her toes. She closed her eyes and felt the warmth travel through her body. Still holding on to Edgas, she turned her hands over and opened them in a gesture of receiving from the Lord. She began to feel a gentle pressure on her chest and warmth spread to her heart and lungs.

She breathed easier now, and she felt the suffocating hopelessness that had settled on her lift. Sweet relief. She took a few deep breaths, thanking the Lord for His goodness and His faithfulness. How quickly He had come to set her free. "Thank you, Jesus," she whispered. "I love you."

I love you too, precious Isabel; you have captured my heart.

MAPUTO, MOZAMBIQUE
UNSEEN REALM

Jesus looked at Michale, and they communicated without words. The guardian stood to his feet and positioned himself behind Isabel. An angel who had accompanied the Lord handed Michale a small vial of oil from the bowl in the Throne Room. Michale poured out the entire vial on top of the sweet missionary's head. It covered her whole body, running all the way down to her toes.

Then Jesus himself reached over and touched her chest. Isabel took several deep breaths. Each one coming easier and easier.

She was free.

Sigh.

She was free indeed!

Jesus leaned over and planted a tender kiss on the top of Isabel's head. He smiled at Michale as he lifted into the air, "She's in for an even bigger surprise. Enjoy her moment." He started to chuckle, then burst into a full out laugh that reverberated around and around the tiny room.

Michale grinned. How he loved and missed that wonderful laugh. And how forward he looked to the day when all who call upon the name of the Lord will join the Heavenly hosts, and together they will live in perfect peace, love, and joy, forever and ever. Oh, that day *will* come; he knew it without doubt. And until then, he renewed his resolve to serve his loving Master well.

THIRTY-ONE

The sun will no more be your light by day, nor will the brightness of the moon shine on you, for the Lord will be your everlasting light, and your God will be your glory. — Isaiah 60:19 (NIV)

"I s the sun setting? It feels like it's not as bright as it was before," Masumi lifted her eyes and gazed out at the horizon.

"There is no sun to set," replied the angel.

"But she's right, look! The sky is turning kinda orange and pink over there," Edgas said, pointing to the horizon.

"What's happening, Abel?" asked Cristen. "It really does look like the sun is about to set."

"God himself is the only light in Heaven," he replied, "and He never sets."

"Is something blocking his light then?" asked Masumi. "Or filtering His light, like a curtain?"

"Did he put on an orange and pink hat?" asked Edgas.

Abel could not suppress his smile, "No, no, and no!" He looked at Edgas on the last no, his blue eyes twinkling.

"Then what's he doing to Himself to change the color of the sky?" asked Henri.

The angel chuckled at first, then laughed merrily. "You are quite right, Henri, God is indeed doing something to Himself!"

Henri was surprised that his guess was closer than the guesses of the others.

Abel continued, "The changing sky is one of the ways He lets us know that it is time to rest."

"Rest? I didn't think people slept in Heaven?" said a surprised Edgas.

"You're right, sleep is not necessary for your heavenly bodies, however some people do enjoy sleep and love to take naps. One of the fun things about Heaven is that you get to do those things you enjoy."

"I am one of those who enjoys naps," laughed Cristen.

"So, our day is coming to an end then?" asked Henri.

"Yes and no. Again, it is hard to explain. Remember, we don't have days like you do on earth. We have rhythms."

The thoughtful group of talkative children suddenly became very quiet.

"Does this mean we are leaving now?" Masumi asked the question on everyone's mind. All eyes quickly shifted to Abel's face, awaiting his answer.

"No. You're journey is not yet over."

There was a collective sigh as four faces brightened in relief.

"HURRA!" shouted Edgas. "I'm not ready to go back—I haven't met Jesus yet!"

Abel grinned, then reached out and tousled the boy's hair, "The Lord is well aware of that, Edgas!"

"This has been a pretty long day," added Henri, "at least when you think of all the things we've done."

"By that standard, it's been the world record of long days," laughed Cristen.

"Yet, I hardly feel like any time has passed." Henri continued. "Living outside of time is so weird."

"You said rest, Abel. Does every one rest, then?"

"Yes, Masumi. All of us enjoy and need some down time. It's really more about enjoying the rhythms of life. Most people recline for a little while and visit with family. Some people love to read and will prop up in their beds or favorite chair to enjoy a good book. Others will enjoy piddling with their hobbies, some like to play games or go to the movies, or whatever. Heavenly bodies don't tire like earthly bodies, and time is not measured in the same way, but we still enjoy the regular rhythm of work, rest, worship, and play."

"What if we don't feel tired, and we don't want to rest?" asked Edgas, a bit concerned he was headed for an unwanted nap.

"There are no rules about what you can or cannot do, only that you rest from your work."

"Wow, look! The whole sky has changed colors now," admired Cristen.

"How *does* God change His light?" asked Henri.

"It is one of the mysteries of Heaven. In a regular rhythm, God will purposely dim His own light, just a tad, and all of Heaven takes on this rosy glow."

"It's beautiful," admired Cristen.

Abel looked around thoughtfully, then said, "You children have had quite a journey. I know exactly where we can go rest."

"But, I'm not tired," said Edgas, still a bit concerned.

"Well, then, you just come along for the fun. I think you'll like where we're going."

"Where is it?" asked Edgas.

"Where are we going, Abel?" asked Henri.

"I thought you said everything was closed," added Masumi.

"Did I? Well, I stand corrected; not everything is closed. There are restaurants, movie theaters, concerts, and those sorts of places that will still be pulsing with activity for a little while longer."

"What about the Throne Room?" asked Cristen.

"What about the Throne Room?" answered the angel.

"Does it close?"

"Never!" resounded the angel. "Our God never slumbers, and activity before Him never ceases. His servants, the angels, along with His children, are always in His presence. Forgive me for neglecting to include the Throne Room as *the* most favorite place to go during the dusk hours."

"Are there ever exceptions to the, 'no working during dusk' rule?" asked Henri.

"Yes, as I mentioned, if you have a restaurant or run a theater, you might be offering your gifts during the dusk hours. And, there are often times when someone's assignments must be continued throughout the dusk period."

"Assignments?" questioned Masumi.

"Yes! All are given assignments, not just angels. God created each of you with an innate desire to accomplish something bigger than yourselves. This is usually referred to as 'your destiny.' Every citizen of Heaven is still fulfilling their destiny; the purpose for which they were created. Personal destiny is not extinguished when a person dies on Earth if they belong to God. It is continued here. People should not compartmentalize their lives; it is one long continuum."

"So, not all the activity we see is fun and games?" chuckled Cristen.

"Not at all, my dear, but as you have seen, much of it is! Remember when I told you that work receives no resistance? Everything you put your hand to will thrive, so even work is enjoyable."

"Like what kind of things?"

"Well, let's see, remember Joseph in the Room of Tears? That was his assignment. And the folks in diamond field?"

"And Gracie at the Golden Corral?" offered Edgas.

"Yes, that's right, Edgas, just like Gracie. There are many more jobs like that all over Heaven, and there are jobs where people are working with angels to record the things happening on Earth.

"Did you know there are even Welcome Centers in Heaven? People run those too, and those *never* close for new residents are always arriving." Abel smiled, "The Welcome centers stay very busy, in fact! Just as we talked about with Gracie, coming to Heaven can be quite the culture shock for some!" He laughed as if remembering something quite humorous and then continued, "Some people are working on preparations for the great *Marriage Supper of the Lamb*, and some people are piloting transports with new arrivals from Earth to Heaven. Some are leading prayer gatherings, some are writing books, and some are teaching. You get the idea."

"Heaven really is a busy place, isn't it?" said Masumi.

"Indeed it is!" replied Abel. "But God will always provide time for you to have fun and for you to rest."

"Oh, that again!" snorted Edgas.

"What about angels?" Cristen turned to look at Abel.

"What about angels?"

"Do you get to rest?"

"Yes, of course! We have many seasons in which we go long periods with no rest, but our Creator is loving and gracious to us. We have ample time to enjoy His goodness. Remember, angelic beings were not created in God's image. He has made us with different abilities and with different needs than humans. But *rest* assured," he smiled as he emphasized the word 'rest,' "He is well acquainted with our needs and He takes very good care of us, too."

"Where do you live, Abel?" asked Henri.

"In the City of Angels!"

"Of course! Why didn't I think of that? Of course you would live in Los Angeles!"

Abel laughed at Henri's joke. "God has created a wonderful home for His servants, the angels. It is a beautiful dwelling place in a whole different dimension, and it's absolutely perfect for us. One day when you return, perhaps He will let you visit."

"Oh, I sure hope so!" said Edgas. "Would you show us around?"

"It would be my honor. Now, who wants to go see the place where we will rest this evening?"

"Me!" said three, with Edgas adding, "I guess...as long as I don't have to sleep."

"Then let's quit jabbering and get going!"

○

PARIS, FRANCE
1:05 p.m.

"I want to believe like you do, Alison."

"You can, Maman."

"I do believe in Jesus, honey. I have chosen Christianity as my way to God, but I think there are perhaps many ways to God. Some people have a hard time accepting a god that sends people to hell."

"No, Maman! You have it upside down. God is not sending people to hell; He died in our place to *save* us from hell! He doesn't want anyone to go there. He loves us so much, so much, in fact, that He took our punishment *Himself*! No other god did that. There's no other way to God but through Jesus. It may sound nice to say there are many ways, and people might think that they are being kind and accepting by saying that there are many ways—but it's just not true. It's a lie from Satan! Only one God lay down His life for mankind. Only one God poured out His blood. Only one God died in our place. Only one God can help us get through a really bad day. Only one God, Maman, there is only one."

Celeste looked again at her daughter. *Who is this rock of strength sitting beside me? Is she fourteen or forty?* Her heart knew that Alison spoke the truth. She couldn't explain it, but she just knew it was the truth.

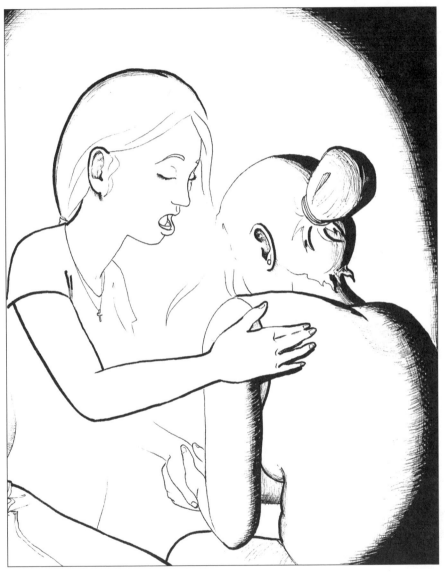

"Jesus we are desperate for you."

"We can lean on Jesus together. I don't have power to get us through this, but God does, and He will help us."

"I want to lean on Jesus like you. I am desperate for His help."

Alison took her mother's hand, and Celeste grasped the dainty hand with both of hers. Putting her free hand on her mother's back, the teen closed her eyes and began to pray earnestly. "Jesus we are desperate for you. We cannot walk this without you. I know you are with us now, for you promise that you will never leave or forsake us."

Celeste hung on every word, hoping against hope that those words were true.

"You have all the power we need to get through this, and you are the only one who can help us; please come and fill this place, and us, with your presence."

Just then, the door opened and a young woman sashayed into the room carrying a stack of papers. The Leonard women sat back in their seats, still holding hands.

"Bonjour, Ms. Leonard." The woman slid into the swivel chair behind the desk. She acknowledged Alison with a slight nod of her head and then turned her attention back to Celeste. She stretched her hand across the table, "I'm Ms. Fitzgerald, I am so sorry for your loss."

Celeste shook the woman's hand but said nothing. Her insincerity made Celeste feel agitated. *Is there anyone here who cares?*

I care, Celeste.

"What'd you say?" Celeste looked at the woman.

"I said I am sorry for your loss, Madame."

"I mean after that."

"I didn't say anything after that."

Celeste stared, confused. She was sure someone had just said that they cared.

"Did you bring your insurance card with you?"

"Yes, I keep it in my purse." Celeste reached in her bag, pulled out her wallet, opened it, and handed the woman her card.

"There are just a few papers I need to go over with you, and then you'll need to sign them in order for us to proceed with your son."

Just a few hundred, Alison thought, looking at the stack of papers on the desk before them. *This is gonna take awhile.* She leaned over to her mother and whispered, "Maman, will you be okay if I went out to pray while you do this? I won't leave you if you need me."

"Yes, honey. You go on ahead, I'll be all right." She wasn't at all sure she'd be all right. The papers before her looked daunting, and she felt like a soggy noodle. But, she didn't want to prevent her daughter from praying. When Alison hesitated, Celeste patted the girl's knee and smiled weakly, trying her best to encourage her, "Go ahead, sweetheart. This is going to take me a few minutes."

"Thanks, Maman. Where do you want me to meet you?"

"How about back in the waiting room?"

"Okay, see you in a few minutes." Alison kissed her mother on both cheeks and slipped quietly out the door. *Hold it together Ali,* she told herself. *Don't loose it here; find a place where you can cry.*

She was awash with emotions. She had longed to share her faith with her mother and had dreamed of her listening and coming to a greater understanding of faith, but this was not the scenario she had imagined. She wanted to be happy about it, but happy was certainly not the emotion she was feeling.

Feeling very alone as she walked the long corridor, Alison suddenly had the strong desire to call her youth pastor. She leaned against the wall and then slid down to the floor, sitting alone in the empty hallway.

"PJ? This is Ali Leonard."

For the next few minutes Alison poured her heart out to the man who was responsible for her strong faith in Jesus Christ.

Pastor Jacque was stunned. He felt like someone had knocked the wind out of him. He loved that boy and couldn't imagine what sweet Ali was going through. "I'm on my way, honey. You are not alone in this. I'll get our prayer chain started for you and your mother right now."

"You don't have to come down here," Alison said, but her heart was crying, *please* come down here. I need your support.

"Of course I'm coming. Don't say another word about it. Now let me pray for you before we hang up."

Alison, with tears streaming again, nodded her head.

"God of Heaven, we come before you right now. I lift up Ali and Celeste to you and ask for your grace to be poured out upon them. Hold them in your arms. Wrap them in your love. Father, we don't understand why this has happened, but we refuse to listen to any accusations about your character. You are good. You are faithful. You are love. And you are with Ali right now. We loose a battalion of angels to fight on their behalf. Send them quickly, Father. We declare that no evil will befall the Leonards. Protect them by your might, oh God. Set a guard about them that no enemy can penetrate.

And Lord, if you are willing, we ask that you bring Henri back to us. You have said in your word that if we speak to the mountain it WILL be moved. Father, we speak to this mountain. We speak to the mountain of death and we say MOVE! We speak to Henri's spirit and say, Henri awaken! Henri, come forth! We know that you can raise the dead, Jesus. You have shown us that throughout your Holy Word. Nothing is impossible to you, NOTHING! But Lord, if this mountain is not to be moved, then we will climb this mountain. We will climb this mountain, and we will lift up our arms and say, 'Show us your glory!' Be glorified in this, Lord. That is the deepest desire of our hearts, that you be glorified. We love you, Jesus, and we thank you for your great mercy. Amen."

"Amen," Alison sighed and then wept. "Thank you, PJ," she finally sputtered. "I really needed that."

"I got your back. See you just as soon as I can get down there."

THIRTY-TWO

Let not your heart be troubled; you believe in God, believe also in Me. In My Father's house are many mansions; if it were not so, I would have told you. I go to prepare a place for you. — John 14:1-2 (NKJV)

A white stretch limousine was parked in a circular drive on a golden street near the American Prayer Assembly; and a young man, neatly groomed in a tweed coat and cap, leaned against the driver side door, waiting. As the sojourners approached, he stood up straight, tipped his hat, bowed slightly, and opened a wide passenger door. "Welcome children. It would be my pleasure to take you to your next destination."

"Are we riding in that limo?" Henri asked excitedly.

"Of course! You heard the man," Abel answered. "Climb on in! You've had a long journey! I thought you'd enjoy the ride."

"But, I'm not tired," Edgas reminded.

"So you've told us!" laughed the angel. "Climb in anyway!" Abel jokingly pushed Edgas from behind.

It was no surprise that the luxurious limo was clean and polished to a bright glean. The children ecstatically obeyed and climbed inside. Abel sat shotgun but had to recline the back of the seat all the way down in order to fit his wings inside.

The chauffeur was the nicest man. While the children opened cabinets, fixed themselves ginger-ales, ate cheese and crackers, pushed one button after another, stood up in the sunroof, waved to other vehicles traveling the golden roads, and chatted excitedly, he pointed out landmarks and beautiful vistas they shouldn't miss.

The children found out that he was from England and had been a cabbie. He loved chauffeuring people around and couldn't get over that this was his assignment in Heaven.

"He's being modest," added Abel. "Haven Moore drove a black taxi on the streets of London. That's a big deal because drivers go through rigorous training to get their badge. They have to pass a test called *The Knowledge,* and it can take some people years and years to pass the test. Haven passed it in only two and half years. Being a black taxi driver is like having a mental GPS of London in your head. No matter what famous landmark or what backstreet hotel, Haven could get you there—without a map, atlas, or GPS."

Haven blushed under Abel's praise and thanked him for his kind remarks. "I'm just thrilled that I have the honor of toting you around."

"Did you have to pass a test to be a limo driver in Heaven?" asked Henri.

"No, thank goodness! After having studied so hard for my license in London, I could scarcely believe it when the map of Heaven's golden streets just flooded my noggin'. It happened immediately upon receiving my assignment here. It's too good to be true. I have to pinch myself every now and again."

"Well, here ya go!" Haven announced after driving a little ways through another amazing neighborhood of mansion-sized homes. The children hopped out and thanked Haven for the wonderful trip in his limo. He smiled and started to wave goodbye but stopped. "Wasn't your shirt red before?" he asked Edgas.

"Why, yes sir, it sure was!" Edgas laughed, adding, "How come I never see my shirt change?"

"Well, it tis a lovely color now. Looks like the color of the ocean. Well, I'll be off. Toot-a-loo." He hopped into the driver's seat, rolled down his window, and waved goodbye as he drove away.

The children waved and called goodbyes until Haven disappeared from view.

"What's on my shirt this time," asked Henri, pulling it out again for a better view.

"It looks like a surfer shirt," said Cristen.

"Surfer? Are we going surfing?" Henri's eyes darted to the angel.

"Really, Henri. Surfing? In Heaven? What will you think of next?" Abel's eyes sparkled wildly.

"You are a great big tease," laughed Cristen, pushing Abel lightly.

He hugged her in return. "Who, me?"

"Yes, you!" laughed Edgas. "We heard about surfing in the Valley of Forgiveness, remember? We know you're teasing us! Sooo are we going surfing?"

"Hey, look at Masumi's shirt. It just lost another petal." Abel pretended great interest in the flower on Masumi's shirt.

"Go ahead, Abel, change the subject! We'll find out soon enough!" Cristen laughed.

"And, Cristen, I think you might just fly off if you're not careful!" Able continued his unsuccessful distraction techniques.

The jolly group shared a hug, turned, and started walking down the street arm in arm. They so enjoyed each other's company. How they would miss each other when they went back to Earth! The thought was too unpleasant, so no one let themselves go there, each determining on their own to just stay in the moment.

The rosy glow permeated everything, and with it came a kind of peace that the children had not yet experienced. They followed Abel slowly, walking and gawking at the lavish homes.

A young girl in a sweet white dress with a wreath of flowers in her hair was playing on a long green lawn in front of her home. Her white mansion sat back on a hill and was bordered by the prettiest landscape of blue and pink and red and yellow flowers, the very ones braided in her hair. There was an inviting marble bench nestled among the flowers and a white swing hanging from a low branch of a great tree. Bright flowers climbed the ropes holding the swing.

The sojourners were just about to call out a hello when they saw that the young girl was playing with dozens of butterflies. They stopped walking and watched her with great interest. There must have been fifty or more brightly colored butterflies fluttering about her, each different in both pattern and color and all larger than any butterfly the children had ever seen. The darling child caught one in her cupped hands, released it, and then quickly caught another. Whenever she held out her hand or a finger, a butterfly would land on it, then giggling she would throw her hands in the air launching it back into flight.

When she noticed her audience, she quickly held her arms out, and a group of butterflies landed on them. With a big smile, she ran right over to show her guests. She spoke to the butterflies, "Meet my guests," and instantly the butterflies fluttered off her arms and hovered in front of the visitors.

"Hold out your hands, and they'll land on you," she instructed. The children did as she advised, and to their delight, the butterflies landed on their outstretched hands.

One landed right on the tip of Cristen's nose. She turned slowly to show the others. When they were looking at her, she crossed her eyes as if she were trying to see the butterfly which caused an eruption of happy giggles.

"My name's Kate; what're yours?"

The friends introduced themselves, and then Kate introduced each butterfly by name.

Suddenly, Masumi screeched and pointed to a black and white fur ball ambling on the grounds of this child's mansion.

"A skunk!" yelled Henri, trying to decide if he should hightail it down the street.

The visiting friends stared in unbelief as the plump skunk headed across the lawn and right towards them.

"Don't be scared," said Kate to her wide-eyed guests. "He's my friend."

Cristen turned a shocked face to Abel. "He's cute, but, uh…is he de-skunked?"

"Not quite," replied the angel, his mouth twisting into a mischievous smirk. In truth, he was fighting to hold back his laughter.

"Okay, this is Heaven," reasoned Masumi, "but everything in me says we should run in the other direction just as fast as humanly possible."

"You mean spiritually possible which is probably really, really fast!" Edgas chortled.

"Oh, don't worry about him being a skunk," said the girl. "He's harmless."

Before the words left her mouth, the skunk turned and lifting his tail, began to spray the children.

The group screamed as one, flinching and shielding their faces from the attack. But then, to their great surprise and delight and relief, a most beautiful and unusual aroma saturated them.

"You've been skunked," laughed Abel, his eyes twinkling wildly.

"We've been what?" Cristen exclaimed.

"Skunked!" Kate laughed with the angel and then scooped her skunk friend up in her arms. "It's one of the funniest surprises in Heaven, don't you think?"

The surprised foursome could not agree more.

"So, instead of a nasty odor, skunks in Heaven smell good?" Henri looked from Abel to little Kate and then back to Abel.

"Yes, Henri," replied Abel. "Skunks don't need to repel any enemies in Heaven, but they're still skunks. Skunks were made to spray, so your infinite Creator lets them use their natural defense mechanism to release a lovely fragrance instead. It's one of His many ways to let a creature be a creature without being a creature, if you get my drift!"

"Does every animal use their natural defense mechanism in a different way here?" questioned Masumi.

"You've got it!" laughed Abel.

"So camels and llamas and alpacas don't spit?" Cristen was eager to know.

"Well, they spit all right," laughed Kate. "But their spit turns into big rainbow bubbles. Camels are hilarious. But my favorite is the porcupine!"

"Oh, what does a porcupine do?' Edgas was captivated with wonder.

"You go ahead and tell them, Miss Kate," urged Abel.

Kate started to speak and then doubled over with laugher. Curiosity fully peaked, all eyes were on the girl as she tried to rein in her giggles. Taking a deep breath she said, "Feathers! Instead of pointed needlelike quills, each quill has a soft feather on the end. The feathers stay hidden until the porcupine raises his quills, then out pops the feathers. He looks like the funniest, roly-poly bird you ever saw!"

The laughing group shook their heads as they tried to imagine what it must look like. Glories upon glories upon glories.

Kate added with genuine enthusiasm, "Eternity will *never* be dull with such a creative God!" She stroked the skunk and held it out for the others to pet.

The guests were beginning to understand just how true that statement was. They certainly never started their day thinking they'd be sprayed by a skunk with a lovely fragrance!

"Is this your mansion, Kate?" Masumi turned her eyes and admired the lovely grounds.

"Well, kinda," the girl answered. "It's actually my great-grandfather's, but I live here with him. That is, until my mommy comes home. Then I'll move into her mansion, and she can finish raising me."

"Remember at the Valley of Forgiveness," added Abel, "I told you that the Lord lets children grow so slowly that even if the parents died of old age, they won't miss any part of watching their child's development! That's how precious your Heavenly Father is, and how much He loves families."

"I'll get my own mansion one day," Kate beamed with joy, "but I don't want it yet. I just want to be with my mommy for a while. I can't wait for her to get here, and then we'll be together forever and ever! And while I wait for her, I'm collecting beautiful things I know she'll just love, and I put them in her mansion. And guess what? It's almost ready!"

"We toured a mansion and saw a room full of gifts waiting for someone," Cristen said, remembering how that room was piled high with gifts. "It never occurred to me that some of those gifts could have been placed there by an excited child waiting for their parent's arrival!" A deep sense of gratitude washed over her.

After saying goodbye to Kate, the group continued down yet another opulent street. Every home was unmistakably a mansion and spaced generously apart from its neighbor on huge sprawling lawns, peppered with the most amazing flowers. Each mansion was unique in its architectural design but similar in its astonishing, jaw-dropping, beauty. Many of the mansions had broad verandas, terraces, or porches completely encircling them. Some had decorative columns supporting the roofs and extravagant domes, and some had lovely steps curving down to pearl paths through manicured and lush lawns. Some were of a Spanish design with red tile roofs, and some looked like a villa from the Tuscan hills of Italy. There was a style for every taste in architecture.

Abel unexpectedly announced, "We're here!" He turned and headed up a pearl path to a mansion that was playing hide and seek among overhanging branches of a large and quite beautiful tree.

It was a multistoried home made of white marble with a broad porch around the first floor and a wide veranda encircling the second floor. Several balconies were positioned off of bedrooms on the third floor, but they were on the back side, and the children were not yet aware of them.

As the group approached the front door, they heard an exclamation of surprise. "They're here, they're here!"

A lovely woman with bright eyes and a warm, beautiful smile appeared in the open doorway. She clasped her hands in joy, looked right at Cristen and said, "Oh, happy day!"

"Cristen's jaw dropped. "Meme? What are you doing here?" she squeaked.

"I live here, baby," Meme's smile could not have been any bigger if she had tried. She reached out and hugged her granddaughter tightly. "Welcome to my home."

As soon as the words were out of her mouth, a wagging tail caught Cristen's eye. She looked down, and her jaw dropped again. "Puddin'?" She looked at her grandmother with wide eyes. "Puddin's here with you?"

"Oh, yes, dear. She was waiting on the steps for me when I arrived. Jolly and Jazz and Gator and Muffin and JiJi are here, too!" Cristen just shook her head in disbelief.

"I didn't know if our pets made it here to Heaven or not!" exclaimed a still-shocked granddaughter. She reached over and pet each one of the dogs she remembered from her many visits over the years to Meme's house.

"Of course they do! Well, I don't know if they are the same ones or if God created new ones and gave them the same memories, but nevertheless, they are the same to me, and I love them."

"And I sure didn't expect to see you again. I mean, until I came back for keeps."

"I know, sweetheart. Isn't this a fun surprise? God is so good to us." She smiled at the others, "Welcome, all of you! And why are we still standing in the doorway? Come in, come in! I'm so glad you're here. You've had a busy day, I'm sure! Come in and rest; refreshments are on the back veranda. Now don't let these puppies trip you."

Meme linked her arm through Cristen's and led the group into her amazing home. She leaned in close and whispered, "Smells like y'all've been skunked!" Her easy laugh echoed around the great foyer.

PARIS, FRANCE
UNSEEN REALM

The angels continued to fight, strengthened by Alison's words. Suddenly, every demon in the room was pushed back and tumbled to the ground. Truth came pouring out of Alison's mouth straight from the Holy Spirit within. Full of power and anointing, she spoke truth to her mother, shattering the lies.

These words of faith poured out of her spirit as Rivers of Living Waters, and it flowed across the room. Every demonic being jumped back to escape the heavenly current.

Capri looked up and thanked the God of Heaven. He and Heston would wash in the refreshing water when the battle was over. It would heal their wounds and cleanse them from any putrid slime they had been exposed to.

Proclamations about the goodness and character of the Lord poured over Celeste, like water on a thirsty ground. Her mother heard and believed and instantly a flame burst to life within her.

Demons screamed in terror.

The tiny demon attached to Celeste's head, released his hold and ran for cover.

Then to make matters worse for the Kingdom of Darkness, Alison called in reinforcements. As her pastor began praying, angels were released to come to the aid of Capri and Heston, and immediately the two guardians changed sides of the ball and now were playing offense instead of defense.

Several flashing swords appeared in the room followed by angels of light sent on assignment. Heston unsheathed his own sword and began delivering debilitating blows to the demons that had not fled, and his sword continually hit its mark.

Shrieks of pain rang out, splitting the air as the sword sliced one demon after another. By now, most had fled in excruciating pain.

With their swords drawn, the readied angels completely encircled the mother in the room and the daughter in the hallway. There was nothing getting past them—not no way, not no how.

The women felt invisible arms of love wrap around them and hold them. Another angel entered the hospital carrying a vial of what looked like oil. He took it to Alison and poured it out over her head, then he flew to Celeste and poured it out over her head as well. Comfort.

Capri, with a band of angels encircling the girl, followed Alison to a bench situated in front of the hospital. A motion above him drew his eye up, and he immediately broke into a wide smile. At the same time, he thumped his fist into his chest and bowed low. At the gesture, every one of the angelic guard did the same.

Jesus. Jesus had come to speak to the young girl. It was a joy beyond measure for the Heavenly Hosts.

Jesus smiled and nodded to each one. He held out his hand to Capri, who reaching out, took the proffered hand and clasped his Master's hand in his own.

"Well done," said the Master with a smile. He then sat down next to Alison and pulled her close to his heart. The guards stood to their feet and hedged in the pair.

Capri leaned close and whispered, "Alison, Jesus is here. Open your ears to His voice."

THIRTY-THREE

Before the throne there was a sea of glass, like crystal. — Revelation 4:6a (NKJV)

A comfortable breeze kissed their faces the moment the group stepped inside the airy villa. A light-colored, hardwood floor polished to a gleaming shine extended throughout the home and was cool to their feet. The foyer opened to a spacious living room with a high open-beamed ceiling that was at least twenty feet high. To the left of the living room and divided from it by a large white marble island was a beautiful open kitchen with large countertops, workstations, and luxurious cabinets. The entire back of the home was opened to the outside with not a door or window in sight. The living room spilled seamlessly into the back patio and garden blending them in an easy uninterrupted flow. Sumptuous white chairs, sofas, and lounges abounded and were sprinkled with colorful pillows. The villa was simply and tastefully decorated with just the right touches of colors and patterns that played all the way out into the garden. A splash of color here, a cluster of flowers there, nothing was overlooked or overdone.

An infinity pool, surrounded deliciously by bright swaying palms and other luscious plants, was positioned invitingly across the back of the house overlooking the most spectacular sight of all—a panoramic view of the Crystal Sea. Wildly sparkling rainbows shot out of the sea's pristine waters that were hemmed by a white, unspoiled beach. The sight, like so many others the children had seen on their journey, was absolutely breathtaking.

"You live on the ocean?" asked an amazed granddaughter.

"Yes and no," laughed Meme. "It looks like the ocean, doesn't it? It's actually a sea, *The Crystal Sea.*"

"We've heard of it," said Cristen, "but I never pictured it looking like this. And I've sure never seen a sea with rainbows shooting out of it like fireworks!"

"It's more sparkly than anything we've seen so far, and that's saying a lot cuz everything we've seen so far sparkles like crazy!" Edgas said, eyes glued to the light display. Then laughing he added, "Crazy, crazy, crazy, crazy, crazy!!"

"It looks like the River of Life, only bigger," commented Masumi.

"That's because the great river which flows directly from God's throne throughout all of Heaven empties into the sea," said Meme.

"I thought the River of Life sparkled, but this is incredible! There must be a billion diamonds in the water!" Henri admired.

"Oh, at least!" said Meme.

"Really?" asked Cristen.

"Really! You can scoop diamonds up by the handful. They are precisely what gives the water its remarkable sparkle," she faced Edgas and continued with a giggle, "and crazy, crazy, crazy rainbow fireworks."

The group shared a laugh.

"Your home is fantastic! I could move right in!" said Masumi.

"Well, come on then! I love to have guests in my home, and you are welcome any time."

"Me, too?" asked Edgas.

"Of course, you, too! All of you!"

"You don't have any windows?" asked Masumi, walking towards the back patio.

"Oh, goodness no! I don't want anything between me and that view, and besides I love the sound of waves lapping up on the beach."

"I guess homes in Heaven don't need windows. I think Abel mentioned that earlier," said Henri.

"Even if you have windows, there is absolutely no reason to close them," added Meme. "Our weather is perfect. There's no chance for rain, there's no dampness, or mold or rust or mildew, and best of all, there's zero chance of a break-in. We are all perfectly safe in Heaven."

"Some folks don't have roofs either," said Abel.

"What? Why?" asked Cristen.

"Nature lovers," explained Abel. "They'd rather be outside than in."

"Oh, Meme! I'm so happy for you!" exclaimed Cristen, hugging her young grandmother tightly. "You always loved the beach. Some of my favorite memories are of our family vacations at the ocean."

"Thank you, my dear. Those are some of my favorite memories, too. God is such a good Daddy and loves to delight His children. He knows exactly what will make our hearts skip a beat! He sure choose the perfect place for me!"

Edgas starting laughing hysterically, and the others looked at him questioningly.

"What's so funny?" asked Henri.

"I just started thinking that this home is a paradise in paradise!"

"Oh, I love that! And it's true. I live in *the* paradise vacation home!"

"Who's singing?" Cristen turned to see where the lovely voices were coming from.

"Oh, honey, those are just my flowers," Meme said, as if it was the most normal thing in the world for flowers to be singing. "Noisy little happy things." She led the children over to one of the walls in her living room. "They love to greet me whenever I come home, and now they are greeting you because you are my special guests."

The children gaped in amazement at the lovely, singing, pink and yellow tropical blossoms growing right out of Meme's living room wall.

Edgas was the first to find his voice. "Hello little singing flowers! It's very nice to meet you, and thank you for the song! It's very pretty."

The others smiled and repeated the thank you, not quite computing that they were really talking to singing flowers.

A painting caught Masumi's eye; she covered her mouth and shrieked.

The others turned to see what had shocked her. The painting was of a sailboat with the wind in its sail, zipping across the Crystal Sea. There were dolphins jumping out of the water beside the boat. It was a lovely painting. And then, right before their eyes, it came to life. The water splashed, the sea salt sprayed, the sails billowed, the boat sailed, and the dolphins jumped in and out of the boat's wake.

The children stood in front of the painting, spellbound.

Meme laughed, "I know, it surprised me too first time I saw it. All the pictures in my home do that. Whenever you stop to look at them, they spring to life. Awesome, isn't it?"

Edgas could not help himself; she had set him up. He wagged his head and muttered, "Weirdly awesome."

The familiar joke broke the children's trance-like state. They giggled and looked for more pictures. After a minute, Meme herded her guests towards the back veranda. "Now go on outside, all of you. You can look around later, but right now there's more than just refreshments waiting on the veranda for you."

<hr />

TOKYO, JAPAN
8:07 p.m.

Evil spirits had done their work well over the years for Michi had listened to many of these lies since birth and solidly believed them. His heart wanted to believe the truth the stranger spoke, but his head had embraced the lie for so long. Besides, was it really a lie? After all he really *was* a loser. He could list out a string of failures over his lifetime. Michi heaved a deep sigh. Yes, he was a fool, an idiot. He was impatient which made him, quite obviously, a bad brother. Of that there was no doubt—he wouldn't be sitting in this stupid waiting room right now if that weren't true. He was a terrible son; he was smart mouthed and rebellious, and worst of all, he had killed his parents' precious daughter! He was a failure—at everything. No, his life was not worth living. His parents would be much better off without him. The *world* would be better off without him. He should just kill himself. He had no reason to live. Besides, he'll be hated by everybody. Heck, he hated himself. He was a murderer. He should have been the one to die, not Masumi. Well, he would take care of that. He'd make that right at his first opportunity.

He made a decision right then and there to put himself and the world out of its misery; he'd kill himself. And by an act of his will, he bound a seed of suicide to his soul.

THIRTY-FOUR

For the gifts and the calling of God are irrevocable. — Romans 11:29 (NKJV)

"SURPRISE!"

As soon as the children walked out on the veranda, a large group of family and friends jumped out from hiding places and came rushing towards them. The group squealed with joy at the unexpected but delightful surprise of seeing again some of those they had said goodbye to at the Gate of Heaven.

Grands, great-grands, cousins, aunts, uncles, friends, teachers, and new acquaintances were all there to party with the visiting children.

"They've been skunked!" someone shouted, bringing a spattering of laughs, snorts, and giggles as everyone in the room remembered their first encounter with one of Heaven's fragrant skunks.

The next portion of their journey was spent visiting, laughing, story telling, eating, and playing games with those they loved and missed so much. Young and old alike filled Meme's home, veranda, garden, pool, and beach with all sorts of joyous activities. It was a party these children would never, ever forget.

Platters of fresh fruit and tasty appetizers abounded, as well as some of the children's favorite sweets. Someone, it turned out to be Henri's great uncle, was grilling delicious smelling hamburgers and hotdogs, and there was grilled fish, plank salmon, and lobster, too, for those who enjoy eating fresh seafood when they visit the Sea, which hands down included an excited Edgas. Abel reminded the children that all the food in Heaven is made of light, and that they weren't really eating animals. The children couldn't tell the difference, and thought it pretty awesome of God to save the animals and make delicious food out of light.

Henri's grandmother delighted the children with a description of her mansion and some of the others she had seen. Grandmama, as Henri calls her, is an artist. She said that adjoined to her mansion is both an art studio and an art gallery. People can come to her home and paint in her studio where she spends much of her time painting, or they can stroll through her art gallery. If someone likes a painting, she gives it to them and paints another.

"It's just like Abel told us," Henri said excitedly.

With Puddin' sitting quietly at her feet, Cristen's friend, LuAnn, sat beside her and held her hand; how great it was to be together again. Her Aunt Leigh, the piano teacher, was also at the party. Cristen looked at Abel, "You knew she'd be here! That's why you gave me that funny look when I mentioned her."

Leigh told the children that she did indeed teach piano, and they were welcomed to her music studio any time, which was adjoined to her mansion, just like Abel had thought.

The girls smiled and told Leigh their plan to take joint lessons together and that they had to remember to invite Abel and the boys to their first concert.

"Oh, that will be wonderful," Leigh agreed. "My performing studio is huge, and it's filled with dozens of very grand, grand pianos. It is amazing actually, for whenever I want to play a song, I sit at my piano, think of the song I want to play, and the music sheet just supernaturally appears. I truly have no idea how it happens, but I do know that we still get to exercise faith in Heaven.

Everett Power, Edgas' caregiver Isabel's dear father, was also at the party. He told the kids he was an avid golfer and that when he arrived in Heaven, he discovered he had his very own golf course as part of his mansion! "You are welcome anytime, children. People come and play golf on my course all the time, and it's always free," he smiled proudly.

Masumi's Sunday School teacher, Kazuko, said she loved to garden and spent most of her time puttering around in her yard. She had acres and acres of beautiful flowers, and she never had to worry with weeds or pests. She had a flower shop as part of her mansion. People sometimes order arrangements to be sent to someone special, just like they do on Earth. Birthdays of loved ones who are still on Earth are a big event that families may celebrate with a special floral arrangement. Everything she makes she gives away freely.

Soon other guests had pulled up chairs and joined this conversation by adding some of their own experiences and discoveries. The children found out that, not only are pets waiting for loved ones when they get to Heaven, but many times little children are waiting on the steps. Sometimes parents don't even know that they have lost a baby through miscarriage, and when they get to Heaven, they discover that child waiting for its parents to come and raise them. Also, babies many times are handed right to the mother at the Gates of Heaven. The visiting group had learned a little about this in the Valley of Forgiveness, but still, this information amazed them. It made their hearts soar with love for the goodness of God.

They discovered that everyone has their very own mansion because everyone has a different gift, and their mansion is designed around that gift. People can visit each other as often as they want and stay in each other's homes. But, because there is no marriage in Heaven, husbands and wives do not live in the same house. They do remember their life together and are generally the best of friends. They probably live right next door or very near to each other. And families love to get together, and they do—a lot!

They also found out there's a beautiful place modeled after the Old American West with purple mountains and unusual landforms. People can go on cattle drives, eat off a chuck wagon, and experience the fun of cowboy living with none of the dangers usually associated with it.

Cristen's great-grandfather told an amazing story about a fire that once destroyed his home on Earth, but more importantly, it destroyed some very special keepsakes. One of these was a family Bible that had been passed down to him from *his* great-grandfather. When he arrived in Heaven, that very Bible was waiting for Him on the nightstand next to His bed. Then after, he continued to discover other things, like special photos he had lost in the fire. He has since heard that God has done the same for others.

Edgas' friend from the orphanage said he found out whenever you stop doing something that was important to you on Earth, he called it "laying it down in obedience to the Lord's call," that God will let you "pick it back up" in Heaven. For instance, if you like to take pictures but God tells you to preach instead, then God will have angels take those pictures for you and when you get to Heaven, those pictures will be there waiting for you. And in Heaven, you can have a really fancy camera and take all the pictures you want.

Cristen's Great-Aunt Priscilla and Great-Uncle Bruce live right next door to each other. They both love to cook, and they share a restaurant and a dream kitchen between their homes.

Masumi's friend also has a restaurant, and he told the kids that people come from all over Heaven to enjoy his renowned sushi, rice, and other traditional Japanese dishes. He said there are restaurants like his all over Heaven where you can enjoy the delicious dishes of different countries. Henri wanted to know if there was a French restaurant. "Of course! Hundreds! It's a favorite here!" he answered.

"Ooh, I love Italian food," crooned Cristen.

"Hundreds of them, too! You can eat pasta and pizza and gelato to your heart's content, my dear."

"Yum, I can't wait!"

"If we eat to our hearts' content, won't we get fat?" asked Edgas who had never had an ounce of fat in his life.

"No, sir, not in Heaven."

"It's all made of light," Abel reminded them. "You cannot overeat light."

"No wonder we haven't seen anyone who is overweight," said Masumi, reflectively.

The children grew more thrilled over Heaven with each new account.

A darling little boy about eight years old and very handsome came up confidently to Masumi. He had a head full of dark, almost black, shiny hair and looked perhaps to have some slightly Asian features.

"You don't know me, but my mommy and your mommy are friends. I grew up in America because my daddy is an American, but my mommy is from Japan."

That explained the beautiful features.

"My name is Daniel."

"Well, hi, Daniel, I'm Masumi," she pointed to her nose, "and I am very happy to meet you."

"I died in a drowning accident, and I came to your party to ask you to give my mommy a message. I heard that you're not staying here yet."

Masumi immediately remembered hearing her mother tell of this little boy's death.

"I would be glad to do that, Daniel. What do you want me to say?"

"Tell her that God did not take me away from her but that he knew my time and that He welcomed me home. Tell her that I didn't suffer because Jesus came and took me immediately. Tell her I'm not lonely and that Jesus taught me how to swim and that I'm not afraid of the water anymore. Tell her that I love to swim now, and I don't want her to be sad around pools. I want her to rejoice when she sees them because they remind her of me and of the beautiful place where I am living. Tell her that I love her and that I go to the Portal often and that I am waiting here for her and Daddy to come play and swim with me."

Masumi hardly knew what to say. A lump stuck in her throat as she remembered how painful this child's departure from Earth was. But here he stood, very much alive and very healthy and happy. "That's a wonderful message, Daniel. I will be sure to remember every word of it and relay it to her just like you said it."

"Thank you, Masumi. Jesus told me that you would."

Wow, Jesus was talking to Daniel about her visit. That amazed her. Masumi opened her arms, inviting Daniel in for a hug. He came forward, and she embraced him warmly. "I know this message will make your mother so proud of you. If I ever happen to meet her face to face, I will pass along this hug as well."

Daniel beamed with joy and ran off to swim with the other children in the infinity pool.

Masumi looked at her friends who had heard the whole conversation, and they just grinned and shook their heads. There was no end to their amazement.

"It's time," said Meme, gathering all the guests on the back veranda. "Come, come, children. You don't want to miss the show; it's especially for you!"

Everyone stood and looked out over the Crystal Sea. Almost immediately, a burst of bright color sailed high up in the sky and then exploded in a fountain of falling light. Fireworks! One after another, exploding colors flashed across the sky, lighting up the Crystal Sea and reflecting off its surface as far as the children could see in all directions. All eyes were on the sky, and all faces aglow as the show continued.

"I've never seen fireworks before," said Edgas, his bright, brown eyes shinning with the wonder.

"I have but never anything like this," Cristen replied.

"I guess I started with the best again," Edgas laughed.

"You sure did!" Cristen smiled and hugged her young friend.

The guests seemed to "just know" when the party was over, and in no time at all, they had thanked their hostess, said their goodbyes with many hugs and kisses, and gone off to their own homes. It was bitter sweet saying goodbye, again, and each of the children was grateful that they would one day return to this wonderful place, never to be separated from these loved ones again.

Meme suggested a quiet time and showed her guests to the third floor bedrooms, girls in one, boys in one, angel in one. The bedrooms were spacious and tastefully decorated in coastal decor. All three rooms had two king-sized beds, two lounging chairs, two bedside tables, one large sofa, a writing table, a bookshelf full of books, and a balcony with two comfy chairs overlooking the Sea.

The bedrooms had doors to the hallway for privacy but no door or window to the balcony. When the angel had closed his door, he looked at the furniture and chuckled. Although very generous by human standards, he would need to push the beds together in order to fit comfortably. Just as well, he wasn't planning to recline here anyway. He immediately walked to the balcony, spread his wings and took flight into the rosy sky. He had an appointment to receive his next instructions.

Meanwhile the girls took turns indulging in a bubble bath, not that they needed a bath for they were in no way dirty. It was just that the Jacuzzi tub was so enticing. When Masumi took her turn to soak in the tub, Cristen took the opportunity to check out the books on the bookshelf.

One of the books that caught her eye was entitled *My Baby Girl*. She opened the book and squealed, shocked to find that it was her mother's baby book. In it were recorded all the milestone events of her mother's life. But not just recorded with pen and ink. Every event popped up off its page as a living scene in hologram form. Within the hologram, Cristen could actually watch her mother say and do those things recorded. She saw her mother take her first steps, she saw and heard her mother say her first words, she saw her first hair cut, and so forth. Cristen laughed and cried as she watched the hologram movie of this adorable, chubby, baby girl's memorable firsts. She closed the book and closed her eyes, saying a quick prayer for her precious mother. *My goodness, Heaven is truly supernatural.*

"Masumi!" Cristen couldn't wait to show her the book.

TOKYO, JAPAN
UNSEEN REALM

Failure bared an insidious smile, revealing a perforated row of stained, yellow teeth. His plot was working. Michi was buying that suicide was his only option. Yes, he was buying it hook, line, and sinker. Cliché' or not, Michi was taking the bait.

As soon as Michi came into agreement with Failure's suicide plan, the dark figure dropped a black seed into the layers of Michi's soul. He cackled hysterically at the pathetic boy. Failure knew the seed would now take root and grow. Michi was as good as dead. The demon sat back, exhausted. Mission accomplished. He was also very glad he had averted another severe beating; he exhaled heavily, filling the waiting room with a putrid stench.

"You really are a stupid idiot!" The demon poked Michi, mercilessly, hoping he had an audience witnessing his victory; "I've defeated you, you stupid little human. You think you're so smart, don't you? Ha! You'll *never* be as smart as me," he boasted. Then puffing out his pride-filled chest, he strutted victoriously around and around the boy. "Where's your God now, boy, huh? Where's your God?" Looking around, he muttered under his breath, "Nobody will ever call me a fool again, nobody."

Raphia's stomach turned over at the boastful performance. "Well, pride does goeth before destruction," he chortled to himself, quoting the verse from the sixteenth chapter of Proverbs. He would have loved nothing more than to demonstrate this verse to this pest and shred the nuisance right here and now; but he had to admit, The Holy One's way of bushwhacking His enemies was much more rewarding.

He watched the little rooster and knew he was about to have a rude awakening. "Where was the boy's God?" Oh! He was right here with Michi and Raphia, and He was about to show off His power!

A seed of suicide is dropped in Michi's soul

THIRTY-FIVE

Give unto the Lord the glory due to His name; Worship the Lord in the beauty of holiness. — Psalm 29:2 (NKJV)

The rosy glow retreated and was replaced by the brilliant blue of before. The children had thought the Sea sparkled wildly in the twilight of dusk; they had no words to describe what they were witnessing now. Without doubt, it would have been blinding on Earth, impossible to gaze upon. But as it was, with heavenly eyesight, its flashes of light and color shooting into a perfectly blue sky was absolutely mesmerizing. Shore birds flitted about everywhere singing out their morning songs of praise. It was another perfect day, or whatever it was—a rhythm—in paradise.

One by one the children, sniffing the air with gladness, gathered on the veranda where juice and warm cinnamon buns awaited.

"I followed my nose," laughed Henri, "and my eyes—they led me right here to these ginormous cinnamon buns. It's still weird how we can both smell and see aromas."

Unnoticed, Abel had only recently returned; He floated down the winding staircase, as if he'd been in the villa all along and added, "Makes it easy to find the bakeries, Henri, when you can follow the wafting aromas."

"Well, I bet that's true," Henri laughed, hoping for a chance to try it out later. Meme was in her wide open kitchen happily cooking something that smelled delicious while the children sat on the white veranda sofas and talked excitedly, reviewing the many marvelous things they had seen and done thus far on their journey to Heaven.

Pulling their special stones out of their pockets, they showed them to Meme when she stepped out onto the veranda.

"Abel said we could keep them in our pockets; aren't they beautiful?" cooed Cristen.

"Oh, they are just lovely, and I'm so glad you showed them to me."

"Abel said he was told to show us some of the glories of Heaven, and boy, did we sure get to see a lot of *glories,*" Edgas told Meme.

Meme nodded, swallowing a laugh and thanking the Lord for this delightful visit as she went back to the kitchen to take something out of the oven.

"Did you remember to thank the Lord for your wonderful journey so far?" asked Abel.

"Oh, yes!" replied Cristen. "Masumi and I got on our knees together and thanked Him for His goodness towards us."

"We did, too," said Henri with Edgas nodding beside him.

"Look everybody; look what I found in our room!" Cristen excitedly showed the group her mother's baby album. It sprang to life when she opened the pages, astounding the boys just as it had the girls.

"How does it do that?" Henri wondered.

"It's supernatural!" Abel's voice carried a smile.

"That's exactly what I was thinking," laughed Cristen.

Meme called the group over to a dining table on the other end of the veranda. The table was artfully set for breakfast with a combination of cobalt blue and aqua blue glass on white china and little aqua blue glass bottles and jars filled with dainty pink and yellow flowers. It looked like a picture out of a magazine.

"I wouldn't have thought to put these two blues together," said Cristen taking her seat, "but they compliment each other so well; I just love it!"

"Thank you, baby. You know, I wouldn't have thought of it either, but I took my inspiration from that view." Hands full of steaming platters, she nodded at the sea.

"Oh, my!" Masumi exclaimed. "You're right; the sea is both of these blues."

"It makes me think of pictures I've seen of the Caribbean waters," Cristen added.

"Except for the flashes of diamonds shooting out of it," laughed Henri.

"You're right, Henri, except for that small detail!"

Abel looked out over the water. "The darker cobalt color is deep water and the aquamarine color is shallow."

"Well, I guess putting those colors together was God's idea!" Edgas laughed, taking notice of the line where the deep and shallow waters met.

"I think these colors are so peaceful. I love your veranda, Meme. Forget my own place; I think I will just live out here on your veranda when I come back."

Meme, eyes twinkling, leaned down and whispered in Cristen's ear, "Maybe you'll live right next door, honey. Wouldn't that be something?"

Cristen felt her heart soar with the possibility. She beamed at her grandmother and nodded enthusiastically.

Meme served her guests the most delicious breakfast any of the humans had ever eaten. It was a feast of heavenly proportions, and the children enjoyed every last bite.

Before long, the sea that stretched before them was bustling with activity. Both white and colorful sails speckled the panorama; skiers and tubers passed by, pulled by fancy boats; several jet skis sprayed streams of water into the air as they played among the boat wakes; a hovercraft practically flew across the surface; and a large ship glided smoothly across the horizon. Oh, how the children wanted to get out there and play with the water enthusiasts.

Abel, sensing their desire said, "I think we have time for a swim before we head out."

Edgas' "HURRA!" was probably heard by passengers on the ship out at the horizon!

The children graciously thanked Meme for the delicious breakfast, carried their plates to the kitchen, and screamed when they saw that they were clean before they even reached the kitchen sink.

"Oh, thank you for the help, children. Why don't you just put them back in the cabinet for me?" she said, putting her pots and pans away.

"Are you kidding me?" Henri almost shouted.

"Kidding you about what, honey?"

"The dishes and pans clean themselves?"

"Oh, that. Yes, yes, they do. Isn't that marvelous? I'm so used to it now that I forget that's not how it is on Earth. No, nothing stays dirty here; there is never any clean up. Sounds like Heaven, doesn't it?"

"I'll say!" The shocked children agreed.

Across the veranda, past the infinity pool, and down the grassy hill the visiting sojourners excitedly headed to the beach—with five happy dogs running and jumping along beside them. What a pleasure it was not to have to put on sunscreen or drag a towel.

It was a lovely, crescent shaped beach with several thatched-like umbrellas and comfortable beach chairs dotting the soft white sand. Every home on this stretch of beach had it's own path directly to the shore. Shells were in abundance, free for the taking, and of such beauty as to thrill any collector. The dogs rushed onto the beach and straight into the water, playing joyously in the surf. The waves gently lapped the children's feet when they put their toes in to test the water. Just as expected, the temperature was perfect.

Diving into the waves, the children headed out—with Abel joining their swim this time—into the deeper water.

"Hey, it's not salty," Cristen licked her lips.

"Too bad it's too calm for surfing," commented Henri. "Hey! That reminds me, *are* we going surfing?"

"Sorry to disappoint you, Henri."

"But his shirt is a surfer shirt," protested Edgas.

"It's a surf shirt, and you are playing in the surf, are you not?"

The kids laughed.

"True, you got us on that one," Henri admitted, "but is there really a surfing place called Wipe Out?"

"Yes, the surf park is one of the favorite pastimes of daring teenagers. You'll have to check it out when you come back."

"Oh, yeah, I'm gonna check that out for sure," Henri grinned and nodded.

Cristen's face registered surprise, "I'm sure it's called Wipe Out for a reason, Henri."

"Hey, we had to die to get here, remember?" Henri wiggled his eyebrows in his silly way which caused an eruption of laughter.

"True," answered Cristen.

"Well, I think *this* area is perfect for swimming," commented Masumi.

"I got an idea!" Edgas exclaimed. "If it's not named yet, let's call this beach Paradise in Paradise! I'm from a town on the beach, and it's got a port with lots of ships and stuff, and it's nickname is Pearl of the Indian Ocean, but it's certainly no paradise!"

"Pearl of the Ocean? That reminds me!" cried Masumi, suddenly remembering something Meme had said. While the others watched, she dove underwater and scooped a handful of tiny stones off the bottom. Surfacing, she grinned and opened her hands revealing a large dollop of sparkling diamonds!

"Those aren't pearls!" laughed Cristen.

"Hey! I know! Let's call this place, Paradise in Paradise, the Diamond of the Crystal Sea!"

Edgas' friends agreed. "So dubbed," said Abel, winking at Edgas.

Henri, Edgas, and Cristen now dove down to get their own fistful of diamonds. They tossed them high in the air, giggling with glee as the facets caught the light and glistened wildly, some landing in their hair like thrown sand. Who would even have considered tossing diamonds into the ocean for the simple pleasure of seeing them sparkle? They are much too valuable on Earth for such foolishness.

The name of the great Sea was fitting in many ways. For one thing, its water was as clear as crystal. The children went under again and this time stayed down a while, enjoying the wide variety of beautiful fish. They excitedly pointed discoveries out to each other. With the ability to breathe underwater, the children could stay under as long as they wanted. They felt very much like scuba divers exploring an undersea world but without the inhibitions of any kind of gear.

They spotted a pod of dolphins playing near them. Delighting the children with their antics and acrobatics, they jumped and splashed, flipped in the air, and skimmed backwards across the water with their strong tails.

Following Abel's lead, the children each took hold of a dolphin's dorsal fin as it swam beside them. The playful dolphins pulled the friends quickly through the water. Before long, the kids were riding on the dolphins, like water cowboys, and their shouts and laughs and giggles resounded across the water and into the lovely villa where Meme had busied herself with a project.

Hearing the joyful commotion, she ran to watch them at play. What fun it was to witness the pure and simple joy of children. No wonder Jesus said that you must be like a little child to enter the Kingdom of Heaven. How glad she was that Heaven is so fun and child friendly! Even adults in Heaven get to act like children, and with strong, youthful bodies, they can enjoy every bit of it just as much as the kids do. *As a matter of fact*, she thought, *why am I up here in the house when I could be down there playing with dolphins!*

To the delight of the children, Cristen's grandmother came running down the path, out across the sandy beach, and plunged into the sea, joining them in their fun. It was hard to remember that she was Cristen's grandmother when she didn't look or act much older than them!

"Watch this," said Abel. He floated on his stomach, face in the water, with his arms out to the side. His feathers looked a little bit like giant swans floating on the water. All of a sudden, two dolphins swam quickly up to him and placed their bottled noses into the soles of his feet, pushing him with such speed that his upper body was quickly out of the water. With his arms still spread, he shouted, "I'm superman!" He flew across the water without using his wings. The boys couldn't wait to try the trick. To their great delight, when they laid face down in the water just like they'd seen Abel do, the dolphins came and pushed them across the top of the water, too.

When Abel said it was time to go, the children said their farewells to the dolphins and obediently swam to the shore. They were again surprised at how their bodies, hair, and clothes dried almost immediately. As they walked back up to the villa, they discussed the issue of heavenly clothes with Cristen's grandmother.

"Abel showed us someone's mansion that's almost ready," Cristen told her grandmother, "and there was a whole closet full of clothes hanging there waiting for her. Did you have clothes hanging in your closet when you arrived, too?"

"Oh, yes, dear! I had a beautiful wardrobe, perfectly fitted, waiting for me."

"You've had on something different each time we've seen you," added Masumi. "You were wearing a gorgeous green gown when you met us at the Gate. Last night you were wearing a fun bright teal and yellow dress, and today you are in a pink pants outfit."

"Oh, the clothes are so lovely here; they're made of the finest fabrics that never wrinkle or stain, and they are so soft you almost forget that you have them on."

"Abel also told us about the white gowns that everybody gets," Edgas said, happy to contribute to the conversation.

"Oh my, yes! Did he tell you that each one is adorned beautifully with special stones in recognition of what we have done for the Lord during our time on Earth?" The children smiled and nodded.

"We saw some of those!" Edgas added excitedly.

"We also saw some that were plain," said Henri. "Abel said that the people wearing those might have gotten saved on their death beds."

"That's true. But even the plain ones are beautiful."

"Abel said that those people are just happy to be here, so we don't need to feel badly for them."

"That's true, too." Meme's face lit up as she continued, "Some of the gowns, let me tell you, are simply works of art and could rightly be hanging in a museum. I'd pay to go see them, wouldn't you? But you don't have to because everything is free! Anyway, we can choose when we want to wear them, but most people choose to wear the white robes when they go to the Throne Room or to a Portal.

"A Portal? What's that?" asked Henri as the group reached the Veranda.

"Yes," said Masumi. "Daniel mentioned the Portal in his message for his mother."

"I will take you to one of the many Portals before you go," answered the angel.

The children seemed satisfied with that. They had learned to trust Abel completely, and so they turned their attention back to Meme.

"What about the pants you're wearing now?" asked Cristen. "What are those called?"

"These are tunic pants. They are very popular up here and are much better suited for certain activities than the robes."

"Like swimming?" commented Masumi.

"Yes, like swimming and like riding on the roller coasters!"

The children looked at her excitedly, "Someone mentioned roller coasters at the Valley of Forgiveness. Then there really are roller coasters in Heaven?" asked Cristen.

"Oh, yes! Great big, really fast, really high, really thrilling roller coasters!"

The children grinned back and forth at each other and then looked pleadingly at Abel.

"I don't believe those are on our agenda, but believe me, you can ride them as much as you want when you return!" he said, watching their faces fall. "Don't be disappointed; there's still plenty of adventure in store."

"Oh, children," Meme chimed in, "God is always adding new and exciting things here. His creativity never ceases, and we will have all of eternity to enjoy the things He is preparing for us. Just think of the possibilities of what might be here when you return!"

They were standing on her veranda now and knew it was time to say goodbye and leave her beautiful Paradise in Paradise, Diamond of the Crystal Sea. Cristen hugged her grandmother tightly, and as she did, Meme smothered her with gentle kisses. Then she whispered in her ear, "Tell your momma hi for me, and tell her that I love her with all my heart."

Next, Meme kissed each of the children on the cheek and promised to visit them at the Portal. She thanked Abel for bringing the children and blessing her with their happy visit.

With one last hug goodbye, the excited group walked about a mile down the road to a large dock where they boarded one of those hovercraft boats they had seen out on the sea. Before long, they were scooting across the water to an unknown port of adventure. They spotted the back of Meme's villa and waved enthusiastically to her as they passed her lovely mansion.

"I love you!" Cristen called out, blowing a kiss in the direction of the villa.

"I love you, too!" Meme whispered. She reached out and grabbed the invisible kiss, holding it close to her heart. "I love you so much, baby girl, and I'll be waiting for your return."

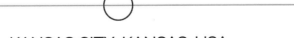

KANSAS CITY, KANSAS, USA
6:10 a.m.

"Father God, we come before you, humbly. We thank you that you are the same yesterday, today, and forever," Pastor Mac's eyes were shut tightly, but instead of his head bowed toward the floor, his chin was lifted slightly upward toward Heaven. "Jesus, you healed everyone that came to you, everyone who asked, everyone who believed, and you are still in the miracle working business today. You are no respecter of persons; what you do for one, you will do for another. We bring Cristen before your throne, Father. We ask for your mercy. We ask for your healing power to touch this precious daughter of yours. So we bring the cross of Jesus Christ and everything Jesus accomplished in His death, burial, and resurrection, and we appropriate it right now by faith for Cristen and her family.

"It says in your word, Father, that what we bind on Earth is bound in Heaven, and what we loose on Earth is loosed in Heaven. So in the name of Jesus, we bind the plans of the enemy. We bind every demonic spirit sent to attack Cristen and this family. We bind sickness and disease. We bind every lying and deceiving spirit that would accuse God and every thought that would raise its head above the powerful name of Jesus and the knowledge of God. Fear must go, NOW! In Jesus' name!"

Scott found himself looking at Pastor Mac as he prayed. He was amazed at how natural it sounded, and how much Pastor Mac seemed to believe everything that he was speaking. Scott thought he felt his spirit lighten, as if hope had actually entered him. *Hmm, maybe there's something to this prayer thing after all.*

"And Father, in Jesus' name," Pastor Mac went on, "we loose angels to go into that operating room and minister to Cristen. We loose angels to guide the doctors' hands and to bring him wisdom and skill. We loose angels with healing in their wings to touch Cristen. We loose angels to stand guard and fight off any demonic spirit that would try to attack her.

"We confess that we *don't* understand this trial, Father, but we *do* trust you. We confess that we *do* know you're nature and your character. You said you came to bring life and that it was your enemy, the devil, that came to steal and to kill and to destroy. We ask for life, Father. We ask for life.

"Give Will and Elaine, Scott and Margaret, and the boys at home grace for today and download a gift of faith and hope into our hearts. We trust you, Lord. You are good and trustworthy. Bring your peace. We ask all these things in the precious name of Jesus. Amen."

"I don't understand what's happening, Lord, but I confess that I trust you." Elaine found the words pouring out of her heart. "I let go of Cristen and place her into your loving and very capable hands. Thank you for dear friends willing to go to war with us. And, as Pastor Mac has taught us, I come boldly to the Throne of Grace in my time of need, and I boldly ask for, and I receive, abundant grace. Give me the grace, Father, that I will need for whatever comes my way today."

At that moment, Elaine physically felt her fear vanish and a tangible peace fill its place. For the next few hours, she was wrapped in an unexplainable bubble of grace. She had no idea whether Cristen would live or die, but she knew whatever happened, it would be okay. She knew Cristen would be okay. She knew *she* would be okay.

THIRTY-SIX

For by one offering He has perfected forever those who are being sanctified.
— Hebrews 10:14 (NKJV)

When the joyful seafarers disembarked the watercraft, Abel unfurled his enormous wings and leaped into the air, lifting easily off the ground. Hovering over the children, he said, "Follow me," and then began to fly slowly away.

The children stared after him for an instant and then exchanged puzzled glances. Abel, keeping low to the ground, glanced back to see if they were coming. He grinned and motioned them with his hand.

Edgas immediately tore off after the angel, and the others were quick to follow. When Abel saw his brood running after him, he increased his speed.

"Hey, wait up, Abel!" Henri pumped his arms and legs as hard as he could.

"Follow me!" the booming voice replied.

"How?" yelled Henri.

"Slow down, Abel! We're trying!" Cristen called, running as fast as she could; but no matter how fast her wonderful, spiritual body could go, she and the others could not catch up with the flying angel.

Masumi abruptly stopped running. *Worship!* "Hey guys, STOP! We don't have to run; we can float on worship, remember?"

"That's right! Good thinking, Masumi!" shouted Henri.

"Do you think it'll work?" Edgas looked from one friend to the other. "We were already in the air last time."

"Let's do it; it can't hurt to try!" Cristen encouraged.

The group began to express their love and gratitude to the Father in songs of worship. To their great delight, the wispy ribbons once again flowed from their lips, but this time, the wisps swirled around them, lifted them off the ground and up into the air, and began to carry them across the skies of Heaven.

"I wonder if we're going to the Throne Room?" Cristen's eyes were wide with excitement. She surveyed ahead, but only saw endless blue sky and Abel laughing.

When the worshipers caught up with their leader, he nodded his head in approval. "Well done," he said, eyes sparkling with the pride of a teacher.

"Masumi thought of it," said Edgas.

"Then let's give credit where credit is due; well done, Masumi."

Masumi blushed and Edgas beamed.

Abel took the group by the hands, like before, and they soared with him through the majestic blue sky. Beneath them lay indescribable beauty in all directions.

They cruised along rapidly then slowed as Abel asked, "Who wants to go solo again?"

"ME!" they chorused.

On the count of three, they released their grips and instantly began to drop altitude.

"Worship!" Abel reminded as his group sank farther and farther away from him.

"Oh yeah!" laughed Edgas. He and the others began to sing, releasing ribbons of worship. The next instant they were floating along beside Abel, buoyed on their worship. It was an amazing experience, and they really enjoyed the thrill of flying solo. They waved and called to anyone and everyone they saw. Suddenly, Abel began to fly faster and faster. The kids kept their eyes glued to the angel who was by now a good distance ahead of them. Leaning forward, they began to pick up speed and close the gap.

Edgas pulled ahead of the others.

"Hey, girls," said Henri, passing them, "don't be golden eggs!" He laughed but then pulled up, in very gentlemanly fashion, allowing the girls to catch him. But instead of joining him, they put their heads down and zoomed past!

"Tootle-loo, Henri!" Masumi teased, waving her fingers over her shoulder.

"Later, golden egg!" laughed Cristen.

"So that's how it's gonna be, is it?" he said, but the girls didn't hear him over their peals of laughter.

Henri—secretly enjoying their teasing—now determined to pass them by; he pumped his arms and legs with all of his might. He looked quite comical, but his method worked, and he picked up great speed.

"Well, look who's flying!" boomed Abel's jolly voice as Edgas and the girls caught up to him. "I knew you'd figure it out; again I say, well done."

"Bye bye, all you golden eggs!" called Henri, passing the group in a blur. He waved his fingers over his shoulder just like Masumi had done.

"Whoa! Slow down, cowboy!" the angel shouted after him. "We've arrived at our next stop!"

Abel took the others by the hand, and the group descended, landing lightly in front of a large marble archway. Abel folded his wings behind him while he and the others kept their eyes on the flying boy.

Henri tried to stop, turn around, and head back all at the same time. The result was a plummeting to the ground and a head over heels tumble down the golden road.

His startled friends gasped.

"Are you hurt?" Cristen yelled, running towards him followed by some very concerned friends.

He was not at all hurt, not even his pride. He jumped up with a planet-sized smile and brushed off non-existing dust. He thought he must have looked hilarious and laughed good-naturedly about it as he jogged back to the group.

Abel burst out in a hearty laugh, his deep tones resounded down the golden street and his shoulders bobbed up and down with merriment. His jolly laughter was so contagious that the children soon found themselves rolling on the street, laughing hysterically—next stop temporarily postponed.

"I guess it's gonna take some practice learning how to put the brakes on this pony," Henri said, making a motion of pushing car breaks while pulling back on horse reins.

"Indeed," replied Abel, wiping his eyes.

After a collective deep breath and contented sighs, the friends stood up and followed Abel through the marble archway into an extremely large courtyard. The courtyard had a beautifully designed, marble, gold, and gemstone path which spiraled through it from a point in the center. Gorgeous, dark, green topiaries stood like sentries around the walled interior. Flowers grew right out of the ivy-covered walls while lovely blooming trees of Redbud, Magnolia, Cherry, and Dogwood hemmed in the courtyard in an eye-pleasing arrangement. Extraordinarily large planters filled with stunning floral arrangements added to the overall sense of peace and beauty. Marble benches had been strategically placed around the courtyard inviting guests to sit and enjoy this lovely place. Beautifully carved marble tables, some short and close to the ground and others quite tall, were also placed about the courtyard.

Men and women gathered around these tables and benches in groups of three to four, deeply engaged in conversation. Although they were serious in their discussions, their faces shone with joy.

Some of these men and women were holding scrolls in their hands or had spread the scrolls open on a table before them. They appeared to be examining the scrolls carefully, and their intensity made them seem very scholarly.

Others had their noses buried deep in beautifully bound books.

"Who are these people?" whispered Masumi to Abel.

"Yeah, and what are they doing?" asked Henri, in his lowest voice.

"These dear people are very special to the Lord," answered Abel.

"Are they the disciples?" asked Edgas.

"Why do they have scrolls?" asked Cristen.

"No, if you mean *the* disciples, as in the ones who walked on the Earth with Jesus, but, yes indeed, they certainly are disciples." He said to Edgas and then to Cristen, "They have scrolls because they are learning. You see, this is a classroom, and those scrolls are their textbooks."

"A classroom?" Henri exclaimed, a little too loudly, "No way!"

"Yes, way!" answered the angel.

"It's not like any classroom I've ever seen before," said Henri.

"We shouldn't be surprised, Henri," chuckled Cristen. "Nothing is like *anything* we've ever seen before!"

"Good point," replied Henri.

"So, these are students?" asked Masumi. "They look more like teachers."

"Students? Oh no!" moaned Henri. "Do we have to go to school when we come back? Are we going to school now? Is that why we're here?"

"You will *always* be learning, Henri!" said Abel. "Even if you don't sit in a classroom."

Abel had a serious look on his face, but he couldn't hide his smiling eyes. "Some of these people are teachers, Masumi, and some are students. I told you that these are very special to the Lord. Every one of them had a mental disability when they lived on Earth. Most of them were children with Down's syndrome or other brain function disability. The ones who have been here the longest are teaching the newer arrivals. Many of the things that you take for granted, they are only now coming to understand. Their minds are like eager sponges, absorbing everything about the world, about Heaven, and about the Lord. They love being students! They love being teachers! And they *love* being in this classroom!" He directed that last statement to Henri.

"How wonderful!" Cristen felt her heart swell.

"Well, if you've got to go to school, this would be a very lovely classroom," admired Masumi.

"Yeah, but still, I can't believe they love school!" whispered Henri.

Just then, a handsome, young man with dark brown hair and twinkling, brown eyes came rushing over to greet them.

"Abel!" he called out, breaking the whispered quiet of the courtyard. He grabbed a hold of Abel and hugged him tightly. "Welcome, my dear friend. It's so good to see you! And who are these that are with you?"

"These are my good friends Masumi, Cristen, Edgas, and Henri. They have come to visit Heaven, and I have the great honor and privilege of showing them some of Heaven's glories. Children, meet my friend, Ricky."

"It is so nice to meet you," Ricky said, then looking at Henri he added, "Cool Superman shirt!"

"What?" Henri looked down and grinned at the flying superman on his shirt.

"Our shirts change all the time, but we never see it happen," laughed Edgas, noticing his purple shirt.

The girls grinned and shook their heads as another petal fell from Masumi's back.

"Oh, what a fun treat. I know you must be very special to the Lord since you have been given Abel as your tour guide. Now, don't tell anyone I said this, but," he leaned in and whispered his secret, "he is my most favorite angel!"

"Now, Ricky, don't confuse the children; there are no favorites in Heaven!" laughed Abel with his arm still snuggly around the young man's shoulders.

"Oh, I know God doesn't play favorites, but I think we people still have our favorites! I do like all the angels, but you must know, Abel, there is a tiny place in my heart reserved just for you."

The children looked back and forth from Abel to Ricky, trying to figure out what was going on between them.

Ricky hugged Abel again and then turned to offer the children an explanation. "You see, when I lived on Earth, my mind didn't work like other people's. I had Down syndrome; have you heard of it?"

The children nodded, and Ricky continued. "Well, although my body grew up, I remained a very young child in my mind. I could write my name and simple words, but I never learned to read."

"I don't know how to read very well, either," interrupted Edgas.

"Really?" Ricky replied, looking at Edgas with kindness. "Well, don't worry one bit about that; you will learn how to read here. It's easy. Besides, you have a perfectly functioning brain, and of course, our wonderful teachers make it so much fun!"

A wide smile broke across Edgas' face. He was thrilled to know he would learn to read.

"Anyway, I had the added difficulty of being born with a hearing disability, so I never learned to speak well either. Communication was hard for me; my family and teachers had to play a kind of charades to figure out what I was saying. My parents loved me very much, but because of my multiple handicaps, they felt that the best thing they could do for me was put me in a boarding school where I could get the full-time attention that I required. Of course, I didn't understand that. All I knew was that I missed the people that I loved the most, very much."

Ricky looked over and smiled at Abel, then continued, "That's when I met Abel."

"Yes," Abel continued the story, "the Lord sent me to be with Ricky. I would come to him, especially during times of loneliness. The Lord allowed Ricky to see me on occasion." The children looked surprised. "God opened his spiritual eyes, and we became friends. No one else could see me, and Ricky did not have the ability to explain what he saw."

"Abel was a very well kept secret." Ricky smiled and winked at the children.

"In our times together," the angel continued, "Ricky would show me some of the things he enjoyed, like pictures of his family, a game he was playing, a book with pictures he was looking at, or a puzzle he was working on, and we would laugh together. I told him stories about God. Ricky loved Jesus, and it was evident to all who knew him."

Abel looked intently at each of the children, who were listening to this story with rapt attention. The four had learned that when Abel looked at them in this manner, he had something very important to say to them, so they paid close attention to his words.

"The childlike faith of one with Down syndrome is meant to be an example to the whole world. They have a sweet, childlike innocence and a purity about them that is to be envied. What precious souls! They are genuinely happy, they love everyone, and seldom meet a stranger. They don't hold onto a grudge or an offense, they are always ready to forgive and forget, and they bring joy wherever they go. It is not only sad, but tragic, that so many people misunderstand the purpose of these very special children and do not see their value. Some people don't even think they should be allowed to live, and snuff out their lives in the womb. Those people are to be pitied, for they have no idea of the blessings that these children bring."

Abel reached out and embraced Ricky again and said, "This young man has been the biggest blessing to me; I love him with all of my heart! And what a joy it is to see him among the most favored in Heaven!"

"Hey! I thought you said there aren't any favorites in Heaven!" laughed Ricky.

"Well, maybe, just maybe, I might have been wrong about that; why don't we settle it this way: your gracious, merciful, loving Father will more than make it up to those who suffered injustices on Earth for He is lavish in His rewards to those who suffered righteously. For do you not know that the first shall be last, and the last shall be first?"

Ricky blushed slightly and smiled back at Abel. "God has restored everything to me, and I am so thankful for who He created me to be."

Edgas fidgeted for a moment unsure if he should ask the question on his mind, but he decided to go ahead and risk it, "Ricky, I was just wondering if you ever saw your family again after they sent you away?"

"Oh, sure I did! I went home to visit often, and they came to see me every chance they got. I have a wonderful family, and I know that they loved me very much. I now understand that they were doing the very best for me that they knew how to do, but that doesn't mean that it didn't hurt, or that I didn't miss them, or feel lonely."

"Did they ever know your secret, that you saw angels?" asked Cristen.

"Well, actually, I think they did." Ricky smiled sheepishly. "Several times they saw me talking to an 'invisible' person. Once they saw me call Abel over to look at a picture in a book. I can still remember my mom's face as she looked around to see who in the world I was talking to. Then she smiled and said, "Ricky, are you talking to your angel?" She was half kidding, but I think after that, she suspected that I sometimes saw angels."

"Ricky has a praying Mama," Abel added. "Her heart was broken when Ricky left home. She spent many hours before the Lord asking him to take care of her little boy. Perhaps it was the earnest prayers from the broken heart of a loving mother that allowed me to come and be with Ricky. Never underestimate the power of prayer."

"Ricky, can I ask you another question?" said Henri, hesitantly.

"Absolutely, ask away."

"Well, I hope this isn't inappropriate, but," Henri hesitated.

"Go on, it's okay," encouraged Ricky.

"Well, I thought that people with Down syndrome all kinda looked alike; how come you don't look like that?"

"That's a very legitimate question; don't feel bad about asking it. You're right; people with Down syndrome have very distinct facial features, a result of a chromosomal abnormality. But when I arrived in Heaven, I no longer had that feature, or any of the other Down features. I guess this is what I would have looked like if I had not been born with Down's."

"You see, children," added Abel, "there are no defects, no abnormalities, and no diseases in Heaven. The deaf can hear, the blind can see, the dumb can talk, the lame can walk, and those who are missing limbs are made whole. Everything is just how it should be. Everything is perfect."

"And I don't have AIDS anymore!" said Edgas joyfully.

"Glory to God!" Abel reached down and swooped Edgas up in his large arms, spinning him around in a full circle. Edgas squealed with delight like a little boy in his daddy's arms.

"Now, that's worth celebrating!" said Ricky, as he and the others grinned at the happy boy.

KANSAS CITY, KANSAS, USA
UNSEEN REALM

When Pastor Mac started to pray, the atmosphere in the room immediately began to shift. He spoke truth from the Word of God, and as he did, a spiritual sword formed out of his mouth. The humans had no idea that this was happening. They didn't know that many things done in the natural realm produced very real results in the spiritual realm. Praying the truth of the Word of God is one of those things. It produces a two-edged sword that is formed right outside the human's mouth. The angels will take that sword and immediately go and fight the spirits of darkness in answer to that prayer.

Obed, upon seeing the sword, reached out and grabbed it. "Thank you," he said with a wide smile and a nod.

Pastor Mac continued praying, and the guardians watched as another sword formed, and likewise Innesto took it, "Thank you very much," said he.

Another sword formed, and again it was taken by one of the guardians. "Thanks P-Mac!" Tangoori's grin was contagious.

By the end of the prayer, every guardian, including Chacomel, was holding a two-edged sword in their hand. Now, with great joy, the protectors were on the offensive, no longer the defensive.

By the forming of the second sword, every demon had fled the room.

In answer to Mac's prayer, several forty feet tall, mighty, Host of Heaven were sent to the hospital. The demons were no match for the Host. The warring angels reached down and pinched up the scrawny demons that had been assigned against the Maples family and snapped them in fetters of iron, according to the prayer of faith. One of the Host leaned down and peered at the spirit of Fear, and it took off running as far away from the hospital as it could get.

As Elaine prayed, a bubble of light floated into the room and wrapped itself like a garment around her. Grace. The heaviness lifted completely off the woman and she instantly felt a peace that passed all understanding.

"Thanks P-Mac!"

THIRTY-SEVEN

God is not unjust; He will not forget your work and the love you have shown Him as you have helped His people and continue to help them. — Hebrews 6:10 (NIV)

Henri, Edgas, Masumi, and Cristen said their goodbyes to Ricky and walked with Abel up one gleaming golden street after another. And although each street shone with the same rich, translucent color, the journeyers never saw any two buildings that looked alike. Some buildings towered high into the sky, some sprawled for blocks, some looked like a faceted jewel, some looked modern, some futuristic while still others had a warm country feel. There was certainly an architectural style for any and every taste. But even with the multitudes of style diversity, nothing stood out as awkward or out of place. There was an integrated flow, a cohesion, joining all of it in perfect harmony. Perhaps it was the landscaping that tied all the quilt pieces together. No matter, the overall effect was beautiful, and ministered deeply to the children.

The visitors chatted exuberantly, never tiring of the new "wow" that took their breaths away around every corner.

Abel pointed out men and women whose names the children recognized from the Bible. They were beyond thrilled to not only see but also greet many of them! These great men and women, famous for their lives of faith, didn't act like superstars. No, they walked as ordinary people; some even stopped to say hello to the children. And although some of them seemed busy with important business matters, most were chatting and laughing with friends as they went in and out of restaurants and galleries. The weird thing, according to Henri, was that none of them were dressed in what he called Bible clothes but had on stylish clothing just like everyone else.

A motorcycle headed towards the children, and the handsome, young, helmetless rider smiled and waved to the children as he zipped by, his thick, red hair flowing freely in his wake.

"David." Abel said it so casually he might as well have said, "David Nobody," but the children didn't hear 'David Nobody' and their jaws dropped to the ground. Four heads turned to watch the rider disappear.

"As in KING David, David?"

"On a motorcycle?"

"Awesomely Weird!"

"No Way!"

"Way. And why not?" Abel could not stop the grin that spread across his face and his eyes were dancing wildly, "He is not the king here. He's a citizen, free to enjoy Heaven, just like you.

The four friends just shook their heads and chuckled. They had just passed King David, or rather he had passed them—on a motorcycle! Unbelievable!

"You'll often see him out on joyrides; and while he's out, he usually looks for someone to serve, for he's discovered that serving others is what brings him the most pleasure."

While watching the motorcycle disappear around a corner, Edgas thought he spotted that sneaky angel again. "Hey guys," he whispered, "I think there's an angel following us." He nodded in the direction of a guardian. The guardian turned abruptly and went inside a shop.

"There are angels everywhere, Edgas. Why do you think that one is following us?"

"I've seen him a lot, and he's always staring at us. That's why."

"That's weird," said Henri.

"Maybe he's learning how to give Heaven tours and is taking pointers from Abel," chortled Masumi.

Abel pursed his lips to keep from laughing. *You've been caught red handed, Sancto, my friend. Better tighten up, or better yet, just come out of hiding.*

Sancto heard Abel's thoughts and rolled his eyes. He knew Abel was laughing at him. Ugh, he didn't like getting caught. He'd tighten up all right, because the last thing he wanted to do was spoil the surprise.

Up ahead, a group of teenagers came laughing hysterically out of a shop. They were pointing at each other, and their laughter was infectious. All of them had a bright crop of dyed hair: blue, green, red, pink, orange, and purple. It totally surprised the children, and they looked at Abel.

"Hair salon," he answered the question written across their faces.

"You can dye your hair here?"

"No, way."

"Way. And why not? God doesn't care what color your hair is."

"He doesn't?"

"No, why would He care? He loves you. He cares about the color of your heart. So, tell me, who looks at the outward appearance?"

"Man!" the four chorused.

"Very good, my students," Abel smiled. "Man, not God."

"So, people get their hair done in Heaven?" Cristen was stunned. The thought had never occurred to her.

"Sure they do."

"Can we go?" Henri asked what they were all thinking. Four expectant faces looked up at Abel.

"Oh, why not? It only takes a blink."

They walked through the open arched door and were greeted by two adorable young women, sisters named Sara and Cara who invited them to hop up into the chairs that were centered on a small round platform above the floor. Each chair faced a large, beveled mirror.

There were buttons and gadgets at each station which looked like something out of a futuristic movie. The women introduced themselves and then went to work right away. After learning what style each of the children wanted, they stood up on the platform, grabbed scissors, and began pushing buttons. When it was time to turn the chair, the platform moved instead of the chair. The women swished effortlessly around the children. It seemed they only needed to think where they wanted to be, and the platform swirled obediently in response. Circling this way and that, Sara and Cara gave each child the exact style requested.

"Do you want a color?" Sara asked with a smile. "I think you saw the group that just left."

"I do!" Cristen decided immediately. Her friends took a moment to consider, but in the end, they all decided to color their hair.

Sara and Cara pulled out long baton like instruments and after asking what color each child wanted, they turned a dial and waved the baton once over the child's head. After it passed over, their hair was dyed! Cristen's hair was pink, Masumi's purple, Edgas wanted yellow hair, and Henri had chosen green.

They looked in the mirror and laughed at themselves—and each other.

Henri scrunched his nose.

"Don't you like it, Henri?" Cara asked observantly.

"Well, I like it, all right. I'm just wishing now that I had said blue. I think I might like blue better. But, no worries," he smiled up at Cara. "Green is still fun."

"No one leaves our salon unhappy." Cara smiled broadly, "Watch this."

The sweet beautician waved the baton back over Henri's head in the other direction, and his hair went back to its original color.

"Whoa! That's weird." Henri laughed, startled.

"Blue it is." Cara turned the dial again, waved the baton over Henri's head, and instantly he had blue hair. "What do you think?"

"That's more like it!"

"Anybody else?" Sara held her baton out.

"I *love* the color, but can you make my hair a little longer?" Cristen asked.

Sara turned a dial and waved it over Cristen's hair. "Voila!"

Cristen gawked in the mirror, amazed at the instant growth of longer hair.

"Where're all our hair clippings?" Masumi examined the floor then looked at Cara for an explanation. But before the hair stylist could answer, Edgas exclaimed, "They must have evaporated just like the fruit and pits and stuff cuz there's no trash in Heaven!"

"That's right," laughed Sara. "There's never any clean up!"

The happy children thanked Sara and Cara for the great cuts and fun colors, thanked Abel for letting them make a pit-stop, and then left the salon laughing and pointing at each other just like the group that had left before them.

The golden street now led them to a widespread campus.

"Can you tell us where we are going?" asked Henri.

"To school!" laughed the angel.

"Well, I like your kind of school," admitted Henri sheepishly.

The angel laughed and tousled Henri's blue hair.

"Now that you've seen some of the men and women of the Bible in the flesh—"

"You mean in the spirit, don't ya?" interrupted Edgas.

"Quite right, thank you, Edgas." The angel cleared his throat and began again, "Now that you've seen some of the men and women of the Bible, in living color, I think you'll enjoy seeing a memorial built to honor all Heroes of the Faith."

Abel led his little group through a large arched doorway into a beautiful marble building that wasn't much more than a very, very, *very* long hallway. Covering both sides of this hall were carved images of the faces of men and women, much like a sculpted relief. Names were embossed above their faces, and a brief description of why their faith captured the Lord's attention was inscribed below.

"This is *the Hall of Heroes*," said Abel.

When the children stood before a face, they were surprised to see how realistic it was. Every face had been sculpted in such a way as to appear to come out from the wall in living 4-D images. The skill of the heavenly artisans can be compared to nothing on Earth. The children could scarcely believe that the person was not actually standing before them. They walked the long hall taking time to read many of the names, excited when they recognized one of them, like Abraham, Moses, Joseph, Boaz, John the Baptist, Stephen, Peter, Paul, Barnabas, Abigail, Deborah, Elizabeth, Mary, Esther, Rahab, Ruth, John Wesley, Noah Webster, Martin Luther, Charles Finney, and on and on it went.

After exiting the memorial, Abel said, "Now let's go see *the Hall of Super Heroes*."

"I think we've already seen all the Super Heroes; didn't you read the names of the men and women on that wall?"

"Yes, in man's view, those were definitely Super Heroes. Let's cross over here and see who the Super Heroes are from God's point of view."

They crossed the street and entered another building. This memorial was much grander in beauty and in scale. "The Lord wants all to know that He highly honors the ones who have made it into His Hall of Super Heroes," said Abel.

It was similar to the other memorial, only this time the entire body was sculpted, not just the face. Again, the curious children began walking down the lovely hall reading names and looking at the beautiful faces of the ones enshrined here. They recognized very few, if any, of the names. The description under each Super Hero read, "Prayer Warrior."

Abel explained, "These are men and women who devoted themselves to prayer and intercession. They believed that God heard their prayers and that their prayers made a difference in the lives of others. Therefore, they prayed relentlessly for God to have His way among the peoples and nations of the Earth, they prayed earnestly in the Spirit, and they prayed for God's will to be done on the Earth as it is done in Heaven. Many times, these Prayer Warriors didn't know who or what they were praying for, but that didn't stop them. They prayed anyway. Hours upon hours, days upon days, years upon years were spent on their knees and in their prayer closets. They may have gone unnoticed by the inhabitants of Earth, but rest assured, dear ones, they had the eye of Heaven upon them. And God not only heard their prayers, but He highly esteems these Super Heroes."

The children were surprised by this revelation and this great memorial. What a thrilling joy to know that *anyone*, no matter who they are or what their situation in life, can be enshrined in the Hall of Super Heroes!

Abel had a few more surprises up his great sleeve for the children before they left the city; two of which were interactive and quite fun.

First, they found themselves inside a hologram. It took them completely by surprise and immediately had them giggling hysterically. The hologram just happened to be an advertisement for an upcoming movie, and it was positioned in front of a theater in such a way that people could actually enter and actively participate in the ad. This particular ad was for a futuristic Star Wars-type movie, and the children found themselves sword playing with light sabers.

The second was a supernatural wonder of great proportion. They went into a room that was full of small circular platforms one or two steps up off the floor. In front of each platform was a large, three-sided mirror and a stand with one, large, push-button on it. Abel had Henri step up onto one of the platforms while the others stood around the circle and watched. The second Abel pushed the button, a light streamed down from above Henri and completely engulfed him in its cylinder shaft.

Immediately, the children squealed with surprise. Right before their eyes, Henri's ethnicity and clothes changed. He looked like an African boy, wearing a colorful robe and sandals. Even his skin tone and the color and texture of his hair had changed.

"Hey! You look kinda like me!" exclaimed Edgas. "I guess we are really brothers after all!" Edgas snorted and then doubled over laughing at black Henri.

"This is so weird!" Henri excitedly turned to Abel for an explanation.

"Here, you can see what it feel likes to walk in another man's moccasins."

Henri stuck his arm out of the shaft of light, and it returned to its original color. Every part of him that was in the light remained changed. "Weird, weird, awesomely weird," he muttered as he twisted and turned, checking out his image in the mirror from every angle.

When Abel pushed the button again the light disappeared, and Henri was back to himself.

"That was awesome!"

"Let me try!" cried Edgas.

"Off with you!" laughed the angel, scattering children around the room. They ran from platform to platform, laughing and squealing with delight as they watched themselves transform into someone else. The only thing that remained the same were their eyes.

When they had each morphed into every possible nationality and ethnicity, Abel said it was time to go.

"Hey, Henri, was that awesomely weird or weirdly awesome?" said Edgas, with a snort, as the little group walked back outside.

"Yes!" Henri laughed.

"Who's ready to visit the Portal?" asked Abel.

"Me!"

"I am!"

"Are you going to tell us what it is now?"

"Yes, Masumi."

The children smiled at each other, excited that another mystery was about to be revealed.

"There are Portals all over Heaven where residents can go anytime they want and view their families on Earth."

"Like at the Acts of The Faithful Arena?" asked Cristen.

"Very much like that but more specifically tailored for each person."

"What do you mean?"

"When you look in the Portal, whomever you are thinking of will appear. You will be as close to them as if you were watching them from their ceiling. It is a way that God lets His children stay connected to their loved ones."

"Oh, dear, can they see you if you are being bad?" asked Henri.

"Yes, Henri, they can see everything you are doing when they come. But don't you worry because they don't worry, nor do they get upset if they see you sinning or being a stinker. Remember they live in Heaven where there is no worry or fear. However, if they see you involved in a sinful activity, they will pray for you and declare that you become the man or woman of God that He has purposed for you to be, and they will declare God's perfect will to be done in your lives."

"That's pretty cool," said Edgas.

The children now approached a gigantic building. They walked up a grand flight of steps to enter. When they got inside, they felt *very* small for the building was so big they could not see the wall on the far side, nor could they see the ceiling above them. The room was abuzz with excited declarations and shouts of jubilation.

Angels were hovering everywhere and multitudes of people were coming and going. Most of them were wearing a fresh, clean gown made of the purest white material, just like Meme said they would be. These white robes were filled with the light of God, and they reflected His brilliant light much like a white sandy beach reflects the noonday sun. They were not quite like the angels' garments of light, but were very bright just the same. Many were garnished extravagantly with beautiful gems.

The first thing the children saw was a large monitor at the base of a simply huge column. On the monitor were names and pictures of faces, scrolling by like a ticker tape. "These are the names and faces of those that are about to come to Heaven," Abel explained. "This is one way family members know to go and meet someone at the gate."

So that's how they know! thought Cristen, amazed.

"And on this monitor over here," the angel led the group to an identical monitor at the base of a column on the opposite side of the entrance, "are the names and faces of the people who are about to be saved! When their faces appear, a call goes out to all their friends and family to get to a Portal as fast as they can, so they can witness their salvation."

"Wow," said Henri, "so there really is a great cloud of witnesses?"

"But, of course," said Abel. "If the Bible says it, you can believe it to be true!"

"But it's not really a cloud," said Edgas.

"Not an actual cloud. That is a descriptive word because they are looking down on you from above, like a cloud," answered Abel.

"Well, with all the white gowns and the angels about, it kinda looks like a cloud, of witnesses, I guess," said Edgas.

In the center of this great room, raised high above everything else was a large opening about the size of a football field. There were beautiful marble steps completely encircling the opening and a gorgeous golden railing, somewhat like the railing on a balcony, that also encircled it. Scores and scores of people were standing around the railing looking down into the opening, many were leaning way over, and all were completely engrossed in what they were witnessing.

"What do they see?" asked Masumi.

"When they look over the railing, they immediately see whoever they are thinking about, and whoever that person is with. And as I already told you, they are as close to them as the ceiling in their home. But they not only see their loved ones, and their natural environment, but they also see the spiritual realm, as well. They see the activity of the Holy Spirit working in the lives of their loved ones and drawing them to repentance. They see the Heavenly Host sent to help them. They can actually see the words of faithful prayers. They see the words of God spoken over their loved ones for God says that His Word does not return to Him void without accomplishing that which He sent it forth to do, and they see the demonic spirits sent to lie and confuse them. From this vantage point, the citizens of Heaven have a perfect understanding of the situation their loved one is in and can declare God's purpose, in perfect agreement with the will of God, over them."

Abel led the children up the steps, but when they looked over the railing, all they could see was a cloudy mist.

"There's the cloud," exclaimed Edgas, then added, "but I don't see anything else, and I'm thinking about Isabel right now."

"Me, either," said Henri, and the girls agreed.

"It is not for you to see," explained Abel. "Not yet. It is only for the ones who are already living here. But, I want you to carefully observe those who are here watching."

The children watched. And just as Abel said, they saw people pointing down into the mist, declaring God's will over their loved ones. They saw excited faces beholding those they held dear. They heard people cheer and saw them being congratulated by others at the Portal because a family member had received the gift of eternal life through Jesus Christ.

They also saw a man throwing rose petals into the portal. When Cristen asked the man about it, he said it was his wife's birthday. Then he leaned over and sang the Happy Birthday song to her.

"How sweet is that?" Cristen said to Masumi after she told her what the gentleman had said.

"Your family never forgets you," said Abel. "They will come here to check on you, to wish you happy birthday, and to declare God's will over you. The Father makes sure they never miss a wedding or the birth of a new baby or when you're telling someone about Jesus. If you're celebrating—they're celebrating."

The children were quiet, reflecting over what they had just witnessed as they left the Portal.

"Remembering this place will probably help me behave a little better," laughed Henri, interrupting the thoughts of his friends. "Knowing that Grandmama can come and watch me anytime will help keep me on the straight and narrow!"

"Ain't that the truth!" agreed Cristen. "And it helps me understand how God sees and knows us intimately and yet still loves us."

Abel smiled, pleased at his little group. He felt very proud of how much they had learned during their short time in Heaven. He would miss these kids very much. He shook that thought and announced, "Who's ready for some cheesy pizza?"

PARIS, FRANCE
1:15 p.m.

When she reached the waiting room, the chairs where she and her mother had been seated were occupied. She looked around and decided that the crowded waiting room was not were she wanted to be; a little more privacy would be welcome. She glanced this way and that, trying to decide which direction to head. Through the large glass window, she caught sight of a vacant bench near the front entrance. Perfect. She could pray there and wait for Pastor Jacque to arrive.

The blast of afternoon air was hot and sticky, but it felt so good to be *outside* the hospital that Alison didn't even notice. She made a beeline to the bench and plopped down on it. She raised her feet and wrapped her arms around her knees. Burying her head in her arms, she began to pour out her heart to her Heavenly Father.

"Lord Jesus," Alison prayed, "I know Henri is in Heaven with you." Tears fell silently down the teen's cheeks as she talked to her Friend and Savior. "I don't understand what is happening, and I don't think I can make it without Henri, but I know that he is in a better place. He probably doesn't even want to come back. But I need him, Lord. I feel so alone. I've never hurt this badly before. The pain is unbearable." Alison lowered her head in her hands and wept. After a while she wiped her face on her shirttail again, making a mental note to find a tissue. *I must look a mess, but who cares?*

I care, Alison. The thought came clearly into her mind, penetrating the muddle and confusion she felt. She knew it was her Lord speaking to her.

"It doesn't feel like it."

I know.

"Why did he have to die, Lord?"

He's alive, Ali.

"What do you mean?"

Henri is with Me, and he is very much alive! Alison could feel the heaviness begin to lift.

"Do you really need him more than I do?" The question was spoken sincerely from her heart, not with disrespect or sarcasm.

I didn't kill him, Ali, but I did welcome him.

"I'm scared, Lord."

Do you trust Me, Alison?

"I want to, Jesus. But I'm so scared. I feel so alone."

I will never leave you or forsake you. The words somehow went straight to Alison's heart, piercing the darkness.

I work all things together for good, to those that love Me and are called according to My purpose. And I know you love Me, Ali. I am working this for good. Don't lose hope, My daughter. For those that put their hope in Me will never be disappointed.

PARIS, FRANCE
UNSEEN REALM

The Word was speaking. The Word—Who took on flesh and became Jesus—He Himself had come to encourage Alison's spirit. The Word had come to impart Truth and Life. The Word had come to shatter darkness. The Word had come to comfort. The Word had come to love His hurting daughter.

Capri, along with the other angels hedging in the pair, basked in His Light — His glorious Light.

The guardian knew well that Henri was only sleeping, that God's plan was not to keep Henri in Heaven, that Alison's grief would be short-lived—*yet*—The Word came to her in her time of need. He was here loving, encouraging, and strengthening her. So great is His love and care. Indeed it is His very nature. It is Who He is.

He is the One who turns darkness to light. He is the One who turns mourning into dancing. He is the One who sets the captives free. He is the One who heals all infirmities and diseases. He is the One who took the punishment for sin upon Himself, the One who took man's place. He is the One whose blood makes it possible for those who believe to have entrance into His eternal Kingdom, being cleansed of all unrighteousness and holy in His sight. This is *The One and Only, Jesus, the Christ.*

And He was here, ministering personally to His precious daughter, His very own possession, a princess, who was hurting so deeply.

He sat with his arm around Alison and pulled her close to his chest. With fiery eyes burning with love and compassion, He spoke to her spirit, sending wave upon wave of holy love over the girl. He answered her questions with no condemnation or contempt but only with love—perfect love.

"I work all things together for good, to those that love Me and are called according to My purpose. And I know you love Me, Ali. I am working this for good. Don't lose hope, My daughter. For those that put their hope in Me will never be disappointed."

Capri, glad to be a witness of this sacred moment, smiled.

THIRTY-EIGHT

And this is love: that we walk in obedience to His commands. As you have heard from the beginning, His command is that you walk in love.
— *2 John 1:6 (NIV)*

After a delicious lunch of very cheesy pepperoni pizza, fresh fruit, and a beautiful chopped salad, the group left the outdoor cafe, thanking the owner—of whose mansion the pizzeria was an extension—for the yummy free meal and began making their way towards a beautiful country hill. Rivers of wildflowers tumbled over the top and spilled all the way down to the bottom.

With exceeding joy, the children raced up the hill, and to their great delight discovered an ocean of wildflowers covering a large, grassy meadow looking like a mosaic quilt of living color. A light breeze filled with a sweet fragrance and a new song greeted the children and continued to wash over them in waves of pleasure. Ribbons of rainbow-worship floated by in the near distance as did hundreds of white-gowned people riding on their worship, looking somewhat like clouds afloat in a pure blue sky.

While the children were admiring the scene before them, a glowing orb of light, brighter than the sun, appeared in the distance and crossed the meadow at great speed. Birds chirped joyfully and flew just ahead of the traveling light as if announcing its arrival. It also seemed as though the tall grass and wildflowers were bending before it. "That's unusual," laughed Henri, "but, hey, what isn't?"

"What was that?" Cristen asked as the orb of light disappeared.

The children looked to Abel for an answer. He zipped his lip, threw away an invisible key, and gave them his, "That's for me to know and you to find out," smile.

"I guess we have to wait again," said Edgas, pretending disappointment.

"I guess so," said Abel, returning the pout. "Why don't you run across the meadow while you're waiting."

That was all they needed to hear. The four took off running and leaping, spinning and twirling through the field of living, singing, sweet-smelling, wildflowers.

When they reached the far side of the meadow, they discovered another one of those unusual gate-markers which the children could have as easily gone around as through. But now they understood that, though unusual, it marked something new and wonderful and might even transport them into a new dimension. They ran to it, curious what the name of this new area would be.

"The Grove of Surrender?" Out loud, Henri read the sign over the gate. "I wonder what that means?"

"Do we have to wait to find that out, too? Edgas turned and looked directly at the angel.

"Not for long," Abel said, taking the lead as he passed through the gate with a curious Edgas right on his heels.

Henri, feigning chivalry, bowed and let the girls go first. "I'm happy to be the golden egg," said he.

In truth, he wanted to see if the others disappeared when they passed through the gate. They did. He ran around the back to see if they were hiding. Nope. It was just like Edgas had said. He came back around and started through, ever so slowly, hoping to witness the change in dimensions; perhaps he could be in two places at once. But the change happened so instantaneously, that one instant he was in the meadow, and the next he was entering an olive grove, thick with ancient trees, heavy with ripe olives. These trees were so large that Abel easily walked beneath them.

Henry discovered the others tittering joyously. Apparently, he looked quite humorous coming through the gate "limbo" style.

He smiled good-naturedly at their teasing and looked around at his new surroundings. "It really is weird how we can be in the exact same place but have everything around us change. Do we time warp or something?"

"No, Henri, as before, we only changed dimensions. The two places are in the exact same spot. Remember, things in Heaven don't take up space the same way they do on Earth. But, don't even try to figure it out; you might hurt your brain." Abel burst out with a laugh at his own joke. "Seriously, though, relax. Your mind will be able to comprehend the spiritual realm when you come back to stay. So for now, just enjoy the fun of it."

Abel led the group into the grove of olive trees and when they were completely engulfed by them, he brought his little hens to a halt. Forming a half-circle around him, they craned their necks back to see the lovely features of his face.

He began to speak in a serious tone, "Children, I have one more place to show you before your visit here comes to an end."

At the sound of those words the children felt their carefree, lightheartedness drain right out of them. The reality of leaving this amazing place hit them like a two-by-four, square in the head. Edgas was no longer pretending; he really did feel disappointed.

"What did you say?" asked Henri, hoping against hope that he had misunderstood his new friend.

"I believe you heard me correctly, Henri."

With great disappointment, the children looked at Abel with pitifully sad faces.

Cristen mustered all her courage and with pleading eyes asked, "Do we really have to go back, Abel?"

"I don't want to go back," Edgas chimed in.

"Me, neither," said Henri, shaking his head.

"Me, either," agreed Masumi.

"I know children. I don't blame you one bit for feeling that way, but, you have known from the beginning that you were just visiting. It is not yet your appointed time to join us here, and Your Father did not keep that from you. Now look me in the eyes." Abel waited.

Edgas was the last to look up. One tear and then another slipped down his cheek. He wiped his face and tried to be brave, but the tears kept coming.

Abel smiled compassionately at the young boy and then continued with great sincerity. "I promise your time will come, and while you wait, you have the unique and very special privilege of knowing, truly knowing, that Heaven exists and that all of this glory—the wonder and beauty of Heaven—will be yours to enjoy."

"Will I still have AIDS" Edgas asked as the tears poured freely now.

Masumi and Cristen instinctively put their arms around him. He was their little brother in every way, and they hurt that he was hurting.

The children looked at Abel. For the first time since arriving they all felt like crying. How could they leave such a wonderful place? As they studied Abel's face, a strong and kind voice came from behind them.

"Come, come children; why the long faces?"

The children spun around towards the resonating voice, but before they could get a good look at the one with the voice, the man reached out and put his hands on their heads. The instant his hand touched them, a jolt of joy and peace flooded their beings.

Immediately, upon seeing the man, Abel slapped his fist across his chest, bowed his towering body toward the ground, and then with utmost grace and humility, stooped down on one knee.

The children's gaze went from Abel to the man whose hand had touched them and discovered they, too, had gone to their knees. The smiling man nodded at Abel who then stood back up to his full nine-foot stature, somehow looking straighter and taller than before. Then the man placed his hand gently under the chin of each child, tilting their faces up. He looked each of them in the eyes. He took hold of their arms and gently helped each child back to his or her feet. For one long moment, no one said a word as the children stared, unabashedly, at the most beautiful being they had ever seen.

The children knew at once that this stranger with the beautiful eyes and head full of curly brown hair, wearing a bedazzling white robe with a purple sash, was not a stranger at all. They all knew instinctively that this was their Lord and Savior—Jesus the Christ.

His eyes captivated them. They were full of fire and passion, yet they were kind and gentle, and emanated pure love. He looked at them as tenderly as a young mother studying her newborn baby for the first time.

The children were transfixed on those eyes. Although, if you were to ask any of them when they returned to Earth what color His eyes were, they could not tell you. Yet, they will tell you that they can never, ever forget those eyes.

He looked intently at each one of them, holding their gazes one by one. They knew that this man knew everything about them; there were no secrets hidden from His piercing view. It was a strange feeling to be so completely known, completely bare and vulnerable, yet without any shame or fear. The children also knew, without doubt, that this man loved them more deeply than anyone had ever loved them, and that He accepted them completely.

Jesus! Oh, Jesus! It's really you! I knew I was going to meet you! And you are more wonderful than I ever dreamed!

Jesus smiled at Edgas, and liquid warmth filled the boy from the top of his head to the tips of his toes.

Jesus! Just as the name formed on Cristen's lips, the man's glorious smile turned directly to her, and she thought she would explode from the joy that filled her.

You're Jesus! I knew you'd be beautiful, but I had no idea.

That marvelous smile flashed Masumi's way. She, too, felt a warmth flow through her entire body, as if energy from His smile had entered her.

Oh, my! Oh, my, it's Jesus!

The beautiful man turned His smile toward Henri.

You know my thoughts! As soon as the realization flashed through Henri's mind, Jesus threw back His head and roared with the jolliest laughter.

"Indeed I do!" replied Jesus, still chuckling. His sparkling eyes crinkled at the sides with the joy that exuded from Him. He smiled again at each one of the children. It was obvious that He found great delight and pleasure in them.

The children continued to stare in awe at the One whom, while living on Earth, they had each made a decision to follow, the One whom they had only seen before with eyes of faith. Now, here they were, standing face to face in His presence, overcome with His beauty, completely unaware of anything else but Him.

Oh, how does one describe this Jesus? He doesn't just love; He *is* love. He doesn't just have joy; He *is* Joy. He isn't just peaceful; He *is* Peace. He isn't just full of life; He *is* Life. He is perfect Perfection. He is wholly Holy. He is righteous Righteousness. He is truly Truth. He doesn't just exude these qualities; He *is* these qualities!

All beauty, *all* goodness, and *every* desirable thing exists through Him and in Him and *only* because of Him. He not only created the Universe, He holds it together by His Word. He is the King of Kings and the Lord of Lords. He is fully God and fully man. And best of all, the children were standing face-to-face in His presence!

Again, they were completely unaware of time. They knew not how long they stood in reverent awe before their Lord. They were dumbfounded by the power of His presence. He was magnificent and glorious, radiating with light, life, and energy. He was breathtaking, simply breathtaking, and He loved them.

"Mmm," said Cristen, breaking the silence. "You smell good, too!" When the others giggled, she realized she had unknowingly verbalized her thought; it had just slipped right out.

"You sure do!" exclaimed Edgas, with the others nodding their agreement.

There had been delightful fragrances since the moment of their arrival in Heaven, but this was far better than any they had yet enjoyed. They inhaled great big gulps of His aroma. They had never experienced such a heady fragrance before. They truly wanted to *drink Him in*!

Jesus acted as if He was surprised and drew Cristen into a big embrace, "Why, thank you, Cristen. What a nice compliment! And you smell nice, too. All of you do. Hmm, let me think...Aude de Skunk perhaps?" He looked at the group's surprised faces and a wide grin spread across His own, and again, He laughed heartily.

With one movement, the others rushed him, laughing and talking at once. He hugged and held each one of them, just as a loving Father would hug a favored child while celebrating a great accomplishment. And every trace of inadequacy in their hearts vanished. These children were loved—unconditionally; they were accepted—completely; they were whole—wholly, and they knew it down to their very core!

Being with Jesus was the most wonderful thing that the children had ever experienced. All of Heaven paled to the way they felt right now. Every wonder they had beheld, every marvel around every corner, every beautiful and amazing thing they had seen and experienced, and been captivated by, simply paled next to Jesus. Those things, as beautiful and lovely as they were, only reflected His likeness. The children, as much as they adored Heaven, couldn't care less if they ever saw another speck of it. They never wanted to leave the presence of Jesus.

"I get it now!" exclaimed a joyful Edgas. "You are the glories! You are the reason Heaven is so wonderful! Heaven is a reflection of YOU."

"You are very wise, young Edgas."

Edgas beamed and blushed under the praise of His Lord.

Henri asked the question on everyone's mind. "Do we really have to go back?" Ugh, he thought his voice sounded small and squeaky as the question rushed out of his mouth.

"It appears that you have enjoyed it here, Henri," said Jesus.

"Yes, Lord, immensely."

"It's amazing!" added Edgas. "That's why we don't want to leave."

"I'm glad you like it, Edgas."

"Like it? Oh, no sir. I LOVE IT!" then he quickly added, "Lord."

Once again, easy laughter spilled from Jesus.

The four friends stole slight glances back and forth, smiling tentatively at first, but Jesus' laughter was just too contagious. They soon found themselves laughing heartily, as well.

Henri caught sight of Abel out of the corner of his eye. The large angel stood back a short distance watching Jesus interact with the children. He was grinning from ear to ear and seemed to enjoy his role as a spectator. Abel, who had only moments before been the most amazing being that Henri had ever known, now shown in his true likeness: a reflection of God's glory. Henri wouldn't have thought it possible, but he witnessed it first hand. He loved Abel so much but now understood the reason for his great love.

Jesus turned to the girls, inviting them to share their feelings as the boys had done.

Masumi was the first to speak up. "Thank you, Lord, for letting us come here," she said, barely audible.

"You're most welcome, Masumi, but there's more that you want to say. Go ahead; say what's on your heart."

Masumi looked down at her feet and then looked pleadingly at Jesus. "I really want to stay here, in Heaven, with you."

"And that's how you feel, too, isn't it, Cristen?"

"Yes, sir, it is," answered Cristen, honestly.

"Well, children, you must know how much that pleases me. I'm so glad that you like it...I mean, that you LOVE it here!" He chuckled then winked at Edgas.

The children looked at Jesus in stunned surprise for they were half expecting to be fussed at for complaining, but Jesus didn't fuss at them at all; in fact, he said he was pleased!

"You're not mad at us?" ventured Henri.

"Mad? Never! I know very well that you would prefer to stay, and I find no fault in that. I have prepared this place for you to enjoy! Hear me well, children," Jesus paused and gazed tenderly at each child. "You will return to enjoy it! Do not let your hearts be troubled. Your time back on Earth is only a breath in the scope of all eternity. You will return more quickly than you believe possible."

He stepped up to Henri, put both hands on his shoulders, and with a gaze that penetrated Henri's soul, Jesus asked him, "What if your going back made it possible for one more soul to come and join you here for all of eternity? Would you be willing to make that sacrifice, Henri?"

Now Henri was the one to look down at his feet. He saw only selfishness in his reflection and was immediately sorry. He marveled later that he felt no condemnation or shame, just godly sorrow. He knew instantly that the Lord knew best, and a willing and obedient spirit began to rise up inside of him. He lifted his head, looked Jesus straight in the eyes, and proclaimed with a clear, loud voice, "Yes, Lord!"

Jesus met his look with a smile that spoke volumes, then he embraced the boy in a warm hug.

He's proud of me, thought Henri excitedly, and he felt his spirit soar. *Jesus is proud of me!*

The others, too, had dropped their heads, averting their eyes when they heard the Lord question Henri. They, too, were confronted with their own selfishness and each examined his or her own heart.

The Lord moved towards Edgas, but just before he reached out to place his hands on Edgas' shoulders, Edgas popped his head up, eyes wide with revelation, "You made that sacrifice, didn't you, Jesus? You left all of this behind! You left your Father, and your angels, and even your throne, and all this beauty to come to dirty Earth, for us. You were willing to leave Heaven, and you're the King! How much more should we be willing to go!"

Jesus broke into a wide grin. He squeezed the boy's shoulders slightly and looking him square in the eyes said, "And I would do it again, even if only for you, my son. That's how much I love you."

Son! Oh, how Edgas liked the sound of that. He thrust his arms out and wrapped them around Jesus' waist, hugging him tightly until the Lord tousled his bright, yellow hair.

Jesus then faced Cristen. "How about you, my daughter?" He placed both hands on her slender shoulders. She looked up and found herself eye-to-eye with the giver of life and of strength and courage. "Are you willing to make that sacrifice?"

"I am," answered Cristen. She was expecting to hear her voice crack, but it rang out true and clear. "I would do anything for you, Jesus!"

He smiled and then hugged her tightly. Cristen knew that the Lord was very proud of her, and it filled her with courage. She realized that she really did trust Him with all of her heart, and she was confident that everything was going to be okay, no matter what.

He then turned to the one child remaining, and placed his hands on her petite shoulders. "Masumi?"

"Yes, Lord?" she whispered without looking up.

"Are you willing?"

"I am willing, Lord," she paused, "but I am afraid. I feel so alone in my country. There are so few who know You. I don't want to be alone."

Jesus cupped his hand under her chin and lifted her face. Pure compassion met her square in the eyes. "There are many others, my daughter. I will lead you to them. And I will be with you; you will not be alone, not ever!" Masumi felt His courage enter her, and she took a deep breath.

"There is one more thing you need to know, Masumi. There is one who needs you very much. Michi is struggling over your death. He is blaming himself and feeling very badly."

Michi! Masumi's hand flung over her mouth as she suddenly remembered her brother and her family. Flooded with the Lord's compassion for them, she instantly realized that going back could indeed make a huge difference in the lives of those she loved, perhaps even a whole nation.

"Oh, Jesus! I'm so sorry; I was being selfish. Of course! I would gladly sacrifice *anything* for Michi and my family!"

"I knew you would!" Jesus embraced this daughter He loved so much. "And I don't think it is selfish to want to stay in My Heaven; I'm very glad that you love it so much."

Masumi's eyes brimmed with tears of joy, and she squeezed her arms around his waist.

"Then it's settled," said the Lord, waving the angel over.

"Abel, I believe you told these children of mine that they had one more place to visit before their journey to Heaven was over."

Abel flashed his trademark smile and answered, "I did indeed, sir."

Jesus looked back at the children and said, "How would you like for me to accompany you?"

"Oh, yes!" they cried, clapping their hands and bouncing up and down with joy!

"By the way," Jesus smiled broadly at the children, "crazy fun hair colors."

In the presence of Jesus, the kids had completely forgotten their hair. When they grinned at Him sheepishly, He grabbed and hugged them tightly, laughing uproariously.

"Hey look! Our shirts have changed again!" Henri said, pointing to Edgas' sapphire colored shirt. He pulled out his own and twisting it, saw the design of an enormous tree with sprawling branches full of broad leaves.

"How come we never see them change?"

Jesus grinned, "We love to surprise our children! Why do you think I said that you must be like a little child to enter the Kingdom of Heaven?"

Cristen's wings began flapping so fast that they pulled her into the air. The group chuckled, and Abel grabbed her ankles to keep her from floating off.

"I think you were right about the adhesive tape, Henri," said Edgas, examining Masumi's shirt. "She only has one petal left, and we will be going back to Earth soon. Do you think we can keep the last one from falling off, so we don't have to go back yet?" Edgas looked over hopefully at Jesus.

"Wait a minute!" Henri said, excitedly. "Turn around Masumi. The back of your shirt has words on it now!"

"Really? What does it say?"

Cristen, back on solid ground, read, "He Loves Me!"

"Oh, I get it!" exclaimed Masumi. "Ha! I had no idea my shirt was playing the 'He loves me, He loves me not' game this whole time! Glad it ended on 'He loves me!'"

Jesus scooped Masumi up in His strong arms and swung her around in a wide circle. "And I do love you!"

She laughed freely, with no hint of cultural reserve or inhibitions.

Then placing her gently on the ground, Jesus declared, "I am in love with each and every one of you."

TOKYO, JAPAN
8:16 p.m.

"It's all my fault," Michi said, shaking his head. "I'm blaming God when I'm the one who killed her. God didn't run out in the street like an idiot; I did."

Self-loathing and suicidal thoughts were circling his head like a swarm of bees. He looked at the kind man sitting next to him. "I can't face my parents," he whimpered. "I killed my sister. I'm the one who should have died, not her. I don't deserve to live. I'm a stupid idiot." Michi broke as sobs racked his body.

Mr. Ninomiya put his arm around Michi, and surprisingly, Michi felt comforted. The boy buried his head on the stranger's shoulder, and the kind man held him tightly and let Michi cry.

"It was an accident, Michi," the man said, after a while.

"I didn't mean to," Michi cried. "I didn't mean to."

"Of course you didn't. It was an accident."

Michi wiped his nose with the back of his hand, spreading snot across his wet and swollen, red face. "What am I going to do? How can I go on?" he asked pathetically. He determined if he didn't kill himself, he would somehow punish himself. He would not allow himself to enjoy another thing as long as he lived, which he hoped would not be for very long. In truth, he just wanted to curl up and die.

"Your parents need you Michi, now more than ever."

"How could they? They don't want a murderer in the house!"

"You are their son, and they love you very much."

"Yeah, their son who killed their daughter whom they loved very much."

"Michi, look at me," Mr. Ninomiya said, gently. Michi turned his despondent eyes to the stranger. "Yes, they will miss Masumi, but they will forgive you. That's what love does."

"But I can never forgive myself."

"I think that is the root, Michi. And that brings us back to Jesus. You *can* forgive yourself because Jesus forgives you. God does not hold any of our sins, our mistakes, even our accidents against us. He forgave us on the cross when Jesus took all of our sins upon Himself. It's not because we're good, or because we've done good things, or because we lived without making mistakes, or because we deserve it in any way. The Bible says that our good works are like filthy rags to the Lord. No, in fact, it's just the opposite; none of us deserve it. Nevertheless, God forgives us, and we are washed clean before him because, in Christ, He counts none of our trespasses against us."

Michi felt a small measure of hope rise in his heart. "I don't know how I can go on. It will be so hard to live without Masumi, always knowing that it was my fault."

"You can with God's help. He will give you the strength to face each new day."

Michi felt a battle raging in his head. Part of him wanted to believe the stranger; it did sound very much like the things that Masumi had told him. Masumi believed what the man said; he was sure of that. But another part of him was resisting. Although, he had to admit, he felt an unexplainable peace settle on him as the man spoke.

"You know, Michi, dying is not the worst thing that could have happened to Masumi. She is a follower of Jesus which means she went straight away to be with Him in Heaven. If she could, she would probably thank you for getting her there."

Michi stared at the man, shocked by his words.

"Heaven is where we all want to get, it's our goal, the finish line," he continued. "This life is filled with heartache and pain, but in Heaven, God wipes away all our tears. There is no sorrow, no pain, no danger, or anything to be afraid of. Heaven is a beautiful place, prettier than you can imagine. Masumi is much better off there than here. She is probably having a blast running and playing with the angels. No, son, don't cry for Masumi. It's okay to miss her, and to weep for yourself, but no need to cry for her."

That thought had not crossed Michi's mind. How could death not be the worst possible thing?

"Michi? May I pray for you?" asked Mr. Ninomiya, tenderly. Michi nodded his head without speaking.

"Father God, I know you are here with us now." Michi glanced up with one eye half expecting to see God standing in the room. "I ask that You would heal Michi's broken heart. He needs You now, Lord. Come and fill him with Your presence. I thank you that Michi is forgiven, he's washed clean by the blood of your Son, Jesus. Have mercy on him now, I pray." Hope and peace began to replace the fear and hopelessness that had been suffocating Michi. Mr. Ninomiya continued, "You are good. You are a good God, and Your ways are perfect. We don't understand what has happened, but we trust You. I know You will be with Michi and give him strength to live each day. Drive away all lying spirits that would torment him. I ask that You would give him a revelation of Heaven, that he might rest in peace, knowing that Masumi is there with You, walking in Your glory."

TOKYO, JAPAN
UNSEEN REALM

The prayer of faith and the spoken words of truth took atmosphere away from the enemy. The Word of God went forth, and as promised, it did not return to the Lord void but began to accomplish their intended purpose.

The small seam in the cloak of darkness burst open, and light flooded the room, directly over Michi, instantly repelling all demons within its beam.

Every one of the demons in the waiting room were taken by surprise and shrieked with fear, running and shielding their eyes from the holy, blinding light. Oh, how they despised the Light!

The Kingdom of Light had come to rescue Michi from the Kingdom of Darkness, and darkness cannot hide from the light but will flee from it every time.

"Noooo!" The ruling Fear screeched and then let out a stream of horrific profanities. *How did this happen? Who did this?* He glared at Failure, hatred seething from his eyes, and then he saw the stranger among them. The man was glowing, bathed in heavenly Light. *One of the guardians! You Fool! How did you let him slip by you?*

Another flood of profanities. There was no way to penetrate that Light. Michi was off limits.

Darkness had been bushwhacked by Light.

THIRTY-NINE

On each side of the river stood the tree of life, bearing twelve crops of fruit, yielding its fruit every month. And the leaves of the tree are for the healing of the nations. No longer will there be any curse. The throne of God and of the Lamb will be in the city, and his servants will serve him. They will see his face, and his name will be on their foreheads. There will be no more night. They will not need the light of a lamp or the light of the sun, for the Lord God will give them light. And they will reign forever and ever.
— Revelation 22:2b-5 (NIV)

With Abel flanked on one side and Jesus on the other, the children instantly found themselves on a wide and spacious plateau of a strikingly beautiful and very high mountaintop. How they got there, they had no idea. One instant they were not there, and the next they were.

The mountain was blanketed with thick blades of rich, bright-green grass and exquisite sprays of colorful flowers unlike any they had yet seen. These flowers were unquestionably singing, and some were larger than the children! Everything turned in their direction and bowed towards them. *Jesus!* They were with Jesus, and all creation recognized and honored Him! It was amazing! It was thrilling! It was right, and good, and honorable, and holy! It was another moment in a long lineup of moments that the children would never, *ever*, forget.

The mountain had a gentle incline on every side, rolling down to multiple valleys below. At the Lord's suggestion, the children turned and discovered a large observation deck. Excitedly, they ran to it and climbed its marble steps to a lovely marble deck encircled with a golden railing. From this high vantage, the children had a thrilling vista of many of the things and places they had seen and visited.

As they surveyed the scene below, a gentle breeze played with the group's hair and lightly rippled Jesus' robe and Abel's feathers. They were quite a lovely sight to behold, silhouetted against the brilliant blue sky. Thrills of joy ran through the children as they recognized sights and pointed them out excitedly to Jesus. They chattered enthusiastically as they relayed some of the things they had seen and done since arriving in Heaven.

They saw the sparkling ribbon of the River of Life as it wound its way through all of Heaven and emptied into the shooting diamonds of the Great Crystal Sea. They saw water activity on the sea, people floating on worship, angels zipping about, and transports of all kinds busily going here and there. They saw a sliver of a roller coaster track nestled between tall trees and a large playground filled with happy children. They saw the great foursquare wall with its twelve gates of pearl and the forever stretch of countryside beyond it. They saw snow covered mountains in the distance and large wide-open plains. They saw the wild sparkle and glistening shine of diamonds, gemstones, and gold everywhere as it flashed and shone from buildings, streets, clothing, mansions, memorials, riverbeds, and so on and so forth. They even saw the sparkle of other cities off in the distance where they had not yet journeyed. There was so much to see! The children could have stayed and gazed forever, but at the Lord's urging they waved goodbye to the world of Heaven.

Climbing down the marble steps, the first thing they noticed on the plateau which stretched out before them was the crystal-clear River of Life. Up here on the mount, the River was broad and flowed with a smooth and even fluidity, almost appearing as a sea of glass. It certainly was not the rushing river of the valley that had washed and rolled over their beautiful stones.

"There is a river whose streams make glad the city of God, the holy place where the Most High dwells." Abel's deep voice brought Psalms 46:4 to life. Surely, the children would never read the Word of God the same after their tour of Heaven.

Seeing the River, Cristen's eyes excitedly followed it upstream. Certainly, *now* she would find its source! She quickly tracked it through the tree-lined avenue, up to the highest point of the plateau, where a great light swallowed it up, or perhaps more appropriately, poured it out. This great light was almost too much to gaze upon even with heavenly eyes. Could this light be coming from the very Throne of God? Was this light God, the Father, Himself? Cristen trembled with excitement. She decided that it had to be just that, the very Light of God.

Abel walked up behind her and quoted Revelation 21:23, "The city does not need the sun or the moon to shine on it, for the glory of God gives it light, and the Lamb is its lamp." As he was saying *Lamb* he dropped to one knee and bowed his head to acknowledge Jesus. The children weren't sure how to respond, so they, too, dropped to their knees and bowed their heads.

"Bless you children," Jesus said, tenderly. He nodded his head to Abel who immediately stood back up, and then He touched each child's brightly cropped head and scooped them together in his arms. "You are my delight."

On each side of the Great River grew spectacular trees of tremendous proportion, bearing such fruit as the children had never seen before. Thick branches, full of large waxy leaves, extended both up and out in every direction. Traversing beside the trees were wide avenues of pure, translucent gold.

Myriads of angels could be seen on the mountain, some hovering, some flying, and some standing post. There were angels with flaming swords, there were angels with scrolls, there were angels that didn't look like anything the children had ever seen before; and many of the myriad of angels were singing triumphant, glorious songs of praise. Everywhere the children looked were angels, angels, angels, and more angels—too numerous to count.

Abel's deep, clear voice rang out again, "But you have come to Mount Zion, to the city of the Living God, the heavenly Jerusalem. You have come to thousands upon thousands of angels in joyful assembly." This time Abel quoted Hebrews 12:22.

The tapestry of music and singing which had been their companion since arriving in Heaven, now swelled to a great crescendo. It would have been deafening by earthly standards. A million voices and instruments joined as one: melodies, harmonies, rhythms, and notes blending in perfection. The compositions were so much more advanced and complicated, so far and above, so beyond anything ever conceived on Earth. Who could have known that history's greatest composers had only scratched the surface of music composition? Their best works are like a child's rendition of chopsticks compared to the Heavenly musical arrangements. Oh, how it made their hearts soar in worship and adoration!

Looking around, the children also saw a company of saints, most of whom were dressed in their shining white robes. Many were coming up the mountain along its golden streets while others were ascending on the grassy slopes, and still others, were riding on their worship floating directly to the Throne Room.

The entire scene was so overwhelming that the children fell before Jesus, faces to the golden street, and worshipped their magnificent Lord.

"Oh, how beautiful and how wonderful you are."

"You are worthy to be praised, Lord Jesus!"

"You are righteous and holy in all your ways!"

"Your name is above every name!"

The children found praises springing forth out of their spirits. They weren't even sure if they spoke them out loud, all they knew was that they couldn't have held back their hearts of love and gratitude if they had wanted to. It was the most natural and right thing to give the Lord honor and praise. So, right there, on the heavenly pavement, they worshipped and praised the Lord with complete abandonment.

Abel could contain himself no longer. As before, he launched like a rocket, spiraling as he rose higher, and higher, and higher until all at once he shouted, "Praise the Lord on high! Praise Him all ye people and heavenly host! Praise His name forever and ever! He is worthy to be praised!"

The children watched, delightedly, as their beloved friend darted across the highest Heaven, worshipping the Lord in his own way, but likewise, with pure abandonment.

In the presence of the Lord there is fullness of joy and pleasures in his right hand forevermore. The thought came unexpectedly into Masumi's mind as she watched Abel soar. She had learned that Scripture when she first arrived. *Fullness of joy,* she thought.

I understand what that means, now. This joy is different from any joy on Earth, and it's certainly much different from happiness. Just like the Scripture says: it's full, complete, and total. That's what I feel with Jesus.

Jesus smiled at her, and she knew that He knew exactly what she was thinking. *How strange that you know all my thoughts, Lord, but when I think about it, isn't that the way it is on Earth? You have always known my thoughts, nothing has changed in that regard, only my understanding of how true that reality really is."*

Again, the Lord gently laid His hand on each child's head, blessing them. One by one, He kissed them, tenderly, on the forehead and smiled into their eyes and then began walking towards the Great Light. "Come along, children."

The children came along, indeed. Right beside their beautiful Savior, they skipped and giggled with irrepressible joy. Edgas reached out and grabbed the Lord's hand, holding it tightly as he skipped along. Now there were others who, upon seeing Jesus, worshipped Him as well. Some fell to His feet, others sang out praises, and some of the little ones threw flowers in front of Him. It was glorious. Jesus greeted all of them, calling each and every one by name. He gave hugs, patted heads, and waved and smiled. It was obvious that every person adored Him and that He loved all of them, as well. It is noteworthy to mention that no one tried to pull Him away from the visiting children; there seemed to be complete respect for others' time with the Lord, and there was no selfishness or jealousy.

One precious little girl, she looked to be of Asian descent, ran up to Jesus and thrust an armful of daisies, or some such flower, into His hands. He thanked her, scooping her up in his arms and twirling her around twice before setting her down with a kiss on the cheek. She wrapped her little arms around his neck, kissed Him right on the mouth, and then ran off giggling with pure joy to gather some more flowers. Before long, she was back with two small bunches she had picked from the hill; one she gave to Cristen and the other to Masumi. The delighted girls thanked her, and then she hugged them with as much affection as if she were their little sister, so pleased that her gift had blessed them; she turned and ran off to romp with the other children. Cristen and Masumi looked at each other and found themselves giggling with glee.

"Isn't she adorable, Masumi?"

"Yes, she is precious! Don't you wish her parents could see how happy she is? They would not be able to mourn for her, only for themselves!"

Jesus looked over at the two girls and said, "You are becoming wise."

The girls felt heat rush to the top of their heads from the unexpected compliment. Oh, how they loved walking along with Jesus!

It was slow moving through the adoring throng, but they made steady progress. The children took advantage of the slow pace to take in the scene of worshippers and the unimaginable beauty around them.

As they walked up the wide golden avenue under the gorgeous trees, they found themselves walking alongside the mighty River of Life, as they had done in the beginning of their journey. It sparkled wildly, as before, but the flow was so peaceful it seemed a different River all together.

Masumi, Henri, Cristen and Edgas peered into the River and were startled to see their reflections as clearly as if the River were a mirror. That was the first surprise. The second surprise was that their hair had returned to its natural color, and the third surprise—which was the most surprising of the surprises, was that in their reflections they were each wearing a simple, yet stunning, white gown. Jolting up, they saw that, indeed, their clothes had changed into beautiful white gowns. Oh, the thrill of surprises!

They were clothed in righteousness and simply glowing with joy, making each one of them strikingly beautiful.

"We look the same, yet so different," commented Cristen.

"I know, I was just thinking that I wouldn't have recognized myself!" laughed Henri.

"I never thought myself very pretty before," said Masumi, "but Jesus has made me beautiful."

"You are very beautiful, Masumi!" said Cristen.

"So are you, Cristen, truly beautiful," her friend returned the compliment.

"Except for the hair salon and that other place we went to where we could change our looks, I never really had a good look at myself cuz the mirrors at the orphanage were old and cracked and anyway they were up at Isabel's house, and once when I saw myself, I was so sick that I looked terrible, so I kinda avoided mirrors after that," said Edgas. "But, boy is it fun to know what I really look like!"

"You are one good-lookin' boy, Edgas!" said Cristen, smiling lovingly at Edgas. Oh, how she would miss him and his run-on sentences.

There were several places along the River Walk where the flowing movement of the river distorted the children's reflections like a fun-house mirror. They laughed outright at their comical looks! Abel joined in the fun; the children doubled over in fits of giggles to see him short and fat. Sweet Abel let the children take their time, for none of them were in a hurry for this wonderful journey to end.

Drawing closer to the Great Light, the children noticed a stupendously large tree standing majestically in the center of the plateau. It looked to be of the same kind as the trees lining the avenue, only many, many, *many* times the size. The towering tree, like its smaller variety, was heavily laden with succulent fruit. It had perfectly formed broad leaves running along the length of the branches which spread out spaciously in all directions from an enormous trunk, giving the tree a rich, deep, and bright green hue. It was as tall as any skyscraper and seemed to be watching over the whole plateau.

"The Tree of Life," boomed the familiar voice of their beloved friend. "Its leaves are for the Healing of the Nations." Abel answered their question before they even asked.

The children looked past the Tree towards the Great Light, and now realized, with great certainty, that the "one place left for them to visit" was the very Throne Room of Heaven! They were headed to meet the One Who sits on the throne. Indeed, the One from Whom the River of Life flows. The Creator of all things visible and invisible. Cristen trembled from head to toe with excitement, and then she noticed the others were trembling, too. She reached out and took Masumi by the hand. Her friend seemed relieved to grasp hold of Cristen. The girls set their small bouquets down on the lush grass, and grinned as the flowers instantly took root. Then Masumi took Edgas' hand while Cristen took Henri's. Together, the friends stood and gazed at the stunning site rising before them.

"Where's Jesus?" asked Masumi, suddenly realizing that He had disappeared.

KANSAS CITY, KANSAS, USA
6:17 a.m.

Will was reluctant to leave Cristen's room, but there was no way this large group could all remain in there. It was just too cramped, and besides, there weren't enough seats. After assurances from the nursing staff that they would find them in the larger surgical waiting room on the second floor if there was any news at all to report, the group moved their base.

Elaine appreciated the distraction of her friends and family, but Will was restless. How could he small talk when his daughter's life was at stake? He excused himself and left them to walk and pray in the hall.

"You want company?" Jon poked his head out the door.

"I just need to be alone for a few minutes to gather my thoughts and pray but thanks."

"Okay, man. Holler if you need me." Jon understood his friend's need and let him go with the promise to hunt him down if any news came in.

Will paced the hall. His mind was thinking crazy thoughts, thoughts and accusations against God. He felt guilty even thinking them. He knew God loved him; he knew God loved his girl. He knew God was good and trustworthy. So, why was it so hard to trust Him? Will tried to pray, but every prayer circled back to accusations and threats and fears and begging and pleading and promises. His thoughts were like buzzing flies swarming around his head. He tried to brush them away, but it was no use; he was infested with them.

Jesus! Make it stop! Help me Lord. I'm going insane, Father. Please help me! His spirit cried out through the cacophony of lies.

Before long, he had paced through several corridors and found himself quite a distance from the waiting room. As he turned to head back, a door with a small stained glass window caught his eye—a chapel! He was immediately drawn to it. He quietly cracked the door and peeked inside. *Empty! Thank God.*

The room was small and comfortable with a peaceful feeling. The lights were low, and a few lit candles flickered inside red glass votives on a small table alongside the opposite wall. A lovely stained glass window depicting a resurrected Christ ascending into Heaven on a cloud—his nail-scarred hands extended—hung behind an altar on which stood both a hand-carved wooden cross and an open Bible. There were several rows of worn wooden pews with padded kneeling benches that pulled down from underneath them.

Will slid into the second row and lowered the kneeling bench. He knelt, placing his elbows on the back of the pew in front of him and gazed at the lovely window.

"Living Lord Jesus," Will began, "I'm desperately in need of you. Please, please help me." He was thankful that he served a God Who *was* a living, risen Lord; One Who hears his prayers and cares deeply about his pain and troubles. He knew, without doubt, that the Lord loved his Cristen, more than he did even, but here was his first real opportunity to test that faith.

"I want to trust You, Lord, but I'm struggling. I'm so scared she's going to die. My head is spinning. I'm angry. Yes, I'm mad. I'm mad at You for allowing this to happen. There, I said it. But I don't want to feel like this, Lord. I hate that I feel like this. Where's my faith? I know You are good, but I'm so afraid You're going to take her and that I'll never get over it, that I'll never forgive You. Yes, I will. Oh, God! I'm so sorry; please forgive me. I guess I'm afraid that I will always hold this against You. Oh God! I need Your help. I'm so confused. I want to trust You, but all I really want is for my Cristen to be well, to get married and have kids, and live a long and happy life. I do believe You are good, Jesus, I do believe You are *for* me, please. *please*, help my unbelief." Will lowered his head to his arms and sobbed.

When the tears of release had subsided, he leaned back against the seat, wiped his eyes, and stared mindlessly at the cross. The buzzing was gone, but now his mind seemed blank of all thoughts. Suddenly, it was as if someone opened a window in the ceiling. Light, filled with millions of bright, colorful, confetti-like, glittery bits, rushed into the room streaming down on him like a spotlight. It poured over him, flowing more like a strong river current than a light beam. Will wanted to close his eyes and let the heavenly light bathe him—cleanse him—but he couldn't take his eyes off it. He was completely captivated by it. The light poured and poured and poured over him until he found himself breathing easier. He inhaled deeply. My, the chapel smelled nicely. He inhaled again.

William?

Startled, his spiritual ears pricked to attention. *Yes, Lord?* He felt his heart responding to that still, quiet voice within.

Do you trust me, son?

Yes, Lord, he answered, and he knew it was true.

Cristen is with me.

He was surprised by the peace he suddenly felt and the calm in which he asked, *Is it her time, Lord?*

She is a delightful girl. You are a marvelous daddy, William, and I'm so proud of you.

Will knew that his daughter was dead. The confetti light continued to stream over him, and all the while he continued to have a supernatural, unexplainable peace. But even so, he found his heart asking again, *But is it her time, Lord?*

Will didn't hear anything. He waited for the Lord to respond. He was just about to repeat the question when the river of confetti-filled light shifted off of him and beamed down on the open Bible. Will's eyes were wide and his jaw dropped slightly as he watched the beam move to the altar, but only a few seconds passed before he jumped up to examine the holy book. He was sure the Lord wanted him to read something. His eyes followed the narrowing light and these words fairly leaped off the page at him. "When Jesus came into the ruler's house, and saw the flute players and the noisy crowd wailing, He said to them, 'Make room, for the girl is not dead, but sleeping.' And they ridiculed Him. But when the crowd was put outside, He went in and took her by the hand, and the girl arose."

Will stared dumbfounded at the illuminated page. He shook his head, blinked his eyes, and read Matthew 9:23-25 again.

The girl arose? She was only sleeping. Are you saying it's not her time, Lord? Is this my answer?

Will felt a strange sensation deep inside of him, like an echo of sorts, reverberating off the walls of his heart. His whole body trembled. He was sure he heard something along with the echoing vibration. He looked around the chapel and strained his ears. All was peacefully quiet. He looked up at the stain-glass depiction of the risen Christ. Their eyes met, and Will felt as if Jesus Himself was peering into his soul through that joyful picture. Will dropped to his knees and gawked. How could a picture look at him with such love and joy and compassion, and yet he felt all of those things penetrating his being.

The reverberating sensation returned and this time the accompanying sound was unmistakable—laughter. Laughter! Shock registered on his face as a rumble of laughter filled his spirit. It was hearty and deep, full of merry joy, and it grew in its intensity. Will was sure it shook the chapel walls, if not the whole hospital. Indescribable joy flooded him. He began to chuckle along with the unseen source of laughter until he found himself doubled over with tears of joy streaming down his face. Like a little child, he rolled on the floor consumed with joy.

He knew without doubt, as the sound of laughter continued to resound within him, that the God of Heaven had enjoyed delivering this surprise.

Will lay on the floor for a time, soaking in the joyful presence of the Lord. No one entered his sanctuary. He raised his arms toward Heaven and thanked God, over and over again, for this amazing and unexpected gift.

When he was finally able, he stood to his feet. His face spread in a grin that could not be wiped away for days on end as he reflected on this holy experience.

Elaine! The thought smacked him in the head. Oh! He had to go tell Elaine. Filled with joy and a thankful heart Will jumped to his feet, and then leaping high in the air, he pumped his fist and shouted, "IT'S NOT HER TIME! IT'S NOT HER TIME! Thank you, Lord! It's not her time!" Then he tore off to find his wife and the others to tell them the great and wonderful news.

FORTY

At once I was in the Spirit, and there before me was a throne in Heaven with someone sitting on it. And the one who sat there had the appearance of jasper and ruby. A rainbow that shone like an emerald encircled the throne. — Revelation 4:2-3 (NIV)

"You will see Jesus again before you leave," Abel smiled, knowingly, at the children. "We're to go on from here without Him."

The four friends walked hand in hand with Abel's large frame looming behind as he guided them across the highland towards the Great Light.

They discovered that the Light was coming from a mountainous edifice with a central rotunda that was so tall its dome could only be seen from a great, great distance.

Situated on high, it towered majestically before them—for it was, is, and always will be, the largest structure ever established—and it shone more brightly than any other building they had seen since arriving in Heaven. Light blazed, engulfing the atmosphere with its glory; for indeed, the Source of all light dwelt there.

"*The Holy Throne Room of the Living God,*" proclaimed Abel, his voice filled with pride and admiration. "Nothing is above it, and as such, it is the crown of everything in existence."

The children made their approach, silently, completely spellbound by the extraordinary beauty.

The Holy Throne Room of the Living God was glorious. It was of white alabaster, pearl, marble, and ivory, inlaid with gold and diamonds, and was created to reflect His glory with radiant brilliance. Massive pillars surrounded the circular rotunda while six broad sets of pearl steps descended from large, magnificently detailed, opened, arched doorways. Bordering the steps, seven crystal clear waterfalls tumbled over beds of diamonds and gold as they flowed out from the Throne of God to all of Heaven.

As the Great Light emanated from the Throne Room, it reflected off the alabaster, pearl, marble, ivory, gold, and diamonds with such a display of dazzling brightness that it was hard to look upon, even with heavenly eyes.

Throngs of people in their shining, gem-studded, white gowns were rejoicing all over the Throne Room grounds. Ribbons, ribbons, and more ribbons of colors continuously approached the building and appeared to be swallowed up by the Great Light.

Thousands upon thousands of angels flew in and out of the Great Light singing out joyous praises to God with energetic vigor, as if they would burst if they didn't release their praises.

A new and different mood was in the atmosphere; Edgas looked questioningly at Abel, hoping that he would offer him an explanation.

Abel knew the children were feeling the atmospheric shift and smiled reassuringly at Edgas. "It is holiness that you are feeling. You are about to enter the Holy of Holies. No sin can enter. Only those who have been washed clean by the blood of the Lamb can stand in His presence."

Cristen remembered that somewhere in the Bible it says that no man can see God and live. Now she understood why—holiness. A prayer left her heart, *Thank you, Jesus, for dying for me. Thank you for covering me in your blood, so that through you, I may stand before the God of Heaven—and live.*

As if moved by an invisible force, the children found themselves at the foot of the massive structure. They slowly began making their way up the pearl steps, gawking at the cascading waters flowing down on their right and on their left. They timidly approached the opened doors, crossed over the arched threshold, and entered the Great Light.

They simply were not prepared for what awaited them, even though they had read about it in the Book of Revelations. The children saw a scene similar to the one depicted in Scripture, the very same one John saw in his revelation, but seeing it in person was nothing like reading about it in the Bible.

Abel immediately coaxed the children through the doors and led them to an open spot. The scene before them was so overwhelming that it shook them to their core. Blazes of splendor and beams of glory flashed before them. They immediately fell flat on their faces, in reverent awe and worship. Holiness seemed to press them to the floor. The very Light of God surged through their bodies. The children felt purified and holy as The Light penetrated every part of their being. By and by, they were able to stand to their feet, holy children of God, reflecting His image.

Silently, they stood, taking in the sight that will be seared in their minds forever. Filling the heart of the Throne Room, not pushed way in the back against a wall, but in the very center of the room—high and lifted up—probably ninety feet up, or more, was a great pearl platform. The platform was partially encircled by a golden, banister railing. Upon the platform was a large throne, and upon the throne wrapped in glorious light sat the God of the Universe, the Great I Am, the Alpha and the Omega, the Beginning and the End. The glory of God, which emanated in waves from within Him, appeared as a cloud of light. This glory cloud overshadowed the throne and hid the Father's face as with a veil. Flashes of lightening and rolls of thunder proceeded from the Great Throne, along with love, which rode on the waves of glory. Over and over these waves of love crashed upon the children's hearts, rolling through their beings like an ocean's tide. It was wonderful and intimidating all at the same time. Yet here they stood, holy, washed in the blood of Jesus, standing bolding before the Throne of Grace.

Some of the worshippers were trying to be struck by the lightning being discharged from the Holy One. That was different. Abel told them later that the lightning was actually God's passionate love. He said that love would build inside of God until He could no longer contain it. It would then burst forth as flashes of lightning bolting straight from His heart. And the reason people ran to be hit by the bolts was because it felt like they were struck by a million megawatts of love.

Cristen, being the Kansas girl, had a random image run through her head. She saw Dorothy with her friends the Scarecrow, the Tin Man, and the Lion standing in the great room of the Wizard, shaking in their boots as the large screen before them projected a scary face and booming voice that boasted, "I am the great and powerful Oz!" For Dorothy, it turned out to be nothing more than smoke and mirrors. *But I am standing before the One who truly IS great, the One who truly IS all-powerful, the One who truly IS God, the Creator of the Universe and everything in it, and although He IS incredibly fearsome, I feel absolutely no fear, only love and joy and peace.* She was struck with an overwhelming appreciation for His great goodness and mercy. *He has the power to do anything He wants, yet He chooses to love us, to forgive us, and to be merciful and patient with us. How great and awesome are you, my God!*

Along with the light and the glory cloud, a rainbow encircled the One who sat on the Great Throne. But as Cristen looked at it more closely, she realized that the rainbow was not static, like one you'd see in the skies of Kansas after a rain, but seemed to have a life of its own. It radiated in every direction, like visible breath, in and out of the One on the throne.

At the center of this rainbow—where she supposed God's face would be if she could see it—the rainbow was bright white, then it gradually became golden yellow. Extending from the yellow, was a narrow band of emerald green which bled into a very broad band of striking teal. The teal gradually shifted into a narrow band of bright sapphire blue. But of those colors, teal was the one that stood out the most. Later, when the children asked Abel about it, he told them that the Apostle Paul had said, "Like unto an emerald," because he did not recognize the color teal.

Streams of shimmering light teeming with colorful, radiant sparkles—looking something like brilliant bits of brightly colored glitter—burst with great energy in every direction. The glitter-filled light poured over the children like a river as they gazed upon the beauty of the God of Heaven.

Jesus—Light of the World, King of Kings and Lord of Lords; Word made flesh; Emmanuel; Yeshua; the Way, the Truth, and the Life; Good Shepherd; Prince of Peace; the Vine; Lion of Judah; Lily of the Valley; Rose of Sharon; Bright and Morning Star; Messiah; Redeemer; Captain of the Hosts; the Door; the Cornerstone; Bridegroom; Living Water; Bread of Life; Lamb of God Who was slain before the foundations of the world; the One and Only Who laid His life down and gave it up as a ransom for the sins of mankind; the Resurrected King—gloriously arrayed in splendor and majesty, was seated to the right of His Father. The children were surprised to see that He did not have His own throne but shared the same throne with the Great I Am!

Surely this man is the Son of God! Masumi gazed at the radiant man, full of strength and authority, seated at the right hand of His father. He, like the Father, was filled with light, and He shone like burnished bronze. He was magnificent—perfectly magnificent. His pure, white robe of the finest of fabrics was illuminated with glory; His sandaled feet looked strong and tan.

Can this possibly be the same Jesus Who just walked with us? As soon as the thought passed through Masumi's mind, Jesus turned his head, looked directly at her, and smiled. *It is Jesus!* Masumi bowed, face to the floor in worship.

When she looked up again, she found she could not stop gazing at God the Son. She was captivated by His beauty and majesty.

He wore a simple golden sash which spoke loudly of his great humility. This was not a pompous, proud King, lording over his subjects. No indeed! He was the embodiment of humility: the greatest One in all of existence, wrapped humbly in human skin, clothed in simplicity, yet more glorious than King Solomon or any king who has ever lived.

On his head was a royal diadem, a crown that He alone, in all the Universe, is worthy to wear. He was beautiful, simply beautiful.

And on the Father's right was a presence that was difficult for the children to describe. Although His body was invisible, there was no doubt He was there—for living colors swirled and twirled around his form like tongues of fire. The children knew immediately it was the Holy Spirt, the third person of the Godhead.

The children discovered the Holy Throne Room of the Lord Most High to be indescribably magnificent, full of wondrous and unusual things, like no place else in Heaven or on Earth. They learned that no citizen of Heaven would ever be turned away from coming into the Throne Room, for no matter how many millions upon millions came at once, the living walls would enlarge to make room for them all! Yes, in the Throne Room there will *always* be enough room for one more.

Rows of luxuriant golden pillars supported the enormous opened dome. When the children looked up, they could not see the top of the dome because of its great height. The walls of the Throne Room were white and inlaid with beautiful, shining gemstones and luxurious gold. There were plenty of grand, elaborately carved chairs for those who might want to sit, but most people were either on their faces or dancing in abandoned joy, or running to be struck by the lightening!

Now, as the children gazed upon the Lord, Abel came up and whispered, "Inside God is eternity. He did not appear somewhere in eternity, but eternity itself comes from Him. If you could step inside God, you would not see bones and organs like you have inside of you, but you would see endless eternity. You would see the stones of fire which is his heart burning with love and passion; you would see mountains and indescribable beauty; you would see the wispy spirit-lights of children, not yet born, playing in the River of Life and riding on beams of glory. Yes, God Himself, not the throne, is the source of the Living Water which flows freely, carrying its life giving properties throughout all of Heaven. The heavenly fount springs from eternity within Him. You can see it gushing forth from beneath His throne. Now look down." The children looked at the floor. "Do you see how the water flows beneath the floor? It crosses the Throne Room and flows out to Heaven via the cascading waterfalls you passed coming in. Then, a confluence of the waters takes place out on the plateau, and it becomes the Mighty River of Life."

The children studied the floor of the Throne Room, noticing that it was made of a clear, crystal material.

"It is often referred to as *the Sea of Glass*," said Abel. "It can be opened at the Father's bidding, making the water available to the worshippers. Whenever that happens, the saints rush into it. They laugh and splash joyfully, playing and soaking in its life-giving waters."

The children were stunned as much by the fact that the floor could be opened as they were that people laughed and played and *splashed* in this holy room!

Abel now drew the children's attention to the rings of beautiful, crystal-clear steps which ascended to the throne platform from every direction. Countless numbers of people were sitting and standing all over the steps captivated by something. Abel told them that people were witnessing the wonder of creation. When the children returned baffling looks, he explained, "God is always creating. It is His nature for He is the great Creator. When you look down into the crystal steps, you witness the creation of something fabulous taking place somewhere in Heaven. As you can tell, most people find this captivating."

As the children looked at the beautiful steps, they noticed a pearl kneeling-step positioned along the top rung immediately beneath the golden banister railing around the platform. It was covered in beautifully embroidered fabric of *living* purple, blue, teal, and golden threads which shimmered wildly and seemed to move with life.

A golden altar of immense proportions was centered near the front of the platform, supported by angels with outstretched wings at each corner.

Directly under the altar was a fountain of crystal-clear water that danced in a great pearl basin.

Directly behind the altar and the fount and centered directly in front of the Throne of the Lord were seven golden lamp-stands burning brightly, each having a flame of a different color. Abel pointed them out and explained, "These are not the Holy Spirit, as some assume, but eternal beings created to serve God in His Temple. You can see where the Holy Spirit is standing in unity with the Father and the Son."

When the children looked again at the Holy Spirit, they saw a very large basin of oil positioned beside Him. Every so often, the Holy Spirit would touch the oil, and when he did, angels would fly down and dip large vials into the oil and then fly off with them. "They are on assignment," explained Abel. "They are taking His oil down to Earth to minister to the people."

The children also witnessed angels carrying beautifully bound books which they presented before the One Who Sits On the Throne. They guessed they might be some of the heart prayers from one of the Rooms of Tears. They laughed when twelve angels came in carrying a very large canvas painted with bold and bright colors. They immediately knew it was a painting made on Earth by someone dancing their praises, but it was so large that it surprised them. They looked to Abel, and he mouthed the words, "Worship Dance Team."

Round about the Father and Son, seated on smaller thrones, twelve to a side, were four and twenty elders arrayed in white garments and on their heads were beautiful crowns of gold.

Henri pointed to them and asked Abel, "Are those the disciples and sons of Israel?"

"No," the angel replied. "These, too, are eternal beings, created to serve the Lord in His Temple, not honored humans as some suppose."

"Isabel thought they were the disciples," said Edgas.

"Yes, most people think that they are. But John, when he described the scene in Revelations, didn't see himself sitting there, did he?"

"Oh, good point," said Edgas.

There was so much to see, the children could not possibly take it all in. Abel had told the children, during their sojourning, about some of the strange looking angels but seeing them was a whole other thing. Multitudes of angels including the seraphim and cherubim were present and worshipping the Lord with great joy. There were angels with blue fire coming right out of their heads, just like Abel had described, and they flew in and out of the cloud of glory over the Throne singing praises to the Lord of Heaven. There were angels who only had one giant eye, and some that had a band of eyes encircling their heads. Some of the angels were very small and seemed to twinkle with tiny flecks of blue and green light, and some angels were so big they could not fit in the Throne Room, even as big as it was.

Hundreds of angels now flew in carrying large, decorative vases of what looked like liquid gold. The fascinated children watched as the flying angels poured the liquid gold into a great bowl before the Father. Again, Abel leaned in and said, "That is worship that they have collected from all over the Earth. Some was collected during church services, some collected at small gatherings, and some from lone individuals."

And still more angels came carrying vials which they poured into another bowl before the throne. "These are the prayers of the saints," said Abel. And the children watched as the prayers rose up out of the bowl and swirled as incense before the Holy One. Immediately, the entire room was filled with a most wonderful aroma.

But the strangest sight of all, and quite frankly, the most terrifying, was the four living creatures positioned under the four corners of the armrests of the throne. They stood upright, facing the Father and the Son, and wore lovely, gossamer-sheer gowns with high collars. Three of these beings had the face of an animal—one a lion, one an eagle, and one an ox—while the fourth had the face of a man. They were bleached white from their constant proximity to the Throne, and they had six wings each. Every wing was fully covered in blue eyes, reminding the children somewhat of the design on the fantail of a peacock. They also had blue eyes all over their bodies and even under their wings. Their hundreds of eyes never blinked for they had no eyelids, and if that wasn't strange enough, each eye moved independently of the others—seeing and recording everything at once.

The Throne Room was electric with joy and filled with pageantry. The children had never in their lives seen such joyous celebration. Music filled the air as people and angels were praising God in song with both voice and instruments. Large, beautiful, sheer banners hung about the room. Smaller banners and ribbons and streamers waved as people were praising God with dancing. The dancers, male and female, had beautiful fluid movements and were a joy to watch.

Abel later told the children that Jesus loves to dance and that He'll often come down and dance with His people. He said they enjoy all kinds of dancing in the Throne Room, not just the worshipping kind, but waltzes, and folk dances, and Greek dances, and line dances, and jitterbugs, and well, all sorts of dances. He said the Throne Room was the happiest and most fun place you'll ever be.

Several worshippers ran by the children carrying large flags. On the first flag was an image of a lion, on the second a trumpet, and on the third flag was a dancer. It seemed normal enough, until the lion lifted its head off the flag and roared, the trumpet came out from the fabric and trumpeted, and the dancer began to leap across the panel. The children were flabbergasted then burst into joyful applause. They looked around in hopes of spying more flags and banners, and to their delight, every banner, no matter what it portrayed, supernaturally sprang to life.

There was also a place in the Throne Room where worshippers could check on their loved ones and cheer them on. Along the wall on the Western side of the room was one of those Portals. This Portal had the same purpose as the other ones scattered about Heaven. The only difference was that it was positioned upright in the wall. And the same thing happened; whomever the person was thinking of, they instantly were as close to them as the person's ceiling. There was great celebration taking place at the Portal—someone must have just accepted Jesus as their Lord!

The children watched all the activity with utmost interest. Dancing, laughing, running, singing, praising, gazing, and most surprisingly, even eating! This Holy Throne Room of the Living God was not like any of them had expected, and certainly not like any church they had ever attended. The Throne Room was holy, make no mistake, but it was *the* most uproariously joyful and fun place to be. Now the children understood why going to the Throne Room was at the top of everyone's list of most favorite activities.

Abel leaned over to the children and quoted Psalm 16:11 again, like he had at the beginning of their journey, but this time they had a fuller understanding of its truth. "You make known to me the path of life; you will fill me with joy in your presence, with eternal pleasures at your right hand." Then he added, "Children, as you can see, worship is not demanded of you, or even required. No, quite the contrary, it is the requited heart response to a magnificent God!"

Quite unexpectedly, a spontaneous song of worship began in which everyone in the room simultaneously participated. It was as if they were caught up as one. The sounds of harmonious praise grew strong as it lifted to the Father and Son.

Cristen looked at the platform. *Where's the Holy Spirit,* she wondered? And then she saw Him, at least she saw the swirls of color around Him. He was moving at great speed around the entire Throne Room, through the very bodies of each worshipper. Cristen turned to Abel for an explanation, and he whispered, "He can enter the spirit man, Cristen. That is how you can be one with Him. The Father and Son can enter you, too and you them. That is the secret of being One with Christ."

Cristen knew there was profound truth in what Abel had just told her. She determined she would meditate on it later. Right now, she had just figured out that the Holy Spirit's movement is what had quickened the spontaneous praise, and she wanted to join in with the heavenly chorus.

The cloud of glory thickened as the praise crescendoed from the hearts of the worshippers.

Suddenly, the four Living Creatures cried out with one voice, "HOLY, HOLY, HOLY IS THE LORD GOD ALMIGHTY! WHO WAS, AND IS, AND IS TO COME!"

As soon as the creatures cried out, thunder and lightning erupted from the Father, shaking the walls and foundations of the building. It was as if something within Him was responding to the praise filling the room. Then, the twenty-four elders sitting on their thrones fell to their knees in worship, casting their golden crowns before the Lord. The worshippers stopped singing for the glory of the Lord billowed into the room with such power and majesty that every one fell prostrate before their God. The glory was so thick that it was impossible to move.

As the glory settled, a still flat-on-the-ground Henri, lifted his head to gaze at the glorious Light spilling from the Throne. It suddenly struck Henri, again, just as it had in the olive grove when he had first seen Jesus, that all of the glorious things he had seen on His visit to Heaven—every sparkling, shining, glowing, dazzling thing that had amazed him—was only reflecting God's glory and light. In and of themselves, they were nothing! It was only in the reflecting of God's light did they become amazingly beautiful. Everything in Heaven, absolutely everything, was created to show off His glory! The river, the grass, the trees, the flowers, the wall, the stones, the gems, the gold, the tears, the buildings, the diamonds, the sea, the robes, the people, and even the angels were all a reflection of Him. *Wow!* he thought, *God, the triune God, is the glory of Heaven!* And as his heart worshipped, he changed that thought and directed it to the One and Only. *You, O Lord, are the Glory of Heaven!*

And of the whole Earth, too, Henri. The powerful voice came rumbling into his thoughts, or did it rumble down from the throne? His eyes widened as he stared at God the Father sitting upon His throne.

All of creation reflects my glory, my son. You, too, were created to reflect my glory.

Henri lowered his face to the floor; the God of Heaven and Earth was speaking to him.

Henri? God was calling his name from the rumbling thunder.

"Yes, Father?" He found himself saying and then questioned himself immediately at calling this Holy, rumbling power a name so familiar. Perhaps he should have said, "Yes, God," or, "Yes, Holy One," or simply, "Yes."

Henri? He hesitated, unsure how to answer.

Henri, I am your Father; that is a perfectly acceptable name for you to call me. Henri felt a lump wedge in his throat.

Henri?

"Yes, Father?" Tears welled up from somewhere deep inside of him. Henri did not have a relationship with his own father and didn't realize until this moment how desperately he wanted and needed a father.

You will find a reflection of My glory in all of creation. When you return to Earth, I want you to look for it. As you do, I will help you find it. I also want to show my glory through you, my son. You will reflect and shine my glory to those around you.

"I would love to reflect your glory, Lord! If you will help me, I will gladly do it!"

I want you to tell your family, your friends, and those that I bring to you that I am a God Who cares. I know their needs, and I am never too busy to care for them.

"Yes, Father," Henri whispered, keeping his gaze low.

Meanwhile, the whole scene unfolding before him floored Edgas. Even knowing that this day was upon him, even as it was that he had prepared his heart to meet Jesus, he was not prepared for this! Glory, majesty, and power! This is the One Who, when he spoke the world into existence, said, "Let there be light!" and a fireball proceeded out of his mouth! This is no wimpy God Who Edgas found himself stretched out before on the floor.

Edgas? He thought he heard his name, but it sounded a lot like thunder.

Edgas? He did hear his name, and it did sound like the rumble of thunder.

"Yes, Lord?"

I love that I am your Father!

Flabbergasted, the talkative boy could not speak.

Edgas?

Edgas swallowed, hard, "Yes, Lord?"

I love that you are my son!

Edgas began to weep great big tears of joy. "Me, too!" He choked out.

There are no orphans in my house, came the rumble straight to his heart. *Look around you, Edgas.*

Edgas picked his wet face up off the floor and looked around. The throne room was full of people who had come to worship their God and King.

Behold your family, my son!

At that moment, the rift in Edgas' soul was mended. He felt whole and complete for the first time in his life. He leaped to his feet, wild with joy, and danced with all his might, in complete abandonment before his Father. And the God of Heaven laughed with pure delight.

KANSAS CITY, KANSAS, USA
UNSEEN REALM

Waving "so long" to his comrades, Obed stayed with Will as the man began wandering the hospital corridors. The orders to lead him to the chapel had come, so the guardian began the task of getting his human charge to the right place at the right time. It wasn't easy; the man was surrounded by lying, accusing demons. Obed knew that Will was struggling with his thoughts; he himself had to listen to every fiery dart being launched at the man. But the demons were too preoccupied with their assault to realize that it was Obed who was taking them all on a journey towards the chapel.

Two large and mighty angels were posted at the door to the chapel; no demon of darkness was allowed to interfere in this room, not today. It was off limits, and the powerful presence of the enormous warriors was an easy reminder.

By the time the nasty demons saw the chapel and the towering lights protecting it, it was too late. Will and Obed passed through the door.

Spewing profanities and raging with anger, they had to release their captive. Furious that their plan had been foiled, terrified of the warriors, and most terrified of the punishment awaiting from their own hierarchy, they fled.

Immediately, another large angel entered and took his post. He was so large that one sandaled foot covered the entire chapel. His job was to keep the chapel invisible to any other wandering souls until the God of Heaven had had His way. There would be no interruptions.

Obed continued to minister to Will. He stood directly behind him—the pews were of no concern in the spiritual realm—keeping his hands firmly placed on the man's shoulders.

Will poured out his heart to the Lord, being totally honest with God and with himself. Afterwards, he wept. It was a soul-cleansing kind of weeping. An angel with a beautiful vial collected his tears and flew straight off to take them to the Room of Tears. Obed knew that the heartfelt tears of a loving father were very precious to the Lord. He also knew God was getting ready to answer the man's heartfelt prayers, in a big way. A way that very few had ever experienced.

Obed's heart soared with joy as a Portal—directly from the Throne Room—opened above the little chapel. A river of light, infused with brilliant rainbow glitter, bathed the angel and human alike. Obed lifted his face to welcome it, for he knew it came from the Great Creator, Himself. How Obed missed being in the Throne Room of Heaven.

God Himself had called this meeting. Accompanying angels poured in from the open Portal. Obed heard the beautiful sounds of Heaven, smelled its fragrance, and relished its light. He felt honored to be a part of this encounter and grinned with joy at the sight of his dumbfounded human.

The heavenly light continued to rain down on Will. Obed was thrilled that Will could see it although he knew that Will had no idea that it poured forth from the Father Himself.

William?

Yes, Lord?

Obed heard the spiritual conversation between The Holy One and William. He could not hear the thoughts of humans, but when their spirits spoke, he was privy to that voice.

Do you trust me, son?

Yes, Lord,

Cristen is with me.

Is it her time, Lord?

Obed wanted to shout out a joyful, *NO!* But he held his tongue.

Cristen is a delight, son, and you are a wonderful Daddy. I'm so very proud of you, William.

The guardian felt proud, too. He had been with Will since the moment his spirit had been sent to Earth. He had watched him grow up, get married, and become a dad. He agreed, wholeheartedly, with God.

After the light moved to highlight the Bible verse, Obed laughed with joy as Will jumped up to examine the book. He again heard Will's spirit. *The girl arose? She was only sleeping. Are you saying it's not her time, Lord? Is this my answer?*

Oh, that laugh! The God of Heaven was laughing! Obed missed that laugh more than anything. It was wonderful, and it sounded like the layers of many waters. It shook the room. It shook Will. It echoed around the Throne Room and reached down into that little chapel.

The Creator's laughter was that of pure joy. Not the hyenical laugh of an angry or vindictive God as many humans suppose but that of a joyful, happy, loving Father. Obed knew that laugh well, and it was contagious. The guardian joined the citizens of Heaven, many who were watching from the Portal, and they laughed uproariously with the One who created laughter.

And then came The Word. He stood up from the throne and walked right into the chapel. Obed slapped his fist across his chest, dropped to one knee, and bowed to the ground as the King of Kings entered the room. The Word acknowledged the guardian with a smile and a quick nod and then went straight away to the stained-glass image of Himself which hung over the altar. Stepping on thin air, Jesus stood in the picture and lined up his eyes with that of His image on the glass; He then opened up the spirit realm to allow Will to see His eyes and only His eyes. Jesus looked at the man with great compassion for his suffering. Unconditional, perfect love radiated from the holy eyes of the Son of God. Will dropped to his knees, undone by His love.

And still the laughter from the Father rolled on and on like the waves of the sea. The Holy Spirit flooded Will's spirit with indescribable joy and supernatural peace, encouraging every fiber of the man's being. Before long, Obed's charge was rolling on the floor like a little child, consumed in laughter as the joy of the Lord overcame him.

Will gave no thought to the scene he created. He was too filled with joy to care. Not that it mattered, for the angelic guards would see to it that no one or no thing would interrupt his soaking in the presence of God. Will felt certain that his precious Cristen would not die, but at this moment, he knew that if dying meant living in the presence of what he felt now, it was not a bad thing. In fact, he was fully convinced it was a good thing. A very, very good thing.

The Lord spoke the name *Elaine*, and as Will registered the thought, he stood to his feet and jumped four feet in the air and then ran to tell his wife the wonderful news. Obed laughed as he followed his favorite person in the world out of the chapel.

And then Obed heard the sounds of Heaven disappear as the Portal snapped shut.

Will dropped to his knees, undone by His love

FORTY-ONE

The one who is victorious I will make a pillar in the temple of my God. Never again will they leave it. I will write on them the name of my God and the name of the city of my God, the new Jerusalem, which is coming down out of Heaven from my God; and I will also write on them my new name. — Revelation 3:12 (NIV)

Masumi, Cristen, Edgas, and Henri had no idea how long they were in the Throne Room. It didn't matter. They wanted to stay right here forever, where this God of Love ministered personally to each one of them. Oh, what peace! Oh, what joy! Oh, what love! It was indescribably fulfilling and intoxicating.

You're all I want, you're all I've ever needed, you're all I desire! Cristen thoughts poured from her heart.

Masumi responded with similar heartfelt sentiments. *Fairest Lord Jesus, you're all I want, you're all I've ever wanted, you're all I'll ever want.*

Those who think that worshipping You is boring have too small a perception of Who You truly are, thought Cristen.

Oh, I agree, answered Masumi. *"I didn't understand that before now; I had no idea of how great He is."*

I could stay here forever, thought Cristen, turning to look at Masumi. She was surprised to see that Masumi was a few feet away from her and could not have possibly spoken to her just now. *What in the world? Can Masumi hear my thoughts?*

Masumi turned and looked at Cristen with a most bewildered look. *Do you know my thoughts?* she asked, without speaking.

Cristen silently nodded her head.

The two girls stared wide-eyed at each other. Then they howled with laughter. Henri turned to see the laughing girls on either side of him and suddenly felt as though he was eavesdropping on their conversation.

How are you guys doing that? he thought, but before he verbalized it, Masumi answered with a thought. *It's another miracle!*

What's going on? asked Edgas, drawn into the nonverbal conversation.

Listen, thought Henri, directing that thought to Edgas. *We can communicate our thoughts to each other!*

"Cool!" yelled Edgas out loud, causing a ripple of laughter to roll through the crowd.

The four friends were amazed that they could still be amazed, and they continued to carry on a silent conversation.

Unnoticed, Abel slipped in behind them. When Cristen saw him, she cried out, "Abel! We can understand each other's thoughts!"

"When you see Him, you will be like Him," quoted Abel, then he added in thought form, *"There are many times in Heaven when no words are necessary."*

That's so weird, laughed Henri. *It's a good thing our thoughts are without sin up here; I'm not so sure I'd like all of you in my head back on Earth!*

Ah, but remember young Henri, the Lord is always in your head. He knows every thought you have ever had, so guard your heart and your mind.

Abel gathered his young charges. They huddled together expectantly as he stretched his long arms around all four shoulders. He turned them towards the throne, standing proudly behind his precious troop. Their shining faces looked expectantly towards the throne.

Jesus, full of power and shining brightly, stood to his feet and stepped down from the throne He shared with the Father and descended the steps all the way down to the Sea of Glass. The worshippers parted like the Red Sea, opening a path for Jesus. He walked straight to His beloved children huddled in Abel's arms. Abel released them.

"I hardly recognized you without your colorful hair!" He laughed joyously. "Did you enjoy your visit?"

"Oh, Yes!" they chorused heartily. "Very much! It was wonderful!"

He looked at them kindly, His amazing eyes sparkling with warmth and love and joy. "Go in peace, children, and remember, although you are leaving Heaven, my presence is not leaving you. I am with you always, and Holy Spirit will be your Comforter, your Teacher, your Guide, and your Helper until the day you return. And know without doubt, We await that day with great joy!"

One by one, Jesus took each child in His arms, and hugging them closely, whispered secrets into their ear. He tousled hair and plastered kisses on their heads and cheeks. Standing with His arms around them, He looked off, as if He could see far away in the distance, and cried out, "Chariot! Arise!"

PARIS, FRANCE
1:20 p.m.

Celeste finished signing the papers and let out a deep sigh. She was exhausted. Something had changed inside her, she could feel it, but still she was exhausted.

Ms. Fitzgerald had left her and now returned to check on her. She seemed nicer than she had before. Unusually nicer.

"Have you finished?" she asked kindly, with no hint of frustration.

"Yes, only just."

"Is there anything else I can do for you, Ms. Leonard?"

Celeste was about to say no, when she had a sudden and strong desire to see Henri. "Can I see him?"

Ms. Fitzgerald looked surprised.

"I didn't get to say goodbye." Tears sprang into the grieving mother's eyes.

Ms. Fitzgerald was deeply moved with compassion, and she answered, "Of course."

The woman led Celeste down another long hallway to a very lonely part of the hospital. It was cold and had an empty feeling. She knocked on a door, and a man wearing a lab coat opened the door right away. "Yes?"

"The mother would like a few minutes to say goodbye to her son."

The man was about to say that that would be impossible for he was just about to begin his examination, but when he looked at the grieving mother, he was moved to pity. "Mais oui, bein sur. Yes, of course," he heard himself saying. "I'll be back in five minutes."

Ms. Fitzgerald and the man left the room and stood outside the doorway. Celeste silently, reverently, made her way to where her son lay on a cold table. The room felt like a tomb. Surgical type instruments were laid out on a tray beside him. She wheeled the tray out of the way, then slowly reached out to touch her boy. He was as cold as the room. She peered deeply at his beautiful face. Even with his eyes closed, she could tell that he was gone. "Where are you, Henri? I don't see you."

For the first time in her life, she realized that the human body was only a shell: a place to house the real person. She knew immediately that Henri was not trapped inside but had been freed from his body, and this thought brought her a great deal of relief.

Leaning over, she gently kissed him on both cheeks. "Come back to me, Henri," she whispered. "Please come back to me."

Bursting into fresh tears, she fell on his stiff body and wept.

"I love you, son. I love you so much. I'm not ready to say goodbye, but I am forced to say it!" Celeste collapsed to the floor, her hand still holding his. She could not leave him; she would not leave him until they carried her out.

FORTY-TWO

And Elisha prayed, "Open his eyes, Lord, so that he may see." Then the Lord opened the servant's eyes, and he looked and saw the hills full of horses and chariots of fire all around Elisha. — 2 Kings 6:17 (NIV)

In immediate answer to the Lord's call, what appeared at first to be a blazing comet streaking across the expanse of the heavenlies, came a golden chariot pulled by two enormous, white horses and driven by an even more enormous angel with thick, brown hair and piercing brown eyes.

Gaping as it approached, but without fear, the children at first thought a ball of fire was coming to consume them for it was impossible to tell what was coming at them with such great speed. The large, muscular horses fitted with golden bridles and golden reins and decorated with colorful ribbons, moved like the wind. So nimble were the horses that they appeared to float on air, easily pulling the massive chariot behind them. The charioteer, skillfully guiding the horses and chariot, brought them to a full stop right in front of the wide-eyed children.

The angel, standing in the chariot with golden reins in his large hands, was as chiseled as the horses he steered, more muscular and powerful than any angel the children had yet seen. His folded wings towered above his head and the breadth of them filled the front half of the chariot.

"Oh! How beautiful!" breathed Masumi.

"A Chariot of Fire!" exclaimed Cristen. "Just like it says in the Bible!"

The group gathered in Jesus' arms gazed at the blazing chariot before them; they could not tell if, indeed, it was on fire, or if, perhaps, the gleam of the golden carriage was brilliantly reflecting the light of the Lord. The chariot itself was in no way consumed, nor did it radiate any heat.

"Is this what carried Elijah to Heaven?" uttered Henri, his voice full of wonder.

"Oh, the glories of Heaven!" squealed Edgas as he clapped his hands and bounced up and down in pure delight.

The angel, his face gleaming like polished copper, thumped his fist across his chest and bowed to Jesus. He faced the children, and addressed them in a deep resonating voice. "It is time for your journey home, young ones. Embark!" Gracefully, he breezed to the rear of the open chariot, extended his arms, and with a smile as enormous as his stature said, "Masumi, Cristen, Henri, and Edgas, welcome aboard!"

He then reached down through the fire, or the fiery reflection, whichever it was, and extended his hand, first to Masumi. She hesitated only an instant, and then reached up and took a hold of his hand. With a gentle grip that engulfed her whole arm, he easily swung the petite girl into the chariot; she passed right through the fire, unharmed. He then repeated this gesture with each of the others.

They were about to ride in a Chariot of Fire—just like Elijah! A thrill rushed through them!

The instant each child stepped into the chariot, they were back in their bluejeans and T-shirts. Masumi's shirt remained the same with "He Loves Me" and one pink petal on the back, Cristen's angel wings were flapping exuberantly, Henri now had a horse and fiery chariot design, and Edgas' shirt was a beautiful teal, the color of the throne room.

They turned to say their goodbyes to Abel and were delighted to see that he had joined them in the chariot. Smiles spread across each face for none of them were yet ready to part from their dear friend.

"You're coming with us?" asked Edgas.

"Of course! It's not every day I get to ride in a chariot! You didn't think I'd let you have all the fun, did you?"

The children rushed him, hugging him at once. He wrapped his arms around the happy children, and then threw back his head with his resounding laugh. Oh, how these kids would miss him and his wonderful laughter.

Picking up the golden reins, the charioteer looked over his shoulder and asked, "Ready?"

"Yes!" they cried with one voice.

"Hold on then...here we go!"

The angel clicked the reins and commanded, "Onward!" Immediately the horses sprang into motion. The startled children grasped tightly to the sides of the chariot as it took off in flight and quickly picked up speed. Abel spread his wings protectively across the open end of the chariot keeping them safely onboard.

The children leaned over the sides, waving goodbye with all their might to Jesus and the Father and the Holy Spirit and all the Heavenly Host and all the worshippers. To their great delight, every living being in the Throne Room waved goodbye to them.

The Chariot of Fire with its very special passengers raced once around the inside perimeter of the Throne Room. It then soared straight up and out through the open roof. The children watched the majestic Throne Room—the Crown of all Creation where the Lord of Heaven and Earth is seated above all things created—grow smaller as they left the plateau and flew swiftly over the magnificent City Beautiful.

It was bittersweet, taking in their last views and sounds and smells—at least for now—of Heaven. They saw the River as it rushed from the Throne to offer its life-giving waters to all the citizens of Heaven. They saw the Tree of Life standing tall, offering its life-giving nourishment.

The children continued to wave and call out goodbyes to people and to the beautiful things they had seen and visited.

There were other Gates of Pearl, and the children saw several. Not all of them opened onto a sprawling meadow like the one they had entered but right into the city itself with its gleaming streets of gold. Each gate they saw had sentries with flaming swords standing post. Abel had told them that there were twelve gates each made of a single pearl, with three gates, evenly spaced, along the four walls that define the perimeter of the New Jerusalem. They had seen the name *Judah* on the gate they entered and had learned each of the gates had one of the names of the twelve sons of Israel. Abel had also told them that the names of the twelve apostles were written on the foundation stones. Oh, there was still so much to learn about Heaven. They couldn't wait to come back!

With cries of enthusiasm, they pointed things out to each other, giggling and squealing with delight.

"Look at those mountains full of fall leaves!" Cristen pointed.

"Those are *the Mountains of Spices*," said Abel. "It always looks like autumn there, and the aroma of different spices change as you ascend the mountain."

"And there is a whole range of waterfalls over there," said Masumi excitedly. "My goodness, I can't even count them there are so many."

"That's called *the Valley of the Falls*," explained Abel. "If you love waterfalls, you'll probably live there. The homes perch seemingly precariously over the falls and even rotate so that no matter where someone goes in their home, they will never miss the view of the falls."

Again, the children were amazed that they were still amazed. A bittersweet feeling began to wash over them, and they were fairly quiet during the rest of the journey as they reflected over the many, many things they had seen, experienced, and learned.

Skimming across the meadow now, it appeared that the children would be departing Heaven through the same gate they had entered, but instead of going through the gate, they went up, up, up, and over the pulsating wall. Now on the other side of the wall, the chariot quickly headed out into space. The children turned and began to see the sphere of the heavenly world take shape. Edgas had been the only one to see this amazing sight. They stared in awe at the huge, floating, diamond-like sphere amazed that they had just been tourists there. The music faded almost immediately, and they could only watch as the intensity of the blazing light, the shine, the sparkle, and the glow of the heavenly paradise grew smaller and smaller until it faded from view.

It seemed as if they flew with light speed, or faster, through the Universe. Enraptured, they lifted their chins and faced the wind as it blew through their hair. Despite their bright and fiery chariot ride, the darkness closed in upon them. They had been in such wondrous light for so long, their eyes had to adjust to the darkness. Suddenly, the air around them was filled with the twinkling lights of millions of stars. Then a blue orb came into view, and the chariot headed right towards it. Closer and closer it rushed at them until they burst upon it. They were home—or were they? The Chariot of Fire was flooded with sighs. Would Earth ever feel like home again?

TOKYO, JAPAN
8:21 p.m.

"Michi, can I lead you in a prayer of repentance?" Mr. Ninomiya asked after he finished his prayer for the boy.

Michi, feeling an overwhelming peace, nodded his head in agreement.

"You have a real enemy, son. As we've already discussed, the Bible says that it's the devil who comes to steal, to kill, and to destroy. It is the devil's plan to steal your life, your joy, and your destiny."

"Yeah, and he killed Masumi."

"That's right. God didn't kill her, but He did welcome her home. And now your enemy wants to kill you by getting you to take your own life."

Michi's head shot up. *How did you know that?* he thought to himself. Tears sprang to his eyes and he fought hard to hold them back.

"The enemy's biggest weapon against us is his lies. He spouts lies into our thoughts and mind. And if he can get us to believe them, they become a stronghold in our lives. His lies are from the pit of hell, Michi, and they stand in complete opposition to the truth of what God says."

Michi nodded his head, beginning to understand.

"God says He loves you very much and that your life has value. He has given you great purpose, and He has good plans to give you a future and a hope. There is nothing you can ever do that can separate you from his love, but your enemy wants to steal that from you. When you agree with what the enemy says about you and with what the enemy says about God's character, you allow him to deposit a bad seed into the soil of your soul."

"And the seed takes root? Just like a real seed takes root in soil?" Michi wiped his wet eyes with his hand.

"Exactly. And then the seeds grow into a tangle of weeds and bad fruit. But when we believe the truth of God's word, Heaven plants good seeds in the soil of our souls, and they take firm root, producing a good and healthy crop."

"How do I get the bad seed out?"

"God has made a way, and it's very easy. It's one of the keys to the Kingdom, Michi. It's called Binding and Loosing. God says whatever you bind on Earth will be bound in Heaven, and whatever you loose on Earth will be loosed in Heaven."

Michi listened very carefully.

"All you need to do is repent for believing and embracing the lies, and then by an act of your will, which just means you want it very much, loose the lies from your soul and embrace the truth."

"I want to do that."

"Then repeat after me. Father, I am so sorry for believing the lies of the enemy."

Michi squeezed his eyes tightly, clasped his hands in his lap, and repeated every word. "Father, I am so sorry for believing the lies of the enemy."

"And for believing that my life is not worth living."

"And for believing that my life is not worth living."

"Please forgive me for embracing these lies as truth, for I now see that they came from the pit of hell."

Michi felt hope rising in his heart and echoed the prayer with renewed energy.

Mr. Ninomiya went on, "I want to live, Jesus."

Michi burst into fresh tears. After a moment, he drew in a deep breath and said, "I do want to live; I really do!"

Mr. Ninomiya opened his eyes and smiled kindly at Michi. "I know you do, son." Then he continued leading Michi in his confession:

"You have purpose and destiny for my life, and my life is not over."

"You have purpose and destiny for my life, and my life is not over."

"I am a living testimony to the saving power of Jesus Christ."

"I am a living testimony to the saving power of Jesus Christ."

"And by an act of my will,"

"And by an act of my will,"

"I loose the seed of suicide out and away from my soul."

"I loose the seed of suicide out and away from my soul."

The angel, in human form, lay his hand on Michi and said, "Be GONE in the name of Jesus!

Michi's eyes popped open. He thought he felt something leave him, but he wasn't sure.

"And now," the angel continued, "I bind to myself the truth of God's Word that says I am fearfully and wonderfully made."

Michi closed his eyes and continued repeating Mr. Ninomiya's words, embracing them as his own.

"And that His plans for me are for my welfare to give me a future and a hope,"

"And that His plans for me are for my welfare to give me a future and a hope,"

"And that there is nothing I can ever do that will separate me from God's love for me."

"And that there is nothing I can ever do that will separate me from God's love for me."

"In Jesus name, Amen."

"Amen." Michi exhaled deeply. He felt free, maybe for the first time in his whole life. He WAS free!

Mr. Ninomiya reached over and hugged Michi, and the boy, with all his might, hugged him back.

"Thank you, Mr. Ninomiya," Michi whispered as they ended their embrace. "Thank you for taking time to care about me. Your words have made a huge impact."

"They are the words of your Heavenly Father, Michi. He loves you very, very much. I was sent in answer to a prayer, you know."

Michi looked at Mr. Ninomiya in surprise.

"You were *sent?*"

"Yes, son. Your sister had a dream last night. A dream in which she saw herself dead in your arms. She woke up shaken and prayed earnestly for you this morning, not for herself. She did not know if the dream would come true, but she asked the Lord to send an angel to help you if it ever did come true for she knew you were new in your faith, and it would shake you to your very core."

Michi's mouth dropped open.

FORTY-THREE

For I am hard-pressed between the two, having a desire to depart and be with Christ, which is far better. Nevertheless to remain in the flesh is more needful for you. — Philippians 1:23-24 (NKJV)

The blazing chariot with its occupants of angels and children flew right over the bustling city of Tokyo. The large city was unmistakable with its bright, flashing neon lights, its busy traffic jammed streets, its maze of railroad tracks and subway stations, its houses and apartments tightly packed together, and its unending stretch of buildings and skyscrapers. Masumi had always thought it was an exciting city, but it no longer held its charm to her. As she looked over Tokyo from her perch in the chariot, it seemed dingy, artificial, cold, and stale.

The charioteer directed the horses down to street level and then suddenly flew right through the walls of a large hospital. He pulled up on the reins and brought the flying vehicle to a halt right outside the doors of the ER.

Masumi knew that this was the end of her heavenly journey. She turned and faced her new BFF's whom she loved like family. In fact, they were family. She looked each of them in the eyes. Finding no words to say, she bowed deeply then reached out and hugged Edgas, Henri, and lastly Cristen.

The girls held their embrace, fighting back tears, until Abel softly interrupted, "It's time now, Masumi."

She turned and wrapped her arms around his waist, burying her head in the folds of his garment. He held her tightly, picking her up in his arms, his wings still open from his protective posture on the flight. Lifting up off the chariot, Abel flew her right into the ER. The children watched, amazed that they could see right through the walls as if those walls weren't even there.

When Masumi lifted her head from Abel's chest, she was surprised to see herself lying on a table. The room was filled with medical personnel working feverishly. Abel set her down on the table, right on top her body.

"Weird!" whispered Henri, watching from the chariot.

The familiar expression made Masumi giggle, and she turned around and waved a final goodbye to her friends.

"Goodbye, Masumi!" they called.

"We'll miss you!" yelled Edgas, feeling very sad for the first time since the Olive Grove.

"I love you!" said Cristen, a lump rising in her throat. "I love you so much!" she repeated, barely audible.

Masumi turned and looked at Abel.

"Ready?" he asked.

"Yes," she inhaled deeply. "I'm ready."

She started to lie down and then popped back up, "Wait! I almost forgot!"

She thrust her hand in her pocket and pulled out her smooth and shiny, deep crimsony-pink stone. It was still beautiful although without the heavenly light it was not nearly as sparkly as it was before. She held it out to Abel. "Here, this belongs to you." She smiled, "Thank you for letting us keep the stones in our pockets."

Abel smiled back at Masumi, and then his eyes began to dance. He gently closed her open hand over the stone, patting it tenderly. "Keep it!"

Masumi looked up at him incredulously. "Really?"

"Really."

Masumi felt the cool stone in her hand, and a big grin spread across her face. She looked up at Abel, her eyes filled with thanksgiving.

"Ready, now?" he asked quietly.

She gazed at the stone then clasped both hands around the precious treasure. Nodding her head, she answered, "Yes."

After one last wave to her friends, Masumi lay back on the table, folded her arms on her chest, took and deep breath, and closed her eyes.

Abel reached down and took her hand in his.

Immediately, she felt herself being pulled towards her body. It was such a strange feeling; the room began to warp and the large angel, still holding her hand beside her, became faint and hard to see. She smiled one last time at Abel, and barely felt him squeeze her hand before hearing someone yell, "I think I have a heartbeat!"

TOKYO, JAPAN
8:23 p.m.

Michi stood staring at the man with his mouth wide open. Masumi had prayed for him *this* morning? *What?* He was trying to understand what Mr. Ninomiya was saying when three things happened all at once.

First, Michi's parents came darting into the waiting room, frantically searching for Michi. A new flood of tears rushed to his eyes the moment he caught sight of his parents. He bounded across the room and threw himself into their arms, sobbing. He needn't have worried about what he would do when they came; in their arms was the only place he wanted to be.

At that exact same moment, a smiling doctor entered the room calling for the parents of Masumi Suzuki. The huddled family, burdened with grief, looked at the doctor who quickly bounced over to join them. What an oddity. Here was this grief-stricken family and a jolly doctor who looked like he could float on the air with joy. What was his deal? Didn't he know how to treat a grieving family?

And, at the very same instant, Mr. Ninomiya vanished. Michi turned to invite him over with the family to hear what the doctor had to say, but he wasn't there. Where could he have possibly gone? Surely he wouldn't have left without saying goodbye. There were no other exits besides the one that his family was clustered in front of. He could not have passed without being seen. Oh, the implications! The man vanished into thin air. Michi scanned the room again, perhaps he was leaning down or...no! He was nowhere. Mr. Ninomiya had disappeared! Michi's head was swimming.

Was he an angel? Is that what he was telling me?

Michi, with shock registering on his face, was turning back to his family when he heard the doctor say something with great joy. The oddest sound squeaked out of his mother, and she almost fainted. Her husband held her tightly as her knees buckled to the floor.

"What did you say?" Michi said, turning his full attention back to the happy doctor.

"Your Masumi is not dead but alive!"

An atmosphere of joy and celebration erupted in the waiting room. Not one person, no matter how sick they felt, held back their smiles of joy. Many of those waiting came over and offered their sincere congratulations to the young boy—the young boy so filled with joy—who only moments before was suffering excruciating, heartbreaking pain.

"Thank you," Michi whispered, looking up.

TOKYO, JAPAN
UNSEEN REALM

Raphia transformed from Mr. Ninomiya back into his real self: a holy servant of the Most High God. He was accompanied by a glorious flock of holy, shining beings singing praises with one voice to the Holy One.

The demons screamed and fled, hating how they had been duped. Shame scrambled, hunting furiously for a shadow to hide in, but none could be found. The glory of Heaven lit up the atmosphere, and his hideous form was exposed no matter where he ran. Fear was too busy seeking his own hiding place to go after the moron. But be assured, Shame would pay a costly price for his folly. Very costly.

Zimbu rushed to give Raphia an angelic high-five. They had done it! And once again, their faithful Master had come through for these humans the angels had grown to love. They were happy — so very happy!

All of Heaven celebrated the victory of the one soul; one precious soul in the sight of the Lord who had been rescued from the clutches of the Kingdom of darkness.

Each and every person in that waiting room had been witness to a bonafide miracle. Guardians joyfully dropped pearly white seeds of faith into the souls of their human charges, knowing that it if any fell on good soil, it would take root and reap a harvest in due time.

The heavenly choir sang out more praises and hallelujahs!

Raphia shot like a bullet into the atmosphere, spinning in a tight corkscrew. He was bursting with exceedingly great joy and shouted out his own praises and hallelujahs. He had been privileged with a rare gift, the opportunity to do what very few angels ever got to do: share God's truth face to face with a living human. He was thankful that Gabriel had entrusted him with this gift. He was thankful that His Creator and Master had entrusted him, as well. And, most of all, he was overjoyed that Michi had received his message.

High in the atmosphere, over and above all the joyous celebration, Raphia's voice could be heard as he shouted out, "I LOVE MY JOB!"

"I LOVE MY JOB!"

FORTY-FOUR

Do all things without complaining and disputing, that you may become blameless and harmless, children of God without fault in the midst of a crooked and perverse generation, among whom you shine as lights in the world... — Philippians 2:14-15 (NKJV)

"Where'd she go?" asked a wide-eyed Edgas, witnessing Masumi's spirit disappear as it merged and reunited with her body.

"Weird!" Henri said, again.

Abel returned to the chariot while the children watched the events in the ER. Masumi began to stir, and the shocked doctors whooped with elation.

"The doctors will worry that she has suffered brain damage," said Abel, "but will soon discover that she is perfectly whole. She may have a headache for a day or two, but they will watch her well and keep her comfortable."

The children absorbed the information, not taking their eyes off of Masumi for a second.

"What language are those people speaking?" asked Cristen.

"Japanese," replied Abel.

"But I can't understand them; I thought I could understand Japanese now?"

"Yeah," replied Henri, "I thought I could, too."

"Perfect communication is a gift of Heaven." Abel's explanation was simple and to the point.

After a moment, Henri ventured, "So, if we were to somehow find each other, like sometime later, we won't understand each other?"

That thought had not crossed their minds, not until now, and every head jerked back to Abel waiting for his response.

"That is mostly true, Henri."

They felt their hearts sink.

"How can something be mostly true?" asked Edgas. "Isn't something either true or not true?"

Abel laughed and pulled Edgas into a hug. "It is true that you will not automatically understand each other's languages, but it is not true that you would not be able to communicate. You're smart children. If somehow your paths were to cross, I'm sure you would figure out a way to talk."

"Abel?"

"Yes, Cristen?"

"Will our paths cross again?" She looked up at him with hopeful eyes.

"I do not know the future, Cristen."

"Oh," Cristen looked down at the floor of the chariot. It seemed that with every passing moment she felt less and less of the exuberance of Heaven.

"But," he said, "it is not forbidden."

Cristen's head popped up, and her eyes met the sparkle dancing from Abel's eyes. "Really?" she shouted, a new excitement thrilling her.

The boys felt it too.

Henri's mind was rushing with ideas. "OK," he said, "we can email each other. I think there are programs that can translate words into another language."

"Really?" Cristen shouted again. "That's a great idea! What is your email address?" Henri told her his email address, she repeated it back to him and was sure she could remember it, then Cristen told Henri hers. They turned to ask Edgas what his was and saw a downcast face.

"What's the matter, Edgas?" asked Cristen.

"I don't have one of those. I don't even know what you're talking about. How will I ever find you guys?"

Henri reached over and hugged Edgas then looked him square in the eye. "I will find you Edgas, I promise. Whatever it takes, little brother."

Edgas hugged him back, warm tears streaming softly down his cheeks. He knew Henri loved him and meant what he said. Even if he never saw Henri again, on Earth anyway, it was a great feeling to know that he had family and that he was loved.

Cristen reached over and hugged Edgas tightly. "And we'll find Masumi, too!" she whispered. "God willing, we'll find a way to connect *and* communicate. We are family now."

"I live in an orphanage called *All God's Children*," Edgas offered hopefully. "In Maputo, Mozambique."

Abel watched the interaction between his kids and felt his chest swell. He would miss these precious ones; *What a day of rejoicing it will be when they come home.* Positioning himself as the rear guard, he nodded to the charioteer.

The children grasped tightly to the sides of the chariot as the driver commanded, "Hold on!" Before the chariot whisked them away, the children took once last glance over at Masumi lying on the operating table. Cristen blew her a kiss.

Once again, an exhilarating wind met their faces as they sped along above the clouds. In seemingly no time, they were close to Earth, heading towards another city.

Henri was the one to recognize familiar landmarks this time and knew they had reached Paris and it would soon be his turn to say goodbye. He swallowed—hard.

Cristen was delighted to fly over the Eiffel tower and Arch De Triumph. They paled to the beauty of heavenly buildings, but still, they were famous landmarks, and she was thrilled to have this bird's eye view of them. Henri pointed out some other places of note, like the Louvre and Notre Dame as Edgas and Cristen eagerly took it all in.

"Do you see the Hunchback?" Cristen said.

"The who?" said Edgas. "Where?"

Cristen and Henri chuckled. "There was a book about a man who lived in that building," pointed Henri. "It was just a pretend story."

"Oh," Edgas smiled. There were so many things he wanted to learn.

As in Tokyo, the chariot flew right along the streets of Paris until they came to a large hospital. When Henri looked towards the hospital entrance, his heart skipped a beat. Sitting on a bench in front of the building was his twin sister, Ali. She had her arms wrapped tightly around her knees. Henri could tell she had been crying...a lot.

"Ali!" he called out. "Ali! I'm back!" She made no acknowledgement, so this time he yelled, "ALISON! IT'S ME, HENRI!"

"She can't hear you, Henri." Abel scooted to his side and put a hand on the boy's shoulders.

"Stop the chariot!" demanded Henri. "Let me out right here, I want to go to her!"

"I'm sorry, Henri. That is not allowed. Come on, let's get you back to your body, so you can be reunited with your family."

"She's so close," he said sadly, suddenly feeling an ache for his sister and mother. "It's weird that she can't see us." He looked around at the others in the chariot, a little embarrassed over his outburst. "Sorry, I guess I got a little excited."

"Your sister is very pretty," said Cristen.

Henri blushed. "Yeah, she is, but don't tell her I said so! She would have enjoyed being with us in Heaven. She really loves Jesus, I'm surprised the Lord took me for a visit and not her."

"Well, I can't wait to meet her someday. Tell her I know we'll be good friends."

"She will love both you and Masumi," said Henri, earnestly.

Just like before, the charioteer drove the horses right through the walls of the hospital. Henri kept his eyes on Alison until he could no longer see her. It was so strange to have earthly feelings again. Even though he was still in his spiritual form, he could tell that he was becoming more like his old self. Although, he knew he would never be *just* like his old self. He had met Jesus, and this trip to Heaven would have a never-ending impact on his earthly life.

The moment Henri took his eyes off Alison, he turned around and faced his own body lying motionless on a table. "Whoa, that's Weird!"

"Now, *this* is where you may get off," laughed Abel.

Henri turned to his friends. "I'm sure gonna miss you guys!"

Edgas grabbed a hold of him and hugged the daylights out of his friend. Then Henri gave Cristen a big hug and kissed her on both cheeks. After that, he turned to Abel. "I'm ready now."

Abel, boring a hole into Henri's eyes, put his large hands on Henri's shoulders and said, "I have watched you become a young man today, Henri. I'm so proud of you."

Henri threw himself into Abel's arms. "I am really gonna miss you, Abel. I love you."

"I love you, too, Henri."

With Abel's large arm around Henri's shoulders, the two jumped down from the chariot and walked over to the teen's body. Henri sat down on the table prepared for what was to happen, having just watched Masumi disappear into her own body. He looked around the room—it was void of people. There was no hospital staff scuttling about. They must have left him for dead, he guessed. He shrugged his shoulders and waved one last time to his friends.

He was just about to lie back on the table when he spied a dainty hand beside him. Startled, he quickly looked at it and discovered it attached to his mother, collapsed on the floor beside him! His heart immediately broke for her. His best day ever had been her worst. He turned sad eyes to Abel who was gazing at him compassionately. "I guess it was selfish of me to not want to come back," he whispered.

"No, Henri. It was not selfish; it is the blessing of Heaven." Abel smiled softly. Henri contemplated that a moment.

"Hey!" Henri suddenly blurted, holding up his lovely turquoise-blue stone. "Do I get to keep mine, too?"

"Yes!" Abel laughed, "Oh, how I'm going to miss you, Henri. Yes, of course! The stone is yours to keep!"

"Cool! A souvenir!"

"Are you ready to go to your mother and sister?"

Henri looked over at his mother crumpled on the floor. She looked just miserable. He never knew how much he loved her.

"I was born ready," he answered with a smile, and then he began to feel a downward pull. Everything started to go fuzzy, and he knew he was being drawn back into his body.

Just as it was with Masumi, Cristen and Edgas could not take their eyes off of Henri as they watched him slip into the mold of his very still and silent body. And right before they could no longer distinguish between the two Henris, a warped and wobbly "Weeeiiirrrdah!" reached their ears and they doubled over in laughter.

KANSAS CITY, KANSAS, USA
6:25 a.m.

Dr. Art and his team seemed to be fighting a losing battle. The girl had flat-lined, and they were working feverishly to revive her. At first he prayed under his breath, but as they struggled to revive the girl, and time was slipping away from them, he began crying out to God for His help and His mercy, not caring what anyone on his team thought. He was not out to win a popularity contest. No, he did not care what they thought of him; the girl's life was at stake. Perhaps, just perhaps, God would bring her back. He had witnessed Him do just that on several occasions. Maybe today He would do again.

"No, Lord! No, Lord! Save her. Help us, Oh God! I ask for your mercy. Bring her back to us, Father! Don't take her, not this one, she's so young. Help us, God!"

Art looked at his nurse and nodded. She applied the electric paddles one more time.

"Please, God!" Art could feel panic start to overtake him. She was gone. Too much time had passed.

Then something began to shift. The panic subsided, and a tangible peace filled the air.
I'm with you, son.

Father, what do you want me to do? Art sent the question without words.

Finish the surgery. Do not try to revive her again.

This did not make sense in his natural mind. He should be applying the paddles again, not finishing a needless surgery if the girl was dead. But, Art knew at this point there was nothing he could do for the girl. He might as well follow what he believed to be the leading of the Holy Spirit.

"Let's finish the surgery," Dr. Art commanded.

The group looked at him questioningly, but all did as he asked, and each went about doing his or her part of the surgery.

Art felt his hands moving, almost as if by an invisible force. Skillfully—amazingly, intricately—he finished the procedure and began the process of stitching her up.

KANSAS CITY, KANSAS, USA
UNSEEN REALM

According to the faith of the pastor and the prayers of the people, the Heavens opened above the ER. Light flooded the operating room along with several swift angels, all set on their different assignments. One touched Cristen on the head, one touched her wound, and one touched her feet. Another angel began speaking words of encouragement over the entire room and everyone in it.

Ten or more large angels came with flaming swords to stand as a wall—a hedge of protection—around Cristen and everyone in the room. Every demon fled at the sight of them, and not one of them dared to return while the Heavenly Hosts stood guard.

There was a pause of angelic action while the Lord spoke to Art. The heavenly beings knew the Creator had leaned in closely to whisper to the doctor, and they bowed their heads in response.

I'm with you, son.

Father, what do you want me to do?

Finish the surgery. Do not try to revive her again.

Every angel heard the silent conversation. They also knew that the girl would soon return to her body and they could feel their excitement rising. This was fun.

Ziv was proud of his human. In the midst of the chaos and near panic, he had not only cried out to God for help but had heard the Lord and obeyed His directions.

The guardian took over the doctor's hands and guided him as he finished the surgery.

The angels on assignment ministered peace, kept the demons at bay, and readied Cristen for the miracle working, resurrection power of Christ.

All knew that Jesus was getting ready to show up and show off in a big way, and this group of humans were going to have a front row seat for the show.

And here came the Chariot of Fire now!

FORTY-FIVE

For to me, to live is Christ, and to die is gain. — Philippians 1:21 (NKJV)

The Chariot of Fire sped across the Atlantic Ocean whose foamy waves were illumined by the light of a full moon. It was beautiful but nothing like the sparkle of the Great Sea. The group rapidly reached land and then flew over the Appalachian Mountains whose wooded peaks, covered in moon shadows, were playing hide and seek with the clouds. From high in the chariot, the remaining two children saw the speckled lights of many towns and cities looking like they were shining through pinholes in a thick, black blanket. In seemingly no time, the horse and chariot along with its precious cargo, flew through the walls of a hospital in the middle of Kansas City, Kansas. Not surprisingly, the charioteer brought his horses to a stop in the hallway right outside of the operating room.

Cristen immediately saw her body lying on the operating table, surrounded by doctors and nurses. She knew the ropes by now. Unafraid, she turned and hugged Edgas. "I love you, little brother." She kissed him on the cheek and whispered in his ear, "We'll find you." Edgas squeezed her tightly. Oh, how he would miss this big sister.

Abel looked at her with those wonderful twinkling eyes of his. "Ready?"

"Ready." Cristen took a deep breath and lifted her chin.

Then Abel picked her up in his strong arms, flew her through the walls into the operating room, and set her down on top of her body, just like he had done with Masumi.

Edgas watched from the chariot. Now he was the one with a lump rising in his throat. He lifted his hand slowly in a final gesture of goodbye as a tear slipped unbidden and rolled down his cheek. In one swift motion, the Charioteer moved over behind Edgas, placing his large hands on Edgas' shoulders. The instant the angel touched him, Edgas felt strength surge through his body, and the loneliness that had started to invade took immediate flight. How wonderful it was to be comforted by the angel's kindness. He suspected he had been unknowingly comforted by angels many times in his life.

Cristen blew Edgas a kiss and then threw her arms around Abel's neck with a hug that said more than a thousand words. Oh, how she loved Abel, and how much she would miss him and all the wonderful things about him, like his wisdom, and his smile, and his wonderful laugh. "I love you," she whispered.

"I love you, too," he whispered back. "Keep your eyes open, Cristen. You never know when you may entertain angels unaware!"

Shocked, Cristen released her strangle hold and leaned back, looking curiously at the beautiful angel. "What do you mean? Will you come and visit me like you did Ricky?" she asked, incredulously.

"It's not mine to say or to know. I'm just saying, keep your eyes open; you never know!" Then he flashed those pearly whites in a glorious smile, and Cristen felt a rush of excitement surge through her.

"Oh, I'll keep my eyes open, I promise!" she said, returning his smile. She reached into her pocket. "Do I get to keep my yellow stone? Like the others?"

"Yes, of course! Like Henri said, it's a cool souvenir!" Abel chuckled.

"Oh, thank you, Abel. Thank you for everything!" And with those last words she felt a pulling towards her body. She did not resist the pull but lay back on top of herself and faded from Edgas' sight. Edgas, supported by the charioteer, watched quietly as she returned to her earthly shell.

Suddenly, great commotion broke out in the little operating room.

"She's back!" someone cried out.

"Oh! Thank God!" breathed another.

"It's a miracle!" cried someone else.

Edgas couldn't understand a word of it, but no language was needed to see that they were very excited as hugs and high fives, along with tears of joy, were shared in that little room.

FORTY-SIX

You will show me the path of life; In Your presence is fullness of joy; At Your right hand are pleasures forevermore. — Psalm 16:11 (NKJV)

"All aboard to Mozambique!" The smiling charioteer cried loudly, startling Edgas a bit, and then immediately the chariot began to pull away.

"Hey! Wait for me!" laughed Abel, leaping in the air and landing dramatically in the flying chariot. He took his position as rear guard and called out, "Well, what are you waiting for; let's go!"

Edgas held on tightly and smiled at Abel, enjoying the good-natured teasing between the angels. He took one last glance at Cristen, but in an instant she was out of view. "Goodbye," he whispered softly. "Goodbye, my sister."

The Chariot of Fire zoomed one last time over cities, towns, mountains, and an ocean until it sailed over the continent of Africa. Edgas ran back and forth from one side of the chariot to the other taking in the sights of Africa, most of which he had only heard about. The sun was high and bright over an African savanna. Edgas squealed with delight as he and Abel saw giraffes, elephants, rhinos, crocodiles, a running cheetah, and a pride of lions. The charioteer enjoyed slowing his pace for Edgas' enjoyment.

"Thank you," Edgas said to the charioteer. "This is really awesome, not as awesome as Expedition Park because that was unbelievably awesome, but still this is really awesome!"

After allowing Edgas ample time to enjoy spotting and viewing the animals, the charioteer picked up the pace and reached Mozambique within seconds. High in the air, the chariot unexpectedly stalled. Edgas peered over the side expecting to see another animal but saw instead a city far below hemmed along its beaches by the Indian Ocean. Wondering why they had stopped, he looked questioningly at the charioteer and was surprised to see the angel wearing an unusually large grin.

The boy turned to Abel and immediately recognized the look on the angel's face. It was the look he wore when he was up to something, and that something always proved amazing.

"Whaaaat?"

"I've a surprise for you," Abel said calmly.

"What?" Edgas asked again, hardly believing there could be any room for yet another surprise.

"We have brought you home last for a reason, dear one."

The boy just stared at Abel, completely baffled.

"Edgas, how would you like to come back with us and begin your life in Heaven?"

"Wh-wh-what?" Edgas stammered.

Straight faced, but with a hint of mirth dancing in his bright blue eyes, Abel looked at the boy.

"What?" Edgas excitedly repeated himself, scared to trust his two ears.

Silence.

"ARE YOU KIDDIN' ME?"

"No, I'm not kiddin' you," and indeed the angel's face looked quite serious.

Edgas' head was swirling. Could this possibly be true? Was he really to go back with the angels and live in Heaven? For real? He squinted his eyes and looked intently at Abel.

"ARE YOU KIDDIN' ME?" He shouted again, apparently unable to come up with anything else to say.

Abel could not withhold his merriment; he had looked forward to this moment since he first met the enthusiastic boy. He threw back his head and howled with laughter. When at last he could speak, he wiped the tears of joy from his eyes and said with a bow, "Your Heavenly Father says your mansion is ready!"

"But, but, Jesus said I had to go back!"

"You will, but just long enough to tell Isabel goodbye. We will wait for you and then carry you home to live with us, forever."

A smile curved across Edgas' shocked face as he realized, indeed, the angel was not kidding. He was really going home!

"You're not kiddin'?" He asked one last time, just to be sure.

"Not kiddin'!"

"HURRA!" The joyous shout erupted from Edgas' small frame and resounded throughout the heavenlies. Jesus and the Father heard it, and knowing exactly what was happening, looked at each other and laughed heartily.

High above Mozambique, Edgas leaped into Abel's strong arms. The beloved angel spun the boy around in a wide circle, and the two laughed with unbridled glee.

"You're coming home, Edgas, you're coming home!"

"HURRA! I'M COMIN' HOME!" Tears of joy streamed down Edgas' dark cheeks. "Jesus! I'm comin' home!"

MAPUTO, MOZAMBIQUE
1:26 p.m.

For how long Isabel had been holding the child and singing, she had no idea. Her heart was so full it had to express itself in worship. It was one of the best things she knew to do when she didn't know what to do.

The nurse had peeked in the room several times and observed her missionary friend rocking and singing quietly to the boy, so she'd left them alone, having no idea Isabel was rocking a lifeless child.

Looking down at sweet Edgas, dead in her arms, Isabel knew it was time to release him and let him go, and she was finally ready. He was gone, and clinging to his dead body would not bring him back, not that she wanted to bring him back. He was home! She had seen the joy on his face and was quite sure, even if given the choice, he would not want to come back.

"Father, I commit the spirit of precious Edgas Isaac into your loving hands. I thank you that you have already received your son."

She stood up slowly, her muscles stiff and achy from sitting in the same position for so long. She held him close to her chest, and then kissed his temple.

"Goodbye, dear Edgas," she said, gently laying his thin, frail body down on the cot. "I'm going to miss our talks about Heaven and your contagious enthusiasm. I'm a little jealous that you get to see it first. I love you, sweet boy." She reached out and rubbed his curly head one last time before turning to get the nurse.

Suddenly, Edgas bolted straight up in the bed.

Isabel jumped a foot in the air and was about to scream when he called out to her, "Isabel, Oh, Isabel! It's more wonderful than we ever imagined!" His eyes were bright and full of life. Isabel had never seen such joy in her whole life; he was brimming over with joy and his face was shining like the sun. This must be how Moses looked when he came down from meeting with God on the mountain, she thought.

She rushed back to him, her heart all a flutter. She grabbed him up and hugged him, and he hugged her back with the strength of a grown man. He stood on the cot, bouncing up and down in his excitement.

"I just came back to say goodbye. I just found out that I get to stay in Heaven, but the others had to come back. I thought I had to come back, too. But I don't."

"What others?"

"My new bestest friends, Henri, Masumi, and Cristen. I've been all over Heaven with them, Isabel. They're from other countries, and they're really nice! They treat me like I'm their little brother, and I kinda am because we're family now. Abel the angel showed us all around! He's right over there, in the chariot; can you see him?" Edgas waved to Abel and Abel waved back.

Isabel turned her head and saw only a wall.

"He's waiting for me, anyway he took us to meet Jesus and God and see the Throne Room, and he took us on a journey all over Heaven, and we saw the River of Life, which looks like liquid diamonds and is full of beautiful gemstones! And the Pearly Gate is one big huge pearl and the streets are really made out of gold and you can see through them! I can't wait to show you Heaven, Isabel. It's so fun and it's so beautiful and there is so much to do. I'll be waiting for you at the big glowing wall cuz I'll know you're coming cuz you're picture will come up on big screen at the Portal. I think the wall might be alive, cause, well *everything's* alive, and I know the Temple is alive because it opens up to make room for all the people that come to worship and people can float on worship and it'll take them right to the Throne Room and God sits in a rainbow that comes in and out of Him and you can't see His face real well but it looks like the sun and the River of Life flows right out of His throne! Oh! And I saw my friends from the orphanage, too...they're all there and they're so happy, and everyone loves to sing in Heaven, you should hear the music! It's unbelievable, Isabel! You'll love it! Speaking of music, I can play a trumpet now and I sound pretty good, too. And Heaven smells really nice and Jesus smells even nicer and there's lots of different kinds of fruit that grow on one tree and they're delicious, but so is the ice cream and the pizza and the seafood. Heaven is just so AWESOME! And I saw your tears, Isabel. An angel brought them to a special room and put them in a bottle and poured some out on a book of heart prayers and took them to God in the Throne Room and I saw my tears, too. Did you know that angels collect our tears? Oh, and there're horses that look like white statues and they worship Jesus, and I rode on one and there're tons of animals in Heaven! I even met a lion and a fawn and I swam with dolphins in the Crystal Sea after the party at Meme's house. Abel said we could name her place Paradise in Paradise, Diamond of the Crystal Sea. It's prettier than our beach cuz there's no dirt or nothin' and it has diamonds on the bottom instead of sand. Henri and I shared a room there and it had a big comfy bed but we didn't sleep we just talked about all the cool stuff we'd seen! And there's lots of birds, too, and they sing songs with words and monkeys are there and Little Fella rode on my back. Then we swam in a rainbow and dove off a really high dive into the lagoon, well actually we jumped and we got to see the Acts of the Faithful Arena and we prayed with some guy named George for America, and, oh! There's an awesome playground and a roller coaster in the amusement park. Oh, and I know how to fly! We float on worship, did I already tell you that? And there's beautiful homes just waiting for us called mansions and Jesus is so beautiful and so nice and He called me, 'Son!' Oh, I can't wait for you to come, Isabel!"

Isabel's head was swimming. She tried to follow what Edgas was telling her, but it came at her so fast she didn't catch the half of it. But what she did catch was his contagious joy.

"That's wonderful, Edgas!"

"I gotta go, Isabel. There's a Chariot of Fire waiting to take me back," He hugged her tightly and then kissed her on both cheeks. "Don't be sad for me, Isabel. I'm not sad. I *was* sad when I thought I had to come back, and I wasn't sure if I'd still have AIDS or not, but since I can stay, I'm not sad anymore. Well, I told Jesus I was happy to make the sacrifice and come back if he wanted me to cuz *He* made that sacrifice for us, right? He left being King and all, so if *He* could do that, I knew *I* could come back. But Abel just told me that I don't have to, so I'm pretty happy about that."

He sat back down on the cot and looked at her with the world's biggest grin. "Goodbye, Isabel. I'm going home now. Always remember that I love you, and Jesus loves you, too. I'll visit you at the Portal and I'll come meet you at the gate! And, oh! I met your dad; he's real nice and said to tell you hello. He looks real young and lives on his own golf course. Okay, I gotta go now. One more kiss." He jumped up and squeezed the life out of Isabel, then kissed her and sat back down. "Goodbye, Isabel. I love you! Goodbye!"

His body fell back on the cot. Kerplop! And he was gone—again.

Isabel stared at his body. She made the funniest noise as a laugh and a cry burst from her throat at the same time. She clamped her hand over her mouth as if that would keep it from happening again. She stared at him for a full minute, frozen, not knowing what to do, or especially, what to think. Was he really gone, or would he pop back up and start rattling off to her any second?

At length, she decided that he was truly gone. She leaned over, and after kissing his still smiling cheek, closed his eyelids. Hesitantly, she reached down to pull the sheet up over him, and as she did, she noticed a glimmer coming from his small hand. *What in the world?* She pried his little hand open. To her great astonishment, it held a beautiful opal-like stone, white with brilliant colors throughout. She took it from his hand and held it up to the light. It glittered and sparkled like nothing she had ever seen before. *Where did this come from? How did you get such a stone?*

Her eyes widened with realization. *It's from Heaven; you brought me a stone from Heaven!* She looked at it again, amazed. Gazing at Edgas' lifeless body, she mouthed, "Thank you, Edgas, for everything."

Overflowing with a taste of heavenly joy, Isabel turned her face towards Heaven. With everything in her, she knew it was there; it was somewhere beyond the stained ceiling. A prayer bubbled up from her grateful heart. "Thank you, Lord. I am overwhelmed by your kindness and goodness towards me. Bless little Edgas, and thank you for letting him tell me of his amazing journey." She shook her head slowly, giggled, and then glanced at the stone in her hand. Clutching it to her heart, she declared, "I will treasure this lovely stone always. It's simply *out of this world*!"

FORTY-SEVEN

But you have come to Mount Zion and to the city of the living God, the heavenly Jerusalem, to an innumerable company of angels, to the general assembly and church of the firstborn who are registered in Heaven, to God the Judge of all, to the spirits of just men made perfect, to Jesus the Mediator of the new covenant, and to the blood of sprinkling that speaks better things than that of Abel. — Hebrews 12:22-24 (NKJV)

As the flaming chariot approached the gates of Heaven, Edgas saw a sight that surprised him. Thousands of angels were flying in the atmosphere around Heaven, calling out their welcome, and hundreds of people were gathered outside the gate to welcome him home, as well. The first person he saw was Jesus. Jesus Himself had come to welcome him home! He then saw Father Abraham who had also come to welcome him. He saw all of his friends from the orphanage, Joseph from the Room of Tears, Gracie, Meme, and all the guests from her party, including Everett, Isabel's father. He also saw some of the children he had met on the playground, Tanner the Ice Cream man with his daughter, Jordan, the angel music instructor, and all the children from the music lesson group, Haven the limo driver, Kate the butterfly girl, and Sara and Cara, the hair stylists. Edgas had never felt so loved in his whole life!

Jesus came right to the chariot and held out his hand. Edgas grabbed hold of it, and jumped, but instead of landing on the ground, he landed in Jesus' arms. Jesus spun him in a circle and planted a kiss on the top of his curly head.

"Welcome back, Edgas, my son." Edgas clung to his neck, thanking him over and over again for letting him come back.

When at last the Lord put him down, Edgas saw that he was again wearing the beautiful white gown, but when he bowed his head to look at it, he saw that it was covered in beautiful, living gems. It was spectacular, and Edgas was overwhelmed with joy. He lovingly touched some of the gemstones and then turned his smiling face to Jesus.

"You earned them all," his Lord's face shone with pride. "You were a very good soldier, Edgas. You fought the good fight, and you won. Congratulations, my boy."

Edgas beamed. He felt like a superstar. Everyone hugged him, kissed his cheek, tousled his curly head, or patted him on the back. He turned and smiled at Abel with a grin that almost broke his face! "Wow!" was all he could manage to say.

Abel smiled at the boy and then said, "Edgas, there is one more that I want you to meet." Abel held his arm open, inviting another angel over.

Edgas' mouth fell open. "You're the angel that was following us!"

The angel burst out laughing. "Yes, I was! You weren't supposed to catch me, dear Edgas."

Abel patted his fellow on the back and doubled over laughing. When he caught his breath he said, "Edgas, I'd like to introduce you to your guardian angel, Sancto."

Edgas' eyes grew wide.

"I have been with you always, my dear Edgas. I would not have missed your introduction and adventure in Heaven for anything!"

"So, you were with me the whole time?" Whether Edgas meant his whole life or his whole adventure in Heaven, it made no matter for the answer to both was a resounding, "YES!"

Edgas flung himself into Sancto's arms. "Thank you for watching over me, thank you so much, my dear Sancto. Sancto," Edgas rolled the name around on his tongue. "I like your name."

Sancto's eyes filled with happy tears. He picked up the boy, grateful for the opportunity to finally hold him. He hugged him tightly. "You are more than welcome. I love you, dear Edgas, and I like your name, too."

He set Edgas down, and with his large hands gently on the boy's shoulders, he turned him in the direction of the living wall.

Peering past the open Gate of Pearl, Edgas recognized another familiar angel standing behind a familiar golden table. And on that table he recognized a familiar golden book with a familiar name etched on the cover—his very own.

Just like he had done before, the angel opened the top cover of the book and held it up before him like a hymnal. But before he could make his announcement, Jesus stepped in front of him, spread open his arms, and with a great big smile and his shining eyes twinkling, said, "Edgas Isaac Seca, enter the joy of your Master!"

And the crowd went wild.

THE END

...Or is it just the beginning?

AFTERWORD

I am beyond grateful that God has revealed Heaven to so many. I could *never* have written this fiction without their revelations. To the following I give my heartfelt thanks for bravely and boldly sharing your adventures of Heaven, your study of Heaven, and/or the narrative of others' adventures, so that we, too, might have a tiny peek into that eternal Kingdom and joyfully set our mind on things above.

Randy Alcorn, *Heaven* and *The Treasure Principle*
Eben Alexander, M. D., *Proof of Heaven, A Neurosurgeon's Journey into the Afterlife*
H. A. Baker, *Visions Beyond the Veil* and *The Three Worlds*
Mary K. Baxter, *Revelation of Heaven*
Capt. Dale Black, *Flight To Heaven: A Pilot's True Story*
Todd Burpo, *Heaven Is For Real*
James L. Garlow and Keith Wall, *Encountering Heaven and the Afterlife: True Stories
    from People Who Have Glimpsed the World Beyond*
Trudy Harris, RN, *Glimpses of Heaven: True Stories of Hope & Peace at the End of
    Life's Journey*
Kat Kerr, *Revealing Heaven I* and *Revealing Heaven II*
Virginia Lively, *Three Months In His Presence: A Housewife's Extraordinary Encounter
    with Jesus...A discovery that can change your life!*
Judith MacNutt, *Angels Are For Real: Inspiring True Stories and Biblical Answers*
Crystal McVea, *Waking Up in Heaven: A True Story of Brokenness, Heaven and Life Again*
Mary C. Neal, MD, *To Heaven and Back: A Doctor's Extraordinary Account of Her
    Death, Heaven, Angels, and Life Again: A True Story*
Don Piper, *90 Minutes in Heaven*
Dennis and Nolene Prince, *Nine Days in Heaven: The Vision of Marietta Davis*
George G. Ritchie with Elizabeth Sherrill, *Return from Tomorrow*
Richard Sigmund, *My Time In Heaven: A True Story of Dying...And Coming Back*
Rebecca Ruter Springer, (revision by Jann Bach) *Heaven: My Dream of What Heaven
    Might Be Like*
David E. Taylor, *My Trip To Heaven: Face To Face With Jesus*
Choo Thomas, *Heaven Is So Real*
Bruce Wilkinson, *A Life God Rewards*

For more information go to:
www.heavenwins.org